KT-361-958

A Sister's Struggle

Mary Gibson was born and brought up in Bermondsey, where both her grandmother and mother were factory girls. She is the author of the bestselling *Custard Tarts and Broken Hearts*, which was selected for World Book Night in 2015, and four other novels, *Jam and Roses, Gunner Girls and Fighter Boys, Bourbon Creams and Tattered Dreams* and *Hattie's Home*. She lives in Kent.

Also by Mary Gibson

Custard Tarts and Broken Hearts

Jam and Roses

Gunner Girls and Fighter Boys

Bourbon Creams and Tattered Dreams

Hattie's Home

Mary Gibson

A Sister's Struggle

First published in the UK in 2019 by Head of Zeus Ltd

Copyright © Mary Gibson, 2019

The moral right of Mary Gibson to be identified as the author of this work has been asserted in accordance with the Copyright, Designs and Patents Act of 1988.

All rights reserved. No part of this publication may be reproduced, stored in a retrieval system, or transmitted in any form or by any means, electronic, mechanical, photocopying, recording, or otherwise, without the prior permission of both the copyright owner and the above publisher of this book.

This is a work of fiction. All characters, organizations, and events portrayed in this novel are either products of the author's imagination or are used fictitiously.

9 7 5 3 1 2 4 6 8

A catalogue record for this book is available from the British Library.

ISBN (HB): 9781788542616
ISBN (E): 9781788542609

Typeset by Divaddict Publishing Solutions Ltd

Printed and bound in Great Britain by CPI Group (UK) Ltd, Croydon CR0 4YY

Head of Zeus Ltd
First Floor East
5–8 Hardwick Street
London EC1R 4RG

WWW.HEADOFZEUS.COM

For Amelia Mary Bartholomew

London Borough of Hackney	
91300001070318	
Askews & Holts	
AF	£18.99
	5958635

1

Hunger

Winter 1930

Ruby was hungry and Dad hadn't come home again. Her brothers, ten-year-old Eric and little Davey, sat at the kitchen table, staring at her. They were hungry too. But she had nothing to give them. She went outside to the food safe but no miracle of loaves and fishes had occurred and it was still as empty as the last time she'd checked. There wasn't a scrap of food in the house, nor a penny to buy any and, at twelve years old, she was still two years short of being able to earn one. She came back into the kitchen and Davey began to whimper. She picked him up. 'Shh, I know, I know you're hungry, love. Just wait a minute and Ruby'll find you something to eat.'

She handed Davey to Eric, who hoisted him over his leg and began to violently toss him up and down while singing 'Ride a Cock Horse to Banbury Cross' while she crept downstairs to Aunt Nancy's. She wasn't a real aunt, just the neighbour who lived in the lower half of the house who looked after them when her father, Dodge, wasn't home, which was increasingly often.

She gave a hesitant knock on the basement kitchen door.

'Excuse me, Aunt Nancy,' she asked, when the woman opened the door, 'can you spare a bit of bread and milk for our Davey?'

The woman's bright smile faded. 'Oh, love, has your dad left you without nothing in the cupboard again?' She shook her head. Nancy had six children of her own and a bull of a husband who was a casual on the docks but hadn't been called on for weeks. 'You know I'd have you in here for tea with my lot, if I could, love, but I've got nothing but bread and drip to feed me own tonight and your dad ain't been near nor by.' Aunt Nancy's gaze slid away from Ruby, who knew what that meant. Dodge hadn't paid the woman for looking after them this week, perhaps longer. Often, when Dodge missed a payment, Aunt Nancy would feed the Scully children from her own cupboard.

'Oh, that's all right, Aunt Nancy, we've got bread and dripping ourselves,' she lied, and Aunt Nancy put a hand to her cheek.

'Hang on a minute.' The woman hurried into her kitchen and Ruby heard her husband's loud voice. 'What you doin' feeding his kids when we've got nothing for our own, you silly mare?' She couldn't hear Aunt Nancy's muffled response but the woman returned with a slice of bread and dripping and a bowl of condensed milk with crusts soaking in it.

'This is all I can spare, love. I'm sorry it ain't more. Off you go now – and you make sure your Eric has a wash; I see him with a tide mark round his neck the other day, black as Newgate's knocker.'

'Thanks, Aunt Nancy.' Ruby gave the woman a kiss on the cheek.

Aunt Nancy hesitated, then, 'And if your dad don't come home tomorrow morning you'll have to go up the Methodist Mission in Tower Bridge Road. They'll give you bread and cocoa, but for gawd's sake don't tell Dodge! He won't take no charity – not less it's from me,' she muttered, raising her eyebrows, which made Ruby feel that she should say something in her father's defence.

'He's away working. He'll give you our keep when he comes home.'

Aunt Nancy took in a deep breath and retied the wraparound apron which bisected her thin frame, pulling it even tighter so that her waist seemed to disappear altogether. She shook her head. 'Working? He does his best, love. We all do, but you're old enough to know times is hard. You just be in that queue early tomorrow. There'll be hundreds in front if you don't!'

'Is it really free?' Ruby was almost hoping Aunt Nancy would say no and then she wouldn't have to even consider it.

'Course it's free.'

'How come?'

'It's the Mission!'

As she made her way back upstairs to her brothers, Ruby tried to remember the last time she hadn't felt hungry. She couldn't. But whenever she complained about it to her father, Dodge Scully would remove his left sock and point to his misshapen big toe.

'See that toe, gel? That toe'll tell you all you need to know about hunger. You don't know what hungry is, darlin',' he would say.

And if she insisted she really did know, because she hadn't had any tea, he would wiggle his misshapen big toe at her, which would make her laugh for a moment and then screw up her face in disgust, for it was an ugly toe, without a nail, and resembled a squashed banana. Then he'd retell the tale she'd heard a hundred times, of a night during the war, when, while he slept in a muddy trench, a rat had gnawed through Dodge Scully's boot and taken a bite out of his big toe. And when he'd woken up he hadn't cared a jot about the pain in his toe because his stomach hurt more from the hunger. 'That rat must have been bloody starvin', Ruby, if he could face eating his way through my smelly old boot to dine on my cheesy toe! But I was hungrier 'an him!'

Eric insisted the story was a barefaced lie, that he'd heard Uncle Jim say Dodge had shot off half his big toe to escape the trenches; but Ruby would still feel bad about complaining that she'd had no tea.

The one thing that made Dodge angry was having to accept charity, especially if it was church charity. It wasn't that he'd never been forced to accept a handout from the 'bun house', it was just that the very mention of charity was the tinder that sparked his normally happy-go-lucky temperament into rage, so the last place she'd be going tomorrow was the Mission.

She pushed open the kitchen door with her foot and gave the boys a triumphant smile.

'See? I told you Ruby would find you something!'

Ruby woke up hungry. It was a hunger so fierce it had penetrated her dream of the fat rat that lived inside her and was gnawing its way out of her stomach. But just as the sharp teeth took another bite at her she jolted herself awake. She sat up with the metallic taste of blood in her mouth. She had bitten her own lip. Groaning, she lay back down, tears beginning to trickle down her cheeks, pooling where her neck met the pillow. She rocked herself quietly. What was she going to do?

Beside her, two-year-old Davey slept peacefully, each breath puffing out his pink lips. His head rested on her shoulder and she pushed aside the curling tendrils of dark brown hair from his forehead. He was a beautiful child, but sickly, with skinny arms and spindly legs that barely held his feather weight. The three Scully children slept, top and tailed, in one bed and she edged aside Eric's smelly feet which were on a level with her nose. They needed a good wash. She'd have to ask Dad for a sixpence for the Grange Road baths when he got home.

She glanced at the long sash window, the rotten frame loose and the curtains, which had been threadbare even when Mum was alive, keeping out none of the cold. They blew in and out with every chilling gust of wind. Through the window she could see the bell tower of St James's church opposite. The bells were silent, resting. She always loved to hear them, chiming out hymn tunes on Sunday mornings or pealing for special services. The bells were so close that their ear-splitting tones would echo round their three small rooms, reverberating against the thin brick walls, setting sash windows trembling. She loved their sound.

But she also loved it when they were resting – great lumpen iron things set on massive wooden beams within the bell tower – waiting for the hand that would set them into motion, and release their music to heaven. On Sundays there was never the prospect of a lie-in. The sound of St James's bells woke everyone, churchgoer and heathen alike.

But whatever the day, the hands on the church tower clock were never still. Now they edged towards five o' clock. She waited until the creeping morning light grew strong enough to penetrate Eric's pale-lashed eyelids. The boys would be hungry when they woke – and their hunger would be even harder to bear than her own. Dodge could say what he liked: the pain she felt was definitely hunger and the hungry rat was feasting on her. She licked the salt tears and pretended they were soup. It was torture to lie here, knowing the queue for a free breakfast at the Bermondsey Central Hall was already forming and they couldn't join it. Hundreds of children were already there in the dawn light, the promise of a good breakfast keeping them warm on this bitterly cold morning. The idea of provoking her father's rare, fierce temper was daunting but the thought of another day without any food was worse...

She waited until the morning sun stroked Eric's blond hair to silver and a finger of light caused his lids to flicker open. Then she wasted no time. If she delayed, she might change her mind. While his sky-blue eyes were still clouded with sleep, she dragged him from the bed and shoved shorts and shirt into his arms.

'You ain't got to have no wash this morning, just get dressed.'

The pain in her stomach was urgent now, demanding as a bawling child and just as difficult to ignore. As if on cue, Davey let out a wail. While she dressed him she pacified him with a piece of rag dipped in the remains of last night's condensed milk. Eric had pulled on his clothes and she spat on her hands before wiping them around his neck. Then she spat on them again and plastered down his fine, blond hair which stuck up like a pale dandelion seed head. Slipping into her frock and shoes she glanced in the mirror above the mantelpiece. Her small-boned face and pointed chin was framed by straight, silver blonde hair, chopped into a rough bob by her own hand. She hastily ran the comb through it. In lieu of a wash, she rubbed sleep from her eyes, which were exactly the same sky blue as Eric's. Only Davey had inherited their mother's dark hair and warm brown eyes. Dodge insisted that she and Eric were descended from Vikings, like him. By which he meant that their grandmother had fallen for a Scandinavian sailor off the docks which resulted in Dodge's birth nine months later. The sailor had felt the call of the sea shortly after and was never seen again. 'She named me after me father! He dodged the bullet, didn't he?' her dad would laugh, bearing his absent parent no ill will.

Ruby surveyed the three of them and pulled a face. Mum would never have let them go out with dirty faces or unwashed clothes.

'It'll have to do,' she muttered. 'Come on, Eric!' She grabbed Davey's hand and dragged him out of the house at a trot.

The breakfast queue outside the Bermondsey Central Hall already stretched back across Decima Street, snaking down Tower Bridge Road, past Edwards Bakery and Manze's Pie and Mash shop. The smells of doughnuts sizzling and pies baking assaulted her. It seemed cruel that hungry children should have to shuffle forward, wreathed in such tantalising smells, and the odours gave urgency to those, like them, at the back of the queue. She felt the pressure of bodies behind her, leaning forward, with nowhere to go. A steel bootcap caught the back of her heel as a large red-headed boy pushed forward. She shot a look behind her, but he was a head taller and oblivious to her, his eyes fixed firmly on the doors which had just opened.

Her stomach grumbled, a long, low lament which was picked up by Eric's. The girl in front of them spun round, a friendly grin on her face. 'Someone ain't had no tea last night!' she said, with a wink and grabbed Ruby's forearm, squeezing it as if to make sure she was a solid human being. 'Good gawd, there's nothing of you! You're skinnier than me!'

Ruby gave her a weak smile; she didn't have the energy for more. The girl was indeed skinny and tall, her features rough-hewn, with high cheekbones and a broad nose and wide-set brown eyes. Her unruly brown curls had been stuffed under a jaunty red beret. 'I'm Ida Turpin,' she said. 'You ain't been here before, have you?'

Ruby shook her head and felt tears prick her eyes. She wanted the girl to shut up, to turn away and face the front and not see how ravenous she was, how she hopped from one foot to the other to distract herself and how she wanted to moan in protest at the hollow ache inside.

'You just follow me,' Ida said, shuffling forward. 'Hang on to me coat – there'll be such a crush at the door and this lot'll eat *you* three for bloody breakfast, you're so green.'

There was a slow surge and Ruby felt fists and elbows digging in her back, urging her on. Soon the surge became a stampede. The big, red-headed boy dodged around her and barged his way forward, knocking over a boy wearing calipers as he went.

'Oi, oi! Stop pushing in, you bully!' Ida shouted after him. Ruby bent to help the child, but an older, curly-haired boy was already getting him to his feet. 'He's all right, I've got him – he's my brother.' The boy shot her a grateful smile as the tide of bodies bore her forward. She grabbed hold of Ida's coat, gripping it so tightly the girl gave an exaggerated cough and clutched at her throat. 'You're strangling me!' she spluttered.

Feeling for Ruby's hand, Ida dragged her along. Davey stumbled but Ruby scooped him up and then shouted, 'Stay with me, Eric!'

The river of hungry children squeezed through the entrance doors, passed the double staircases leading to the great hall, then turned, carving a course to a huge meeting room which was set up as a dining hall. Thirty long trestle tables covered in white paper were quickly filled by hundreds of children. The scraping of chairs, the excited high-pitched chatter, the shouts of laughter pierced the vaulted hall as women in floral aprons began placing slices of bread onto the tables, two slices for each child, one covered in thick beef dripping and the other in strawberry jam. Then came mugs of hot cocoa. Sick with desire, Ruby dipped her head to inhale the smell of fresh bread and sweet chocolate. She lifted a slice to her lips and was surprised to feel a sharp flick on the side of her head. It was Ida.

'You have to wait for grace!' Ida said. Seeing Ruby's confusion, she gave a surprisingly deep laugh. 'Don't tell me you don't know who Grace is!'

Ruby blushed. 'I ain't stupid! We always say grace indoors.' Why she'd lied she had no idea. She always felt she should know everything. After all, she was in charge of the boys and Dodge had told her when Mum died that now it would be her job to keep the home going, especially with him being away so much.

The steward stood at the head of one of the tables and said a short thanksgiving, but it was nothing so eloquent as the silent prayer Ruby offered as she bit into crusty bread and salty beef dripping. 'Dear Jesus, thank you thank you thank you,' she prayed, understanding for the first time what the love of God really meant. Gratitude filled her stomach with each bite of bread and each burst of strawberry and chocolate sweetness on her tongue. If she'd been able to remember a hymn she would have stood on the table and sung it to the entire room. Instead. she felt an unexpected tear trickle down her cheek.

Ida paused with her mug of cocoa at her lips. 'What are you crying for, you silly 'apporth?'

'I'm so grateful,' Ruby said, swallowing her tears. She turned to Davey, pretending to help him, but his two slices were already gone.

Eric ate his bread and dripping more hesitantly.

'Don't you like it?' she whispered.

He ducked his head, then swallowed the bread with a great gulp as if it were a stone.

'Don't tell me he's gonna cry too!' Ida scoffed.

Ruby shot Ida a fierce look and shook her head. At which the girl's face grew serious. 'Sorry!'

For Eric really was crying and Ruby knew it wasn't from gratitude but from sheer shame. 'It's all right, Ricky, Dad won't find out,' she whispered.

'I don't want to come here again. It's horrible,' Eric mumbled. He was screwing a piece of bread into a ball and he lifted the mug of cocoa to hide his tears.

'It's only till Dad gets back,' Ruby said softly. 'There's nothing at home.'

Eric turned to her fiercely. 'I ain't coming here again. Dad says we don't need charity!'

It was only now that Ruby realized half a dozen children on their table bore a striking resemblance to Ida. It seemed they were her younger brothers and sisters and all were happily munching their way through breakfast. Ida regarded Eric. 'You're right. God helps them that helps themselves. Don't you want that?' And when Eric shoved his slice of bread and jam away, she tore it in two and offered half to her youngest sister and half to Davey. Grabbing at it with two small hands he gave her a wide-toothed grin of appreciation. Dad couldn't blame *him*, Ruby thought – he was far too young to understand what charity was.

Which was just as well, because breakfast was the only meal they had all day and when Dodge still hadn't come home by evening she took Ida up on an invitation the girl had given her at breakfast.

'If your dad don't come home today, you meet me back here

when the market closes and I'll soon show you how to get some grub!' she'd promised.

So that evening, Ruby left Davey at home with Eric and walked to Tower Bridge Road. The market was packing up for the day and there was a bustle of awnings being lowered and stalls being trundled back to their lock ups. Ruby spotted Ida's red beret first and then three smaller Turpin girls standing beside her. Ida's gaze was roving to and fro. When she spotted Ruby, she smiled and beckoned her over. She sent three of her sisters running in different directions and then turned to Ruby. 'You come with me. Do what I do.'

Ruby followed her to a greengrocer's stall which was surrounded by small piles of vegetables and fruit in various stages of decay. 'Just pick up as many 'specks' as you can,' Ida ordered. 'We'll sort 'em out later. There y'are – get them, quick!' She pointed Ruby to some brown-skinned pears and a few mottled apples a stallholder had thrown to the ground. Ruby popped them into a bag she'd made out of her coat and then snatched up some green-ended potatoes and a handful of limp cabbage leaves. She had to fight another girl for a couple of squashy carrots, but she wouldn't let go and eventually her sharp-boned elbow sent the other girl crying to her mother, who was gleaning at the other end of the market.

They scoured the pavements and cobbles till the last of the stalls had discarded their waste for the road sweepers and then Ida sent her sisters home with their booty, insisting on walking home with Ruby. She showed her how to make a soup from the vegetables and how to cut out the bad bits of fruit and stew them up for their tea – and Ruby was left wondering at the girl's kindness. The following morning Eric didn't complain when she insisted they must go to the Mission for breakfast again. But he regarded the bread and cocoa as if they were poison, then folded his arms and stared at the ceiling. 'I ain't eating nothing,' he said and closed his mouth tight shut.

His mute misery was painful to witness and Ida, who'd made sure they were on the same table, whispered in her ear, 'Take this!' Ruby felt a halfpenny pushed into her palm. 'Tell him you're paying today.' Ruby had noticed that some children placed a halfpenny or penny beside their mugs. Ida quickly explained that sometimes parents sent along a 'contribution' with their children if they could afford it. Ruby pushed Ida's hand away, but the girl hissed. 'Do you want him to starve?'

Ruby took the coin and placed it beside Eric's plate. She tugged at his sleeve.

'We're paying today, Ricky, see?'

He sniffed and said gruffly, 'Why didn't you say so? I could've looked forward to me breakfast!'

On the way out, and behind Eric's back, Ruby saw Ida pick up the halfpenny and put it in her pocket. Ruby's eyes widened and Ida put a finger to her lips.

Between the Mission and the specs, Ruby kept herself and the boys fed, but Dodge had been away almost a week and rent day had come and gone. Mrs Nash, the landlady, who occupied the top two floors, wouldn't be put off forever. Fortunately for them she was one of the many women of all ages that Dodge could charm, but without his silver-tongued presence Ruby worried Mrs Nash would start to worry if she'd ever get her ten bob. Ruby hoped it was in Dodge's pocket, wherever that was. Ruby had never known exactly what he did for work. She couldn't say, like other kids, that her dad was a docker or a driver for Peek Freans biscuit factory. Dodge simply told her he did a bit of this and a bit of that and would be drawn no further and she'd worked out that much of his money came from the horses. His overnight trips away were usually to racecourses in various parts of the country. Sometimes Dodge came home grim-faced and empty-handed, but this evening, as she sat waiting, praying she wouldn't have to spend another day fobbing off Mrs Nash, he came home with a smile on his face and a wad of money in his pocket.

He held out his arms to her, lifting her off the chair, swinging her around, as if she were no older than Davey.

'Where's the boys?' he asked, setting her back on her feet.

'In bed, Dad, where d'you think? It's gone nine o' clock!'

'Is it? Lost track of time.' He was emptying his pockets onto the deal table, which she'd scrubbed to a bone white. The notes uncurled from a roll.

'Didn't do bad at all, darlin'. Aunt Nancy been looking after you?

Ruby nodded. 'Yes, Dad.'

'I'll drop her a few bob when I see her.'

He was putting money into old tobacco tins. One was marked 'Rent', another 'Gas', another 'Coal' and another 'Food.' He looked up and smiled. 'Should keep us going for a bit, eh, gel?' He put the rest of the wad into his trouser pocket.

He was a good-looking man. She remembered the way her mother had teased him because he'd never leave the house without looking in the mirror and putting a comb through his crisply cut fair hair – which he would never Brylcreem because he said it dulled its bright colour. He had the large, limpid blue eyes his eldest children had inherited and his suits were always well cut, though now, as he took off his jacket, she noticed his shirt cuffs were frayed.

'Give us your shirt, Dad. I'll mend it.' She held out her hands and he looked at her properly for the first time.

'You're shooting up, love. That frock's too small. You sure your Aunt Nancy's been feeding you?'

'Course.'

'Well, here...' He pulled out some silver. 'You go down Tower Bridge Road tomorrow and get yourself something that fits. And none of that second-hand rubbish – something new!'

She kissed his cheek, which was bristly with a day's growth. 'Thanks, Dad.'

But even as she thanked him, she knew she'd put the money into the tin marked 'Food' instead. She had vowed never to let the boys suffer again as they had these past days – and she knew, from experience, it might be months before Dodge came home with a wad again.

'I'll just have a shave, darlin', while you mend me shirt. Then I'll be out of your way. Got a bit of business at the World Turned Upside Down.' He winked and mimed a drinking action.

He stropped the cut-throat razor on the leather strap that hung from a hook by the sink and lathered up his face. She loved to watch her dad shaving; the fluid strokes through the lather fascinated her. He always played to the gallery, with a flamboyant flourish of the blade and a little finger stuck in the air. When he was finished he would invariably offer his newly smooth cheek to be kissed. He liked the closest of shaves. Now, he drew the razor up under his chin and she could hear the faint crackle as the blade bit into stubble. He was wiping lather off the blade when Eric appeared at the kitchen door. Still holding the razor, Dodge threw his arms wide for his welcome home.

'Hello, son! How've you been?'

He was a demonstrative father, expecting a kiss or a hug at every meeting. Eric launched himself at his father, but instead of the looked-for embrace, Dodge received a furious head butt to the stomach, then Eric began to pummel his father, sending him reeling backwards. The razor flew from Dodge's hand and spun like a silver sycamore seed through the air, spiralling till it glanced Eric's cheek, slicing a red line across his flesh.

'Hold up, son! What you doin' of?' Dodge's normally musical voice was discordant with shock.

'Don't you call me, son! You're a bloody useless dad. We've been starvin' hungry here and had to go to the Mission!'

Eric wiped blood from his cheek and the sight of it seemed to calm him. He picked up the razor and lunged.

Ruby threw herself in front of Eric just before he could slice Dodge. He struggled with her briefly until her pleas penetrated his rage. She locked her eyes on to his and saw him suddenly realize what he was doing. He tossed the razor at his father's feet. 'Get yourself all spruced up and piss off to the pub, Dad, it's all you're good for. Ruby's looking after us now. We don't need you!'

Dodge was not the sort of father who beat them, but his fuse once lit could be fierce. Now, his face flushed bright red and his lips tightened as he wrapped the leather strop around his hand and went to lay it across Eric's shoulders. Ruby put out a hand to prevent him and felt the strop sting her own palm. Eric charged out of the kitchen, his sobs reaching them from the bedroom

Eric had never been a violent or rebellious child and now Dodge's look of anger had turned to shock and mirrored her own. He bent to pick up the razor and turned on Ruby.

'What the bloody hell d'you take the kids to the Mission for? I don't want you having nothing to do with church and we don't need charity! You don't take a blind bit of notice of me! I'm too bloody easy on you. I should get the strap out more often, like other dads, then you'd listen.'

'I'm sorry, Dad. I didn't know what to do, we had no food and it was only breakfast... We was so hungry!'

'Why didn't you go to Aunt Nancy, then?'

'She didn't have nothing either – you didn't pay her.'

Her father passed a hand across his forehead and sat down heavily, a dazed look on his face.

'You do your best, Dad,' she said, believing it with all her heart. She saw his lower lip tremble and she rushed to put her arms around him. He let the razor clatter to the floor and his blue eyes pooled with tears.

'Well, me best ain't good enough, is it, Ruby?' He wiped his eyes with the back of his hand, picked up the razor and turned back to the shaving mirror. 'You'd better go and see to him,' he said.

He drew the blade across his still lathered cheek and she saw red seeping through the fluffy soap. It could have been Eric's blood, but the razor trembled so much in Dodge's hand, it could just as well have been his own.

2

The Mission

Winter 1930–Summer 1931

After that, Ruby made sure Dodge never knew she took her brothers for a free breakfast at the South London Mission every day – even though her father had filled up the housekeeping tins, this wasn't something she could rely on happening regularly. Often he would fill the tins in the morning and empty them again by evening. And Bermondsey was packed with missions. There was Arthur's Mission and Gedling Street Mission, the Bermondsey Gospel Mission, the Cambridge University Mission, the Oxford and Bermondsey – the list was endless. Dodge always said the reason you always found a Mission opposite a pub was to catch the drunkards inside at their weakest and the wives waiting outside at their most desperate.

This morning Ruby was heading, as usual, to the Methodist South London Mission, at Bermondsey Central Hall. The brick building, vast and, to Ruby's eyes, magnificent, was topped by a castellated tower and dominated one end of Bermondsey Street. It didn't look anything like a 'proper' church in Ruby's opinion, not like St James's. In one corner of the building was a public dining room and, in the other, a women's club. Great wooden entrance doors ranged beneath a sweeping stone arch and inside was a lofty octagonal hall with a gallery and an orchestra platform. On Sundays, and at Mother's Meetings, you could hear, all the way up Tower Bridge Road, nearly two thousand voices singing hymns. Ruby had passed it often but had never been inside before the breakfasts.

She and Eric used to go to the Sunday School at St James's Church when Mum was alive. That all ended when she died having their Davey, and Dodge refused to let them go after that, insisting the church had never helped his Rachel when she needed it and he wouldn't have his children going there. A lot of things had ended when Mum died – school ended, more or less; playing in the street without a baby on her hip ended; feeling like a child herself ended – the only thing that never ended was her love for her mother and the physical memory of her arms around Ruby. Mum had been a great cuddler of all her children, whatever their age. When she died, it was as if all the life Ruby had ever known came to a full stop. Sometimes she felt just like one of those resting bells atop St James's Church, waiting for a hidden hand to start her life into motion again.

She thought the Mission was the best place she'd ever been. Everything there was in its right place. There was order and abundance, a never-ending stream of bread, cocoa, loving smiles and helping hands. Even when it was packed with four hundred hungry kids, squawking like raucous, rowdy fledglings, Ruby still felt a sense of calm.

This morning, after she and Ida had played out the charade with the halfpenny for Eric's benefit, Sister Evelyn drew Ida aside on their way out.

'My dear, you shouldn't pretend to pay...'

Ruby was by her side, but Eric had already run out into the street.

'Sorry, Sister,' Ruby said. 'Ida only does it for my brother – he's like me Dad, he hates taking charity so please, don't tell us we can't come again!'

Sister Evelyn gave both the girls an unexpected hug. 'I only meant, it's not *obligatory* – you don't *have* to pay! But Ida, you've done a kind thing for your young friend. You've spared his pride,' Sister Evelyn said. *Let not thy left hand know what thy right hand doeth*! And when Ruby looked puzzled she said, 'It's a verse from the Bible; don't you know it?'

Ruby flushed, conscious of her near-heathen status and her less than fluent reading skills. But Ida grinned and said, 'I'm a Catholic, we don't read the Bible.'

Sister Evelyn laughed. She had very short curly hair and smooth pink cheeks which had a fine pale down on them. She reached into her pocket and pulled out a small tract.

'You two must come to the Sunday School!'

Ruby nodded and took the tract, but Ida shook her head. 'No thanks, Sister, the priest wouldn't like it!' she said, already hurrying Ruby away.

Once out on the street, Ida asked, 'You ain't going to the Sunday School, are you?'

'I might. It'll be something to do with the boys on Sunday afternoons when Dodge's having his kip.'

She looked down at the tract in her hand, trying to make out the words, but she was struggling now. 'What's this say?' She pointed to a sentence and Ida leaned over and took the tract. It says *Come unto me all ye that labour and are heavy laden, and I will give you rest*.

It sounded good to Ruby. But Ida gave her a puzzled look as she handed her back the pamphlet. 'Can't you read, then?'

Ruby blushed. 'A bit. But I've missed too much school looking after Davey.'

'Don't the school board come round after your dad?'

Ruby shrugged. 'He's always out if they do.'

'Same as my mum's always out when the tallyman comes round.' Ida laughed loudly and Ruby joined in.

'I suppose it is stupid to go to Sunday School if I can't even read the Bible. Besides, there's too much to do at home and Dad probably won't let me anyway,' Ruby added abruptly

'I'll teach you to read if you like,' Ida offered, then added, 'And write, an' all if you can't do that!'

Ida chose the Time and Talents Settlement in Abbey Street for Ruby's schoolroom. The doors opened at 5.00 p.m. and there was a window in Ruby's day then. She persuaded Eric to look after Davey for an hour and after giving the boys their tea, she ran the length of Jamaica Road to the club. The long stream of kids was already filing in through the doors and Ruby hurried to the library. By the time she reached it, every table was full, but Ida was there, sitting at a small table in the corner, a book already on her lap.

Beginning with the alphabet as if she were a five-year-old, Ida made her repeat the letters and sounds, then she tried a few simple words. At first Ruby stumbled over the sentences and despaired of ever making any progress. It was shaming, and she felt that the kids around her, noses stuck in books, must be secretly laughing at her.

'This ain't no good,' Ida declared on their second night. 'Get your coat on, we're going up the roof.'

The flat roof of the building was covered in a tall wire cage. In a borough of thirteen hundred acres and only one sizeable park, playing space had to be snatched from factories and wharf sides. Someone had had the bright idea to put a football pitch and small garden on the Time and Talent's roof. Here, screened from the football game, the girls sat in their coats and scarves on wicker chairs and, in the glare of the arc lights, Ruby followed Ida's tracing finger, not caring how much she stumbled over her words, for the footballers couldn't hear. She and Ida might as well have been alone in a bubble under the stars.

All through the winter months Ida taught her on the rooftop

and later, when the nights got lighter, she showed her how to do 'joined-up' writing. 'Good' was the first word Ruby wrote successfully; over and over again she looped the letters, in a satisfying line.

As soon as she could master *Jolly Tales for Girls*, Ruby made her case to Dodge. It helped that she asked on a Sunday afternoon when the boys were being particularly noisy and Dodge was trying to take a nap after his lunchtime drink.

'It's winter and there's nowhere for them to go, so I want to take them. It's not like a church, it's more like a club,' Ruby said and waited for Davey to shoot past her, followed by Eric on all fours, roaring. Davey loved to be scared or surprised or chased. 'Please can we go, Dad?'

'All right then, for gawd's sake. But if they start asking for money you ain't going no more!'

The excuse of occupying the boys on a Sunday afternoon was not the true reason Ruby wanted to go to the Central Hall Sunday School. She was hungry for more than free breakfasts. She longed for some quality she'd seen in Sister Evelyn. No one in her life had ever seemed so certain or so joyful, not even Dodge when he came home from the pub a bit 'merry', as he called it. He didn't always seem very merry to Ruby and often, after a night at the World Turned Upside Down, she would see him slumped in the chair, wiping tears from his eyes. If she ever asked what was wrong, he'd say, 'I'm crying for your darlin' dead mother, my Rachel.'

From the day Dodge agreed to her going to Sunday School, Ruby made the Mission her second home. Dodge's fears were unfounded. They never asked for money, although at a certain point in the Sunday School they marched round in a circle and put their pennies 'for the poor black children' into a wooden box. Each time a penny dropped, the little figure of a black boy nodded and they sang as they walked, *Dropping, dropping,*

dropping, dropping; Hear the pennies fall! Ev'ry one for Jesus, He will get them all.

It was always an awkward moment for Ruby as they had no pennies. There was no use pretending to put in a coin, either. Any fake pass at the box would not result in a nodding head.

But everything else was free. Free songs, free games, free breakfasts; there were cheap suppers too that she could take the boys to during the cold winter months. Ruby loved it all, even the Sunday services at the Mission – which at St James's Church had been chanted in confusing, old-fashioned language – seemed more like entertainment. The singing was full-throated and lively and for those few Sunday hours Ruby felt transported to another world where everything in life was possible and any problem could be overcome by a prayer or a hymn. Eric was a sullen, reluctant pupil, however, until one day Sister Evelyn provided a second-hand blue uniform and then he jumped at the chance to join the Life Boys, the junior section of the Boys' Brigade.

The love of God, she soon learned, was to feed poor men with ha'penny suppers and clothe the unemployed from the cast-off clothing store. At Sunday School she was taught that *inasmuch as ye have done it unto one of the least of these my brethren, ye have done it unto me.* So, she volunteered for every job she could at the Mission. She arranged flowers and polished the brass, she helped with the little ones in Sunday School and she served tea to the lonely old men and women who stayed for tea after the Brotherhood or Sisterhood meetings. It was the least she could do after all those free breakfasts. If Aunt Nancy couldn't look after Davey, she took her little brother with her and his sunny expression and dark-lashed, brown eyes always made the old people smile.

Ida would come to the Mission when she felt like it. She was a talented grazer of the various charities and settlements and would glean the best pickings from them, just as she gleaned the discarded bruised 'specks' from beneath the fruit stalls in the market. On one Sunday afternoon, early in the new year, Ida was at the Sunday School when the leaflets were given out for the Methodist Girls' Holiday Fund. Her eyes sparkled as they emerged from the Central Hall.

'How do you fancy a week in the country, eh Ruby?'

Ruby shook her head. 'No, you have to put two bob towards it.'

'Two bob! Blimey, I reckon you earn that every week with your brass polishing and your floor polishing!'

'That's our Christian sacrifice.'

Ida snorted and then said enigmatically, 'You just leave the two bobs to me! We need a bleedin' holiday and we're getting one.'

Ida was the most resourceful person Ruby had ever met, but she doubted even Ida could spirit four shillings out of nowhere.

She forgot about the holiday fund until a few weeks later when Ida turned up at the Sunday School and went to the teacher to ask for a holiday form.

'Me and my friend Ruby, we want to put our names down.'

The teacher looked doubtfully at Ruby – she'd no doubt noticed that the little black boy's head never nodded when Ruby passed the box.

'And here's our four bob, all up front,' Ida said, slapping the coins onto the desk and returning proudly to Ruby. Heads turned and there was a low muttering of surprise in the class. Most girls would be paying in instalments.

'Where d'you get it?' Ruby whispered.

'It was a gift from God,' Ida said and smiled enigmatically.

Ruby knew it was a miracle, because everything fell into place that August. Aunt Nancy looked after the boys, Dodge gave her a shilling to spend and she met Ida, along with thirty or so others from the Sunday School outside the Mission. The family's only suitcase was far too big for her to carry and so she put her two frocks, everyday and best, her jumper and nightdress, in an old laundry bag. Ida had her clothes in a small brown suitcase, which Ruby envied. She looked around and was comforted that many of the other children only had bundles. Most of them were in their best clothes and she was glad Aunt Nancy had advised her to put on hers. The noise as they waited for the coach increased in intensity as the time drew near and when it drew up there was a stampede, which Sister Evelyn tried in vain to control. Ida, with her superior height and knobbly elbows, made sure she and Ruby sat together, as near the back as Ida could arrange, then she got out some humbugs. 'For the journey,' she said like a seasoned traveller – though Ruby knew that Ida, like her, had never travelled beyond Bermondsey in her life.

Ida chattered away until they got past the Old Kent Road and then told her they were in the country. But Ruby saw only houses, albeit with more sky and space around them; it was only when green fields ringed by hedges came into view that she believed they were truly in the country and a bubbling excitement overtook her for the rest of the journey in this strange, green world where the skies were enormous and endless. When they finally arrived, she thought she'd come to a place that seemed very much like heaven. From a house, high above a deep valley, she saw cows in fields for the first time and smelt wild flowers in deep meadows. But it wasn't until one humid night towards the end of the week that she finally saw the light.

Sister Evelyn had taken them to hear a famous preacher in an outdoor tent meeting. Perhaps it was his persuasive sing-song voice, or a culmination of all those Sunday School lessons, or the encouraging smile of Sister Evelyn, but at his call to come to the altar rail and decide for Christ, an unseen force seemed to grab Ruby and project her forward. Not really knowing how she had come there, she found herself in the 'decision room', listening to Sister Evelyn explaining that she must ask Jesus into her heart and she realized that all the brass polishing and volunteering in the world could never conjure such a feeling.

Ruby knelt to say the prayer and no sooner were the words out of her mouth than she was knocked forward, her knees buckled and Sister Evelyn caught her. Ruby shook from head to foot and from behind the darkness of her eyes, from the farthest edge of the universe, came a ripple in a pond, concentric waves of light spreading out at unimaginable speed towards her, hitting her with waves of overwhelming love and joy. It was similar to the feelings she'd had when, on cold mornings, she would get into bed with her mother, not so much for warmth as for the comforting arms around her. It was as if all those times had been rolled into a single enveloping embrace and all the air knocked from her lungs was replaced by liquid light. Tears of happiness coursed down her face.

Ruby Scully had been reborn.

When she opened her eyes, she spotted Ida, on her knees, across the decision room and she felt the warm certainty that her friend had experienced exactly the same force of love that she had. Afterwards, she sought her out. She was sitting outside the tent on a little wall, looking down across a moonlit valley. They sat in silence for a while and Ruby put her arm around Ida.

'Oh, Ida, wasn't it amazing? Did Jesus come to you? Did love roll over you like light?'

Ida stared at her, but seemed unable to speak.

'Well, what did you feel?' Ruby asked, impatiently.

'Not a bleedin' thing, love. I want me two bob back!'

For a long time after she returned from the holiday, Ruby's heart was bursting with the sort of universal love for everything and everyone that could not be squashed. She'd be washing Davey as he sat on the draining board or scrubbing at Eric's shirt collars, or cooking Dad his tea, when she'd break into a smile so wide it hurt her face. Her father remarked that he didn't know what they were selling down at the Central Hall but if he could bottle it he'd make a fortune in the World Turned Upside Down.

But for all that, her friend Ida refused all Ruby's pleas to come back to the Mission.

'Oh, Ida. I wished you'd felt it too,' Ruby sighed one day after receiving another refusal.

'It don't matter, Ruby. I've had me holiday.'

'So, are you going to tell me where you got the money for us?'

Ida grinned and appeared to cheer up at the memory. 'Well, won't hurt if I tell you now. I borrowed the poor black babies' box,' Ida whispered with a grin. 'Went collecting down The Blue. Just shook it about a bit - it's amazing how many people will put a penny in a box if it does something!'

'Ida! Ain't that wrong, like stealing from God?'

'*Dropping, dropping, dropping, dropping; ... Ev'ry one for Jesus...* That's what the song says and them pennies brought you to Jesus, so how's that wrong?'

3

The Resting Bell

Summer 1935

The bells of St James's were ringing. Too loudly. A clapper inside her head hit her temples over and over again, so that pain flamed behind her eyes with each clang. No, it couldn't be the bells. It was a weekday. It was just a thumping headache. Ruby turned over in the single bed she now had all to herself. With a groan, she leaned over to pull aside the dividing curtain. Behind it the boys were topped and tailed in the old double bed. Sitting up, her head thudding, she slipped out of bed to check Davey's breathing. It was still hoarse from a bad bout of whooping cough and she'd been up all night, trying to keep him comfortable. He'd lost his toddler's gap-tooth grin and gained a seven-year-old's. He was now a spindly, rather sickly boy, whose smile was hard to coax. When she'd started work three years ago and he'd had to be given into Aunt Nancy's care, he'd cried for a solid fortnight. She wasn't an unkind woman, Nancy, just distracted, and even though her two eldest had moved out, she still had too many kids of her own to worry about. Still, Ruby was all the mother Davey had and it broke her heart to leave him in tears every day.

She felt his forehead. It was cooler, thank goodness. Eric

pulled the covers over his head and gave Davey a shove with his foot. 'He kept me awake all bleedin' night! I'm not going to work today.'

'Don't come it, get up. If I can go to work after the night I've had, then so can you.' She rolled him over till he fell out of the bed, which in turn woke Davey.

'How do you feel?' she asked her younger brother, stroking his hair.

Davey sat up and gave her a reluctant smile. 'Bit better. But do I have to go to school?' He put a hand to his head and squeezed tears from the corners of his eyes.

She pulled him into a tight embrace and kissed the top of his head. 'No doctor for you, then, thank God!' Her thanks as much for saving the doctor's sixpence as for Davey's improvement. 'And yes, you're going to school!'

The minute she entered the yard she heard the first catcall. This morning it came from Terry, a young man who'd once been sweet on her and whose too enthusiastic advances she'd had to repulse.

'Here comes the Bible-basher!' he called to his mate. They deftly spun tall, heavy barrels onto their sides and began rolling them towards her as if they weighed nothing. 'Good job these ain't full of beer – she'd have us signing the pledge, Harry!'

'Mind yerself, Rube, or you'll be going to meet Jesus sooner than you think!' Terry said, grinning at her as the two of them trundled past her with the barrels.

'Morning, Terry,' she said with a smile, screwing up her courage for the next comment from the loading bay boys.

The working day at Crosse & Blackwell's always began with her being forced to run the gauntlet. The factory in Crimscott Street consisted of several slab-like, six-storey buildings, striped with rows of large, metal-framed windows. A huge barrel storage yard wrapped around one of these buildings and she had to cross it to get to the vegetable preparation room where she worked.

Kenny, a loading boy, not much older than Eric, weighed in first. 'Didn't I see you over the Earl of Derby last night, Ruby? I'm sure you was downing a sweet sherry!' he said in a tremulous imitation of an old lady.

She had been at the nearby pub, but only because she'd volunteered for Sister Evelyn's Public House Brigade and had been handing out pledges. She'd tried joining in the boys' banter in the past, but they'd only mocked her all the more, so now she simply smiled and moved on. But as she pushed through the door into veg prep, she was already clenching her teeth together so tightly, her jaw was aching with the effort.

'Here comes Sister Anna with the banner! Mind your P's and Q's, girls!' Minnie Boot never grew tired of drawing attention to Ruby's arrival, but she was used to it after three years. She shed her coat and nodded to Minnie as she made her way through the onion-peeling stations.

'Can't you think of a new one?' The loud voice came from a tall, skinny, curly-haired girl standing at a station near the back wall. It was Ida. Ruby gave her friend a small smile and kept her eyes firmly fixed on the floor.

Undeterred, Minnie sang, '*Come and join us, come and join us... da di da di da!*' in a voice made hoarse by a lifetime of smoking Senior Service.

'Well, you ought to join us, Minnie, we could do with a lovely voice like that in the Sisterhood choir!' Ruby said and then wished she hadn't risen to the woman's bait. It always led to extra teasing and she was too tired for that after her sleepless night with Davey.

'Oooh, the *Sisterhood*!' Minnie said sarcastically, then, 'Who's got bleedin' time to go to church! Some of us have to get home to our kids! But you single ladies up the Mission wouldn't know how to go about it, would you?'

A few of the other girls sniggered and Dora, a girl who was slow on the uptake, asked, 'Go about what, Min?'

'Getting herself up the duff!' Minnie shot back. But by now her audience was dwindling, for most had already started peeling onions and their faces had taken on the intent look of women on piecework.

'No one's had more practice of getting up the duff than you, Minnie Boot!' Ida shouted over at the woman who'd already brought eight children into the world. Ida could always be relied upon to come to Ruby's rescue. Not that she felt in need of help – wasn't it all part of what their pastor called 'a life of Christian sacrifice?' She arrived at her peeling station next to Ida's, grateful for its protective steel bulk. Plucking a white overall from her bag, she tied it tightly around her waist, then tucked her smooth blonde bob under her white hat.

'I've loaded you up!' Ida said, indicating the pyramid of onions piled high in the steel trough attached to her station.

'Thanks, Ida. Davey was a bit tearful this morning and it's put me all behind.' She looked up at the clock; she'd be docked half an hour's pay for being five minutes late.

Picking up her first onion of the day, she began to hum a hymn. *We rest on Thee, our Shield and our Defender, We go not forth alone against the foe…* Not that she saw the women who teased her for being a churchgoer as her foes. They weren't mean-hearted, just bored and she was, after all, fair game – just a bit of light entertainment at the start or end of their long, dull day. But even after all this time she could still feel the sting of isolation and was annoyed to find tears pricking the corners of her eyes. Sister Evelyn at the Mission had said she must suffer her workmates' jokes and turn the other cheek.

'You have to remember,' the deaconess had explained to Ruby, 'some of our most loyal members were once scoffers! The fields are white for harvest, Ruby, and the factory floor is no less a field!'

'How many times have I told you: cut it the *other* way and you won't get no tears!' Ida scolded, thankfully mistaking their cause.

'I can't peel them that way – it'd take me five minutes an onion!' And with two thousand a day to peel, Ruby had to be much quicker than that.

She might peel onions the wrong way, but Ruby and Ida always synchronized their movements and within a few minutes were plucking onions from their piles, tossing peelings into one bin and chopped onions into another, in perfect harmony.

Ida had used her influence with the forelady to get Ruby this job when she'd left school. There was never a question of doing anything other than factory work – Ruby had missed so much schooling while looking after her brothers that she was grateful for any job she could get. Besides, she had her faith and she had the Mission, which was all she needed. It made anything bearable.

'I don't know why you don't give 'em a mouthful back, Ruby. It's not like you're shy in coming forward at home, the way you shout your orders at Davey and Eric,' Ida said.

'Well, if I don't keep the boys in order, no one else will.' Ruby was thinking of Dodge's latest absence. 'And Sister Evelyn says the best way to deal with the teasing is to turn the other cheek.'

'I'd turn the other cheek all right, the cheek of me arse!' Ida roared at her own joke and Ruby couldn't help but join in, which pleased her friend.

'You don't laugh enough, Rube. You should take a day off from being a good girl, you know!' Ida had a mischievous look which Ruby had come to know.

'What are you up to now?' Ruby sliced the onion and chopped it into chunks. 'You're never happier than when you're getting me into trouble.'

'I think you should give the Mission the slip for one night and come out with me.'

'Where? I've got no money for the pictures and I'm not coming drinking with you.'

'Did I say the pub? It's serious stuff! I want you to come to the Labour Institute with me.'

While Ruby had found her salvation in Christianity, Ida had discovered the gospel of socialism suited her much better.

'As me mum always says,' Ida went on, 'there's more churches than Christchurch and it's not only just your Mission doing good works, you know! It's all very well feeding the poor, love, but all them free breakfasts you had and you still ain't got a pot to piss in, 'ave you?'

She had to agree, but that had more to do with Dodge Scully than anything else.

'So, our view is you've got to change the system, Ruby. We're organising a hunger march up to Parliament!'

'I don't know, Ida. Those marches get violent sometimes. Besides, I'm not sure they do much good.'

'So, you're saying I've been wasting my time? How would you like it if I told you all them tracts you hand out go straight in the bin?'

'Sorry, Ida. Tell you what, love. I'll come and hear what they've got to say if you'll come to the next Pleasant Sunday Afternoon up the Central Hall!'

'*Pleasant*? In *church*? Blimey, Rube, them two don't go together, not in my book. I ain't been to church since Sister Bernadette chucked me out of Dockhead for handing out a few leaflets the day our Michael got christened.

'What leaflets?' Ruby asked.

'*Religion is the opium of the people*. That sort of thing. Anyway, I still think the Sunday School teacher at the Central Hall knew how I got the money for that holiday and I wouldn't want to bump into her again. Sour-faced old tart.'

'Well then, that's that' Ruby said, with a set to her jaw which she knew Ida would see as final. After a few seconds silence, Ida said 'Oh, all right then. You've persuaded me.'

Ruby gave a satisfied nod. She didn't feel at all like a persuasive person. The amount of people she'd led to the altar rail could be counted on one hand and when she stood on the witness box down the Blue Market, any listeners soon drifted away. But she could invariably sway Ida.

During dinner break in the canteen, Ida tried to convince Ruby that it was no good just feeding poor working men at the Mission's soup kitchens.

'That's just stopgap stuff. You've got to make sure they've got jobs. Full employment – that's what the Labour Party's campaigning for. Jobs, not handouts.' And Ruby had to concede that perhaps both were needed. It was the sort of conversation they'd been having for years, ever since Ida had ditched the Mission and found her own purpose in the Labour League of Youth.

When they returned to the veg prep room it was pungent with the eye-stinging raw onions, even though their morning's produce had already been carted away to the pickle and sauces building. Now another thousand onions stood between Ruby and the end-of-shift hooter. She'd just put on her overall when she noticed something, which was definitely not an onion, sitting on her chopping board.

'What's this, Ida?' she said, holding it up to the light from a tall metal-framed window behind her. She felt heat rush to her cheeks, suddenly realizing what the object was and who had deposited it on her bench. She knew what a condom looked like. She'd once flicked a packet of three off the top of Dodge's wardrobe with a feather duster. He'd no doubt hidden it where his children wouldn't come across it. But he hadn't considered that Ruby was not so much a child as a housewife and that she regularly dusted every corner of the house, just as her mother would have done.

Minnie curled her stout figure into a ball of hilarity, hooting till she could barely breathe. 'What's that? Tell her, Ida!' And wiping tears of laughter from her eyes she said to Ruby, 'It'll come in handy when you work out what goes where, darlin'!'

Minnie let out another cackle and all the women at nearby stations joined in with her laughter, so that those further down the floor looked up to see what the fun was.

Ida snatched the condom from Ruby's hand and marched over to Minnie. Towering over the woman, her wiry frame had a muscular power that could be intimidating. Now she leaned forward and stuffed the condom into Minnie's overall pocket and prodded the woman with a powerful index finger. 'Why don't you take it home and explain to your old man what it's for? After eight kids I'd have thought *you'd* be clever enough to work it out!'

Now it was Minnie's turn to be laughed at and the woman's smile faded. 'All right, Ida. It was only a bit of fun for gawd's sake.' She backed away.

Ruby bit her lip. She wished that just one day would be different. Ida came back to her station, her breath coming in short angry gasps. She spoke, without looking at Ruby. 'If you don't start standing up to them, Ruby, they'll never leave you alone. I might not always be here.'

'You're not leaving, are you?' Ruby was suddenly aware of just how much she relied on Ida, not just for protection, but for companionship. Ida sometimes felt like her only friend outside of the Mission.

'I'm not saying that; it's just I might want to do something else with me life one day besides peeling onions. And you never know, so might you.'

But Ruby wondered what else there could be for her. For so long she'd felt like the resting bells of St James waiting for something to propel her life forward and then God had moved her, given her a purpose, sometimes given her the very food that kept her and her family alive. The Mission provided the only joy that had entered her life in the sad years since her mother's death. It seemed ungrateful to wish for anything else.

That evening she met Ida outside her home in Arnold's Place. It was a long, narrow alley near the river in Dockhead, crammed with tumbledown, bug-ridden houses. Tonight it seemed as if all the residents were out of doors, which often happened when the bugs were particularly active. Kitchen chairs were ranged along the house fronts and women of all ages sat talking or knitting or nursing babies. Boys scuffled in a game of football with a ball made of newspapers. Men in shirtsleeves stood in small groups, smoking roll-ups and coughing, explosive bursts of their laughter rattling round the alley. Ida emerged from her house and was immediately harried by half a dozen clamouring children, chanting, 'Give us yer mouldies, Ida!', for they knew it was payday and sometimes that meant a few coppers might come their way. They were some of Ida's many brothers and sisters. Ruby had lost count of them because Ida's mother seemed to have one every year and the latest was only a few months old.

'Sod off, you're not getting nothing.' Ida shooed away her siblings and turned to Ruby. 'They've all been allowed to stay out late, no point in putting 'em to bed early – the walls are thick with bugs already. It's the weather, brings 'em out. Mr and Mrs Slipper next door have slept outside on their chairs every night this week!'

Ruby didn't know anyone whose house wasn't plagued with something – either bugs or fleas or rats or mould.

'Ready to see the other side?' Ida asked. 'Have the Sisterhood been praying you won't get lured away by the bolshies?'

'Oh, shut up. We had a speaker at the Young Women's Fellowship told us Christians was the first communists! So we got there first!'

Ida laughed and slipped her arm through Ruby's. 'They think all us bolshies have got loose morals, though, don't they, your Sisters?'

'Not all, just you,' Ruby said and grinned.

The Labour Institute in Fort Road was packed by the time they arrived. Though the numbers couldn't rival the thousands who attended the Central Hall, the atmosphere was oddly similar and Ruby saw a similar light of expectation in the eyes of those looking to the rostrum, where the speaker was about to be introduced. She recognized the excited buzz of conversation as late arrivals took their seats. Something was going to happen, people were sure, something important, that would change everything. Tonight they would hear the truth and it would set them free. Perhaps the similarity she saw was faith...

Even the format of the evening seemed like the services Ruby was used to, for they began with a rousing Labour 'hymn' to the accompaniment of a harmonium. It couldn't compare to the full orchestra of the Central Hall, but again, the fervour was just as real. As they sang about the onward march of socialism, their shining faces revealed an evangelical certainty in the purity of their mission.

'This feels a bit like church!' Ruby teased her friend. 'I think you must secretly believe in God, Ida Turpin.'

'I do. His name's Dr Salter! Anyone who can get us out of Arnold's Place and into a lovely new flat's a god to me.'

Ida explained that the first speaker would be Will James, a leading light in the local Labour Party. He was obviously popular and drew a round of applause before he'd even begun. He was a stocky, powerful-looking young man and spoke in a clear, commanding voice that reached the back of the hall. He gave an overview of what had so far been achieved in highlighting the plight of the unemployed, not just in Bermondsey but all over the country. He spoke about the solidarity of the working man and

Ruby heard echoes of the gospel of brotherly love. But the meat of his talk was a practical plan for the next big demonstration, a hunger march to Parliament, demanding a radical overhaul of the unemployment allowance, which, he explained, at thirty-two shillings for the average man with three children to feed, was 'paltry'. He spat out the word as if it was poison and then repeated it: '*Paltry*!'

At the end of his talk he asked for donations of time and money, for offers of overnight accommodation for the marchers from outside London, or for volunteers to be stewards. As far as Ruby was concerned there was little difference between what he proposed and Jesus's words: *For I was an hungered, and ye gave me meat: I was thirsty, and ye gave me drink: I was a stranger, and ye took me in: Naked and ye clothed me:* which were regularly quoted at the Mission to prick the consciences of potential volunteers in the soup kitchen.

After Will James left the podium and the next speaker came forward, Ruby felt a moment's disappointment. He was introduced as Alfie Diamond, representing the League of Youth. His hands visibly trembled as he held his notes and his voice was indistinct. A few irreverent shouts of 'Can't hear you!' rang round the room and brought a blush to the man's face.

She was used to commanding preachers with powerful voices at the Central Hall. They had a presence, and the rostrum of the Mission was deliberately placed so that it jutted out into the congregation like a stage. The last speaker had exactly that power, but the young man now standing at the front of the hall didn't. He was very young, perhaps only nineteen, and she shifted uncomfortably in her seat. He was broad-shouldered, but he still had the slimness of youth before it filled into manhood. His long, thin face was dominated by a high forehead from which unruly dark curls were swept back. Straight eyebrows framed his most notable feature: large, dark brown eyes which were surveying the room with, what looked to Ruby, very much like terror. He licked his lips and swallowed visibly. The lectern was too low for him and as he struggled to raise it, his sheaf of notes scattered to the floor. Suddenly Ida leaped up and, in a few strides, was at the front, gathering them up. Ruby saw her put a hand on the young man's arm and mutter something in his ear.

When she came to sit down again, Ruby whispered, 'Do you know him?'

Ida nodded silently, for Alfie Diamond had begun his speech again and now, seeming to look at no one else in the room except Ida, he quickly warmed to his subject.

He explained that the League of Youth had committed itself to campaigning for a living wage, for hunger affected not just the unemployed, he said, but those in work too, many of whom were starving for want of a decent week's wage. The League of Youth were determined to end the exploitation of young women working a ten-hour day for a weekly wage of twelve shillings.

'Now – with respect to the previous speaker – *that* is what I call paltry!'

And Will James shouted out, 'Here, here!'

At this point Ruby sat up, for twelve shillings was exactly her wage, the majority of which went to pay the rent on their three rooms. And if Dodge had been bringing home the thirty-two shillings a week in unemployment benefit instead of doing his unspecified 'this and that', she would have thought herself rich.

After the meeting there was a small social gathering worthy of the Band of Hope, with tea and biscuits and not a drop of hard liquor in sight.

'So, what did you think?' Ida asked hopefully. 'Nothing too sinful going on here. Will you join us?'

Ruby gave her a hug. 'I can't give up any of my Mission work, but I'll help if I can. Now *you've* got to come for a Pleasant Sunday Afternoon!'

'Who could refuse an invitation like that?' a voice behind them said.

Ruby turned, recognizing the young speaker, Alfie Diamond. He was holding a teacup in one hand and a biscuit in the other.

'Well, you can always come too,' Ida said, smiling and introduced Ruby.

Alfie got rid of the biscuit with one bite in order to shake her hand. 'I'm not sure an agnostic socialist Jew would fit in at a Methodist Mission! But I've heard a lot about you, Ruby Scully,' he said, exchanging an enigmatic smile with Ida and Ruby wondered what she'd been telling him.

'Hope it's nothing bad?' she said, feeling at a disadvantage.

'Bad? No. Ida says you're a saint. I've always wanted to see if they were real, saints. You look real enough.' He grinned and lifted a plate from the tea table. 'Biscuit?'

Ruby took two.

'Don't listen to Alfie. I just told him about your work at the Mission – soup kitchens and poor men's suppers, cast off clothing club… She does everything!'

Ruby waved her praise away. 'It's not much different to what you do here, by the sound of things.'

Alfie's long, straight mouth curled into a smile, the corners of his large eyes crinkling in amusement. 'No help from God, though,' he whispered and, helping himself to another biscuit, he walked off in the direction of Will James.

'He's a bit odd,' Ruby said to Ida, as she put the two biscuits in her bag for Eric and Davey.

'If you think he's odd, wait till you meet his brother,' Ida said and nodded her head enigmatically.

'Who's his brother?'

'Ocki Diamond. And I think it's about time you met him. He's my chap.'

'Chap! Since when did you have a chap?'

Ida steered Ruby away from the tea table towards a group having a loud discussion by the stage.

Ruby saw the resemblance to his brother at once, but whereas Alfie was like a tall, straight oak sapling, his brother, Ocki, was more a twisted thorn tree. Slighter and smaller than Alfie, it was obvious what had given him the slightly lopsided look. One shoulder was noticeably lower and one leg shorter than the other. She had seen the results of polio often enough to spot its legacy and, glancing quickly down, she could just see a caliper beneath his trouser turn-up. She had a flash of memory – a young boy with calipers, knocked to the ground and his brother helping him up. Could it be the same two? If it was, then Alfie Diamond's scruples about attending the Methodist Mission hadn't extended to their free breakfasts.

When Ida laid one of her formidable hands on his sunken shoulder, Ocki turned to her with a slow smile. 'I'd know that *light* touch anywhere!' he said, pivoting on his calipered foot. His features were enough like his brother's for Ruby to see the resemblance, but they were softer and his smile sweeter. He looked shyly at Ruby.

'Pleased to meet you. Ida said you'd tell her off for keeping me a secret, but don't. You can't blame her for waiting to see if I'd suit, can you?'

Both the brothers had an odd sort of directness, unusual in Ruby's experience. Older men barely spoke to her at all, younger men always addressed her in a mocking way that made her feel useless but these two brothers seemed to be including her in their private view of the world. If it was all a joke, they seemed to be saying, then Ruby was in on it.

She decided she preferred Ocki to his handsomer brother – for defending Ida, if nothing else. But whatever his plea, she wasn't going to let her friend get away with her subterfuge.

'Ida!' Ruby was stunned. Ever since the day they'd met in the free breakfast queue they'd told each other everything. 'How long's this been going on and you've not let on?'

Ida pulled a face. 'Only a fortnight! Well, I didn't know if he was really my type, at first. Didn't seem much point telling you all about him and then he turns out to be a five-minute wonder,' she said, putting an affectionate arm around Ocki's shrunken shoulder.

Ruby's choice of friends was always a source of surprise. Look at herself. They couldn't have been more different, and yet Ida had known from the first minute that Ruby would be a friend. Ida was one of the few who saw past the outside of people and Ruby wished she was the same. The Turpins were what her mum would have called 'rough'. Poverty wasn't a sin, her mother had always said, but you didn't need to be rough with it. And that meant your babies shouldn't be sent out of the house in dirty nappies and unwashed clothes. If you couldn't afford shoes for your children, she would say, then do without yourself. Ida hadn't had it easy.

On the way home she asked Ida about Ocki. 'Did you feel sorry for him?' she said and Ida's eyes flashed with rare anger.

'No, I did not. He's a lovely chap, and clever – sharper 'an one of our onion knives.'

'Hmm. His brother seems pretty sharp too. Are they college boys?'

Ida shook her head, laughing. 'They work at Crosse & Blackwells! But their dad's a bit of a scholar; Ocki says their flat's crammed with books.'

'Books!' Ruby's surprise couldn't have been greater if Ida had said the Diamonds' home was full of silver plate. Books were a luxury most people couldn't afford in Ruby's experience.

'Books,' Ida confirmed. 'Alfie's clever enough, but Ocki's cleverer than him *and* every one of those cocky sods in the League of Youth! He won a scholarship for college, you know, and he wouldn't go because he knew his mum and dad needed his wages. Broke his dad's heart, Ocki said. Alfie told me Ocki could beat Will James to becoming an MP one day.'

Ida's eyes were unusually bright and Ruby thought she saw tears brimming.

'What is it, Ida? I'm sorry if I upset you.'

But Ida shook her head. 'It's not that. It's just he's got such a lot to put up with. His body lets him down, see. He knows what he could be, if he only had the stamina. But he gets tired out and then there's the pain…'

At this point her hard-as-nails friend, who was never knocked back by any circumstances, let tears fall. She batted them away. 'Look at me, worse than our Patsy; that baby hasn't stopped bawling since the day she was born.'

Ruby knew Ida would rather they didn't pursue the subject of Ocki and his frustrated ambitions and they were silent for most of the walk home as Ruby thought of her own, unspecified yearning to be something more. Perhaps she wasn't the only one who felt like a resting bell, with all the chimes and changes silent, just waiting.

4

Looking After Your Own

Summer 1935

When she got home that evening, Ruby was surprised to hear Davey's laughter – not just because it was such a rare thing over the past weeks, but because it was so late.

'Eric? she called as she entered the dark passage from which their three rooms led. 'What's Davey doing still up?'

She threw open the kitchen door and was surprised to see her two brothers both sporting women's fur coats. Davey had a foxtail stole wrapped around his head and his rickety legs were enveloped in a dark brown fur coat that trailed along the floor behind him. He was being chased around the room by Eric, holding a rolling pin as if it were a rifle.

'Look, Ruby, Davey Crockett!' Eric pulled his little brother forward for inspection. 'Davey! Get it?'

'*You'll* get it if I catch you! Why couldn't you just do as I asked and get him to bed on time? I don't get no help from you.'

Her visit to the Labour Institute had unsettled her, perhaps because she'd been shown that doing good wasn't the sole province of the church. It had been simple of her to believe that only Christians wanted to improve the world.

'And what's all this stuff doing here?' she asked. Black,

chestnut, silver and white furs were draped in every corner of the tiny kitchen.

'It ain't my fault!' Eric protested. 'Blame Dad!'

At that moment Dodge came in, carrying a bundle of furs piled so high that his head was barely visible above them. He peered over an intricately whorled black astrakhan.

'Gawd's sake, help us with these, son. They're heavier 'an a sack of coals,' he said in a voice muffled by furs.

Seeing Ruby, he stopped dead.

'They won't be here for long! Don't worry, love. I'll have 'em out of your way in a day or two… Shove over.' He edged past her. 'I'll just leave 'em here for the time being.' He was about to dump them onto the kitchen table.

'Oh no you won't! How am I going to get the meals ready without a table? Find somewhere else for them.'

Dodge's face reddened with the effort of supporting the weighty coats. 'There's nowhere else!'

Ruby ducked around him, planting herself firmly in front of the table. 'They can go on your bed! You stole them, you can get caught with them if the police come knocking!'

'Don't be like that, Ruby.'

She turned her back on him and heard his laboured breathing as he carried the furs to his bedroom.

'And you,' she said, pointing at Eric, 'can help *him* out of that get-up and into bed!'

She plucked the hat from Davey's head.

'You're a spoilsport, you bloody miserable Bible-basher,' Eric muttered as he tore off his own fur coat. 'Davey was having good fun, wasn't you, boy?'

'Fun? With this knocked-off stuff? You won't think it's such fun when Dad's locked up, Ricky, I can promise you that.'

Once Dave was tucked into bed and Eric had stormed out of the house, Dodge reappeared with a sheepish look on his face. 'I only do it for you and the boys, you know, so don't be cross, Ruby love, it spoils your pretty face.'

'Don't try your old soft soap on me,' she said, feeling the heat rise to her cheeks, 'This is not right, Dad!' I can't live on the money you get from thieving—'

'I'm not a thief! I just get stuff cheap and sell it on. It's an honest living, darlin'.' Dodge's shocked expression was so sincere she despaired and resorted to a Bible verse.

'*Better is the poor that walketh in his uprightness, than he that is perverse in his ways.*'

'Oh, my gawd, here we go.' Dodge wiped a hand across his face and sat in the one armchair the Scullys possessed. 'I've told you not to quote that shit at me. I can't stop you going there, but I don't want it shoved down me throat, Ruby. If we got chucked out of this place it'd be a different verse you'd be spouting then – *Better to have a roof over your head than live under St James's railway arch!* That's what it'd be then.' He took out a packet of Woodbines and lit one up, staring morosely at the glowing tip. 'That bloody Mission. I told you, once they get their claws into you, they think they bloody own you. Turning a daughter against her own father. I'd like to see where it says in the Bible that that's all right!' He took a long drag so that the glowing tip extended to ash and she saw his hand was trembling. He sometimes trembled after a late night out, but this was trembling of a different kind. It was so hard for Ruby to be angry with him; sometimes she felt she had three children to look after, not two.

'I'm just saying, Dad, I'd rather starve than steal,' but even as she said it, she remembered those days as a child when she'd cried with hunger and felt the words stick in her throat. What if he was right and her objections to Dodge's moneymaking schemes were all just show?

'All right, then!' Dodge let the cigarette dangle from his bottom lip while he got out the housekeeping tin marked 'Food'. 'Bloody starve then.' And grabbing the pen he used to write out his bets, he added NOT RUBY'S! to the label. 'How's that do ya? Conscience clear now?'

He flung the tin at her. 'I'm going to the pub.'

After he'd left she went into his room and sat amidst the luxurious furs, stroking the silky pelts, her throat tight against the lingering sadness and anger. She hated falling out with Dodge, but he had made a liar of her. For if they found out, there were many at the Mission who would tell her she must shun the proceeds of his stolen coats or whatever the current hookey hoard happened to be, even if it meant starving. At the very least, they would say, she should inform on Dodge to the police. But all the Bible verses in the world couldn't induce her to do that. If Dodge was going to hell she supposed she would have to go with him.

Saturday was Ruby's regular day for helping Sister Evelyn on home visits. She was waiting for Eric to come back from Tower Bridge Road where he'd been to buy his first pair of trousers with his own hard-earned money. She was glad that he appeared to be in a good mood when he swaggered through the door.

'What do you think?' he asked, putting his hands into his new trouser pockets.

'Very smart. I was wondering, Ricky, could you keep an eye on Davey for a few hours while I go home visiting with Sister Evelyn?'

His smile vanished. 'No! I'm going out with me mates later. Why can't he go with Aunt Nancy like he always does?'

'She's gone to a wedding. I don't ask much from you, Ricky. Just once wouldn't hurt.'

Since starting work as a messenger boy at the docks Eric had begun to rebel against her as a surrogate mother. As a child he'd been compliant and docile and she supposed she'd spoiled him. When their mother died in childbirth, Eric, at eight, had been old enough to realize what had been taken from him.

'Why should I have him? I ain't his bleedin' father.'

'You know Dad's working – and less of the bleedin''.'

Eric laughed at her. 'Working? Flogging fur coats in the World Turned Upside Down ain't work, Ruby.'

She looked down at his trousers. 'They're too long.'

He peered at the turn-ups which bagged over the top of his shoes, then took down the mirror from above the mantelpiece, positioning it carefully on the floor so that he could just see the lower half of his legs. 'Too long?' He plucked at the trousers to raise them up.

Ruby nodded and dropped to her knees so that she could turn over the hem. 'See?'

'They do look better like that. Could you take 'em up for me?'

Ruby nodded. 'Of course I *could*.' Then she looked up at him and smiled.

'Oh, very Christian that is! Blackmail, I get it. All right, I'll have Davey, but only for two hours. Then I'm going out with me mates.'

They were visiting Monarch Buildings, in Abbey Street, one of the handful of Victorian tenements in Bermondsey that had eluded the slum clearance. The tenement sat in crumbling bleakness next to the Star Cinema and the posters plastering its frontage, with their peroxide blonde starlets posed against glamorous backgrounds, were a world away from Monarch Buildings. Today the grimy tenement entrance was blocked by a couple of hundred children queuing for the Tuppenny rush. As Ruby and Sister Evelyn approached, the noise of peanut shells crunching underfoot greeted them, as kids dipped into their treats before they'd even got into the cinema. She wormed her way through the tight-packed crowd, clearing a path for Sister Evelyn, thinking of her own childhood Saturdays. Even while her mother was alive, the only way she'd ever managed to get into the Star was round the side entrance when the usherette wasn't looking. And when she was dead, looking after the new baby had supplanted Saturday pictures.

The kids' excited chatter echoed up the cracked-tiled stairwell and followed them to the top floor. These home visits with Sister Evelyn were always hard for Ruby. What could she possibly have to offer Mrs Mongey? She took in a deep breath, steeling herself. The place smelled of boiled cabbage and blocked drains and she felt grateful for their own three-roomed home, which at least had the relief of a small backyard and tall windows. Mrs Mongey had seven children and a husband out of work and the family lived in two rooms which were permanently filled with damp washing, some of it their own, some belonging to other people. Mrs Mongey took in laundry to cover the rent, but there was little left for clothes or food for her children, so the Mission supplied both. They found Mrs Mongey in the bedroom, nursing her two youngest – a boy of eighteen months and a tiny baby girl. Both were suffering from hacking coughs, which sounded to Ruby suspiciously like Davey's. A third child, a girl of four, had opened the door to them, but when Mrs Mongey saw it was Sister Evelyn, the woman attempted to get up from the bedside.

'Stay where you are Mrs Mongey!' Sister Evelyn said, beginning to unpack a bag of groceries, including tea and tinned milk, bread and a jar of jam. 'Ruby go and fill the kettle, there's a good girl. Mrs Mongey would like a cup of tea, I'd imagine.' The bedroom was divided in two by a blanket strung across it, the younger children and their parents sleeping in one half and the three older Mongey boys in the other. The second room in the flat was a kitchen. Jenny, the four-year-old, followed Ruby and watched as she boiled a kettle.

'You're a pretty lady,' Jenny lisped, tugging on Ruby's skirt. Ruby smiled, wondering how anyone, even a child, could believe she was either. Jenny was a favourite with her. Bright and curious, she had an open, sunny nature that seemed at odds with her dreary surroundings.

'And you're a pretty little girl. Have you got a cough too?'

Jenny shook her head. 'Me dad has, though. He's gone out

looking for work. Mum says he's not well enough – he should be in a nasturtium.'

Ruby chuckled and bent down. 'A sanatorium.'

Jenny nodded solemnly. 'I don't want my dad to go to no nasturtium. I heard Mum say he'd never come home again.' Ruby saw Jenny's lower lip tremble and distracted her with a spoonful of condensed milk. When she went back into the bedroom with the tea, she found Sister Evelyn sitting on the side of the bed, comforting a crying Mrs Mongey. The babies were too ill to do more than cough and wheeze and stare mournfully at the adults.

'I'm sure it's the whooping cough, Mrs Mongey. But if you're worried, you must bring them to the Child Welfare Clinic – just as soon as you're able and we can put your mind at rest about the little ones.'

The Welfare Clinic at the Central Hall was free and Ruby helped out there when she could. She hoped the children weren't showing the first signs of Mr Mongey's TB, and she couldn't imagine how his wife would have the strength or time to make her way to the Central Hall, for she looked weak and frazzled herself.

'Perhaps the doctor could come to you?' Ruby offered.

'No! No. I can't afford no doctors coming home here, darlin'. I'll bring 'em all up the Central Hall, I will.' And to show willing, Mrs Mongey hauled herself up from the chair.

Ruby could hear the sounds of the Wurlitzer organ drifting up from the Star Cinema and faint strains of children singing along. The picture show was about to begin and again she felt the clash between the fiction on the screen and the reality facing her now in this fetid little room. Jenny slipped a hand through hers and looked up shyly. 'Are you a film star on the pictures, miss?'

It made Ruby smile. She thought she was plain. She wore no make-up, kept her hair in the same smooth bob she'd worn as a child and, in spite of Dodge's disapproval, her clothes were still second-hand from Tower Bridge Road's old clo' market. She'd been told her clear blue eyes were lovely, but that was Terry, and she couldn't believe a word he'd said to her. If anyone noticed her twice, it was because of her pale blonde hair which, in some lights, was almost silver. Now she crouched down and asked, smiling, 'What makes you think I'm a film star?'

'Cos you got blond hair and you talk nice.' Perhaps working with the missionaries at the Central Hall had softened Ruby's Bermondsey accent. It hadn't occurred to her before.

'Well, I work in a factory, same as everyone else. I go to the Mission – you could come to Sunday School there, if you wanted. It's fun.'

'Can I?'

Ruby picked the child up and carried her back into the kitchen. She gave her bread and jam and told her about the Sunday School, feeling bad, because she doubted Mrs Mongey would allow Jenny to go unless one of her older children could be persuaded to take her.

They had several more visits to make. One was to Mrs Simmons, a housebound old lady who lived in one room, further down Abbey Street. She was a chirpy, bird-like woman, who'd been a member of the Central Hall since it opened almost forty years earlier. She was fond of telling Ruby the story of how she and her fellow factory girls had put away their farthings to buy the great pulpit Bible which still held pride of place at the Central Hall.

'I do like to think something lovely come out of all them hours I spent pouring boiling jam into stone jars at Southwells,' she would say, laughing, showing burn scars on her wrinkled old arms, still evident after decades. She was dying cheerfully, even eagerly. The woman lived in the one room with her daughter, son-in-law and their four children. When they arrived the first thing Mrs Simmons said was, 'Thank the Lord you've come now while I'm on me own, Sister. I don't get a quiet minute to say me prayers in!'

So, after Ruby fetched water from a scullery shared with three other families and helped the woman to drink some broth, Sister

Evelyn said a prayer, then they all sang 'And Can It Be, That I Should Gain?', a hymn which the toothless old lady said was her favourite as it had been the one that had brought her to the decision room. They followed it with 'Are You Washed in the Blood?' to which Mrs Simmons firmly replied: 'I am!'

When they'd finished their visits and were on their way home, Ruby began thinking about little Jenny Mongey.

'Do you think Mrs Mongey would let Jenny go to the Sunday School? If the older boys won't go with her, perhaps I could collect her?' she said.

'That's kind, Ruby, but I don't think she'd have it. She says the children haven't any Sunday Best to wear and she isn't going to disgrace herself by sending them to church in rags.'

'Can't we give them some Sunday Best from the cast-off clothing?'

'She'll take food, but not old clothes because she thinks they carry disease. People draw the line at all sorts of strange places, Ruby. Remember your Eric and how he wouldn't eat the free breakfasts?'

'Eric!' Ruby's hand flew to her mouth. 'Oh no, I left him looking after Davey, I'm late! Sorry, Sister Evelyn, I'll have to run.'

She sprinted through the early evening streets at full pelt and arrived home, her chest heaving and with a stitch in her side. She pounded up the outside stairs to the front door and let herself in. Eric would be livid. She expected to be met by a loud, furious accusation from her brother, but silence was her only greeting as she passed by the two bedrooms and poked her head around the kitchen door. It was empty. She glanced at the clock. She was an hour late. She felt fear tingle down her spine. Surely Eric hadn't gone out and left Davey sleeping alone here? She ran to their bedroom. It was empty.

'Oh, Eric. Where've you taken him!' She licked dry lips, beginning to silently berate herself for leaving Davey in his care. Then she relaxed. Of course, Aunt Nancy must have come back from the wedding already and Eric had dumped Davey on her. She leaped down the inside stairs, two at a time, not caring if she woke any of Aunt Nancy's kids; she just needed to find Davey. But there was no answer to her knock on Aunt Nancy's door. The house was empty. She breathed deeply, trying to quieten her mind and still her trembling limbs. Nothing would have happened to her little brother; God would look after him, she was sure of that, she just needed to think. She sat on the bottom stair, closed her eyes and clenched her hands together in prayer. Sister Evelyn always said a minute's prayer could save an hour of struggle and, almost immediately, she realized that he might have left her a note.

She dashed upstairs. The note was on the kitchen table. Eric had scrawled on the back of an envelope, *I told you I was going out with me mates. Davey's with Dodge.*

'You selfish little tyke!' she addressed her absent brother, crumpling the envelope and trying to banish thoughts of the revenge she could wreak on him. All the simple but effective ways to make his life a misery – like refusing to scrub his precious shirt collars. '*Vengeance is mine; I will repay, saith the Lord,*' she muttered.

There was only one place she would find Dodge on a Saturday evening – the World Turned Upside Down. Once installed, there was no moving him. Poor Davey would still be there at chucking out time if it was up to Dodge. It was a fair walk to the pub and the summer evening had turned chilly; steel-grey rain clouds now scudded across the early evening sun, giving that lurid upside-down light which threatened rain and she wished she'd brought a jacket for Davey – she was pretty certain Eric wouldn't have thought of one. She half ran, half walked through the darkening streets, but before she'd even reached the Old Kent Road fat drops of rain began pounding the pavement, raising the dust of the day, filling the air with dankness and her heart with foreboding. She was soaked in minutes, her thin cotton jacket sticking to her back, her cardboard-packed shoes sodden.

Outside the pub a few miserable children scrunched under the lea of windowsills and doorways, desperate for shelter from the driving rain. But Davey wasn't among them. She was about to ask one of them if they'd seen her brother when her eye was caught by a saturated bundle. It was Davey, hunkered down against some railings at the mercy of the elements. Why hadn't the silly boy at least gone with the others for shelter? She began running, calling, 'Davey, get out of the rain!' But he didn't look up and when she reached him she could see why he hadn't moved. He'd been tied to the railing with a webbing belt. Dodge's. She shook her brother by the shoulder but his head lolled to one side. She knelt beside him, frantically tearing at the belt.

'Davey, love, wake up! It's Ruby!'

His eyes flickered and he tried to smile. 'Hello, Mum,' he said and her heart froze. He'd never called her that, even though she'd been his mother in all but name. Where was Davey now, if he thought he'd seen his dead mother? She prayed he wasn't halfway to heaven, for she'd heard stories of people seeing their loved ones just before they died.

'It's your sister, Ruby; don't you know me? Oh God, where's Dad?' She looked around frantically and saw the little gaggle of children eyeing her with soggy curiosity. 'Can one of you go in the pub and ask for Dodge Scully?' They looked doubtful; if they'd been left here, then either their parents weren't the sort who'd appreciate being interrupted or were already incapable of remembering they had children. Either way, the kids would be in trouble for venturing into the adult's domain. 'Please, my little brother needs help. He's ill!'

One boy of about eleven stepped forward. 'I'll go,' he said, skidding away on his plimsoled feet.

It took only a matter of minutes for him to find Dodge, who rolled out of the pub and searched with futile, drink-clouded eyes until he spotted her. Even then he didn't register what was happening and smiled broadly as the rain splashed great dark patches onto his neat suit. He put out his hands, letting the rain spatter his palms. 'Gawd, when did this start? Hello, Ruby, love. Don't tell me you've torn up the pledge and come for a drink with your old man?'

'What's the matter with you, don't you know you've got a son?' she shouted above the thundering rain.

His eyes widened with shock at her tone. 'Course I know! And don't tell me I treat him any different – I treat all my kids the same! I never blamed him for my poor Rachel. It wasn't his fault, it was mine!'

And she realized he was talking about their mother's death. How could Dodge even think Davey was responsible?

'Well, if this is the way you treat *any* of your kids, you want locking up! What possessed you to leave him out here like this? Help me get this undone!' The webbing had tightened as it got wet and her fingers simply couldn't wrench the knots apart.

Dodge finally ran to help. 'Honest, love, I didn't notice the rain! I come out to check on him once, give him his crisps and a drink, but he was running up and down the street. I only tied him up to keep him safe!' He tore at the knots and, when he'd finally freed Davey, he lifted the boy into his arms, looking left and right, lost in an alcoholic fuzz.

'Take him inside, Dad, *inside*,' she ordered, pushing him through the pub doors. A few people noticed a man with a sick child and moved aside, but most continued their drinking and singing. The pianist was banging out 'My Old Dutch' and Dodge had difficulty making himself heard over the din, but eventually the landlord showed them into a back room. His wife helped Ruby strip off Davey's wet clothes, searched out a blanket to wrap him in and put a small glass of brandy to his lips. Dodge stood to one side, drunken tears sliding down his cheeks now that it had become obvious Davey wasn't coming around.

'I'm sorry, love.' He put a hand on Ruby's shoulder as she knelt to chafe Davey's hands and feet. But she shrugged him off.

Eric was right. Dodge was a useless dad. The words were on her lips, but she didn't utter them. It wouldn't help Davey.

'He don't look good, love. Do you want me to phone for the doctor?' the landlady asked and Ruby nodded.

She looked at Dodge. 'I'll need some money to pay him.'

He dug deep into his trouser pocket and, finding no change, pulled out a pound from his wallet. It was the only note there.

'Is that all you've got?' She shot him an accusing look as she took the proffered note. Either he'd sold very few of the coats or his profits had already been drunk and his shamefaced expression told her which of the two it was.

It was almost midnight by the time Eric returned home. It was odd how much he reminded her of Dodge when he was drunk. He had the same benevolent smile on his face, as if he could love all the world.

'Ruby! What you doing up?' He came to put an arm around her shoulder and gave her a beer-infused kiss on the cheek.

She pushed him away. 'You stink of booze.'

'What? I only had a little drink! Don't give me your Band of Hope claptrap tonight. I've just been enjoying meself, which is what you should be doin' instead of wasting your life at that bloody Mission.'

'Why didn't you stay with our Davey?' Her mouth was dry and her muscles ached from the anxiety of the night.

'That's your bloody fault. I told you *two* hours!' He flung himself onto the armchair, his long legs dangling over the arm. She noticed his new trousers had beer stains on them.

'Well, it's thanks to you that our Davey's laying in there, fighting for his life!' But her voice cracked and the ice in her heart seemed to melt as soon as she attempted to blame Eric.

He sat bolt upright and then ran to the bedroom where Dodge had insisted on staying with Davey. When Eric returned, his face was white.

'What happened? I can't get no sense out of Dad.'

'Dodge tied him to a railing and left him out in the rain. The doctor says the whooping cough's turned to pneumonia.'

'I know he's a selfish bastard, but that takes the cake.' He shook his head.

'*He's* selfish! What about you? You should've looked after him, he's your brother!'

Eric's face flushed. 'That's it, stick up for Dad, like you always do. But if you want to blame someone then point the finger at your bloody self. If you wasn't out seeing to other people's families instead of home, looking after your own, then this would never have happened! It's you's to blame, no one else.'

Dodge appeared at the kitchen door. 'What are you two shouting the odds for? I don't want to hear it, not when my little boy's in there at death's door.' His stricken face crumpled and he leaned against the doorjamb, looking like a puppet whose strings had been cut. She ran to help him, fearing that he would fall to the ground.

'Come on, Eric' she pleaded and they supported Dodge to the armchair where he put his head in his hands and sobbed.

'Don't you two fall out. I'm the one to blame,' he said, 'it's me punishment...'

'Dad, I don't believe God's going to take our Davey just because you sold a few knocked-off furs!' she said, praying she was right.

Dodge sniffed and wiped his eyes with the back of his hand. 'I ain't talking about that, gel, I—'

Ruby put a finger to her lips. She'd heard a noise coming from the bedroom, a whimper, the same noise he'd made as a baby. Davey was awake.

She ran to the bedroom and, as she entered, Davey's dark eyes stared like twin black pools. His gaze found her and his mouth twisted in a cry. He reached out for her, but his hand flopped to the sheet and his eyes closed again. Leaning over the bed, she stroked his hair as she had when, as a tiny boy, he'd had nightmares about a monster who tried to kill him by crushing his head.

'It'll be all right Davey, love, there's no monsters. Ruby's here, no one can get you.'

She was aware of the two anxious figures standing behind her. And then Eric came and slipped his hand into hers. 'He opened his eyes; is that good? Will he be all right now?'

'Please God, he will,' she said, but her heart was gripped with a fearful doubt. What had Dodge done that was so terrible he thought God would take his child?

5

Charles

Summer 1935

She woke to the sound of Dodge's stifled sobs. She'd banished him and Eric in the early hours as their presence only added to the cloud of fear hanging in the room. Sister Evelyn had advised her that on hospital visits it was always best to banish death from a ward as soon as you stepped on to it for, in places of illness, the expectation alone could call death forth. But at some point exhaustion claimed her and she dropped off to sleep for she hadn't heard him come back into the bedroom. Now she listened to her father crying beyond the dividing curtain and was afraid to move a muscle, for then she would have to admit to herself that she hadn't banished death at all.

The low, stifled noise went on and on till she couldn't bear it any longer. With an almighty effort she heaved aside the bed cover and got out of bed. Trembling in every inch of her body, she parted the curtain and crept to where Dodge was hunched over, holding the little boy's hand.

'Dad?' Her voice was hoarse.

Dodge nodded silently, answering her unasked question. 'He's still with us.'

'Thank God.' She let out a shuddering sigh.

'What's God ever done for this family?' Dodge shot her an accusing look. 'He never helped your poor mum and now he's punishing me with my boy's life.'

She felt as if he were blaming her, but she said nothing and, with tears pricking her eyes, she left him there while she went to wake Eric for work.

As the morning wore on, Dodge refused to move and she found herself resenting his presence. He got in the way when she wanted to wash Davey, taking the bowl of water from her and spilling most of the contents onto the sheet. His guilt was like a dark shadow hanging over the bed.

'Come on, Dad, you go and get some breakfast at the café. You're just getting in me way. I'll stay with him.'

'I ain't leaving him! Hear me?'

She got his jacket and hat and shoved them into his arms. 'Either you go or I do! Who do you think's the best nurse, me or you?'

He paused for a moment. 'All right, gel. But you come and get me if anything changes.'

When he'd gone, the room felt lighter. Even Davey's breathing seemed to become easier. She looked down at her brother's pinched little face, remembering the pretty toddler and his infectious grin. Now the sharpness of his nose and cheekbones spoke of years of undernourishment. She stroked his cheek and, in the stillness, prayed properly for the first time since the doctor's pronouncement.

'He's done nothing wrong, you know that.' She spoke to God as she always did in private, as a friend, not as the wrathful God sometimes portrayed in church, not the vengeful God Dodge so feared, but the one who'd come to her on waves of love. 'Davey's always cheerful and he never complains. I know he's not very good at learning the Bible verses, but he's so proud when he does and he gets a bookmark from the Sunday School. Don't take him, just don't!' And she silently invoked all the Bible stories she knew about Jesus loving little children. '*Suffer the little children to come unto me,* you said. *Weep not; she is not dead, but sleepeth,* you said and Jairus's daughter got up!'

But Davey slept on; and when the evening came and he still hadn't improved, she left Dodge in charge and went to the only person who could help.

'Have faith, my dear,' Sister Evelyn said, her face radiant with certainty. 'God hears the prayers of the faithful, and when two or three are gathered together, those prayers are even more powerful! Your voice won't be the only one ascending to heaven, you can be sure of that. We'll have a prayer chain going that will stretch all the way to heaven and back.'

Ruby gazed into Sister Evelyn's bright, believing eyes and took strength. She knew the woman had had her own share of loss: two of her brothers had died in the war. And it was this, she'd told Ruby, that had first made her turn to God.

If there was one thing the members of the Central Hall knew how to do, it was pray – and not just on Sundays. There was the Monday Sisterhood, where two thousand women added a prayer for Davey to their list; at the Tuesday Brotherhood another thousand did the same; and the hundreds at Wednesday Fellowship added their voices, so that Ruby felt God must have been deafened by the clamour of so many prayers. But by the end of the week Davey's strength seemed to be waning rather than improving and the doctor had told them to prepare for the worst.

Sister Evelyn brought the minister with her to their house. The prayer he murmured turned the blood to ice in Ruby's veins. He was giving Davey to God, asking him to ease his passing. Ruby shook so violently she had to grab the bedclothes and make her excuses. She stumbled from the room and went to find Dodge. He was in his bedroom, where he'd spent most of the week. She was glad the minister hadn't seen him. Perhaps she shouldn't be ashamed that Dodge was a thief and a drunkard, but she was.

She found him lying on the bed, fully clothed – and drunk. She shook him till the coins in his jacket pocket rattled and he was forced to look up at her through bloodshot eyes, a line of drool at the corner of his mouth.

'What did you do?' she demanded. 'What could be so bad that our Davey's being punished for it?'

The minister's prayer had shaken her faith in her own loving God; perhaps Dodge was right after all.

'I only wanted to protect him, protect you all…' He swallowed slurred words, letting his head fall back against the pillow.

She thumped his shoulder. 'Wake up, Dad! Confess! Beg for mercy and it'll be all right!' But Dodge was as deaf to her pleas as, it seemed, was God.

She stumbled back in to the kitchen and slumped down at the table, clenching her hands together.

'I'll be Yours forever,' she promised, 'do whatever You ask, give up anything, go anywhere. I've got no life from now on, it's all Yours; just let our Davey live.'

The silence descended, then a red veil behind her eyes brightened gradually until she felt she was staring into bright sunlight. When she felt the hand on her shoulder she thought it might be Jesus, but the gentle jogging was insistent and only too human.

'There's been a change, my dear. You'd better come.'

Sister Evelyn's eyes were clouded with pity and Ruby jumped up. She hurried to the bedroom, where the minister stood holding up the cross which hung around his neck. It seemed to Ruby that Davey's face had plumped out, had almost regained the toddler chubbiness that had made him such a pretty child. But she knew it was an illusion; she'd heard that before death all the worry lines and pain disappear. She clutched Sister Evelyn's hand and the woman squeezed back. Ruby waited, afraid to move.

Then, with no warning, Davey took in one deep, shuddering breath and his eyes flicked open. He stared for a long time at the minister and then turned his fathomless dark eyes to Ruby.

'Why's that man wearing a necklace?' he asked in a hoarse voice.

And Ruby laughed in relief. Letting go of Sister Evelyn's hand, she threw her arms around Davey, squeezing him so tightly that he was forced into a weak attempt to push her away.

'Is there anything to eat?' he croaked, frowning.

'He's always been a hungry boy,' she explained in a mingled euphoria of tears and laughter.

'Of course he has,' Sister Evelyn said, nodding, knowing he'd had good reason.

There was great rejoicing at the Central Hall when the miracle of Davey's recovery was announced from the pulpit. After all her years of quiet service, it was almost as if Ruby had become visible for the first time. For, however hard she'd worked in the Mission, and however faithfully she'd attended, she was only ever one of thousands of faithful. Now the glamour of a miracle hung about her, people wanted to tell her about the prayers they'd offered up and she was grateful, but sometimes wished she could go back to being invisible.

It was at the next Pleasant Sunday Afternoon that she first noticed the muscular young man with close-cut rusty hair staring at her. She had seen him going about church business at the Central Hall, but they didn't move in the same circles. He was often chosen to do the readings, which he carried off with a confidence that Ruby envied. She noticed he would always look up between verses and seem to fix someone in the congregation with his gaze. He'd even given talks, usually about the plight of the poor children of Basutoland where he hoped one day to serve. Ruby remembered thinking he must be a very devoted Christian, to want to go to Africa. Now he was definitely staring at her, and if she hadn't known he was holy she would have thought he was eyeing her up.

They were listening to the speaker talking about plans for the next evangelistic crusade when, in what seemed an unashamed, deliberate way, she saw the young man get up from his seat and make a beeline for her. He nodded and smiled as he made other people in her row stand up so that he could come and take the empty seat beside her. She desperately wished that Ida wasn't sitting on her other side. Ruby turned her head away from the young man as he made himself comfortable in his seat. Ida, who'd finally kept her promise to attend a Pleasant Sunday Afternoon, raised her eyes. Before she could say anything, Ruby gave what she thought was a threatening glare and the briefest shake of her head. The young man's interest was embarrassing enough without having Ida commenting upon it.

But, being Ida, of course she did. In a voice Ruby feared would carry her friend said, 'Keen as mustard – you're on to a winner there, gel.'

'Shh, Ida!' Ruby hissed, wishing she hadn't been so persistent about Ida keeping her promise.

When the speaker had finished, it was time for a hymn and the young man next to her sang in a powerful baritone. He stood with one hand behind his back and held the hymnal in the other, never glancing at it, as he seemed to know all the words. After several more hymns and a closing prayer, she got up quickly, ready to usher Ida out into the opposite aisle, but the young man put a restraining hand on her elbow.

'Hello, it's Ruby Scully, isn't it? I'm Charles Best.' His handshake was firm and his face strong-boned and handsome. But the smile that briefly crossed his face was quickly replaced by a frown. 'And how is your poor little brother getting on? We prayed for him constantly in the Brotherhood. It was a mighty miracle.'

She felt Ida nudging her back.

'Yes, I'm so grateful. Thank you for praying.'

'It's no more than my duty,' he said, and there was a moment's silence that made her feel almost wrong for thanking him. Perhaps he thought she had robbed God of her thanks.

'I'm thankful to God every day,' she added quickly and felt Ida's eyes boring in to her back. The row was emptying and she saw her escape route opening up.

'Nice to meet you,' she said lamely, hustling Ida out into the aisle.

But once they were at the tea table she saw he'd stuck like glue. 'Can I get you some cake?' he asked.

'Yes, ta. That'd be lovely,' Ida said. 'Two bits, one for me and one for my friend.'

Keeping his gaze fixed on Ruby, Charles Best attempted to ignore Ida, but she pressed on regardless.

'I'm only visiting. I usually spend my Sunday nights up the pub,' she said, forcing him to notice her as Ruby squirmed. She knew Ida was having fun at his expense.

'You're welcome, here.' Charles gave a stiff smile. 'There's many a hardened drinker come to Jesus in this place, as your friend will testify.' He looked to Ruby for support. And it felt odd to be put on the opposite side of the fence to Ida, who had only ever been on Ruby's side. Ida smiled broadly, enjoying her discomfort.

While Charles helped them to cake, Ruby tried to step on Ida's toes, but she was having too much fun. As she took a great bite out of a slice of madeira, Ida asked disingenuously, 'Have you got any tracts I can read?' making Ruby blush and choke on her own cake.

Ida slapped her back and Ruby was relieved when Charles pointed them in the direction of a table filled with free literature, before excusing himself, explaining that he was needed at the Crusade Committee meeting.

'Good gawd, whoever stuck the broom up his arse did a good job of it!' Ida watched him go and let out a guffaw, which Ruby shushed, hoping Charles hadn't heard.

'He's a bit stiff, but he was kind about our Davey.'

'Kind? He's got his eye on you, that's all, Ruby. You've got to learn to spot the signs. So, you don't take anything he says as gospel, see? 'Cos holier than thou or not, there's only one thing they want when they've got that glint in their eye!'

'Ida, shut up. The young men here are a different breed to Terry and the loading-bay boys!'

Ida gave a deep sigh and put her arm around Ruby. 'Ah, my sweet innocent little friend. You never needed to come to the altar rail, love, you was born good.' And she gave her a loud kiss on the cheek.

Ida's verdict on the afternoon was that she'd enjoyed the hymns and the cake and the other girls, who she said were good sports, but she hadn't like the talk of a crusade.

'The only crusade I'm interested in is the one for increased unemployment allowance and more jobs and better housing. I think we should take care of our bodies and let God look after our souls. I can understand being a paid-up Labour Party member, 'cos we need the funds, but why does God need your signature on a card and your name in a book in heaven? If He can see inside your heart He knows already.'

'Well, that's what the "Good News" is all about, Ida,' she said, trying for the millionth time to explain, but Ida interrupted her.

'Hang on, I've just realized who he is.'

'Who?'

'*Charles* Best. But when I knew him he was plain old Charlie Best from Barnham Street Buildings. Tidied himself up since then, but I knew I recognized him from somewhere. I daresay that's why he tried to ignore me!'

'I don't think he tried to ignore you. When did you know him?'

'Oh, when we was kids. Our Barney used to be in a gang with him.'

'He was friends with your brother? So why should he remember you?'

'Cos I gave him a good hiding once. I can feel the crack of his jaw now.' Ida rubbed her fist and smiled at the memory.

'Well, it makes sense he'd want to forget you then! What did he do to you?'

'Not to me, to Barney. Shoved him around, treated him like a whipping boy. Anyway, you met him too, you know. Remember that red-headed kid, always barging up the front of the breakfast queue? He's a bully, that one.'

Ruby did have a vague memory, but there were always kids trying to push into the queue. 'But that was ages ago. He's got to be different now – he's a Christian.'

'Leopards don't change their spots. I'd steer clear of him, Ruby, if I was you.'

Her father had been one leopard who appeared to be changing his spots ever since Davey's recovery. He spent less time at the Upside Down and his winnings now always went straight into the housekeeping tins. Life took on a rare peacefulness, which even Eric contributed to by staying out of the house as much as he could. Ruby's time was even more co-opted by the Mission. Sister Evelyn had asked her to do more sessions at the Child Welfare clinic and because God had saved a child dear to her, she felt it only fair. She'd agreed to everything that God might ask of her – now or in the future – in her desperate plea for Davey. So when she was asked to be one of the sandwich boarders for the forthcoming crusade, she agreed without hesitation.

The sandwich boarders had to be young, fit and fearless. They walked the streets, wearing heavy wooden boards which advertised the coming crusade, over their shoulders: *Great Evangelistic Crusade in Southwark Park. Full orchestra, under-cover seating for a thousand people!* Their fearlessness came into play when traversing parts of Bermondsey where gangs of kids harried them, throwing stones and whatever rubbish came to hand; sometimes men and women shouted abuse as they passed along Tower Bridge Road.

On her first evening of sandwich boarding, Ruby and Molly, a friend from the Young Women's Fellowship, arrived at the Central Hall with about thirty other volunteers. Ruby immediately spotted Charles Best distributing boards. She suspected he'd noticed her when he made a show of shouldering four boards at once. She joined the line of volunteers and, when she finally came face to face with Charles, he gave her an encouraging smile.

'Is this your first time sandwich boarding?' he asked.

'Oh no, I've done it every crusade since I was fourteen. I'm an old hand. I like it!'

'Really?' He looked impressed. 'I've been put in charge this year and I've instituted a new policy. It's not right, letting our young women walk the streets unaccompanied, vulnerable to all sorts of—'

'Oh, you don't have to worry about me,' she interrupted. 'People have got used to me. They even call me Sister Anna with the Banner!' she said, laughing. And, in spite of the teasing, Ruby had never been physically attacked on the streets or been at the receiving end of the anger that other girls reported. She wasn't sure why she was spared – perhaps because she always imagined how she'd felt before coming to the Mission. To her mind, all she was offering was the chance of something different from the drudge of merely surviving: some jolly music, in a nice warm tent and, best of all, free tea and cake afterwards. As far as she could see, trouble only started if you acted as if you were better than the people whose streets you walked through. And Ruby could never do that, for she knew she wasn't.

'I know you'd be prepared to take abuse for the sake of the Lord, Ruby, but this year you're not going to have to take it alone. I'm paired with you tonight,' he told her, as he placed the sandwich board over her head and settled it on her shoulders like a yoke.

'But what about Molly?'

Charles looked down at his list. 'Molly's with Peter. Much better if there's a man and a woman together. Some of the toughs need a firm hand. There he is.' He pointed to a lanky boy with less muscle than Molly – who worked in the lime pits at Bevington's and had built up a physique worthy of a docker. Molly raised her eyes at Ruby and went to join the stripling.

Charles chose their route. They would cover Bermondsey Street, London Bridge Station, Tooley Street and finish at Dockhead. It wasn't the easiest of beats, but Ruby might have enjoyed it if she'd been alone, for she liked the bustle of London Bridge Station in the evening, when the bridge became a black river of office workers in dark suits and bowlers, with occasional splashes of colour from well-dressed young secretaries returning home to the suburbs.

As they made their way up Bermondsey Street she was uncomfortably conscious of Charles' silent presence at her side. His smart navy blazer and grey trousers had been pressed, his white shirt collar was immaculate and his tie knot sharp. He walked with his chin tilted slightly skywards and his gaze fixed on some invisible point in the far distance. For a while she wondered if they would make the whole round in silence, the only sounds between them the irregular clacking of the boards. But he'd been the one who'd forced their pairing, so she decided it was up to him to make the conversation.

Eventually he said, 'So, you've been coming to the Mission since you were fourteen – much longer than me. But why haven't I seen you before?'

'I've been coming since I was twelve, really. First it was free breakfasts, then Sunday School and at thirteen I made my decision.'

He nodded, thoughtfully. 'That's a good long time. Have you brought your family to the Lord?'

'My little brother Davey comes to Sunday School,' she answered truthfully, not wanting to mention Dodge's disapproval or Eric's recent anger at her devotion to the Mission.

'Not your parents?' he asked with a frown.

Perhaps he found it the easiest thing in the world to preach to his own family, but she found it the most difficult. When she'd first heard, from the pulpit, that those who didn't confess Christ wouldn't go to heaven, she'd despaired. How could it be that Dodge and Eric wouldn't be where she was? And she couldn't bear to think of her poor dead mother already in hell – she'd been an Anglican and Ruby wasn't sure if that counted – so she hoped God would be merciful. Now Ruby had dedicated herself to saving the others. She'd spent many hours on her knees, but the more she prayed, the more resistant they seemed to become.

'Mum's dead, she died in childbirth with our Davey.'

'I'm sorry, Ruby. It must be hard without a mother to guide you. Still, at least you have one parent.'

'What about your family?' she asked, not wanting to get on to the subject of that particular parent.

His gaze returned to the invisible far point. 'Dead to me. It was painful, but I cut all ties a few years ago. They refused to change their ways. My father's a drunkard and my mother's a gambler – and worse. To my shame, I couldn't turn them to Christ.'

'So, you just left them?'

He nodded. She could see the muscles of his jaw working as he gritted his teeth and released them. '*If thine eye offend thee, pluck it out,*' he said, quoting a verse she'd always found gruesomely disturbing. She wanted to counter with *Honour thy father and thy mother* but she guessed from Charles' stony expression that he was immovable when it came to his parents.

'So, where do they live?' she asked, hoping to ferret out any truth in Ida's memory of him. She was sure it must be false, for to her ears, his accent had very little of Bermondsey about it. His vowels were rounded and he sounded his aitches; a thing was not a 'fing' and he never said 'ain't' when he meant 'isn't'. Either he'd been to elocution lessons or Ida was wrong.

'They live not far from here, actually. Barnham Street Buildings.' His fair, freckled skin was unable to hide the rosy flush that suffused his cheeks. She felt sorry for him; to be so ashamed of his origins must be a burden; and yet, she had to ask herself, was she that much different, desperate as she was to keep Dodge's shady dealings a secret?

'There's nothing wrong with Barnham Street Buildings – nothing that pulling them down wouldn't fix!'

But her attempt to lighten his discomfort failed. 'It's a den of dissolutes, thieves and vagabonds,' he said, unsmiling.

Even the little she knew of the buildings gave the lie to that. She'd had a school friend who lived there whose family was decent.

'Anyway, I brushed that dust off my feet when I was only fifteen and left with nothing. I went to classes at the Bermondsey Settlement and now I'm training to be an accountant.'

'Good for you,' she said.

They had been handing out leaflets to anyone who showed any interest, but she felt she was getting less response than she had done in previous years. In fact, people were crossing to the other side of the street to avoid them. If Ruby had been on her own, she knew she'd have drawn some amused comments and even a few followers, tagging along with her to ask questions or just to enquire about the free food. Outside the Woolpack pub she bumped into a couple of girls from Crosse's and offered them some leaflets.

'Hello, here comes the Bible-basher,' one of them greeted her. 'Wait till Minnie Boot hears about this at work tomorrow. Shall I give her one?' She flapped the leaflet in Ruby's face and then turned away with a giggle and disappeared into the pub.

'Do you get much persecution at Crosse's?' She didn't remember telling Charles where she worked so he'd obviously made enquiries.

She laughed and looked him full in the eyes, and his cheeks glowed again, but the discomfort had a different cause and he looked away. 'Persecution? It's not exactly being fed to the lions! Minnie Boot don't scare me. It just wears me out sometimes.'

His gaze returned to hers, and this time the confident manner had faded. 'Sometimes I get so tired... It's a constant battle when you don't belong in this world.' And she saw his shoulders slump. It was almost like witnessing a knight of old sloughing of his armour.

'Still,' he said and shook himself, 'we have the breastplate of righteousness, the shield of faith and the sword of the spirit to help us!' And he seemed to rise up, encased in his spiritual armour; though Ruby wondered why it should weigh so heavy on his shoulders when it was meant to be made of light...

She found being at London Bridge less exhilarating this year and, buffeted by crowds, they soon turned for home. Halfway down Tooley Street, they were met by a phalanx of working men, dockers by the look of them, marching shoulder to shoulder with not an inch between them, blocking the entire width of the road, holding up buses and pedestrians alike. Their banners protested wage cuts and welfare cuts and proclaimed them to be members of the TGWU. They'd passed the union offices a little way back and she quickly realized this was where the marchers must be heading. There was no way through. She saw Charles glancing at a side road.

'We should cut down there into Crucifix Lane – we can get to Dockhead that way,' she suggested. He stood immobile, his fingers on his lips, beating a tattoo of indecision. What was the matter with him? She swerved to one side as two dockers broke ranks around her and made her own decision. If he wanted to battle against the crush he could, but she wouldn't. She ducked down the side street, looking up at the street name. All at once she understood his hesitation. It was Barnham Street.

He trotted to catch up with her, his face etched with faint disgust and what looked like apprehension.

'Sorry we had to come this way, Charles,' she shouted into his ear as steam trains thundered along the viaduct ahead of them.

'The Lord tests those he loves,' Charles said, as he marched on a little faster than before, forcing her into a trot so that her sandwich board banged uncomfortably against her knees.

'God didn't *make* you go this way, though, did he?'

'Ruby, you surprise me. I don't do anything without the Lord's leading.'

She gave herself the pleasure of imagining Ida's response to this, but kept quiet herself. She had thought it was her idea to come down Barnham Street, but perhaps it was indeed a test from heaven, for the gang of boys that came charging out of the tenement courtyard towards them were screaming like demons from hell.

'Get the Bible-bashers!' they whooped in excited high-pitched voices. 'Grab the boards off 'em!'

Charles didn't waver. He swung his arms like a grenadier guard and marched on. Ruby hesitated, thinking it might be better to run for it, but shamed by Charles's courage, she attempted to keep in stride with him. Soon they were surrounded by a circle of jeering kids and young men. A large boy of about fourteen took a running leap at Charles, lifting his boot and stamping it against the sandwich board. Charles rocked back slightly, but he was impressively built with a solid, muscled physique that would obviously take more than a boot in the chest to rock it. Two more attackers tried to tear the board from his shoulders. 'Gis a read!' one of them laughed. 'Can I take it home to show me old mum?'

Charles clamped his jaw tight shut and took hold of her hand, barging his way through, taking blows to both back and front boards, his trousers tugged at by smaller boys who hobbled him so effectively that he tripped and stumbled to the cobbles, bringing her down with him. Ruby flailed about like a tortoise on its back, unable to find purchase. Then she felt hands grabbing at her, fingers pinching at her arms and worming their way beneath the board towards her breasts.

'Get off, you dirty little sods!' she cried, kicking at the shins of her nearest attacker.

'Ohhh, you Bible-bashers ain't supposed to swear!' A hoarse-voiced young man thrust his face into hers, only to be yanked back by Charles who still lay beside her, hampered by the board and the small boy who sat on it. His face was inches from hers and she saw fury burning in his hazel eyes.

'Get off her, you filthy louts!' he shouted and, with a powerful surge, tipped the boy off and flipped up onto his feet. Tearing the front board off its strap, he spun it around in a wide arc, scattering their attackers. He was like a whirling dervish, spinning and spinning till the whole whooping crowd had dispersed beyond his reach. He helped her to her feet and gripped her hand.

'I thought you said you never had any trouble?' He was breathing heavily.

'I never have before. Must be you!' she told him.

He gave a grim smile. 'Oh, it's me all right.' And his eyes were focused on a figure emerging from behind the gang which had now regrouped at the tenement entrance.

'Need any help, Charlie?' the young man asked, nonchalantly, but his tone wasn't exactly sympathetic. Then, turning to the boys he ordered, 'Clear off you lot, go and find someone your own size.'

The boys walked meekly away and, as the young man approached, Ruby realized she'd met him before, though he showed no sign of recognizing her. Instead he addressed Charles.

'I thought this place wasn't good enough for you now, Charlie. Your mum and dad were telling me only the other day how you were too busy with your Mission work to visit them.'

'My name's *Charles* and you can keep your opinions about my parents to yourself,' Charles said quietly, red in the face. He turned to go, but the young man made the mistake of carrying on. 'I don't call it very Christian to neglect your parents. Your dad's in a terrible state; you should be looking after him.'

Without any warning Charles spun round and smashed his fist into the young man's jaw.

'I told you to be quiet,' he said, looking down at the sprawled figure. 'Come on, Ruby.'

The young man on the ground was tall but slender and she feared Charles had knocked him out.

'Hang on a minute, Charles, we can't leave him,' she said, bending down to see if he was hurt. But he turned onto his back and propped himself up on his elbows as if he was reclining on a beach and not the filthy cobbles of Barnham Street.

'Thank you, kind lady,' he said, pushing back dishevelled curls and giving her a wry smile, which made him wince and put his hand to his jaw. And, as his intelligent brown eyes met hers, she knew she'd definitely seen him before. It was Alfie Diamond from the Labour Institute.

'Has he hurt you?' she asked, looking over her shoulder as Charles, already walking away, called for her to hurry.

Alfie rubbed his jaw and shook his head. 'I've had worse from him in the past,' he murmured.

'I remember you from the Labour Institute.' Seeing him had given her a flash of guilt. 'I've been meaning to come and help with the hunger march but…' She wanted to explain why she hadn't made good on her promise.

'Don't worry. I know your brother's been ill. You'd best go.' He got to his feet and, without another word, strolled away, joining the ranks of dockers marching in Tooley Street.

Charles was obviously agitated as he massaged his fist over and over.

'What were you saying to him?'

'I met him when I went to the Labour Institute with my friend Ida. I'd promised to go and help with the hunger march.'

'You shouldn't get involved with him, Ruby. He's a bolshie troublemaker.'

She wasn't going to argue with Charles; whatever was between him and Alfie Diamond was obviously rooted in the past and Ruby thought it should probably stay there.

'And Ruby, I'm sorry to point this out, but you shouldn't have resorted to bad language.'

She was confused. 'When?'

'Towards those boys.'

She gave him a long stare, waiting for him to laugh, but his expression was very earnest.

'Well, you shouldn't have resorted to violence,' she said, fed up with protecting Charles Best's feelings.

'No. You're right, Ruby. But didn't I say that you'd need protection tonight?'

'Well, thanks for the help, Charles,' she said, silently wondering if she would have had a much easier time without him.

6

In A Pickle

Autumn 1935

As preparations for the crusade intensified, it seemed Charles Best was never very far from her side. He co-opted her onto the crusade committee, but she'd never felt so useless. For her, the hours spent in deciding the spending budget, which chairs to hire and what sort of lighting to use, was time-consuming and dull compared to her work in the Child Welfare Clinic or the Poor Men's Suppers. But Charles assured her that the really important work went on behind the scenes.

'I'd be happy just doling out the tea and cake,' she told Charles before one committee meeting. 'I don't think planning's my strong point.'

'Rubbish. You've made some very good suggestions,' he said and inclined his head to one side, holding the smile on his face for a fraction too long. 'I was wondering, Ruby, w-would you like to come for tea with me after the meeting?' His pale skin flushed and her first instinct was to refuse. She'd seen another side of him during the Barnham Street brawl – and, more importantly, Ida had warned her off him and she'd learned that her friend's intuition could sometimes be as sharp as her tongue.

'Oh, that's very nice of you, but I'm so busy, Charles – I've had to take on extra shifts and there's a lot to do at home, then there's the crusade...' She swallowed hard and saw his face fill with confusion.

'Perhaps another time?' she said.

'Good. Saturday afternoon, then?' he said, with a satisfied nod. 'We'd better be getting started.'

He ushered her into the small meeting room and she felt that she'd been herded by a sheepdog into a pen without ever knowing how she got there.

Later she walked home, her mind full of Charles Best, and what it would be like to be courted by him. She was aware it was a fantasy that could never work. A good part of her life would have to remain hidden – the part that contained Dodge. Her musings made the scene that awaited her at home even more troubling. She found their rooms in chaos. Large flat boxes lined the passage and Uncle Jim – not a real uncle but a lifelong friend of Dodge's who was always game for a punch-up or a chance of easy money – was puffing up the backstairs from the garden with more boxes.

The wooden backstairs were an afterthought to the three-storey Victorian house, put in when Mrs Nash had rented out the lower half to two families. A door was knocked through the second-floor back wall and the stairs led straight to the garden below. But it was a rickety affair and Ruby thought it might collapse under the combined weight of Uncle Jim and his boxes.

'Out the way, Ruby, love, we're bringing them up from the garden.'

The boxes joined two dozen others in Dodge's bedroom, where she found him silently tallying up the contents. One look told her what they were and a wave of anger flooded her.

'Don't bother counting them, Dad, there's twenty-four to the box,' she said, crossing her arms and deliberately blocking Uncle Jim's passage.

Dodge flashed her a distracted smile. 'Good girl, very helpful.'

'I'll give you helpful! Dad, they're Branston Pickle!'

'Seconds! Dented lids.'

She walked over and snatched up a jar. 'Perfect!' she said, tossing it at him. 'We don't send them out with dented lids. You'll get me sacked if the police find this lot.'

'Well, I'm sure the tins was dented.'

'Tins! You've got tins as well? God help me.' She went to inspect the other boxes and let out a long groan. There were tins of beans, soups and vegetables, as well as jars of meat paste, pickles and sauces. It looked as if someone had stolen a Crosse's delivery lorry and passed the entire contents over to Dodge.

'Don't look so worried, love. Have a bit of faith. Just say a prayer I don't get caught.' Dodge winked at Uncle Jim, who chuckled.

'It's not funny. I don't care about you getting put away, but I do care if our Davey has to go into an orphanage because I can't pay the rent while *you're* inside!'

'Shh, you don't have to let her upstairs know all our business.' He jerked his head towards Mrs Nash's floor. 'I'll have to go and sweet talk her as it is, for next week's rent.'

'You're joking!'

She turned abruptly away, slamming the bedroom door so that it shook in the frame. Back in the kitchen she ran to find the rent tin. It was empty. 'Well, that takes the cake.' She stared into the empty tin and then shouted along the passage, 'I'm taking Davey and moving out if this carries on!' She knew full well her threat was as empty as her purse. On thirteen shillings a week she had no way of keeping herself, let alone Davey.

She stamped down the wooden stairs into the garden, hoping the little patch of green, with the silver birch tree her mother had lovingly planted when Ruby was a baby, would disperse her anger. It had given her comfort so many times, as though part of her mother remained with her. Aunt Nancy peered around her scullery curtain and then came out into the yard.

'You ain't going to change him now, love,' Aunt Nancy said, her cigarette dangling from the corner of her mouth. 'He don't know any other way to make a few bob. And he's got a very good heart, your dad. You shouldn't shout at him, Ruby, he thinks the world of you and the boys.'

'Oh, I know he does, but did you see what he's brought home this time?'

Aunt Nancy nodded. 'Crosse's stuff. To be honest, I've had a few jars of Branston off him meself today. But I wouldn't worry. No one round here's going to shop him, not even her upstairs – we'd all have empty cupboards, gel!' And her thin frame was wracked by a phlegmy laugh that ended in a rattling cough.

She began struggling to take down the zinc bath from where it hung on the garden fence and Ruby went to help her. They carried it into Aunt Nancy's basement scullery and Ruby began helping her to fill it with hot water from the copper.

'You know what? You ought to get out more, Ruby. Have a bit more fun. I'll always have Davey if you want to go out with your mates – or a feller.'

It seemed like a sign. Perhaps it was right, after all, that she had agreed to go out with Charles. But next morning at work Ida was unconvinced.

'Oh, you silly mare. A sign? I should think that little punch-up he had with Alfie would've give you enough of a sign!'

'How do you know about that?'

'Alfie told me and Ocki about it in the pub.'

'I didn't think he'd even remembered me at first, and then he said he knew about Davey.'

'Oh, Ruby, you ain't the sort of girl men forget.' And when Ruby gave her a blank look, Ida giggled.

'Poor Charles, he really felt bad about the fight.'

'Not half as bad as Alfie felt; he's got a fractured jaw.'

'No!'

Ida nodded. 'He could have had Charlie up for assault, but he ain't vindictive.'

'Oh, Ida, poor Alfie, what can I do?'

'Nothing for Alfie, but you can do yourself a favour and tell Charles to sod off to Swaziland.'

'Basutoland.'

'I don't care if it's Never Never Land, just as long as he slings his hook.'

The following Saturday Charles insisted on coming to her home to collect her, but she made sure she was ready and waiting for him outside. She'd rather not have to explain why her home was full of Branston Pickle. He was wearing his Sunday-best suit, with a matching tie and handkerchief and new, highly polished shoes. His bronze hair was cut in a short back and sides and he wore a black trilby which made him look older than his years. He wore his clothes with as much confidence as he did everything else, seemed to own the very ground he stood on. He was by far the smartest man she'd seen in the Mission and he stood out in a congregation which was poor enough for the collection plate to be full of coppers and where the steward had to spray unwashed members of the congregation with disinfectant on warm days.

Today was a mild September morning, which was fortunate as the only decent jacket Ruby owned was made of thin blue cotton. The wide collar flaps were trimmed with some white braid she'd added herself and she'd paired it with a mid-calf, straight navy skirt. Both jacket and skirt were from the Mission's cast-off clothing club, but Aunt Nancy had assured her she looked very smart when Ruby dropped off Davey.

Charles offered her his arm in a very gentlemanly way and told her they were going to the tea room in Southwark Park, which suited her as it was within easy walking distance and meant she wouldn't have to sit on a bus. She was conscious that the cheap cotton skirt creased easily, while every part of him looked pressed to a knife edge.

Today their conversation flowed more easily. They spoke about the crusade, his accountancy examinations and his desire to be a missionary in Africa one day.

'I'm only a clerk, but the accountancy pays well enough and it's just to fund my training for the ministry,' he explained.

'I suppose that'll be quite a few years away yet?' she asked.

'Not if it's God's will I go earlier. Eight years at most. I intend to be in the field before I'm thirty; after all, that's when our Lord started his ministry, and after the mission field I'll come home and be a minister of my own church.'

She nodded, impressed that he had such a far-reaching plan for his life. She couldn't see beyond the next payday and hoped he wouldn't ask about her own hopes and dreams. Sometimes, when she was lying in bed in the early morning, before everyone else had stirred, she would get a sudden vision of herself doing work that improved people's lives and made her own more bearable. Something far out of her reach – a housing officer, perhaps, or even a teacher. The visions would be as clear and insistent as the bells of St James's in her mind, but then they would fade to mere echoes, as fleeting as their chimes and soon replaced by the realities of Monarch Buildings or Arnold's Place. Until those were all gone, there were thousands – like the Mongeys and old Mrs Simmons in Abbey Street – whose lives would remain unbearable.

But Charles didn't probe her hopes and dreams; instead he asked if she'd ever considered missionary work herself.

'I put sixpence in the African babies' box every month and a penny for a picture out of the book,' she said, feeling now that this was totally inadequate. But she liked doing it. You had to choose a photo of an African child from something like a book of raffle tickets; you tore it off and kept it in your Bible so you could imagine your donation going to that child. But she doubted it was true; she'd been doing it for many years and always picked the same babies, none of whom seemed to get any older.

'Actually, I'm starting a prayer group for the children of Basutoland; will you join us, Ruby?'

'Oh, yes! I am really interested in African children,' she said, and she thought that perhaps, beneath Charles's rather dour exterior, there really was a kind heart.

They reached the tea room – a green and cream wooden chalet at the edge of the park, in the shadow of the old St Olave's workhouse. Charles chose a table with a view of the flower beds. He drank his hot tea in great gulps, sitting on the edge of his seat and seeming, to Ruby, eager to be outside walking again. His scone and jam was also efficiently demolished so that she felt she must hurry and finish. He pulled at his tie and she wondered how he'd take the heat of Africa if he couldn't put up with a mild English afternoon. The place was crowded and the windows closed and he seemed too large for the table they'd chosen.

'Do you want to go now?' she asked, putting down her scone and wiping a crumb from her mouth.

'Only if you want to; you haven't finished.'

She handed him the plate and he grinned, popping the rest of the scone into his mouth.

They strolled around the boating lake and when he asked if she'd like to take a boat out, he paid the tuppence and took her, with a few strong strokes, to the central island. He'd removed his jacket and she could see sweat rings growing beneath his armpits. He rowed with concentration and purpose, sending the boat smoothly around the island, deftly avoiding collisions with other rowing boats and with the motor cruiser that chugged back and forth on lake tours. She'd lived here all her life and never been able to spare the time nor the money for tea in the refreshment room nor a boat on the lake. If he'd taken her to the Savoy Grill she couldn't have been more grateful.

He bought them ice cream at the lake kiosk and they walked back down the broad avenue of trees, eating the ice cream and listening to the band that was playing to an audience seated on deckchairs.

'Do you want to sit and have a listen?' he asked, flicking his pointed tongue expertly along the ice cream. But she was already getting to know what made Charles uncomfortable.

'You, in one of those!' She pointed to the confining striped deckchair. It would bind him like a strait jacket. 'You'll never get yourself up out of it.'

He shook his head and laughed. 'I am a bit large for those things.'

'I don't know how you managed it, growing up in those two room places in Barnham Street. My friend Alice lived in one and it was tiny.'

His smile disappeared. 'Ruby. I really meant what I said about leaving that place behind. I'd rather you didn't mention it again. It's not something I tell everybody about... I thought I could trust you, though.'

'Oh, I'm sorry. Of course I wouldn't say anything to anyone else about you coming from there.'

He gave a brief nod and she feared she'd spoiled the day. But then he asked if he could hold her hand and, as they walked along the broad avenue, she felt forgiven.

He was so different to her short-lived sweetheart Terry from the loading bay. She felt he would never take advantage of her, nor harm her, and he had his life so much under control; it felt comforting to drift off into the briefest of dreams, as they walked hand in hand, that she might share in that order and purpose.

But her dream was cut short when they arrived back at St James's Road. Aunt Nancy was waiting outside with Davey. She shot Ruby an anxious look.

'Davey's been pining for you,' Aunt Nancy said, giving Charles a nervous smile.

Ruby knew that was a lie, because Davey was playing a game of marbles in the gutter and gave her only the briefest of nods.

'You two better say your goodnights, cos I've got to get to me evening cleaning,' she said, with a half wink at Ruby.

There was no evening cleaning job. Something was wrong and she guessed Aunt Nancy was giving her an excuse to get rid of Charles before it became obvious what the trouble really was.

As she watched him disappear around the corner into Jamaica Road, she turned to Aunt Nancy. 'What's happened now?' she asked, dry-mouthed, dumped back into her chaotic life in an instant. 'Is it Dodge?'

Aunt Nancy nodded, mouthing under her breath so that Davey couldn't hear, 'He's been nicked in the Upside Down, trying to sell a chap a case of Branston. Turned out the feller was old Bill!'

Some tightly coiled spring in Ruby's heart let go and she leaned against the airey wall with a light-headed feeling resembling relief. What she had so long dreaded had finally come to pass. Aunt Nancy waited, wide-eyed, for her response and then all at once Ruby's heart thumped in her chest as she remembered. 'Oh, Lord, no! The boxes! Aunt Nancy, have the police been?'

'Not yet, Jim got here first. He was in the pub with your dad and run all the way from the Old Kent Road.'

Just then Uncle Jim came down the front steps, wiping sweat from his forehead.

'Don't worry, Ruby, gel,' he said, answering her worried look, 'they've all gone. Georgie next door helped me get 'em into Nancy's shed. I've give him a few tins for his trouble – if that's all right with you, darlin?'

'What are you asking me for? I'm not running Dodge's business for him, Uncle Jim!'

'Well, someone's got to, love, while he's away.'

She lifted her eyes to heaven. Was this one of those 'tests' Charles was so fond of telling her about? 'Can't you just get rid of them?'

Uncle Jim sucked on his teeth and shook his head sadly. 'Too hot, Ruby. Best not to try and move 'em at the moment. The Old

Bill will be on us like a ton o' bricks. If they come and search your place, you just act normal.'

'Normal?' She gave a sharp laugh and Davey looked up from his marbles. She guessed she'd have to answer questions about where the Branston had come from and she would have to lie. So, she'd already failed whatever test God had sent her way.

'Oh, I give up. Come on, Davey, it's bedtime,' she said, wearily. 'Thanks for your help, Uncle Jim. But you will let me know when it's safe to get rid of the stuff, won't you? It's not fair keeping them in Aunt Nancy's shed and if Mrs Nash takes it into her head to have a root around we'll be out on our ear.'

He gave her a kiss on the cheek. 'I'll be in touch.'

'And if you find out what's happening to Dodge...?'

'You'll be the first to know, Ruby, love.'

He wiped a hand over his sweaty, balding head. 'He's had a good run, though, ain't he? Made a pretty penny before they've caught him.'

'If he has, we haven't seen much of it, Uncle Jim,' she told him truthfully, and saying goodnight to Aunt Nancy she led Davey up the steps to their front door. He put his hand in hers and raised questioning dark eyes. 'Will Dad be all right?'

'Oh, Davey. Don't start worrying about Dad. He can look after himself.' And she added with a bitterness that increasingly tinged her view of Dodge, 'He's good at that.'

She waited for the police to come, but as the night wore on she began to hope she'd get away without being questioned. When she heard the knock she jumped up and ran in to the passage, trying to remember the well-rehearsed words which would involve the least lies. But it wasn't the police.

Eric came through the door, smiling broadly, his face flushed. He offered her an unusually affectionate kiss.

'Have you been drinking, Eric?' she asked sharply.

'Sod me, can't I be happy? And no, I haven't been on the piss. I ain't Dad!' But his eyes were too bright and she wasn't convinced.

'Where've you been, then? It's so late.'

'One of me mates took me to this rally, it was brilliant.'

'What, a hunger march?' She'd never heard him express much interest in politics, even when Ida was round to spar with.

'No! Labour haven't done a thing for us working people. It was a BUF rally.'

'Oh Eric, not the fascists!' She knew all about the BUF. When she and others from the Mission were on public house crusades, they would often bump into groups of belligerent Blackshirts, standing outside the pubs, trying to sell their magazine and usually failing. Bermondsey's borough flag was red for a reason, Ida had always told her. And only last year, when the *Daily Mail* had been plastered with a 'Hurrah for the Blackshirts' campaign, Dodge had stopped reading it, saying he hated bullies, though perhaps it was because he feared their promised crackdown on crime would curb his activities a little too much.

'Don't turn your nose up like that,' Eric said. 'They'll have this country sorted out in no time. A tea leaf like our dad wouldn't last five minutes!'

'Maybe not, but Eric, while we're on the subject of Dad, I've got something to tell you and I don't want you shouting and hollering and waking up Davey.'

Eric heard her out quietly enough. She'd expected him to rail against Dodge, but instead he leaned his head in his hands and asked, 'Do you think he'll be all right?'

It struck her that where her first thoughts had been for how to keep the family going, his were for Dodge. 'That's what Davey asked me. But what I want to know is will *we* be all right?'

'They can't nick us for something he's done!'

'I'm talking about paying the rent and feeding us. You earn even less than I do. At least I'm guaranteed extra shifts in the

Paste Kitchen till Christmas. That'll pay the rent till then, but there won't be much left for anything else.'

'I'll try and get some overtime,' he said, then slumping to the floor and leaning against her legs, put his head on her knees. 'Oh, Ruby, coming out of that rally tonight, I just had this feeling everything was going to get better. But nothing don't change, does it, not when it comes to Dad?'

Ruby stroked his hair, reflecting that whatever the fascists had offered him, they couldn't promise to change human nature. She tried to dredge up the drop of comfort that he needed. 'That's true, but you know Dad, sometimes he just gets lucky. Maybe he'll get off with a warning.' And that was the best she could offer him tonight.

The following Monday, after their shift in the vegetable preparation room in the 1927 building, she and Ida crossed the yard to the 1924 building and climbed four floors to the Paste Kitchen. Extra staff were always needed here in the months before Christmas and it wouldn't be the first time Christmas puddings had got the Scullys through a lean patch. The chefs who ran the floor wore tall white hats, check trousers and white tunics. Two of them were tipping large pans of dried fruit and great blocks of suet into a deep circular steel vat sited at the head of a long wooden table. She and Ida donned clean white aprons and caps before joining a team of twenty girls, ranged either side of the table. Clouds of nutmeg, cinnamon and ginger rose up as the chefs began emptying bags of spices over the vat.

'Ooh, smell that spice, Ruby!' Ida nudged her as they took their places near the top of the table. Ruby nodded, unable to raise any enthusiasm for a job she normally enjoyed.

'Come on, it's got to be better than having stinking onions under your nose all day! What's the matter with you anyway?' Ida said, giving her a puzzled look.

She shook her head. 'Nothing. I'd better get these set up,' she said, lifting a 2lb weight onto the scales.

'Didn't it go well with Charlie?' Ida whispered.

'Shh, don't make a fuss. Stack me up some basins.'

Ida began loading the table with white china basins, ready for Ruby to fill.

The chefs were now working up a sweat as they stirred the mixture in the steel tub with two huge wooden paddles. They needed dockers' muscles, for the sticky mixture was as hard to work as road tar. In fact, she and Ida always joked that the pudding chefs' sweat was the secret ingredient in Crosse's Christmas puddings and they would always tip each other off when a drop was about to plop into the mixture from the end of a chef's nose. Once the chefs were satisfied with the mix, they filled two smaller steel pans on either side of the table, from which Ruby and the girl opposite scooped ladles of mixture. It was Ruby's task to weigh out two pounds of the mixture on scales, then fill one basin at a time, passing them on for tamping down to Ida, who then slid them along to the rest of the girls for parchment pleating and wrapping the basins.

It was easy work and usually fun because the spirit of Christmas seemed to hang over the kitchen when they were pudding filling. Perhaps it was the smell, or the anticipation, or just because it felt like a holiday after peeling two thousand onions a day. It was mercifully easier on the hands. But as the weigher, Ruby did need to have her wits about her. For it was crucial, in the batch-cooking process, that each basin contain exactly the same weight.

After ten minutes it was obvious that Ruby's side of the table was producing far fewer puddings than the opposite side. And it drew the attention of Sid Bean, the foreman, who patrolled between the benches, inspecting parchment seals and ensuring wrapped puddings were stacked swiftly onto cooking racks ready for transport to the hot room. Any lag in the production caused an immediate log jam.

'Ruby, do you think you could manage to get us a few done by Christmas?' Sid asked her, his tone laced with sarcasm. 'I mean, what would Jesus say about it if there was no Christmas puddings at bleedin' *Christmas*! You in love or something?'

'I bloody well hope not, we're all on piecework!' piped up a girl down the line, who'd been standing idle. Seeing Ruby's blush, Ida took a step back from the table. 'I'll do a turn on the scales,' she said and the foreman nodded. 'Lively then.'

As they swapped places, Ida whispered, 'We're going out to the pub together after work and I don't care if you drink tap water. You need a night off!'

That evening, after Davey was in bed, Ruby met Ida in the St James Tavern. Known to all as 'the Jame'oh', the pub was only a few hundred yards from her house and she'd chosen it because she could get home quickly if she were needed.

'I can't stay long, Ida,' she said, removing her coat and slipping it over the back of the bentwood chair. 'Aunt Nancy'll pop up and check on Davey but I don't want to take liberties; she had him nearly all of yesterday.'

'Here y'are, gel, bitter lemon.' Ida pushed the drink towards her. 'Was you out with Charlie a long time, then? I thought you'd be bored stiff after an hour and come home!'

'He's not boring! I don't know many people with his get-up-and-go. Besides, I think it's more important to be kind than interesting. Do you know what, Ida? He really cares about people in Africa!'

'Pity he don't care about his old mum and dad, then.'

'Oh, Ida I don't want to argue about him. I probably won't see him again anyway, not when he finds out about Dodge.'

'What's your dad got to do with it?'

'He's been nicked.'

Ida's eyes widened. 'Good gawd, no! What for?'

'Tried to sell a case of Branston to a copper.'

Ida laughed, but quickly put her hand over her mouth. 'Sorry, I shouldn't, but surely the silly sod knows how to spot an off-duty flattie by now?'

Ruby shook her head. 'He was probably drunk.'

'So that's why you've been off with the fairies all day. Is he locked up?'

Ruby nodded. 'As far as I know.'

'He might get off with a fine, love.'

'And if he doesn't?' Ruby felt her throat tighten. She knew she should have faith that God would provide. After all, they hadn't starved yet.

Ida put a hand over hers. 'If he gets put away, you won't be on your own. You know I'll always help you out.'

Tears stung Ruby's eyes. 'You're a good friend, Ida. But your mum needs your wages.'

Ida squeezed her hand. 'I may be a caddywack, but even I've heard of the loaves and fishes! We'll get by.'

Ruby gave Ida a hug. 'You always help me bounce back.'

'You do that all on your own. Anyway, I reckon they'll let Dodge out with a court date. He'll probably be home tonight.'

'Let's hope so.' But she felt torn between wanting him home and never wanting to see him again.

'Now, tell me all about your day out with *Charles*. Did he try and kiss you?'

'No, he's a gentleman. We did hold hands, though.' And Ruby gave a small smile.

Ida pulled a disbelieving face. 'A gentleman? I'd lay money that won't last.'

'Ida, you don't understand. He's a Christian. We don't believe in – in doing anything before you're married.'

'He's a man. That's all I need to understand.'

'What about you and Ocki?' Ruby asked, deflecting her. 'Has he kissed you?'

Ida gave a deep sigh and nodded. 'I know he's not what most people would call a catch, Ruby, but he's the best kisser ever – and a bit more than that!'

Ruby blushed. 'You haven't? Oh no, why did you do that?' she asked, jolted by the fear that her dearest friend would go to hell.

Ida laughed. Then, with shining eyes and flushed cheeks, she looked at Ruby and said simply, 'Because I love him.'

Fear vied with happiness for her friend and it was tinged with a little jealousy too, because Ruby had always felt first in Ida's affections. 'Oh, Ida, why couldn't you have waited till you got married?'

Her friend shrugged. 'We might not get married.'

Ruby blinked. 'What are you talking about? Of course you will, if you love each other.'

Ida twirled her glass around on the beer-ringed table. 'There's other ways to live your life. I want to be with him *now*, not ten years down the line when he's got a better job and we can afford to set up on our own. We might all be dead by then! Besides, I don't think it'd go down very well with his mum and dad.'

'Why not?'

'I'm a caddywack.'

'So what? People might not like it, but Catholics marry Protestants all the time these days. My cousin did and they're doing fine. She just had a bit of a tussle about how they'll bring up the kids.'

'But Ocki's not a proddywack, he's Jewish.'

'So what? He's not practicing is he?' Perhaps wrongly, Ruby had assumed that as Alfie had said he was agnostic, Ocki would be too.

Ida sighed. 'No. But still, I wouldn't be his mum and dad's first choice and mine would go bonkers.'

'I'm sorry it ain't straightforward, love, but you're the best fighter I know. Remember when anyone tried to nick your bread at the free breakfasts – they'd be on their back under the table in no time. Why would you let anyone take Ocki away from you, if you really love him?'

Ida drained her stout to the last fleck of foam before answering. 'You might have a point there, love. But nobody's taking him away from me, and marriage… well, it ain't for everyone.'

They walked arm in arm back along St James's Road and when they got to Ruby's house, she kissed her friend goodnight. 'I know the Bible says it's a sin, Ida, but you know what I think? I think if God is love, then loving someone can't be classed as bad as murdering them, can it?'

'You little rebel, you! Charlie'll give you the elbow if he hears you talking like that.'

And Ruby thought she was probably right.

Instead of going straight upstairs, she went down to the basement to let Aunt Nancy know she was home. When the woman answered her door, she had a strange, wide-eyed look on her face and said in an overly loud voice, 'Oh, Ruby, love, come in! There's a constable here in the kitchen wants to speak to you – something about your father. But I told him you ain't seen Dodge in a long time!'

The policeman looked comfortable, sitting at the table with a cup of tea. He was dunking a bourbon cream biscuit and looked up briefly before popping it into his mouth. Biscuits weren't generally available in Aunt Nancy's house, so she must have cracked open the Christmas store and her younger children were staring at the policeman with undisguised envy. He got up, brushing crumbs from his trousers.

'Just a routine call, Miss Scully. Perhaps we could go upstairs?' He looked around at the little faces following the proceedings with undisguised interest. 'Have a word in private?' He thanked Aunt Nancy for the tea and as he bent to pick up his helmet she mouthed at Ruby, 'You ain't seen Dodge for weeks!'

Upstairs, the constable explained what she already knew. 'I'm afraid we have your father in custody on suspicion of receiving and selling stolen goods. Now, he's denied any involvement on your part, but we believe you work at Crosse & Blackwell's, so you understand we need to ask the question: did you help your father illegally obtain a quantity of Branston Pickle?'

Every part of her body was trembling. Her black leather Bible with gold-leaf edges which had belonged to her mother lay accusingly on the table, daring her to lie.

Ruby indicated a chair for the policeman and sat down herself, grateful that her shaking legs were now hidden beneath the table. The policeman's eye was caught by the Bible and she reached out to it for strength.

'Are you a churchgoer, Miss Scully?' the constable asked, with a look of surprise.

'I go to the Central Hall,' she said, gripping the Bible now, though her hand shook visibly.

'I understand you haven't seen your father in some time, Miss Scully, and I can see this has been a bit of a shock for you, so I won't keep you long. Now, can I write down here in my report that, as an employee of Crosse & Blackwell's, you have had nothing to do with your father's alleged crime?'

She couldn't categorically say she'd had nothing to do with the crime – there was, after all, a stash of stolen cartons in Aunt Nancy's shed that she had full knowledge of.

'I *am* an employee of Crosse's, but I didn't supply any Branston to Dad – I couldn't have, I work in the 1924 building.'

He'd only asked about the Branston so she didn't feel she had to address the tinned soup and meat paste, both of which *were* made in the 1924 building.

'Ah, of course, Branston's is made in the 1927 building.' The policeman smiled. 'My mum worked there for years – salad cream. Now, if it's all right with you, I just need to have a quick look round the other rooms. I'm sure there's no need, but it's procedure.'

'Of course, there's only the two bedrooms; Davey, my little brother, is asleep in one...'

'I'll just pop my head round the door,' he said and she led him along the passage.

The only light came from the gas mantle on the stairs. Its soft glow illuminated Davey's untroubled features. 'Handsome little chap,' the policeman said, smiling, then scanned the room.

They went into Dodge's room. Uncle Jim had done a good job of clearing away the evidence, but Ruby spotted a couple of dents in the lino where the heavy boxes had rested. She waited for the policeman to notice them, but he looked inside the wardrobe and behind the curtains before giving a satisfied nod. 'Nothing here.'

Back in the kitchen, he finished writing up his notes at the table. 'I'm sorry to have troubled you,' he said, tapping on the Bible which she'd left lying there. 'I go to the Bermondsey Gospel Mission myself,' he said and she silently thanked God for her mother's Bible.

'It's been no trouble.' She got up to see him out. 'Do you think me Dad'll be coming home soon?'

He gave her a pitying look. 'The evidence is pretty clear, Miss Scully. I think he's looking at six months.'

After he'd gone, she sat alone for a long time, flicking through the Bible, looking for comfort. On the flyleaf her mother had recorded in a clear, looping handwriting the births – and deaths – of all her children. Ruby at the war's end in 1918, Eric in 1920, and two other children who'd died in infancy. Then Davey's birth was recorded in 1928. She looked at the handwriting; it was the same as the previous entries, certainly nothing like Dodge's scrawl, and for the first time it struck her that it must have been her mother who had entered Davey's birth. How had she never noticed it before? It meant that her mother must have lived at least long enough to see her child and record his birth. A wave of gratitude swept through Ruby, that her mother had at least known Davey, if only for the briefest of times. She wished Dodge had been more open to questions about her mother's death. That sparse sentence: 'Your mum died in childbirth' had left her with a lifetime of anguished imaginings. Now she put the Bible's flyleaf close to her face and put her lips to the faded ink, imagining she was kissing the beloved hand that had once held the pen.

A noise made her start and pull away from the Bible. Davey had crept in and was standing beside her.

'Can't you sleep?' she asked, taking him on to her lap.

'I had a bad dream – about Dad. Ain't he ever coming home again, Ruby?'

She rested her chin on his head and he reached for the open Bible. His small finger began tracing the record of births and death. 'This is "Mum-in-heaven's" Bible, ain't it?' he said. 'Tell me all about her.' And he pulled up his knees, curling into a ball, ready to be told the oft-repeated, comforting litany of his mother's virtues. All the minute details that Ruby could remember – the colour of her hair, her warm laugh, how she always smelled of Lily of the Valley and how she loved all her children very much. When she got to this point, Ruby found silent tears wetting her cheeks, because for the first time it could finally be true. Her mother *had* seen Davey and, of course, she had loved him.

7

Crusades and Kitchens

Winter 1935

The final preparations for the Southwark Park crusade brought Ruby and Charles into almost daily contact with planning and prayer meetings and sorties into the streets delivering leaflets. At meetings, people listened respectfully to what he had to say and they would often come to him with questions. Although he held no official position in the Mission, he seemed to have made himself indispensable in so many areas that she wondered how he had the time to fit in his work at the accountants.

He did everything with energy and confidence. As they stacked chairs after one prayer meeting, she noticed how he lifted six at a time so that a hundred chairs were cleared and stacked in minutes. And then he was ready to go on to the next job. But whatever they were doing, he always contrived to spend some time alone with her and then walk her home. And it was on one of these walks home that he confessed to her that he had doubts.

'It's not the Lord, I doubt. It's that a person from my background can ever hope to rise in the church. I haven't had the advantage of a good upbringing or education and that's my cross to bear, Ruby. But sometimes I feel I'm a bit of an imposter.' She was surprised that he seemed really interested in her opinion. He was always so sure of himself.

'I think it's *because* you've had no advantages that you'd make such a good minister! Especially with a congregation like ours, coming from the same background – you can understand them better.'

But he shook his head. 'No, no. They need leaders that can set an example of another sort of life! That's why I've spent all this money on elocution lessons. Our sort are never listened to and a minister needs to be *heard*.'

She felt an aching uncertainty in the pit of her stomach. What he was saying seemed well-reasoned, and yet his words grated in her heart like St James's bells on a practice night.

'I think you've got it wrong,' she ventured and he shook his head, frowning.

'I've made a study of the way institutions work, Ruby. Whether it's accountancy firms, local politics, churches… I think you'll find I'm right,' he said, with a look that made her feel foolish for even suggesting otherwise. He was so far beyond her in experience and education, and he spoke with such authority, that sometimes she wondered why he was bothering with her. But when it came time to say goodnight, she understood that better. He would only ever hold her hand, or sometimes take her two hands in his. Soft hands, nails clean and clipped. She would lean against the airey wall and he would draw her face close to his, so that beneath the street lamp she could see points of light burning in his hazel eyes. His voice would thicken and lower till she had to strain to hear the words, which he appeared to force from a mouth dry with intensity.

'Your hair!' he would say. 'Your eyes! Your mouth!' And with each word of praise he would have to lick his dry lips. It made Ruby feel intensely excited – and confusingly frustrated. She was sure that he desperately wanted to kiss her, but either wouldn't or couldn't. And she also knew that if she should ever attempt to kiss him, he would walk away.

*

During the final week of the crusade Ruby discovered that Dodge had been sentenced to ten months in prison, which seemed harsh enough, but even more so when she heard where they were sending him. Dartmoor. The very word sent a chill up her spine. It was second home to half the mobs in London and it would be impossible for her to visit. But she was given the chance to see him briefly before they transferred him. Unbowed and optimistic, he greeted her with his same old winning smile.

'Now, you're not to worry, Ruby, love. I'll be out early with good behaviour and Jim's gonna see if he can bung a few people, get things moving along. Don't look so sad.' He rubbed his hands together and grinned. 'It'll be like a little holiday for me!'

She couldn't talk to him about how she'd find money for rent and food; it would only upset him and it was clear he could do nothing for them. She wanted to promise she'd visit him, but they both knew she could never afford the fare.

'You and Eric help each other – and look after our Davey, won't you?' He cupped her face with his shackled hand and the cold metal brushed her cheek. 'Just like you always do, gel. Been like a real mum to him, you have. Now bye, me darlin'. See you in ten!' And he gave her a little wave, rattling the handcuffs at her like a child's toy.

All through the crusade she had felt oddly numb. Once she would have been excited just to step into the atmosphere of the great marquee, filled with the prayers of the faithful who had paced out its length and breadth, invoking God's blessing in each corner of the tent. But the threat of Dodge's impending prison sentence had clouded everything. And tonight, now that she knew his fate, all she could think of was her father, locked in a grim cell in Dartmoor. The harmonium was playing 'Nearer My God To Thee' as the massive crowd filed in. A banner over the podium proclaimed the words *For God so Loved the World, that he gave his only begotten Son.* Yet the stirring sermon, the rousing renditions of 'Just As I Am, Without One Plea', the impassioned call to the altar rail at the end, all failed to move her. She took refuge behind the tea table and tried her best to hide from Charles. His fervent excitement would be too much to bear tonight.

But he found her. Eyes bright and cheeks flushed, he rushed up to her.

'Ruby! What are you hiding over here for? We've got so many people coming forward, you're needed in the decision room. Anyone can dole out tea and cake!' He took her by the elbow and steered her away, shoving tracts into her hand as they walked to the screened-off area set aside for quiet chats with would-be converts. The area was filled with people huddled together in twos and threes, whispering, praying, crying. Someone had fallen on the floor in a rapture. Charles steered her around the insensible, bliss-filled body and placed her at a table before calling to the next person in line, a middle-aged woman.

'Sister Ruby will pray with you,' he said, then hurried off to guide more people to their confessors.

Ruby's heart felt empty and she looked at the glowing face of the middle-aged woman with something like pity. The woman, whose name was Aggie, no doubt believed that this night all her problems would be solved. But Ruby knew she was wrong.

'So, you want to decide for Christ?' she asked the woman, her mouth dry as she repeated the appeal from the pulpit.

Aggie nodded, her cheeks wet with tears. 'I do. I do.'

'Well, the Bible says you only need to admit you're a sinner and ask Jesus into your heart. Are you ready to do that?'

She nodded. 'Oh yes, Sister. There ain't not a shred of doubt that I *am* a sinner. I just come out of nick, so enough said. And you don't have to warn me about hell, 'cos that place I've just been in – well, let's just say I learned all about hell and I never want to go back there again! Give me that piece of paper and I'll say the prayer.'

The woman's hand shook as she held the decision card and she choked back tears as, haltingly, she read the prayer from a card. Ruby closed her eyes, but when she opened them Aggie's face was bright with a sheen of golden light. Her rough, prison-cut hair shone like fine silver wire and her eyes widened with joy. Ruby was grateful that she'd had to do nothing. God had done it all, which was just as well, for tonight she hadn't an ounce of faith to offer. She knew she must go through what Aggie should do next: how she must pray every day and tell someone straight away that she'd become a Christian and come to the Sunday service, but instead she found herself staring blankly into the concerned gaze of Sister Evelyn.

'Shall I get the service times for this lady?' Sister Evelyn asked, taking over.

Ruby watched as a beaming Aggie walked away with a tract and her new life before her. She remembered how, on a night like this, she'd worn the same smile. She wished she'd told the woman that it wouldn't always be this easy.

Sister Evelyn perched on the edge of the chair Aggie had vacated and reached for Ruby's hand. 'Sometimes other people's need can be overwhelming and you weren't prepared. Perhaps Charles shouldn't have put you in the decision room without any warning.'

'It's not that, Sister.'

'What is it then, my dear?'

'Promise you won't tell anyone else?'

'Of course.'

Ruby wished her lips didn't tremble so much. 'I just found out me dad's been given ten months.'

Sister Evelyn's face registered shock and pity. 'To live?'

She shook her head. 'In Dartmoor.'

The look of shock and pity didn't diminish. Sister Evelyn knew what this might mean for Ruby and her brothers. 'Can you still manage the rent?'

'I've got extra shifts till Christmas; after that I'm not sure what I'll do.'

'The Mission will help. There's an emergency fund.'

'But I don't want people knowing—'

'No one will judge you for your father's crimes, Ruby. But if anyone should ask, I'll simply say he is absent from the home.'

'I suppose that's been true for a long time, Sister.'

Charles insisted on walking her home. He was almost bouncing off the pavement, he was so excited.

'Hundreds, Ruby! Hundreds saved tonight. It was a mighty revival, just like in Wesley's day. Central Hall will be bursting at the seams by the end of this week! Doesn't it make you feel as though your life's got a real purpose?'

'Yes,' she said, hearing the dullness in her voice. If it had been last year's crusade, she would have easily matched his enthusiasm.

He took her hand and she felt his eyes on her. 'I think you're very beautiful, Ruby.' The sudden change of subject took her off guard.

'I'm not!'

'I never lie,' he said, seriously. 'But it's more important to me that you're a good, moral Christian woman. 'Proverbs 31:10: *Who can find a virtuous woman? For her price is far above rubies*.' He smiled down at her, knowing she would recognize the verse. 'Ruby. There's no one more precious than you, especially not to me.'

She wanted to stop him. But he pressed on. 'I had a revelation tonight, Ruby, and I can't keep it to myself a minute longer. The Lord told me that you're the woman for me!'

She was stunned. 'But Charles, the Lord hasn't told me you're the man for me!' she blurted out.

Charles halted. He had the same confused expression as when she'd first rejected his invitation to go out. As she studied his intense, powerful features and the set of his strong jaw, she could almost read his thoughts. Charles simply couldn't fathom anyone who had a different opinion to his own. Perhaps if she could read him so well after such a short time they really ought to be together, but this didn't seem the right way to go about things. True, she'd only ever had one boyfriend, if you could call Terry that. His main preoccupation had been trying to get the top button of her blouse undone without her noticing. But strangely, she felt even that was an encounter which involved her far more than Charles's proposal just had.

He pursed his lips into a tight white line and then walked on in silence until they reached her house. 'We should pray about it together. Perhaps I could come in. I'm sure you just need some guidance.'

She thought of Ida's confession about Ocki: 'Because I love him' had been the only guidance she'd seemed to need.

'I don't think that's a good idea, not tonight Charles. I'm tired and me dad's away,' she said, repeating Sister Evelyn's words, 'so it wouldn't be right. I'm not saying I wouldn't like to carry on seeing you, but we've only been courting three months. I think it's early days to be planning a future together, don't you?'

He frowned. 'I wouldn't be holding your hand if I hadn't considered the future, Ruby. We'll pray about it tomorrow, then.' He leaned towards her as he spoke, but his eyes told her more than his words. Part of her wished he would just kiss her and then they would both know. Instead, he put his hand on the wall and pushed himself away, muttering a brief goodnight.

She had upset him. And later, as she lay awake in bed thinking of all that had happened that day, her confusion only deepened. Ruby traced a finger down her forehead and nose, resting it on her lips. Charles had said she was beautiful, precious. Her? Ruby Scully, who'd never had two ha'pennies to rub together, precious? It made her laugh out loud, so that Davey stirred in the bed behind the curtain. There was a power in Charles's conviction which attracted her, but she felt no softness when she thought of him. And love had to have something soft about it, didn't it? But the truth was, whenever she was with him it felt her heart was made of iron and he was simply the magnet which drew her.

On the last night of the crusade the response to the altar call was so great that afterwards converts and missionaries alike poured out of the park and into the surrounding streets on a spontaneous great march of witness. All along Southwark Park Road they marched, singing: *And whoso drinketh, Jesus said, shall never, never thirst again*! Then the rousing question was half shouted, half sung: *What, never thirst again?* and the response given: *No! Never thirst again!* At which point a man with a misshapen bulbous nose and a beer belly rolled out of the John Bull Arms and asked Charles in slurred tones, 'What you got to be thirsty for, you silly sod? You're outside a bleedin' pub!'

Charles halted the march and, raising his voice, addressed the procession. 'We've been singing of living waters, but we should be taking the Good News into every pub in Southwark Park Road!'

Ruby's heart sank; she just wanted to get home. But Charles was already splitting the marchers into groups. They would go into as many pubs in the area as they could and invite people back to a late-night open-air meeting.

In the John Bull they were greeted by a lot of good-natured banter and a surprising number who decided that the night's entertainment could be rounded off by a lark with the Young Women's Fellowship. It was probably just bad luck that in the Blue Anchor, the next pub she and Charles entered, they were confronted by Alfie and Ocki Diamond standing at the piano, singing a duet, while Ida joined in from a nearby table.

'Ruby! Come over here and have a drink with us!' Ida shouted, spotting her immediately.

Uncertain what to do, Ruby looked behind her, trying to locate Charles through the smoky fug. Ida got up and, stumbling over to Ruby, greeted her with an affectionate, tipsy kiss.

But Ruby had spotted Charles, his bronze hair shining like a beacon above the crowd at the bar, saw his earnest face as he tried to speak over the group of barracking drinkers. His big-boned, chapped hands held out a sheaf of tracts which someone grabbed and threw up into the air like confetti.

Ida followed her gaze. 'For gawd's sake, Ruby, you should give Charlie boy the slip just for one night and have a good time with me.'

'He doesn't like being called Charlie.'

'I couldn't give a monkey's what he likes and neither should you. He's Charlie Best from Barnham Street, don't matter how much he pretends he's Lord Charles Chumley from Chumptown!'

Ruby giggled. 'Don't,' she said, in a voice that didn't even convince herself. 'Anyway, it's not Charlie – *Charles* – that's been keeping me busy, it's the crusade! There's been hundreds there every night, Ida. We couldn't keep up with the people coming to the altar.'

'Is that before they got their tea and cake or after?'

Ruby shoved her friend's shoulder. 'You're terrible! People don't just come for the food.'

'We used to,' Ida said, grinning conspiratorially, and Ruby remembered the scrawny, lanky girl who'd become her unlikely protector in the breakfast queue.'

'Sorry, I'll have to be going, Ida.' Ida grabbed her hand and refused to let go as Ruby tried to disentangle herself. She tugged harder, just at the moment Ida decided to let her go and Ruby was sent tumbling backward, certain she'd fall flat on the beery floorboards. Instead, she felt a sure pair of hands catch her. She turned her head, expecting to see Charles, and yet knowing, before she'd even seen the face, that these weren't Charles's hands around her waist. His hands would have pressed harder, but never lingered so long and he would certainly not be holding her so obviously against his chest. She tilted her head back and looked up into the irreverent eyes of Alfie Diamond.

'Oooh, Alf, you've got yourself a right catch there!' Ida exclaimed, laughing.

'Last time we met I think she picked me up,' Alfie replied, also laughing, looking into Ruby's eyes. 'It's either me taking a tumble or you – we're a pair!' he said and chuckled.

'Well, you won't get any other sort of tumble with our Ruby,' Ida said.

As Ruby attempted to struggle up and out of Alfie's arms, she saw the inexorable approach of Charles's bronze head. 'Help me up, Ida, quick!'

Ida ignored her plea and draped an arm across Ocki's shoulder. 'We should make up a foursome! Us two and these two, what d'you reckon, Ruby?' she said, giving Ocki an ostentatious kiss on the lips.

'Let me go, let me go!' she hissed at Alfie.

'Sorry, I was only trying to break your fall,' he said, helping her back on to her feet just as Charles arrived. She wasn't sure how much he'd seen, but she wanted to avoid a repeat of the two men's earlier clash and positioned herself squarely between them.

'I'll tell our Barney you said hello, shall I, Charlie?' Ida asked, her voice even and her stare unwavering.

He ignored her. 'I think the others have moved on, Ruby. Let's go. These people aren't interested in coming to an open-air meeting.' And he grasped her hand, his iron grip tightening as he pulled her after him.

'See you Monday, Ruby!' Ida called and, looking back at her friend, Ruby felt a sad tug on her heart as the two halves of her life began tearing steadily apart.

As Christmas approached, the Mission began planning its annual free Christmas dinner at the Central Hall. There had been many years when she and her brothers joined the queue for a turkey dinner, and now it felt strange to be on the other side of the tables.

Charles had been put in charge of the Christmas Dinner committee. 'I think you'll make a valuable contribution, Ruby,' he'd explained when he invited her to be one of the organizers.

But she knew that any one of a hundred other girls could have done a better job on the committee.

'I'm too busy as it is, looking after the family with Dad away,' she'd protested.

'I understand, but you need to make a choice about what comes first, Ruby. When his mother and brothers came to him, Jesus turned to the crowd and said *you are my mother and brothers*.'

She was quiet for a while, feeling the tension between the two worlds that had been nagging at her ever since she'd met Charles.

'It's not just that, I don't want to let Sister Evelyn down on the home visits and Welfare Clinic.'

'We're *all* busy. I'm busy with work and studying till the early hours and I come into the Mission and do whatever's necessary. Ruby, it's a life of sacrifice we've chosen.'

He studied her intently and she felt herself crumble under his scrutiny. 'Perhaps you're right, Charles. I don't sacrifice enough for God.'

He smiled. 'Good. It'll only be a short-term commitment and your contacts at Crosse's will be invaluable.'

'Contacts? What contacts? I'm an onion peeler!'

He shook his head. 'Not *just* an onion peeler, Ruby. You're making *Christmas puddings* – and we need Christmas puddings!'

'Surely you don't want me to half-inch some?' The flippant suggestion was out before she remembered she wasn't talking to Ida or one of her family, and Charles's straight face reminded her that his sense of humour was strictly policed.

'I was thinking you could ask the manager for a donation.'

'You don't know the Paste Kitchen foreman!'

Charles looked deflated and she relented. She hadn't seen him so enthusiastic since the crusade, which she'd managed to spoil for him by tripping into the arms of Alfie Diamond. 'All right. I'll ask,' she promised, without any hope that Sid Bean would be overtaken by Christmas good cheer.

Her next shift in the Paste Kitchen was an evening one. She dashed home to give Davey his tea and left Aunt Nancy to put him to bed, but she was still running late. The light had failed by the time she went back to the factory, but the gates to St James's churchyard weren't locked and so she took the shortcut through. As she passed the lofty, pillared portico she saw the broad-shouldered, slim figure of a man, standing with his hands in his pockets, who swayed slightly as, with his head tilted back, he looked up at the louvred bell tower. Hearing her approach, he shot a look in her direction. His brilliant, dark eyes, almost too large for his face, were framed by straight eyebrows, drawn together in concentration. He seemed to look through her and she was about to skirt around him when he broke into a smile.

'Ruby Scully! What are you doing here?'

It was Alfie Diamond. She pointed vaguely back to St James's Road. 'It's where I live.' She hesitated before asking him the same question.

'I'm looking at the bells,' he replied. 'I volunteered to do some repair work on them. The cradles are in a terrible state!'

She couldn't hide her shock. 'But you're not a Christian.'

He shrugged. 'I like bells. And I don't think the bells mind what religion you are.' He looked up at the tower again. 'I was reading the other day about John Bunyan – he was a good-enough Christian and he was terrified the church bells would fall on his head if he sinned. I don't go much on that idea – what do you think?'

He had a clipped, offhand way of talking, as if she would understand every vague reference he made.

'I don't think they'll *fall* on me, but sometimes I feel just like one of those bells. Only not when they're ringing...'

He turned the wide, dark eyes on her again. 'When they're resting?'

She nodded and her gaze moved back to the dark bell tower. But the white clock face set directly above it brought her up short. 'Oh no, I'll be late for me shift! I've got to run.' She set off at a fast trot, calling back, 'Yes, when they're resting.'

'Mind how you go, Ruby Scully. We can't afford any more slip-ups!' he called back and she smiled as she ran.

She arrived late for her shift and had to join the end of the table as a parchment pleater. Her late entrance hadn't gone unnoticed and, after the shift was over, she had little hope Sid Bean would be inclined to give her any puddings for the Mission, but as the other girls trooped out, she made her request.

'You must be joking! Give you puddings when your old man's in prison for nicking a case of Branston!?' She was taken aback by the venom in his tone. 'You can't get one over on me with your holier-than-thou act. How do I know anything I give you won't just get flogged too?'

'Don't show your ignorance, Sid.' Ida, fearless as usual, was at her side. 'It's not up to you; she'll go upstairs and ask management herself and they'll be glad of the goodwill. Besides, Ruby ain't got a dishonest bone in her body.'

Ruby hadn't thought of going to the management, but she nodded. 'And the puddings would go straight to the Mission, not to me.'

At the mention of management his tone altered. 'I'll ask, but I can't promise nothing. And you, Ruby Scully, sort yourself out. It'll be Christmas soon and you'll still be pleating the parchments!'

*

The Crosse & Blackwell tins in Aunt Nancy's shed had been weighing heavily on her mind and she was desperate to get rid of them. When the management agreed to supply the Mission with enough Christmas puddings to feed three hundred people, Ruby reasoned that their philanthropical hearts wouldn't be averse to donating a larger variety of foodstuffs. And for that she enlisted Ida's help.

'Ruby Scully, I'm shocked. There I was telling Sid Bean you didn't have a dishonest bone in your body!'

'You're not shocked, you're pleased – I can tell by the smile that's splitting your face in half,' Ruby said as they squeezed into Aunt Nancy's shed. 'I'm not sure what we've got here and Uncle Jim put some boxes in the chicken run as well.'

'I'm not getting meself covered in chicken shit for no one's Christmas dinner. Open these up first.'

They discovered turtle and tomato soups which would do nicely for starters, tinned peterkin peas, bottles of gravy browning and redcurrant jellies to go with the main course; large tins of fruit salad and sterilized cream for the Christmas puddings and tinned 'Starboard Lights' after-dinner crême de menthes for the coffee course. The Mission also served a Christmas tea later in the day, and for this they found tinned salmon, potted ox tongue and meat paste.

'How are we going to smuggle these into the Mission?' Ida whispered, though there was no one to overhear.

'You, not *we*. You take it in bags to the anonymous donor drop off point – no one'll recognize you.'

'Only Sister Evelyn or Charlie boy.'

'Hmm, go on Saturday afternoon when Sister Evelyn's on a home visit and then on Friday night when I'm out with Charles.'

'All right.' And Ida grinned. 'I knew you'd break out one day, Ruby.'

'I'm only doing it because I couldn't have it on my conscience if Aunt Nancy got caught with the stuff and this is the only way I can get rid of it all and keep me conscience clear.'

'We're a bit short at the Labour Institute soup kitchen – what do you think of chucking a dozen tins of Mulligatawny and a case of baked beans our way? All in a good cause?'

Once all the Christmas puddings had been made for that year, Ruby's extra shifts dried up and to help cover the rent Eric asked for an evening job as a pot-boy in the St James Tavern, another favourite haunt of Dodge's, so although the landlord didn't really need help, he agreed. Eric's extra money went straight into the rent tin as their landlady, Mrs Nash, was fast losing patience with her excuses. But now the food money tin was rapidly emptying too. One night in Christmas week Eric came home from the Jame'oh with an extra two pounds. He handed it straight to Ruby.

'Here y'are, Ruby. Get us some food in the house for Christmas. I can't live on bread and jam no more. I need feeding up, I'm a man now!' He laughed and flexed his forearms for her to test.

When she felt his muscles, she looked at him with surprise. 'Where did they come from? You don't do any lifting in the dock office.'

'I've been weightlifting at the BUF gym.'

'Oh.' She was less impressed now. She'd hoped he would grow out of his obsession with the Blackshirts. But there was something about a uniform that had always attracted Eric and she could only hope that when he tired of that, he would tire of the BUF.

'Anyway, thanks love, it'll come in handy, but where did you get two quid? Did they give you a Christmas Box at work?'

'No.' And he put a finger to his nose in a gesture reminiscent of Dodge.

'You haven't nicked anything, have you?'

'Not really. What's the point in going hungry when there's two dozen boxes of food in the shed? I just sold a few at the Jame'oh tonight.'

She gave him a disbelieving look. 'You silly 'apporth! Do you want to ruin your life and end up like Dad? Even Uncle Jim wouldn't risk selling them at the moment. And what about all your "New Britain" ideas? How does turning yourself into a villain fit in with that?'

He shrugged. 'It's different when it's your family. We've got to look after ourselves. Anyway, our leader says fascism's all about action. And at least I've got off me arse and done something to help us.'

'Help us? Well, just don't do anything else to *help* us will you?'

It was so unlike Eric to want to emulate Dodge. He'd always been ashamed of the way their father earned a living.

'I can't believe you did that.' She shook her head in disbelief.

Eric slumped down in the chair. 'I was hungry. I need feeding up now I'm doing all this physical fitness with the BUF instructor.'

She believed it was that simple. She hadn't told Eric about the tins of food that she'd 'donated' to the Mission, but it didn't seem fair her own brother was going hungry when she was helping to feed hundreds of strangers. Perhaps she'd made the wrong choice in not shopping Dodge on the day he'd brought home the Crosse's cartons. But it was too late now, she was too involved, and she gave up trying to pretend that if Charles found out what she'd done he would understand.

'Promise me not to sell any more, Eric. It's too dangerous. But you won't go hungry, I can promise you that.'

And so, by the light of a frosted moon Eric helped her ferry tins from the shed up to their kitchen. She opened a tinned meat pudding and heated it up for their tea. Afterwards they tucked into a tin of pineapple and Crosse's Fulcreem custard. Every morsel tasted delicious.

'I ain't complaining,' Eric said, when they were both full, 'but don't you feel guilty, about eating stolen goods?'

Ruby thought for a moment and was surprised that she didn't, not at all. Up until now it had been a matter of conscience not to use any of the tins for themselves, however hungry they might be. But now she told herself that she was, after all, just distributing food to the poor.

8

Avoid All Appearance

Winter 1935–1936

Ruby and Ida moved on to square pickle packing. They always tried to move jobs together and sometimes Ruby felt that Ida's presence was the only thing that kept her sane at work. It was usually Ida who engineered the change, talking to a forelady or chatting up a foreman, to land whatever job was the cushiest or best paid for each season. Square pickle packing wasn't a job that came up very often; some women stayed on square pickles all their working lives because although the wages were obviously never as good as for even the least skilled men's job, among the girls, it was the best paid.

As well as the wages, Ruby found the other advantage of packing the mixed pickle jars was that the time sped by. The task involved using a vacuum pencil to pick up the various pickles and arrange them into a square jar of brine in a defined pattern, with the small gherkins and silverskin onions tucked neatly into each corner. The disadvantage was that Ruby was sure the vinegar was staining her lungs the colour and consistency of pickled walnuts.

Pickle packing was done on the second floor of the 1927 building, not far from Ocki's office where he was an order clerk.

Ruby suspected that one reason Ida had engineered their move was to be closer to Ocki. The factory was so vast that Ruby had not once bumped into either Ocki or his brother Alfie, who worked in the cooperage yard, but Ida contrived to 'bump into' Ocki at least two or three times a day, usually during lavatory breaks.

About two weeks after they'd started in square pickles, Ida came back from a particularly protracted lavatory break with a look of suppressed excitement on her face.

'You've been gone half an hour! You'll be getting the sack if you're not careful,' Ruby whispered when her friend joined her.

'Me Aunt Dora's not going to sack me,' Ida replied, which was no doubt true. Her aunt had been forelady of pickle packing for twenty years and ruled the roost with an iron hand for all but her niece, and by extension Ruby.

'I've been with Ocki round the back of salad cream. He was checking an order that's gone up the spout. Someone's on the fiddle – but that's not what we were talking about. Ocki's asked me to go and live with him!'

'He's proposed?'

'No! We're not going through all that outdated rigmarole. Ocki doesn't believe in it and nor do I!'

'Are you sure about that, Ida? You know how vicious tongues like to wag in this place if you're a bit different.' Ruby reached a vinegary hand to cover Ida's.

'My little friend,' Ida said, with the infectious laugh that had first made Ruby warm to her, 'don't you worry about me, love. I can take on any of the sharp-tongued cows this place can chuck at me. But listen, Ocki wants a celebration, even if we're not getting married. It's still special for us. Will you come?'

'I wouldn't miss it, Ida, not for the world.'

Ida moved into Ocki's rented rooms on the top floor of a house in Fort Road, not far from the Labour Institute and her non-wedding reception was to be held in the Havelock Arms, a large, friendly pub just a few doors away. The landlord had laid on sandwiches and pork pies in a private room upstairs and when Ruby arrived she added her own contribution: desserts of Crosse & Blackwell madeira and champagne jellies, layered with tinned pineapple and peaches. She'd also whipped up a packet of Crosse's blancmange. Ida eyed the moulded desserts. 'Good old Dodge – jellies are on him. We'll raise a glass to him tonight, eh?'

Ruby lowered her voice, spotting some Crosse's girls. 'I'd rather you didn't draw attention to them, Ida. Just in case someone puts a blancmange and a jelly together and makes a lorryload!'

Ida giggled.

'Haven't you got rid of all that bent stuff yet, Ruby?'

'I can only spread it about a bit at a time. Mind you the Mongeys were very happy with the Mulligatawnys. Anyway, how did your mum and dad take the news, are they coming tonight?' The crowd in the high-ceilinged room was largely made up of young people. Some she recognized from Crosse's, others she'd seen during her visit to the Labour Institute.

'Miserable sods wouldn't even let any of the kids come – and Alfie's the only one from Ocki's family here. What gets me is that Mum ain't exactly a regular at Holy Trinity these days and Ocki's mum and dad ain't very strict, so what's the problem? Ocki says it's just like different tribes.'

Ruby chuckled. 'I expect they'll come round. Anyway, how is it, living in the new place?'

'It's a palace, compared to Arnold's Place, Ruby. And Ocki's painted it all up. We've got our own little kitchen with an Ascot and a bath built in under the work bench and there's *two* bedrooms.'

No wonder Ida was pleased. She'd been sharing a bedroom with four of her siblings. 'Two bedrooms! You'll be rattling around in there with all that space to yourselves.'

'Well, not completely to ourselves. We couldn't afford the rent on just our wages. Alfie's moved out of their mum and dad's as well - he's got the second bedroom.'

Ruby detected a slight tone of regret in Ida's voice. 'But you'd prefer to have Ocki all to yourself, wouldn't you?'

'Mmm, but luckily Alfie's out a lot,' Ida said and grinned.

'Are you talking about me, sister-out-of-law?' Hearing his name, Alfie joined them. 'Is she already complaining about my messy habits?' he asked Ruby.

'I was just telling her you're no trouble,' Ida said.

'Don't believe her.' He grinned at Ruby. 'It's flying in the face of all the evidence: whenever we meet I seem to be in trouble.'

Ruby remembered the one occasion when he hadn't ended up on the floor. 'Not always,' she said and saw him smile at the memory of their brief encounter in St James's churchyard.

Ida went to greet more new arrivals and they stood for a moment in awkward silence, surveying the room.

There were guests who didn't look particularly like Bermondsey people. Here, you could be as poor as you liked, but it was a sin not to be smart. Shoes might have holes in the soles but they would be polished. And factory girls like Ruby might shop at the old clo' but would always alter the frocks to the latest designs. Tonight, Ruby saw men wearing expensive tweed jackets with stains down the front, or baggy trousers that hadn't been pressed. She even saw young men with sandalled, none-too-clean feet. She thought they might be student friends of Ocki's, for she knew he studied in the evenings at Morley College.

'Are these mostly Ocki's friends?' Ruby asked.

Alfie's eyes scanned the room. 'Some. A lot are friends of all three of us – from the Party. Do you want to meet some of them?'

For some reason she heard a warning voice in her head – it sounded like Charles's – *Be in the world but not of it*. But with Ida, surely this didn't apply. Ida was her other self; there was no wrong in Ida. But these people were from another world. She was about to say no, when Alfie steered her to a middle-aged man with a domed, bald head who stood surrounded by a coterie of young people. He was holding a teacup in his hand – obviously a fellow abstainer.

'Dr Salter, this is Ruby Scully.' She tried to conceal her surprise. The last person she expected to see at Ida's celebration was the beloved MP for Bermondsey. He gave her a genial smile, put down his teacup and shook her hand. 'Ruby's an active member at the Bermondsey Central Hall, sir,' Alfie said and she noticed a mischievous look in his eye.

The doctor's mild expression sharpened and he gave an explosive laugh. 'Ha! Do you know that the Reverend Kedward at the Central Hall *stole* the '23 election from me, *stole* it with the "turkey vote"? Gave away four thousand turkeys and *stole* all my votes! Do you still give away turkeys at Christmas, by any chance?'

Ruby swallowed hard. Did the good doctor know about her contribution to this year's Christmas dinner from Dodge's contraband? With each repetition of the word 'stole', her guilt was laid bare. She shot a pleading look at Alfie, but his attention was fixed steadily on the doctor. She could see a small smile curling the edges of his straight mouth.

'W-we invite people for free Christmas dinners. I-I was on the committee...'

'Excellent work. Not that I'm worried about anyone stealing the next election. West Bermondsey has again won the London Labour Party shield for the largest number of recruits, due to our young friend here's energetic campaigning. Did you ever meet the Reverend Kedward, my dear?'

Ruby shook her head.

'A good Christian and a devilish political opponent. Doubled the turkey giveaway that year and stole all my votes.' He shook his head, laughing at the memory. 'But Labour prevailed in '24 – and we didn't need a single turkey to do it!'

Alfie had an adoring look on his face as he gazed at Dr Salter. But while he was admiring, she was calculating. Alfie had obviously wanted to tease her with the 'turkey vote' story. She might as well make use of the introduction and she told Dr Salter about the Mongeys in Monarch Buildings. She didn't know where her boldness had come from; perhaps the last visit to the Mongeys when little Jenny had been ill with scarlet fever.

'Could you do anything about rehousing them?' she pressed and saw Alfie's eyes widen and Dr Salter's face darken. Had she gone too far?

'Thirty years of strenuous work in Bermondsey and too little has changed,' the doctor said and looked into Ruby's eyes, sadness in his own. 'My own darling daughter died of scarlet fever, here in Bermondsey twenty-five years ago. I had hoped to eradicate it...' He seemed to be lost in the past. 'She would have been thirty-three, perhaps a mother herself... I'll do all I can for the family, Ruby.'

Then the MP was claimed by another guest and she was left standing with Alfie.

He tilted his head to one side. 'Ever thought of joining the Labour Party?' And she detected a new respect in his tone which was gratifying as she hadn't enjoyed his attempt to rattle her with the 'turkey vote' trap.

'You have your hero, I have mine,' she said.

'Not Charlie Best!'

'Jesus, you daft 'apporth!' And they both laughed.

After the last of Ida's guests had left, Ruby helped ferry back the leftover food to Ida's new home. Ida showed her round the three rooms with pride and Ruby felt that, however sparsely furnished, it had a comfort to it. As the four young people talked about the night's events, Ruby found herself liking the two brothers more and more. There was something relaxing about their attitude to life, and she never once felt that anything she said would be frowned upon or ridiculed. As the talk went on, she realized something was missing. It was a sense she always had that there was something wrong with her. It was then that she thought of Charles and she found her fingers intertwining themselves in to a tight knot.

Friday had become the night when Ruby and Charles went to a 'Happy Evening for Tired Toilers' at the Mission. There was a concert and tea and then Charles would walk her home. She had contemplated not telling him about going to Ida's party at the Havelock, but Ruby knew that a lie by omission was as much a sin as a direct one and tonight he seemed so happy, so on the walk home she decided to couch the confession in a light Charles would approve of.

'You'll never guess who I spoke to the other night.'

'Who?' he asked.

'Dr Salter, the MP! And he said he'd try to get the Mongeys rehoused. So it was a good thing I went—'

Charles interrupted, frowning. 'The Mongeys?'

She reminded him. 'Oh, yes I'll have to put them on my prayer list. But where did you meet Dr Salter?'

'At Ida's party.'

He stopped dead. 'Why was she having a party? I shouldn't think she'd have the money to spend on parties.'

Ruby gave a nervous laugh. 'It was a joint one, for her and Ocki, they're setting up home together—'

'And you went! I'm surprised you even considered it, Ruby. It'll seem like you're condoning Ida living in sin with that man.' He shook his sleek bronze head and tutted.

'Charles, she's my best friend. She would've been so hurt if I hadn't gone!"

'Ruby, I know we're not married yet, but I very much hope we will be. When that day comes I'll be head of the house and it's not right for you to go against me. Do you understand?'

She bit her lip, wondering if it would ever occur to him he'd never actually proposed and she'd never agreed! But she said nothing, wanting to avoid a tussle and desperate to convince Charles. 'I know you don't approve of Ida, but she and her friends do so much good – and Dr Salter's a Christian, you know.'

'Salter's a *Quaker* – hardly a Christian at all! And besides, he's a pacifist. He'll have us ruled by the Nazis if he gets his way. Why was he at Ida's party, anyway?' He shrugged up his jacket shoulders – a nervous habit he had when he was upset.

'Apparently he's taken Alfie under his wing, says he could go far in the Party.'

Charles pulled at his collar. 'I'd rather you didn't associate with the Diamonds. They're commies.'

'No they're not. They're Labour.' Ruby was certain she knew more about this than Charles. 'Alfie's in the Labour League of Youth. Besides, it's going to be hard not to meet them when they're all living in the same house!'

'That's even worse! You'll have to explain to Ida you can't visit her there. If she's really your friend she'll understand. It's the principle.'

They had arrived at the place where they said their goodnights, beneath the gas lamp outside her house. The gas lamp seemed to cast a golden light over the future when Charles would talk of his plans, which now included her.

'Let's not argue. We've got to say goodnight and I won't see you till Sunday.' Ruby looked up into his eyes and his bronze head dipped so that it almost touched the pale gold of her hair.

'I don't want to argue either, Ruby. I only want what's best for you. I love you.' And when he held her hand, he stroked his thumb again and again across the tips of her fingers. She tried to imagine it was his mouth on hers, and she wondered if he did the same.

'I love you too,' she said softly.

She turned her palm over, placing her fingertips against his. She let them rest there. Perhaps if he could feel that she loved him, he would be less adamant about her love for Ida. But instead he jumped back and dropped her hand as if he'd been given an electric shock.

'Ruby, no!' His expression was one of horror. He took in a deep breath and straightened his tie. 'Thessalonians 5:22 Ruby. *Abstain from all appearance of evil.* I don't want you to associate with those characters any more – they'll end up corrupting you and you're too precious. I won't allow it.'

On Saturday afternoon she joined Sister Evelyn for the home visits, something she always looked forward to, not just because of the families they were helping, but because Sister Evelyn always cheered her up and since her last conversation with Charles she had been miserable. Sister Evelyn was quick to pick up on her mood.

'Is it your father, Ruby? Are you missing him?'

'Yes. He's not much help when he's here but I do feel a bit lonely without him.'

'Oh, my dear.' Sister Evelyn dropped her parcel of clothes to hug Ruby, which only succeeded in opening the floodgates of her tears.

'You've had such a heavy burden to bear. And you've done so well, to look after the boys and keep your family together. You'll make some lucky man a wonderful wife when the time comes – and that may be sooner rather than later if my eyes don't deceive me!'

Ruby's sobs deepened.

'What is it? You can speak to me about anything, Ruby.'

And so Ruby told her about the thing that she'd done for the Mongeys and how happy she'd been about it and about Charles's reaction.

Sister Evelyn sighed. 'Charles is a wonderfully committed Christian, but sometimes he can be a little too – too zealous. No doubt his biblical references are correct, but you're only courting, so Charles has absolutely no authority over you. That belongs only to God and the Church.'

'Sometimes it's hard to tell the difference between the two.'

'Between God and the Church? There certainly is a difference, one is fallible.'

'No, I meant between Charles and God.'

'Oh!' Sister Evelyn chuckled. 'Well, I think the same applies!'

When they arrived at the flat in Monarch Buildings, Mrs Mongey hugged Ruby, almost knocking her off her feet.

'Oh, here she is, my angel!' She put her palms either side of Ruby's cheeks and kissed her. 'Sister, you'll never guess what Ruby's been and done. She's only got Dr Salter to help us. He sent round a lovely young feller to look at our rooms and count the kids and he's just been back here, not five minutes ago, to tell us we're being rehoused. We're moving to one of them little cottages in Wilson's Grove and Mr Mongey's getting a job on the council, planting up the flower beds, and it's all thanks to Ruby Scully!'

'That's marvellous news, Mrs Mongey! And well done, Ruby, you should be proud of yourself!'

'Dr Salter seemed upset when I told him about Jenny, so perhaps it's her you have to thank, Mrs Mongey. Where is she?'

Mrs Mongey's eyes clouded with anxiety. 'She ain't getting no better, Ruby, love. That young feller Alfie said Dr Salter would pay for a doctor and he's gone to fetch one. You go in and see her now.'

The bedroom was in shadow and from behind the curtain that divided the room Ruby heard snoring. Malchy, the eldest Mongey boy, happened to be a friend of Eric and Ruby knew he worked nights at the glue factory. As the only member of the family earning any money at all, it was important to let him sleep. Ruby lowered her voice to a whisper, calling Jenny's name.

The little girl lay in the bed she shared with her parents, her pretty face thinner than the last time Ruby had seen her. Her breathing was harsh, her eyes wide open, staring but unseeing.

'Jenny, it's Ruby. I've come to see you.'

With great difficulty the child focused and smiled.

'Hello, miss. Mum says you're an angel. Have you come to take me to heaven?'

Ruby picked up the small hand which was clammy and limp.

'No, I'm not an angel, and you're not going to heaven, darlin'.'

'Am I going to a nasturtium?'

'No, but you are going to a lovely little cottage where you and Maffy and the baby will have a bedroom all of your own. Would you like that?'

Jenny nodded then winced and put her small hand to her head. 'I got an 'eadache. But when can I go to the cottage? Is it in the country?'

'Sort of; it's down by the river and there are trees in the street and a front garden where your dad can plant flowers.'

Jenny's eyes widened further, taken up in the wonder of her new life. 'Tell me about the cottage, miss.'

And Ruby painted the brightest picture her imagination could conjure of the cottage in the garden where little Jenny would be transported very soon.

As she intoned the fairy tale of Jenny's future, she heard a banging on the front door and a simultaneous cursing from behind the dividing curtain.

'Chrissake, I've only just got off!' Malchy's tousled head emerged from behind the curtain. 'Oh, its Ruby! Sorry, blasphemin'. Didn't know you was in here.' He gathered a blanket around himself and padded over to the bedside.

'Ain't she no better?' he asked, wiping sleep from his eyes.

Ruby was about to answer with a platitude when Sister Evelyn ushered in Mrs Mongey and a doctor. She beckoned to Ruby and Malchy slipped back into his bed, leaving the doctor to his ministrations.

In the tiny kitchen the slender figure of Alfie Diamond stood like an elongated shadow, his arms folded across his chest, deep in thought as he stared down at the sleeping forms of Maffy, the little toddler, and the tiny baby, Jessie, asleep in the chest of drawers. Two empty drawers had been pulled out and lined with blankets from the Mission, so that Jenny could sleep alone in the bed with her parents.

'Just as well they've got nothing else to put in the drawers,' Alfie said, in a tone that might have sounded unfeeling.

'Mrs Mongey told me Dr Salter would pay the medical bill. He didn't hang about...'

'Actually, he's in a meeting, so I've paid the doctor.' Alfie jerked his head towards the bedroom. 'If it had been Dr Salter on call he wouldn't have taken a penny. They're not all like him.'

'You did the right thing, Alfie. Little Jenny's bad.'

He nodded. 'I know. How that lump of a lad can snore in the bed while his little sister's dying…' He wiped a hand across his forehead.

'She's not dying! And Malchy's dead tired.'

'Do you always make excuses for people, Ruby Scully?'

He fixed her with his dark brown eyes. They had such a piercing quality she was forced to look away for an instant. Eventually she returned his gaze and said, 'None of us are innocent.'

'*Let him first cast a stone*?'

'You know the New Testament?'

He smiled. 'I went to Fair Street school, same as Charlie Best. We all learned the New Testament, it's just some of us understand it better than others.'

She was at a loss for words. He was such a puzzle to her, and yet it was the sort of puzzle that she felt might hold her until it was solved.

It was two days later that Eric came home late from a BUF meeting. Ruby had waited up late for him. She'd barely seen him all week and she was worried about the company he was keeping. His leisure time these days was spent either on the streets or with his new Blackshirt friends. But someone followed Eric into their kitchen. It was Malchy Mongey and he lifted his head in silent greeting to Ruby.

'Hello, Malchy,' she said, surprised to see him. 'Shouldn't you be at work?'

'He's been at a BUF meeting with me; he's joining.'

'How's little Jenny?'

There was just enough time for Ruby to register Eric's small shake of the head, before Malchy's face crumpled. He broke into heart-rending sobs that shook his whole body. Ruby's blood turned to ice water in her veins.

'No!' she said out loud, not to Malchy, but to God. 'No!'

Malchy fell into her arms, while Eric stood looking on. 'No? You said it. Too bloody right, No! So much for your prayers and your Dr Salter's. That little girl should have been in a hospital weeks ago! That's why Malchy's joining us. Labour's had its chance to sort out this borough and his sister still had to die relying on charity—'

'Be quiet! Your friend don't need a lecture tonight.' Nor, she silently added to herself, a sermon.

She stood with her arms around Malchy till his sobs subsided and then she sat him down and let the sad tale of Jenny's death spill from his grief-stricken heart.

'We thought she was getting better. She was prattling on about the new house and she even let Dad get her up to sit on his lap. And then she just seemed to fade away. I don't know where she got the idea from but she said, "I think I'm going to heaven and Ruby Scully's come to take me." And then she smiled and her little face was so peaceful…' And here Malchy dropped his head in his hands. 'And then she just sighed and went… Oh, Ruby, I don't understand God. Why would he take my lovely little sister? They say some kids are too good for this world. Do you think it's true?'

Ruby's tears were falling now along with Malchy's. His questions were her questions too and she knew all her answers would be inadequate, but still she had to try.

'I think Jenny got the scarlet fever because Monarch Buildings is too packed with families and there's no air, or decent sanitation. I think your family did everything to help her – and I think she's with God now.'

They seemed hollow, comfortless words. But Malchy looked up with hope in his eyes.

'I think so too,' he said. 'But I'm going to do something about it. We can make our country a place where this don't need to happen. We'll have a health corporation and a housing corporation and ordinary people will run it and we'll get rid of the useless politicians and the rich bankers – that's what they said tonight in the meeting, didn't they, Eric?'

He glanced towards Eric, who stood ramrod straight with his back to the wall, his face set like stone. 'We'll take our country back for the ordinary people,' he said, clenching his fist.

'Unless you happen to be an ordinary Jew!' Ruby said, thinking of Alfie and Ocki. And then she had a chilling glimpse of a future where it would never be the meek who inherited the earth – not if her brother had anything to do with it.

9

What's Wrong with Ruby?

Spring–Summer 1936

'I ain't going down the clinic again!' Davey protested. 'I went last week and the doctor said there's nothing wrong with me!'

It was Saturday afternoon and this morning she'd been alarmed to see Davey's temperature was up half a degree.

'You're coming with me. It'll take five minutes to get you checked and afterwards you can go to Manze's for pie and mash while I help out at the clinic.'

The bribe of Davey's favourite dinner was enough to get him out of the house, but he dragged his heels all the way to the Child Welfare Clinic in the Central Hall's newly built annexe. Four days a week, two young women doctors and a handful of volunteers struggled to deal with the hundreds of women and children who came. Saturday was always extra busy and Ruby had to push her way into a tiled waiting room, crammed with prams and pushchairs. She squeezed past screaming twins and stepped around a little girl eating a doughnut. The gathering had more the air of a social club than a medical centre, with mothers standing in line chatting, and babies exercising their lungs.

Sometimes Ruby thought the women brought their kids here just for an afternoon out. And who could blame them? Families tended to be large and in their cramped kitchens and overcrowded bedrooms mothers got no time to themselves. Here, for a precious hour, they could gossip, compare notes on their children's progress, complain and laugh.

Since Jenny's death, Ruby saw her sweet, smiling face in every little girl that came through the door. She'd always loved helping to weigh the babies and measure the toddlers. But today other people's children would have to wait. She was sure there was something wrong with Davey. Let the doctor call her an over anxious 'mother' if she liked but she wouldn't lose another child she loved. She ushered her brother into the bright, tiled consulting room. The young lady doctor, sitting behind a small desk, looked up over rimless spectacles. Dr Scott always greeted patients with a pleasant smile, but today Ruby thought she saw the slightest flash of irritation.

'Ah, Ruby you've brought your brother to see us – *again*!'

She obviously believed Davey was completely healthy. But Jenny's death had precipitated a new sacred daily practice – the taking of Davey's temperature. And Ruby knew it was up.

'I don't want to waste your time, doctor. But you always tell us it's so important to catch scarlet fever early.'

'Let's just see,' the doctor said, shaking her thermometer and putting it under Davey's tongue. Ruby held her breath as Dr Scott removed the thermometer and inspected the mercury through her half-moon spectacles.

'Normal,' she pronounced a little brusquely and began scribbling on a pad. 'Here, Ruby, take this.' It was a note for the dispensary.

'But you said he's normal.'

'He is. It's for you. You look pale and you're too thin.' The doctor paused, softening her brisk tone. 'I know how hard it's been for you lately. You were fond of little Jenny Mongey, weren't you?'

Ruby's even temper slipped into what for her was rage. 'I know I'm a volunteer here, doctor, but I still think I'm entitled to use the service, same as any other mother.'

The doctor reached for her hand. 'Take the tonic, Ruby. I promise you, it *will* help.'

As they exited the consulting room, Davey gave Ruby a triumphant look.

'All right, clever Dick, don't rub it in. It's better to be safe than sorry.'

He gave her an unexpected hug and then stuck out his hand. 'Can I get me pie and mash now?'

She opened her purse. There was only a single shilling left, but a promise was a promise. She handed it to him. 'Pie, mash and liquor and nothing else! And you go straight home afterwards. I'm staying here to help out for an hour.'

At eight, Davey was used to walking and playing in the streets on his own and Ruby lost herself in helping mothers divest their infants of thick woollen cardigans and padded liberty bodices, ready for nurse to weigh them. She loved the mothers' delight as they saw the scales reveal an increase in their child's weight. Here, a baby was only considered bonny if it was chubby. After her stint she made her way to the dispensary. Picking up the tonic, she read the label. *Gives new life to the weary*. Perhaps she'd give it a try after all.

The following week, Ruby, Charles and a dozen other young men and women assembled for the Children of Basutoland prayer meeting. They sat in a semi-circle facing Charles, who invited them to bow their heads and opened with an impassioned prayer for the salvation of the children of Basutoland. She half opened her eyes and saw his face had a pained look as he asked God to bring both children and their parents to the light. Sweat shone on his forehead as he pleaded for the salvation of the innocents, whose misfortune it had been to be born in a heathen land.

Ruby felt no fervour, only a deep-seated weariness. The tonic hadn't helped.

She was aware that all their prayers could be equally applied to Bermondsey children, and indeed, there were other meetings going on which were doing just that. But in spite of all those fervent prayers, all the pioneering efforts of the Labour council, her little friend Jenny had still died. The Mongeys were Christian, not heathen, and yet she had still died. Ruby felt a sense of pointlessness in praying for the babies of Basutoland. Why would they be any more blessed than Jenny Mongey of Monarch Buildings?

While others offered prayers for the evangelistic drive in Basutoland or asked for blessings on the head of Paramount Chief Lerotholi and wisdom for the British Commissioner, Ruby asked for nothing. Instead, she tried to imagine herself doing good in an African village as Charles's wife. What if she did agree to marry him? Would she be allowed to help make mud huts and carry water? That was what she would do best. Or would she be shut away, shaded from the African sun and the natives equally? She doubted Charles would allow her to do her own kind of work out there. Sometimes his idea of her as his 'precious ruby', to be guarded from damage and corruption, irked her. She'd rather be a diamond – a million times tougher than a ruby and far more useful.

But the idea of going to Africa had taken hold of her imagination – perhaps even more so than marriage to Charles itself. The prospect of a life spent making converts rather than pickles had its allure, and when lying awake, feeling like those resting bells in St James's tower, she had begun to dream of Africa. She'd secretly searched out books about the continent in the Spa Road library and had been entranced by the exotic photographs of wide-open plains and mist-covered mountains, raging waterfalls and huge rivers. Grainy photographs of tall, lithe black bodies, shining in the sun, peopled her imaginings. But tonight she struggled to believe she could ever have anything to offer such a place.

She felt tears begin to pool in her eyes and squeezed them tightly closed, damning back the flood. Africa: mysterious and faraway, a fantasy land to which she could fly away and forget that in Bermondsey malnourished children with rickets still regularly turned up at the clinic, where diphtheria and scarlet fever still cut short more young lives than anywhere else in London. So, wasn't the idea of going to Africa as much a fairy tale as the one she'd spun for Jenny of her shining future in that cottage with a garden?

Charles was calling the meeting to an end and came up to her as she gathered her coat and bag, quickly flicking tears from her eyes.

'You didn't pray.' It was a statement but his tone demanded an answer.

She shook her head. 'I wasn't moved.'

'It's not a matter of emotion, Ruby. It's a duty. It's irrelevant whether you feel miserable or happy, you just pray. It's all that's required of you.'

'I was thinking of little Jenny.'

He gave her a pitying look. 'I'm sorry the little girl was taken. But your prayers will never be effective if you're not single-minded, Ruby.'

'Charles! Are you saying it's my fault she died? I did everything I could!'

'For he that wavereth is like a wave of the sea, driven with the wind and tossed. For let not that man think that he shall receive any thing of the Lord. A double minded man is unstable in all his ways,' Charles quoted. 'Your actions haven't been consistent with your faith. I warned you that keeping evil company would have its consequences, Ruby. You need to cut yourself off from godless, immoral socialists like Ida Turpin and those Diamonds. Remember First Corinthians

15:33: *Be not deceived: evil communications corrupt good manners.*'

At that moment she thought she hated him. Yet what if it was true that, if she'd been a purer Christian, more faithful, her prayers would have been answered?

Over the following weeks, the seed of doubt wormed its way in to her mind like a maggot in a rotten apple until she felt she must do something to make a change. *Sacrifice*. She'd heard it defined in a sermon once as costly, painful service. The cost would be a friendship that meant the world to her, the pain would be a loss deeper than words, but the resulting service would be the sort of single-mindedness that would make her prayers effective and satisfy even Charles's rigorous standards.

Finally, one Monday at the start of their shift on square pickles, Ruby held up her red hands for Ida's inspection. Several cuts had been inflamed by the daily drenching of vinegar.

'Ida, look at these hands, they're terrible. I've had to get myself moved off square pickles.' She convinced herself that the excuse was partially true.

'What? Without me?' The look of shock on Ida's face cut her more painfully than those on her inflamed hands.

'You've got to stay here, you and Ocki need the money.' She lowered her eyes as if concentrating on her work and rushed on, 'Anyway, I'm going over to essence of roses. It'll be a big drop in wages, but the doctor said these'll get infected if I carry on here.'

Ida was shaking her head. 'I know we need the money, but listen, I'll ask Ocki if he can get overtime. You and me have always worked together, right from the start.'

'I know we have, but it's different now. You're with Ocki and you're putting away for the future.'

A look of realization dawned on Ida's face. 'Oh, Ruby. I don't want you to think that Ocki's taken your place. I still love you! You're me best mate, always will be!'

Ruby wanted to run far, far away now and Africa wouldn't have been far enough. She reminded herself that the Christian life was one of sacrifice, yet her heart was lacerated as she realized that Ida was as much the sacrificial victim as she was herself.

All week long the tussle went on between Ruby and Ida and eventually Ruby's will proved the strongest. On the day that Ruby moved over to essence of roses, she kissed Ida lightly on the cheek. She knew it for what it was: a Judas kiss.

'You'll have to come round tonight, tell me how you got on,' Ida called after her as she hurried out of square pickles.

'Sorry, Ida. I've got Band of Hope,' she called back, before dashing downstairs to the fourth floor where the supervisor showed her to her bench and the woman working at the next station looked up with a grin.

'Oooh! Look who it ain't. The Bible-basher! She can have a bleedin' bath in essence of roses, it still won't convince me her shit don't stink!' It was Minnie Boot, moved from peeling onions.

The rose essence bottling line required no skill and just enough speed to keep up with the semi-automated process. She missed Ida and comforted herself with the thought that she'd get used to working alone. But it only got worse, and, after a few days of Minnie Boot using her as a butt for her jokes, Ruby kept her head down and on every lunch break made sure she had an errand to do, so that by the end of the week she hadn't seen Ida and hadn't been forced to turn down any more invitations.

After the first week, Ida came to find her. Ruby was cleaning down the steel bench when she felt two large, vinegary palms cover her eyes. 'Guess who?'

Ida spun her around. 'Oooh, don't you smell sweet! You been avoiding me?' she asked with a grin and Ruby felt the blood rush to her cheeks. She saw her friend's smile fade.

'What's going on, Ruby? Have I done something to upset you?'

'No! No, Ida. You've been the best of friends to me—'

'*Been*? That sounds like it's all in the past. I *am* your best friend, ain't I, Ruby?'

Ruby dropped her head. 'I'll never have another friend like you, Ida. But you've got your new life with Ocki and Charles says—'

'Oh, Lord Charles of Chumpton, is it? I *knew* it! I knew Charlie Best would turn you against me one day. What does he say? Stay away from her, she's a slut? Don't you like me no more, Ruby?'

Ruby's throat tightened. 'Don't be silly, Ida. That sort of talk's for kids and it's time to start acting like grown-ups. You've got your beliefs, I've got mine,' she mumbled, turning away and hurrying from the factory floor before Ida could say another word. She walked home, seeing nothing, hearing nothing, feeling more ashamed than she ever had in her life.

She hoped that as the weeks passed it would get easier, that Ida would forget her and things would improve with Charles. The friction over her friendships had been causing them to argue in a way he said was unworthy and which she simply found exhausting. Then one warm Sunday she went walking with Charles in Greenwich Park. The bright day held the promise of unending summer and, as they reached the top of One Tree Hill, she took his hand.

'Charles, I've got something to tell you. I've made the break with Ida,' she said softly. She'd wondered if saying the words would make it any more real, but her voice didn't sound her own. It could have been that of a stranger.

He looked down at her tenderly and squeezed her hand. 'You've done the right thing, Ruby. Your path is set like an arrow now, straight and true, like mine. We can go on together now and I'll have no doubts in my mind about your steadfastness. I love you, Ruby.' His voice was thick with adoration. 'I think the Lord is telling me we should marry sooner than I'd planned.'

'But Charles, you've never asked me!'

'Oh, Ruby! Did I need to?' He took both her hands in his. 'Ruby, my precious girl, will you marry me?'

She felt his hands trembling as he waited for her answer and glanced away to the broad, winding Thames as it meandered down to the sea, picturing herself leaving on the boat with Charles. She imagined looking back to the foreshore where Ida, Dodge, Eric and Davey were waving goodbye.

'Yes. Yes, I will marry you, Charles,' she said, and was flooded with the longed-for certainty and single-mindedness that she'd craved.

Charles dipped his bronze head and she felt his mouth on hers for the first time, his lips insistent, almost relentless, now they had finally been unleashed. There was a headlong, hungry questing, which she tried to answer with her own kisses. But when he pulled back, his expression was still hungry and she wondered what it would take to drive that hunger away. The wide sky above them had seemed to expand and the grassy hill to descend so that only liquid air supported her. Perhaps this feeling of incompleteness was what it meant to love a man.

At any other time, she would have gone straight to Ida to talk about Charles's proposal and the confusion of emotions it had set up in her. But that was impossible now.

There was something wrong with her. Of this she was sure. Her friendship with Ida had weakened her faith, so that her prayers for Jenny had been ineffective. And so she'd cut herself off from Ida. But still there was the nagging sense that nothing was in its right place in her life. There's something wrong with you, something lacking, the preacher had said, and it can only be put right if you ask Jesus into your heart. And so she had. But that had never made her feel blameless or complete and every week a new lesson or verse convinced her there was still something about her that needed mending.

She decided to speak to Sister Evelyn after Sunday Service, but Sister Evelyn immediately invited her to tea that evening. The woman lived in a tiny flat next to the Central Hall and though her door was always open to the Young Women's Fellowship members, Sister Evelyn wasn't allowed favourites so invitations to tea were rare. Sister Evelyn believed in sharing the poverty of the majority of the congregation, so Ruby took with her some remnants of the Crosse & Blackwell contraband: a jar of strawberry jam and a tin of salmon. Charles would say this was evidence of her double mind, but she'd long since silenced her conscience about the cartons in Aunt Nancy's shed. She was simply distributing food to the poor. Sister Evelyn met her with a bright smile and a kiss on the cheek.

'Oh, Ruby, this is kind, but I can't take them. You shouldn't be robbing your own cupboards. I'm providing the tea today!' Ruby felt a pang; if only Sister Evelyn knew who exactly Ruby was robbing. The woman ushered her into a small living room, where the table was already set with bread and butter and a plate of scones.

'Oh, Sister Evelyn, you've got the bread all ready, so we can make salmon sandwiches and the jam will go with the scones! Besides, the boys have gone right off jam.'

Eric had only this morning complained that he was sick and tired of living off bread and jam and so Ruby told no lie.

'And what about you, Ruby, dear, have you gone off jam?'

Ruby was genuinely puzzled. 'What makes you ask that?' She released the cap and stuck in a spoon, putting a generous dollop onto Sister Evelyn's plate.

'You seem to be getting thinner and thinner, my dear, and I worry you're so intent on feeding up those boys you've been neglecting yourself.'

'No! Of course I've not. Eric's getting an extra pound a week now – not that I like where it's coming from – he's been put in the BUF defence force.' She shook her head, remembering the argument she'd had when he told her he was joining the 'bully boy' wing of the party that policed political meetings and was responsible for the punch-ups that featured in the papers. 'Still, he's putting the pound straight into the food money tin.'

'You're worried about Eric, is that what's been wrong?'

'Why do you think that something's wrong?' Ruby said, pushed almost to tears by the woman's gentle probing.

Sister Evelyn got up. She took down a scallop-edged mirror that hung on a chain above the fireplace. It was heavy, backed with wood, and the woman struggled to position it far enough away so that Ruby could view almost all of her seated form.

'What do you see?' Sister Evelyn asked.

Ruby's forehead creased in a frown. 'I see Ruby Scully.'

'And how does Ruby Scully look to you?'

Sister Evelyn's voice had taken on a tone that brooked no argument.

'A girl. Blonde hair,' she said aloud. 'Blue eyes.' Her voice wavered as she saw that there were dark rings beneath them.

'Do you see a healthy, robust sort of a girl?'

'I've never been big-boned, Sister, and you know the last few months have been a struggle, to find the housekeeping…'

Sister Evelyn put down the mirror and, coming to her, lifted Ruby's arm and set it alongside her own. 'Ruby, I'm not a great eater myself. But this arm of mine is twice as thick as yours. Doesn't that show you that you might well have gone off jam yourself?'

Ruby lifted uncomprehending eyes to her mentor. 'I honestly can't see the difference, Sister,' she said, feeling that there was something here that was definitely wrong with her and she must be the last to know what it was.

'Well, perhaps I'm mistaken,' Sister Evelyn said unconvincingly and passed her the plate of sandwiches. 'Now, what is it that you wanted to talk to me about, Ruby?'

'You're right. I do think there's something wrong with me, all the time, Sister, but it's not my skinny arms. I feel worthless.

Charles says my prayers for Jenny weren't answered because I was lacking in faith. He says I've been double-minded.'

Sister Evelyn pursed her lips.

'You must never think you're worthless, though we're all of us unworthy. You must remember that the hairs of your head are all numbered and you're very precious to God, Ruby.'

Ruby looked shyly at the woman. 'Sister Evelyn, Charles has proposed and I said yes.'

Sister Evelyn gave her a quizzical look. 'You don't seem entirely happy about it?'

'He's just so – so sure. He knows exactly what God wants of him, where he should go, what he should do, and he seems to know what I should be doing too. I – I feel like one of those birds on a leash: I'm flying around and around, but only as far as he wants me to go.'

'And that irks you?'

'Sometimes, yes.'

'Marriage isn't for everyone, Ruby. Think carefully about what *you* want. I've had a very happy single life, serving the Lord in Bermondsey. I loved a man once, a conscientious objector during the war. He died carrying a wounded soldier to an ambulance,' she said, with a small tremor in her voice. 'He was everything to me. But I sometimes think that if Arnold had lived I shouldn't have had such a fulfilling life – no, not half the life I've had. But perhaps for you it's different and it isn't so much marriage that doesn't suit you as...' She paused before continuing, 'I suppose I shouldn't say this, but not all Christian men are like Charles Best, my dear; there might be someone more compatible.'

She was walking in St James's churchyard by the light of a full moon. Though the gates were locked there was a gap in the railings that she'd slipped through. Although it had been almost two months since their conversation, she often found her thoughts returning to Sister Evelyn's suggestion that there could be someone more suitable for her than Charles. Tonight, those words played themselves on a loop, keeping her awake till she'd eventually been forced to slip out of bed, put on her coat and go out into the quiet street. She had hoped for a mild night and a silent hour to clear her jumbled thoughts, but instead a sharp wind blew Alfie Diamond into her path again. She heard him humming a tune before she saw him emerging from the church, swinging a canvas bag of tools.

He jumped at the sight of her. 'Ruby! I thought you were a ghost!'

Perhaps she did look a bit ghostly with her pale hair and light grey coat.

'I'm solid enough,' she said, 'though Sister Evelyn seems to think I'm wasting away.' She tried to smile.

'What's wrong with you, Ruby?' Alfie asked, coming closer

'Everything,' she answered truthfully.

'I've been meaning to come and see you,' he said, putting down the tool bag.

'Have you?'

'Fancy coming up to see the bells?'

'What, now?'

'Why not? I've been up there replacing some of the rotten woodwork in the frames since practice finished.'

'I never heard the bells!'

He laughed, 'Be grateful they muffle the clappers for practice! Well, what do you say?'

'All right, if it's allowed.'

He grinned. 'The bellringers went off with the key, but I don't need it.' And with a shoulder barge and a quick twist of the handle he shoved opened the side door.

She followed him up stone steps to the gallery, then steep wooden stairs. They emerged into a high, square room, with deep, arched recesses in each wall.

'This is the ringing room,' Alfie said, going to light a paraffin lamp.

Light bounced off the whitewashed walls, revealing a number of holes in the ceiling, from which hung striped fluffy bell ropes.

'So, where are the bells?' she asked, disappointed.

Alfie pointed to the ceiling, 'Up there!'

'Oh! Can't we see them?'

'All in good time,' he said, offering her the single chair and settling himself down on the dusty floor. 'First of all, I want to know who told you that everything's wrong with you? I thought once you'd got the "I'm saved" thing under your belt, you were OK – all your sins wiped away?'

'Yes... but you can slip back.'

'And when you slip back, you're all wrong again?'

'Not *all*, but mostly I suppose.'

'Seems a waste of time to me. First the missionaries come and tell you you're living a life that's all wrong and they can put it right and then, when they've got you in church, they tell you you're all wrong again!'

She rubbed at her forehead. 'There's more to it than that. And look at all the good work the Mission does. Soup kitchens and clinics and charity boxes—'

'Socialists do all that too, except we don't blame the *people* – we tell them the truth. It's the system that's wrong, not them, and we've got to change it ourselves!'

'Of course, but you have to change people's hearts first.'

'So, tell me about this backsliding, when did you do that?'

'Oh, all the time!'

'All right, what's the latest sin you've committed?' He gave a mischievous smile. 'Pretend I'm your confessor.' Then his expression grew serious. 'Honestly, I'm interested to hear about this horrible crime that makes you feel everything about you is wrong?'

'First off, I gave a load of knocked-off Crosse's tins to the Mission *and* the Labour Institute – don't tell anyone!'

Alfie nodded. 'Of course not. I'm the confessor! Besides, I already heard all about that. Go on.'

'I missed my morning prayers for weeks because I was too busy fussing over Davey, taking his temperature every five minutes.' She saw him smile.

'Don't laugh. That showed a real lack of faith, Charles said.'

'All right, go on.'

She frowned. 'I probably shouldn't tell you this, but – but I've been kissing Charles Best.'

He gave a look of mock horror. 'Kisses? For that man? Now that *is* a sin – a sinful waste of kisses.' And his laugh seemed to bounce off the bells in the tower above them.

'Don't make fun of me. It's a serious thing for us. We might be engaged, but Charles believes kisses like that should wait till after we're married. He's mortified every time it happens.'

Alfie stuck out his lower lip.

'So, doesn't he have anything to do with these kisses, or do you get all the blame?'

'He says I provoke him.'

Alfie had been leaning back on his hands with his long legs stretched out on the floorboards, but now he drew them up and dropped his chin to his knees.

'Well, Ruby, a beautiful woman will provoke a man, no doubt of it. But he's not obliged to act on it. I should think he'd only have to take one look at your silvery hair or your sky blue eyes…' He paused awkwardly, looking as if he regretted his words, and then went on, 'But you can't do much about the way you look, Ruby, not unless he wants you to walk around with a bag over your head!'

'Perhaps that's why St Paul said a woman's glory is her hair and we should keep it covered.'

Alfie gave an impatient sigh. 'There's the problem, Ruby! Even I know the Methodists are one of the few churches where a woman's free to speak and work alongside men – and you end up with Charlie Best! The only thing wrong with you, Ruby Scully, is your judgement when it comes to men.'

'You sound just like Ida.' She chuckled, while feeling a pang of longing for her friend. She was surprised to see his expression harden a little.

'Which brings me back to my question: what's this big thing you've done wrong, keeping you from sleeping, sending you walking through churchyards at this time of night?' Before she could respond, he answered the question himself. 'Ida! If you've got anything on your conscience, it's Ida.'

Ruby groaned to think that he'd so easily seen through her weakness. 'I miss her so much, Alfie. I never wanted to hurt her!'

'Well, you did. You've turned your back on the best friend you'll ever have, Ruby Scully, and she's heartbroken.'

Ruby scrambled up, disturbing the dust on the ringing room floor, sorry she'd trusted him.

'You've got no right to blame me! Sometimes there's hard things you have to do, to be true to your conscience.'

'Don't you mean Charlie Best's conscience?'

'When we're married it'll *have* to be this way. He won't have me associating with – with certain people. I just thought it would be less hurtful to make a clean break now. You know I shouldn't be talking to you, either, don't you?'

For answer he got up, brushing the dust from his trousers. 'Want to see the bells now?' he asked, taking her by surprise.

Intrigued in spite of herself, she nodded and followed him to a ladder which ascended through a trapdoor into the bell tower.

'I'll go first and give you a hand up.' His foot was already on the lowest rung and, mentally silencing Charles, she followed Alfie. How often had these bells broken the Sunday morning stillness, awakening her to the innumerable possibilities of all the years ahead of her?

Alfie disappeared through the trapdoor and then extended a hand to help her up the last few rungs and into the bell chamber itself. At first she could see nothing, but then her eyes became accustomed to the pale moonlight which streamed through the louvred arches of the tower. The bells filled her vision, massive and unmoving, slumbering giants waiting to be woken. She tipped her head back and began counting the rust-stained shadows.

'One, two three...' Silently she counted the rest. 'Ten? I never knew there were so many!' she whispered, for the place seemed to demand a sacred silence, a silence to be broken only by the bells themselves. He came nearer.

'What's wrong with them, Ruby?'

Puzzled, she squinted at each of the variously sized bells. 'I can't tell. I thought you said you'd fixed them?'

'Yes, I've done enough repairs to the frames so they can still just about be rung safely.'

'So, what's wrong with them then?'

'There's nothing wrong with them. It's just that they're not ringing. I've got a riddle for you. Is a bell still a bell when it's still?'

She wrinkled her nose and laughed. 'I give in, Alfie, you'll have to tell me.'

'Well, if it was never ever rung, wouldn't it just be a bell-shaped lump of metal that had once been a canon at the battle of Waterloo?'

Wind whistled through the louvres and she stared at the bells; and instead of their chimes she heard the canons' thunder of their earlier incarnations. Then the wind dropped and there was only silence.

'No. They're not bells if they don't ring.'

He gave a little clap, which found a resonance in the nearest bell and set up a faint humming. 'Nothing's ever anything unless it moves, changes.'

She turned her gaze away from the bells, realizing that all the while he had been talking about her, not the bells. Now she looked him full in the eyes, which reflected back the moonlight.

'You know that when they ring the bells the tunes are called "changes"?'

She nodded.

'Time to make a change, Ruby.'

10
Honour Thy Father

Summer–Autumn 1936

She was left feeling both exhilarated and unsettled by the encounter with Alfie Diamond. His words had rung with a truth she couldn't dismiss, but weeks passed and still she couldn't find the courage to tell Charles she desperately wanted to be reconciled with Ida. She'd been pondering all the ways it would be wrong to visit her friend while keeping it a secret from Charles, when she received an unexpected visit.

'Can I come in, Ruby?'

It was Charles. At her door! He'd never before suggested coming in to her house because he would consider entering a young woman's home without her parents present as one of those 'appearances of evil' to be avoided at all costs. He stood on the doorstep, ramrod straight, a fine trembling visible in the hand that gripped his hat and his nostrils flaring as if he needed to take in more air. He sighed a deep outbreath and asked again, 'Can I come in, Ruby?'

'Are you sure, Charlie?'

'Charles! That's the name I was christened with! And I *was* christened, even though my parents are as godless as the heathens of Basutoland!'

She didn't know why she'd called him Charlie, it had just slipped out, but she'd only made his agitation worse.

'You do know my dad's still away?' she warned him, not wanting him to blame her later for not giving him all the facts. 'Eric's out, Davey's downstairs with Aunt Nancy – I'm on me own.'

He nodded and she led the way to the back kitchen. He looked around, taking in the sparse furnishings, and she saw his eye fall on her mother's Bible on the kitchen table. He took it up, flicking through the gold-edged pages.

'Sit down. What's wrong, Charles?' she asked, sitting beside him. Putting a fist to his mouth, he bit into his knuckle – and then he did a thing she'd never once seen him do. He bowed his head and began to cry, in great, heaving sobs that shook his powerful, bowed back. He covered his face with both hands and said something, which she couldn't hear.

'What's happened?'

'My father's died,' he said and choked on a sob.

'Oh, Charles, I'm so, so sorry.' She stood up and pulled him into her arms, letting his head rest on her breast. 'My poor Charles, when did it happen?'

'My mother sent a boy to fetch me and he said the place was covered in blood and I'd better come. Ruby, I thought she'd finally murdered him! I ran all the way to Barnham Street. Mother was crying and Father was on the floor, his face covered in blood. There was a bucket beside him. He'd vomited up his liver, Ruby. Drunk himself to death – finally. Just as I'd always told him he would.' He was overtaken by another heaving sob.

'I'm so sorry you never made it up with him before he died,' she said softly, but he looked up at her with incomprehension. 'Made it up? I don't care about that! He wasn't saved, Ruby! He's rotting in hell! I'm only upset because I couldn't save him.' Charles fell from the chair onto his knees and grabbed the Bible with one hand and her with the other. 'I need guidance, Ruby. Mother's asked me to go to the funeral.'

'Well, of course, you should go!'

'Pray with me.'

He pulled her down onto her knees and opened the Bible. 'Show me, Lord, what I should do. Give me a sign,' he prayed and turned the pages. Then placing a finger on the page that had fallen open, he read: *And call no man your father on the earth: for one is your Father, which is in heaven.* See, Ruby? I *knew* I was right to do what I did. He was no father of mine.'

'I don't think it means that...'

'Are you trying to teach me what the Bible means?' he snapped. 'You're a woman, you're not to teach a man! Another one, you'll see.' And he flicked wildly through the pages till his eye fell upon another verse: *Lord, suffer me first to go and bury my father. But Jesus said unto him, Follow me; and let the dead bury their dead.*'

She couldn't think of a sadder thing than that Charles should let his mum mourn alone. 'But it's only talking about *fathers*, isn't it?' she ventured. 'What about mothers? Three! You always say look at three verses.'

He flipped the gold-edged pages again, closed his eyes and let his finger rest on another verse. He opened his eyes and read: '*Honour thy father and mother*. No, no, that's not it!'

'But it says honour your mother and your mum asked you to go. Charles, go to the funeral.'

He thumped the Bible with his clenched fist. 'You don't understand. She always took his side. That man! He's still got me by the throat, even from the grave.'

She took his hand. 'Perhaps it's time to forgive them, Charles.'

'Will you come with me?' His look of anguish tore at her heart. What torments must he have suffered to make him hate his parents so much?

She was surprised that he actually took her advice. She borrowed Aunt Nancy's best black coat and hat, lucky that the woman was as thin as a rail and the clothes fitted her. But once dressed for the funeral in the old-fashioned clothes, Ruby was glad vanity wasn't one of her besetting sins. But it was a funeral, after all, and who would be looking at her?

When Charles came to collect her his agitation had abated. He was paler than usual and the stony planes of his face revealed little. He wore a new black suit and tie with a black trilby and he paid for a tram, though normally they would have walked. He led her up to the open top deck, even though the sky was overcast and rain was threatening, saying that he needed the air.

'How are you feeling?' she asked, once they were settled.

'I haven't seen my mother for six years and I was hoping I never would again. I'm trusting the Lord.'

'Charles, what did she do to you?'

'That's not important – it's what she did to herself.' His top lip trembled. 'She went off with another man when I was ten and left me with a drunkard father who beat me black and blue as if it was my fault and then was foolish enough to take her back. She's a slut.'

'But if she was sorry enough to come back to you both—'

'Ruby, you're too soft on people. There are no excuses for what she did. Anyway, the chap chucked *her* out. But I'm not going to rake it all over. I've just come to give her another chance to save herself.'

Ruby wanted to say that that was up to God, but she didn't want to push Charles, not today.

When they arrived at his childhood home, a tiny flat, the woman who greeted them took her by surprise. She hadn't expected this tall, stout, smartly dressed woman, her red hair streaked with grey and drawn back in a bun. She wore a shapeless black hat which looked as if it had been bought on the same clothes stall as Aunt Nancy's.

'Charlie, love, you've come!' She threw her arms around him.

Ruby felt him recoil. True, his mother wore make-up, which Charles disapproved of, but Ruby could see no evidence of the sluttish gambler he'd portrayed. Still, who could ever guess the secret life of a family? Everyone said Dodge was a charmer, but that had never made him a very good father.

Mrs Best surveyed her son. 'Your dad would have been proud of you,' she said and Ruby saw she bore the same stoical expression as her son. Whatever emotion Mrs Best was feeling today was hidden well. She looked at Ruby. 'Ain't you going to introduce your young lady to me, Charlie?'

'This is Ruby, Mother. We're to be married.'

Mrs Best gave a satisfied nod. 'I'm glad you found someone, son. Come in, don't stand on the doorstep.'

She showed them into a small kitchen scullery and Ruby noticed there were two doors leading off to bedrooms. An odd assortment of chairs, probably borrowed, were ranged around the walls and mostly occupied by whispering women, who sat with their coats and hats on, handbags on their laps, cups of tea in their hands.

'You were lucky – you had a bedroom all to yourself!' Ruby whispered.

He pulled at his collar. 'I wouldn't give a dog a bedroom in this place. Did you see the filth around the rubbish chutes?'

She winced as his voice boomed loud in the tiny space. This was home to many of the women sitting near him, but none of them showed they'd heard his insult. 'I'm just going outside for a bit of air,' he said and she got up to go with him, but he stopped her. 'I'll stand with the men outside. You stay here, talk to my mother.'

When he'd gone, one of the women around her couldn't hide her curiosity. 'Is Charlie your chap, then?'

Ruby nodded and the woman swiped her index finger up under her nose. 'Oooh, you're honoured. He's too good for us lot. That woman –' she dropped her voice and pointed to Mrs Best who was making tea at the stove '– she idolized him, *idolized*! Spoilt rotten he was. She even come back to be knocked about by her old man 'cos she couldn't bear to leave that boy. Shit's her thanks.' The woman folded her arms and nodded her hat at her companions who nodded theirs back in agreement. 'Still, you must see some good in 'im,' the woman said after some consideration.

'I see a lot of good in Charles.' Ruby felt she should defend him, though she had no reason to think the woman was lying about his mother. 'He's dedicating his life to serving others and – and I love him,' she said, almost fiercely.

The woman sniffed and tucked in her chins. 'His mother loved 'im, darlin.'

The hearse arrived and there was a car for the family. This was not normal for a Barnham Street funeral and she wondered if Charles had paid for it. As she followed Charles and his mother, she saw the whole courtyard of the buildings was ringed with neighbours. Some came to shake Mrs Best's hand, but all ignored Charles. It hurt her to see how much he was despised in this place. But he fixed his gaze above them and lifted his head. She could only imagine that he felt a martyr for his faith.

Only when his father was being lowered into the ground at the cemetery did she see Charles falter. He gripped her hand and she whispered, 'Go to your mum.' For Mrs Best had begun to weep. She had obviously forgiven her husband's 'knocking her about'. But Charles didn't move until it was time to return to the tiny flat for a funeral tea, which by Barnham Street standards was sumptuous.

'We've got red salmon *and* ham,' Mrs Best said proudly to Charles, as if ham could possibly wipe away all his bad opinion of her. The tea seemed interminable to Ruby. The men stood outside eating all the salmon sandwiches and drinking whisky, whilst the women formed a team, whipping away cups and plates, washing them up and returning them to their owners, for no one person in Barnham Street would possess so much crockery. Charles fitted into neither group. He sat awkwardly with a plate on his immaculately trousered leg and ate nothing. In the end Ruby joined the women. Charles wasn't talking to her or anyone else so she might as well be of use to his mother.

'When you two getting married?' Mrs Best asked.

'Oh, I think we should wait at least a year, but I know Charles wants it to be sooner.'

Mrs Best gave her a long look. 'You'll need the patience of a saint with that one, darlin'. Come with me.' She beckoned her into one of the bedrooms. There was a double bed over which was hung a small crucifix. Ruby was surprised; Charles had described his parents as heathen. Mrs Best took down a box from the top of the wardrobe. She opened it to reveal a length of ivory lace. 'This was my wedding veil. I want you to have it.'

And before she could object, Mrs Best had clipped the veil to her hair, fluffed it out over Ruby's shoulders and led her to a mirror. Ruby's sky-blue eyes gazed back at her from the froth of lace and she tried to imagine if Charles would be proud of her as she walked down the aisle towards him and their new life together. She would become Mrs Best, respected wife of a Methodist missionary and the thought made her feel that same, arrow-like certainty she'd had when she accepted Charles. She took off the veil so that she was plain Ruby Scully again and handed it back to Mrs Best.

'I couldn't take it.'

'Oh, but you look so beautiful in it! Is it that your mother wants you to wear hers?'

Ruby shook her head. 'Mum's dead.'

'Oh, you poor thing. It's hard to be without a mother. I suppose my Charlie's told you about the wrong thing I did, all them years ago. He never forgive me. But I come back, didn't I? Never wanted him to grow up without a mother, you see…' She smoothed the veil. 'Still, me and his father, we had a bit of happiness, in later years.' She sniffed and Ruby thought she would begin to cry when Charles put his head through the door.

'Your guests are leaving, Mother.'

When she'd shown out the last person and there were only the three of them left, they sat in silence, broken only by the distant shouts of kids in the courtyard.

'They should be in bed,' Charles said.

'You was always in bed be nine,' Mrs Best said. 'I made sure you had your sleep so you was fresh for school.'

'Fair Street school was for factory fodder. I educated myself at night school after I left home,' Charles said.

'Me and your dad did what we could.'

Charles bit his lip. 'You don't have to remind me what he did, and really, Mother, I didn't come here to pay my respects to Mr Best. I came here to save your eternal soul. I don't want to have you on my conscience as well as him.'

'You always did have a cruel tongue, Charlie. I hope Ruby here is listening.'

He leaned closer to his mother, his face taut with urgency. 'Why won't you accept Jesus as your saviour? It will cost you nothing but an admission of sin and you will gain a place in heaven!' Charles was blindly oblivious to his mother's outraged expression. Ruby felt glued to the chair. His description of salvation seemed more like a monetary transaction, something he might write in his account books, filling in the profit and loss columns.

Mrs Best had flushed red. 'Now listen 'ere, you've come in with your posh voice and your turned-up nose and I've took it. But I've told you before, I've got my religion and you've got your'n. It don't make me a sinner. I go to confession and mass every week! You won't find no one more regular at Dockhead church than me!'

He leaped up with an impatient wave of his hand. 'Mumbo jumbo! The Catholic Church is not the *true* church!'

Mrs Best snatched her handbag and pulled out a rosary.

'God forgive you, Charlie Best. If your dad had let me bring you up Catholic we'd have had *none* of this trouble. You'd have been a priest by now!'

'I'd rather join the Diamonds in the synagogue – at least they don't pretend to be Christian. Well, I've tried. You've chosen your fate, Mother. Come on, Ruby.'

He stalked out of the flat, but Ruby stopped to grasp Mrs Best's hand. 'I'll get him to come back and see you when he's calmed down.'

But Mrs Best shook her head. 'Don't bother, love. You'll only make a rod for your own back. He's a hard man, my Charlie. Just like his dad.'

Charles was already halfway across the courtyard when she caught up with him.

'You said she was a heathen! Why didn't you tell me she was Catholic?'

He stormed ahead of her.

'Stop!' She pulled him by the arm and forced him to face her. 'She's a religious woman! All right, she made a mistake when she was young, but Charles, she loves you! Where's your Christian forgiveness?'

'It's not my forgiveness she needs, it's God's.'

'But she goes to church every week!'

He shook his head and frowned. 'I despair of you, Ruby. The Catholic Church is the anti-Christ; I'll give you a leaflet. Shouldn't be difficult for even you to understand.'

She flushed at the stinging jibe and when they reached St James's road, she didn't ask him in. He reached for her hand, but she quickly withdrew it.

'Ruby, let's not argue about my parents, they're both dead to me now. And I was thinking today about your father. I should really ask his permission to marry his daughter. When's he coming home? I think it's time I met him, don't you?'

'Who's that wants to meet me?' A voice emerged from the gloom beyond the street lamp's glow.

Ruby whirled round. 'Dad! What are you doing here?'

'I live here – unless you've chucked me out and taken a lodger while I've been gone!' Dodge enveloped her in a bear hug. 'Hello, me darlin', I thought I'd surprise you!' He whispered in her ear, 'Who's the geezer?'

Ruby felt an unexpected wave of relief at finding herself in Dodge's arms. 'I've missed you!'

She hadn't realized just how much until this moment, for however unreliable a father he'd been, Dodge's love for her was as certain as the sunrise and just as bright. There was nothing she'd ever needed to do to earn his love, except be herself, and one minute in his arms had washed away the months of worry and struggle she'd endured alone.

As Dodge let go of Ruby, Charles stepped forward and stuck out his hand. 'I'm pleased to meet you, Mr Scully. And the reason I wanted to meet you is to ask you a question.' He looked fondly at Ruby, taking hold of her hand in a proprietary gesture.

Ruby hoped Dodge would keep his mouth shut about being locked up for the past six months.

'Dad, this is Charles Best. We've been courting,' she said and gave him a look which he'd practiced on her often enough when she was a child, and which usually meant Ruby shouldn't tell her mother – or any other authority figure – anything about Dodge's latest dubious dealings.

He squinted at Charles, coming a little closer into the circle of light beneath the street lamp. 'Charles Best? Good gawd, is that Charlie Best's son? Well, I've got a question for you an 'all. Have you seen yer old man lately? 'Cos he owes me five large ones!' He laughed heartily and good-naturedly, but halted at the sight of Ruby's face.

Charles's expression transformed from one of eagerness to dismay, the imperturbable veneer of the day melting like wax in a flame. Ruby gripped his hand, but it slipped from her grasp.

'Pleased to meet you, Mr Scully,' he said coldly. 'Good night, Ruby.' He turned on his heel and walked away, almost at a trot, swiping the black trilby rhythmically against the airey walls as he went.

'Did I say something to upset him? I see you give me the eye, so I never said nothing about being in nick! What's got up his arse?'

She should have cried, but instead she gave into a giggle that became an unstoppable belly laugh when Dodge joined in, so that they both stood doubled up on the doorstep until Ruby knew she must quell her hilarity.

'Of course you said something wrong,' she said and then laughed even louder. 'We've just been to his dad's funeral!'

'Oh, my gawd, no! Trust me to put me size tens in it.' Putting his arm around her, they stumbled up the front steps, laughing all the way along the passage.

In the kitchen, she wiped the tears of laughter from her eyes and went to light the gas mantles. Now she was able to look at her father properly she saw that his abundant fair hair had thinned and his once perfectly fitting suit was now hanging on him. He was a rogue, but he was her father and it saddened her to see what prison had done to him. He was looking back at her wonderingly.

'Gawd, you're looking just like your beautiful mum when she was young, but you're too skinny, love. You ain't been eating enough.' He paused, and Ruby wondered if he realized his absence might have something to do with her weight loss. But Dodge wasn't one to blame himself. 'So, put the kettle on, gel, and tell me what's been going on.'

'I wasn't really laughing about his dad dying, so much as that you knew him!' she explained. 'Charles wasn't pleased…'

Dodge sniffed. 'I could tell that, darlin'. To be honest, I knew little Charlie hadn't seen his dad in years; Big Charlie used to tell me how it broke his mother's heart. I was just having the boy on. Poor old Charlie Best dead? He was a lovely feller – when he wasn't in the drink. How d'ya get yourself hooked up with Little Charlie?'

'He likes to be called Charles now. He goes to the Central Hall.'

'Does he, be'gawd? Charlie Best's son a Bible-basher!'

'Dad! Don't call him that; I get called it all the time and it's hurtful.'

'Sorry, love. But you sure about him?'

'Yes, I am!'

He shook his head. 'He's a cold-hearted bastard to leave his mum and dad in the lurch all them years.'

'Well, that's only because your "lovely feller" Charlie Best used to beat him up as a kid!'

'He was a cheeky, clever little git. Used to run bets for his dad and Charlie always give him a treat for it, but the little git fiddled him rotten. Thought Charlie didn't know about it. That boy was always looking down his nose at you, even as a youngster. I'd steer clear if I was you, love.'

'Don't you start as soon as you get home,' she admonished. 'He's a good man and I love him. The question he wanted to ask was if you'd agree to us getting married.'

'With the corner up I will, gel. You ain't marrying *him*, not for love nor money!'

11

Not For Love

Autumn 1936

Ruby hadn't had a chance to argue with Dodge about his refusal to let her marry Charles. She'd been about to retort that she'd be eighteen soon and then she wouldn't need his consent, but at that moment Davey had woken up and run in from the bedroom. She hadn't wanted to spoil his pleasure at Dodge's return and even Eric, when he came home, had seemed pleased to see his father. But this morning, as she walked to work, the phrase Dodge had used rang in her ears. He'd said he wouldn't allow them to marry, *not for love, nor money*, and she was struck by the question she knew she should have asked herself before now. What *was* she marrying for? Not for money. Charles was a lowly trainee accountant and once he became a missionary he'd be poor. But there was comfort in the idea of a future with an upright man who held a position in society, one that had nothing to do with ducking and diving. Of course she was marrying for love. But Mrs Best had been right. Charles was a hard man, as hard with himself as with other people. Still, in her father she'd seen the chaos a soft man could wreak and didn't want another one of those in her future. And the Charles other people saw was not the one she saw. She was certain that his passion and devotion to her was real. Ruby wasn't frightened to follow her heart, but sometimes she was unsure of it. It was like holding up a map and not knowing which way was north or south. All she had to guide her was faith, faith that she was going in the right direction. But today, as she crossed the barrel yard of Crosse and Blackwell's, she prayed for a compass, something that could point her heart to true north and leave her in no doubt about the path to her future happiness.

As she skirted a barrel taller than herself, a voice called her name. She steeled herself for mockery from Terry and the lads and scurried on, but someone shot out a strong hand pulling her out of the path of a massive barrel being rolled by two hefty coopers.

She looked up gratefully into warm brown eyes that crinkled at the corners. 'Thanks Alfie!'

'You nearly had it! But I'm glad I've seen you, Ruby. Been meaning to come and find you. There's something I need to talk to you about.'

'Sorry, I've got to hurry. I should be clocking on,' she said, fearing another lecture about Ida.

'Well, what about dinner time? Can I see you for five minutes?'

She wavered. She no longer went to the canteen so as not to have to face Ida, and perhaps he guessed that. 'Why don't I meet you outside the 27 building, after work? Just five minutes! It's important.'

Charles wouldn't like it, but Alfie had just saved her from serious injury and besides, something in his voice compelled her. 'All right.'

She spent the morning wondering what Alfie could have to say. She hoped he wouldn't mention Ida again. The death of Charles's father had intervened and she'd thought better of going behind his back and seeing her old friend again. When the hooter went she hurried down to the yard to find out what was so important.

Alfie was leaning against the wall, smoking, when he spotted her and extinguished the cigarette. He pushed himself upright and strolled over. He was as supple and lithe as the silver birch in her back yard and his long, unhurried stride quickly covered the distance between them.

'Don't look so worried; this is nothing that Charlie can jaw you about.'

It was as if he'd read her mind and it made her want to contradict him. 'I'm not a kid, I can still decide for meself what I do or who I speak to!'

'Sorry, shouldn't have said that.' He looked chastened.

'Tell me what's so important, then?'

'Well, I've been pushing a plan, at the Labour League of Youth, and I think you can be a big help, Ruby.'

This was not what she'd been expecting.

'It's a drive to help needy families like the Mongeys but it needs people like you if it's going to work.'

'But how can *I* help? I'm not a party member.'

'The whole point is that you're *not* a member. The thing is Ruby, Bermondsey's full of different organizations all trying to improve people's lot, but there's no co-operation. The Central Hall clinic looked after Jenny, but they couldn't do anything about where she lived. If the family had been brought to the housing department's attention, then perhaps they could have been moved earlier. Voluntary Liaison Officers. That's what we'd call them. All young people, under twenty-one, volunteers in the churches and missions, settlements and youth clubs, even in the communist party, or Catholic charities, or the young Conservatives, for that matter. We'd build up a network and pass on information about the most needy families. A network can do more good than us all working away on our own. What do you think?'

'I think it's a terrific idea, Alfie, I really do.'

'I knew you would!'

'But would I have to come to League of Youth meetings?'

'Not if you don't want to. It's just an exchange of information, we might not be able to do much, but it'll be better than sitting around putting out fires when it's too late.'

She liked the picture he painted and she liked the passion that shone in his eyes too.

'All right, I'll help. After Saturday's home visits and my next stint at the Welfare Clinic I'll write a list of people I think need most help.'

He smiled at her for a long moment and eventually said simply, 'I'm pleased. You can pass me the names at work or you can come to Fort Road, anytime; you know you're always welcome.' He hesitated. 'Did you know Ida's moved to the tin shop?'

Ruby shook her head. 'How could I know?'

'You didn't take my advice then, about going to see Ida?' His dark eyes seemed to pin her to the spot.

'I was going to, but it's hard, Alfie. Things pull you in different directions...'

'Yes, it's not easy to know what's the right thing to do sometimes.'

She was surprised that he hadn't condemned her, and was struck by the difference between him and Charles, who was always so certain about everything.

'But is it things or people that are tugging at you?' he asked.

'Both.' She made up her mind. 'But I can't see the wrong in giving you a few names.'

He gave her an appreciative nod and the lightest touch on her arm before turning swiftly away, but she felt that touch of his hand for a long time after he'd disappeared.

Now that Ruby knew Ida had moved from square pickles she understood why she hadn't seen the familiar head of curly hair from a distance lately. There was no good reason for Ida to have quit the well-paying job in square pickles but Ruby knew it made it easier for her, because the tin shop was tucked well away in the

1894 building, far from essence of roses and far from Ruby. The seventh-floor tin shop – always referred to as 'up in the gods' – actually smelt like the depths of hell. Foul flux fumes permeated it, scraping the lungs raw, while the cacophony caused by heavy machines stamping out lids and cutting can bodies from huge rolls of tin sheet, bruised the ears and dulled the mind. Ruby knew Ida hated the job but now it seemed Ida preferred it to witnessing Ruby's desertion.

This daily dance of avoidance had to stop. It was breaking her heart, so what must it be doing to Ida's? In the days since her talk with Alfie, she'd begun to question whether she really did have any power to make decisions for herself or if she'd just given every choice over to Charles. Almost to prove her own freedom to herself, she determined to speak to Ida.

She decided to wait for her friend outside the 1894 building at lunchtime and when the hooter went she hurried down the stairs and across the yard before her heart could begin to battle with her conscience. But once at the building, her way was blocked. Men and women poured out into the yard. It was more than the usual scrum to get to the canteen or home. This was too orderly, too restrained. Ruby saw too that workers were emerging from the back entrance and congregating in the yard.

'Is it a fire drill?' Ruby asked a girl she knew wearing a solder-stained overall.

'Fire in the tin shop. Sparks from the soldering caught some sacks alight, gone up like a tinderbox!' the girl said with a cough.

'Do you know if Ida's come out?' Ruby asked.

'I never saw her on the staircase. But I'm on can handling, she's on lid stamping. She could have come down the back fire escape. They tried to put the fire out, but I don't know if they managed to.' And the girl pointed to the top floor where black smoke billowed from one of the open windows on the left side of the building.

Ruby dashed to a few groups to see if Ida was among any of them, but no one had seen her. Ruby refused to let panic seize her. Ida wasn't so stupid as to have lingered, she would have got herself to safety. But where? Ruby sprinted around to the fire escape at the back of the old Victorian building. The zigzag iron staircase was alive with moving figures, but when the trail of evacuees petered out, there was still no sign of Ida – and then a loud boom burst from the top floor, followed by a rain of splintering glass. Shards fell like icicles and a foreman standing nearby dragged her out of the path of a spike hurtling towards her head.

'Keep out the way, love! Get clear!'

But Ruby had heard, just before the boom, another sound, a cry coming from the far right-hand corner of the top floor. She knew, without a shadow of doubt, it was Ida's voice.

Ruby pushed the foreman out of her way. 'My friend's up there! I just heard her.'

'Don't be stupid, love. You couldn't hear anyone over that noise.' And though he plucked at her coat, she slipped from his grasp, dashing round to the front entrance and hurling herself into the building before anyone could stop her.

At first it was easy, up two, three, four floors she sprinted as if she had wings on her feet. But at the seventh floor black smoke, thick with the sulphurous flux used in soldering can seams, descended in sooty sinuous streams. She tore off her scarf, shielding her face, before plunging up the next few steps and through the double doors to the tin shop. Ruby was astonished to find the great conveyer belts still running. Jammed with already completed cans, and without the army of handling girls to remove and pack the cans onto pallets, the belts circled and stuttered and shuddered and groaned. She headed for the right-hand corner where the cry had come from. Here it was dark as night. Even the tongues of flame that still had hold on the left side of the floor brought no light.

She took the scarf from her face. 'Ida! Ida! It's Ruby. Where are you?'

She stumbled towards the windows, screaming her friend's name, but her voice was growing hoarse and she felt pain stab her throat as searing smoke cauterized her lungs. *Dear God, let me find her, only let me find her.*

And then a light, which wasn't a flame, seemed to hover like a ball in the air, over by the window. For a moment she thought it might be an angel, but her fume-addled mind was surely mistaken. Still she felt her way to the light, calling all the time, 'Ida! I'm coming.'

She came to a lid stamping machine which had stalled to a halt. Flames in the far corner were bouncing light off a tin lid held vertically in a clamp, like a miniature sun disk in the rosy glow. Then, on the floor beneath the machine, Ruby spotted a motionless figure. She dropped to her knees and saw the pale, smoke-streaked face of her friend.

'Ida! Wake up!' Ruby tried to pull Ida to her feet but immediately understood why she hadn't been able to escape with the rest. A heavy roll of tin sheeting had toppled over, trapping Ida's foot. As Ruby cursed those who'd run and left her friend behind, an accusing voice told her she'd done the same. *Run and left the best friend anyone could have, didn't you?* Now, she tugged at the heavy roll of tin sheet, and with tears of frustration streaming down her cheeks, realized it was simply far too heavy for her.

What if she dies here and you can never tell her you're sorry? the accusing voice persisted.

Refusing to admit defeat, she put her arms beneath Ida armpits and pulled, straining every muscle. 'Ida, come on now, help me. You always help me, don't you? Right from a kid. You was always looking after me. Help me out one more time, Ida, love. Just wake up and push!'

'Ruby Scully, is that you?' Ida's eyes flickered open. 'What you come up here for, you silly mare? I knew you'd get yourself into trouble without me around!'

Ruby stopped tugging at her friend and lifted the curly head, looking into her eyes. 'I don't like to say it, love, but you're the one in trouble. Your foot's stuck under that tin roll.'

Ida took in the size of the roll of tin. 'You ain't going to shift that, Ruby. They'll send someone up soon,' she whispered hoarsely. 'The fire ain't bad, is it? You go down, I'll be all right.'

Ruby shook her head. 'The whole building's been evacuated and I ain't leaving you, I'm never going to leave you ever again.' And she took her friend's face between her hands, looking in to her eyes. 'I'm so sorry, love. I'm so sorry. You didn't deserve it.'

Ida's lips were dry as sandpaper and through her charred throat, she said, 'I know. I know, it's all right…' and then slumped back, her eyes closed.

Ruby saw that the creeping flames had climbed to the dusty rafters. Now the fire had found that highway, she knew it would migrate to their side of the floor in no time. There must be some way she could move the roll. As she looked at its inert circular mass she was reminded, for some reason of the huge cylindrical bells of St James's. So heavy, and yet with one tug of the rope their whole mass could easily be made to swing. Alfie had shown her the mechanism, the frame and wheels which took the strain and transformed a small amount of strength into a greater. The stamping machines were powered by overhead belts that were still running, but Ida's machine had been halted by the lid, held in suspension and jammed in the machinery. In an instant, she knew what she had to do.

She snatched up a soldering tool and, using it to dislodge the jammed tin lid, saw, with satisfaction, the cam belt of the machine begin to turn again. 'I'm going to use the machine belt to pull the roll off you!' Ruby said. 'Hold still.'

'I ain't got no choice about that!' Ida said, her eyes flickering open again. She gave a grim smile. 'Get on with it, then, don't hang about like a tit in a trance.'

Ruby unravelled some of the rope which secured the roll of tin and pulled it up to the machine, then, looping it deftly around the cam belt she tugged it tight. There was a groan and a scraping noise as the machine took the strain and for a minute she thought the belt might break, but then the roll began to shift.

'When it starts to roll off you, I'll pull you out!' Ruby shouted, 'Wait... Wait... Now, Ida! Push yourself back with your other foot.'

The roll moved jerkily and Ida screamed as its weight shifted onto her toes. 'Gawd's sake, Ruby. Stop the bloody machine!'

But Ruby tugged all the harder. 'Nearly there!' She let out what sounded like a roar in her ears and with one final effort she pulled her friend free. Toppling backwards onto the floor, she saw that the flames in the rafters had finally reached them.

Ida was groaning in pain and when Ruby saw the bloody pulp that was her foot, she despaired. 'You've got to get up, Ida. Put your arm round me.' Ruby's ribs screamed in protest as she took most of Ida's weight across her shoulders and strained herself upright. Then, with Ida hopping at her side, she steered them towards the staircase.

Seeing a narrow corridor open through the flames she hesitated, then remembered Shadrach, Meshach and Abednego, how they had walked unharmed in the fiery furnace. She stormed ahead, feeling like a bull charging a red cape, and at the exit she simply leaned both of them forward so that their combined weight swung the doors outward. After stumbling down two flights, Ida was pleading for her to stop, but Ruby ignored her and it wasn't until the third-floor landing that she collapsed, unable to carry Ida a step further. Her arms felt pulled from their sockets and her legs like water. She took a few, smoke free breaths and was back on her knees, steeling herself to continue, when the thunder of boots on stone steps reached her ears.

*

When Ruby visited her friends a few days later, Ida tossed the crutch she'd been using aside and hobbled towards her with a wicked grin. 'Look! Me and Ocki are a perfect match now!'

Trust Ida to make a joke of her damaged foot. 'You shouldn't be putting any weight on it yet!' Ruby snatched up the crutch and gave it to Ida who didn't argue, but leaned on it heavily as she led the way to the little front room in the Fort Road house. Ruby went to warm herself at the fire as Ida flopped down into a chair next to it. Sitting opposite her friend, Ruby took her hands. 'I'm sorry I couldn't come before. But Alfie's been giving me progress reports on you.'

'Oh, I'm fine. But listen, Ruby, are you sure you want to be here? I know what you said, when you found me in the tin shop. But I can't hold you to it.'

Ruby didn't flinch from her gaze. What had been said in a time of danger needed repeating now.

'I said I wouldn't leave you again – and I meant it. It took nearly losing you to bring me to my senses. I don't expect you to forgive me for letting you down but—'

'Don't start all that. You run into a burning building for me – I don't call that letting me down. And I didn't blame you. It's your life, you've got to do what makes you happy and if Charlie don't want you to see me, well then…' Ida's gaze was unwavering and Ruby could tell she meant what she said.

'But it *didn't* make me happy, that's what was so hard. Not being friends with you – well, I've never been more miserable in me life.'

'So, he don't know you're here?'

Ruby shook her head. That was a battle that would have to come another day. 'Sister Evelyn told me once not to mistake Charles for God—'

Ida let out a barking laugh. Her throat was still damaged from the flux fumes of the fire. 'Good old Sister Evelyn!'

'So, if he asks me where I've been, then I'll tell him, but I don't want to fight with him. All I'm saying is that you're my friend and you always will be. I've decided I'm just going to do what *I* think's right in future.'

Ida put her head to one side. 'Just make sure you do what's right for Ruby Scully, too.'

Ruby nodded. A shift had come with the fire. All sorts of voices had clamoured to be heard when she was dragging Ida through the burning tin shop, but Charles's had been completely absent. Instead, over and over she'd repeated Job's lament: *My kinsfolk have failed, and my familiar friends have forgotten me ... and they whom I love are turned against me.* She only wanted another chance to prove to Ida and herself that she was nothing like Job's friends.

When Ruby went to the kitchen to make them tea, Ida called, 'I hear you're going to help with Alfie's new cooperative plan. Is that another thing you're not telling Charles about?'

Ruby could hear a teasing tone in her voice and she smiled to herself. To be teased by Ida seemed a privilege now.

'If he asks me I'll tell him.' She brought in tea and slices of bread and jam on a tray and placed it on a small side table near Ida.

Ruby saw a smile creep across her friend's face. 'Bell tower in the moonlight.' Ida sucked jam from her fingers. 'Very romantic.'

'Does Alfie tell you everything?'

Ida wrinkled her nose. 'He tells Ocki everything...'

'And then Ocki tells you.'

Ida laughed. 'Funny, that. You know, not all couples keep secrets, Ruby.'

Ruby hadn't had time alone with Charles since Dodge's return. She knew he was avoiding her and the conversation about Dodge that must come. She wasn't looking forward to it either, but determined at the next Pleasant Sunday Afternoon to raise the subject. But Charles surprised her. He wasn't there. When she asked among the Young Men's Fellowship one of them told her he'd seemed subdued and had said he was considering going on a spiritual retreat for a time of prayer and reflection about his future. Perhaps Dodge had frightened him off for good. She supposed she ought to have been worried that Charles would leave her, but instead she found herself jealous. She would have liked the luxury of a spiritual retreat herself, free from worrying about the money for next week's shopping or rent, free from Crosse & Blackwell's.

And she had other things besides Charles to worry about, not least her brother Eric who now wore the Blackshirt uniform, proudly showing off his newly honed physique in the regulation tight, black, collarless tunic, grey trousers and broad leather belt. He spent his evenings at BUF meetings and his weekends distributing leaflets or in Black House – the BUF headquarters – body building in their gym. Muscles were a requirement for stewarding meetings – which meant preventing communist infiltrators from getting in or manhandling hecklers out.

One evening, Ruby and her father were sitting in the kitchen listening to the wireless which Dodge had acquired the day after his release. From the wear on the dials Ruby could tell two things: that it wasn't brand new and that Dodge had not been reformed by his prison sentence. They'd never been able to afford a wireless and though she felt sorry for the previous owners, it was too much of a novelty for her to boycott the broadcast in protest. It was a rare night in for Dodge, and Ruby had been guiltily enjoying his company along with Ambrose's orchestra playing 'Until The Real Thing Comes Along' when Eric walked through the door in his Blackshirt uniform with a bloody nose and a grazed cheek.

'What have you done to yourself?' Ruby rushed to examine his wounds.

'It's what I did to the commie that got in my way you should be worried about!' he answered with a swagger. 'I've been fighting to keep this country free and you'll read about it in the paper tomorrow!' He was flushed with excitement, brushing away her ministrations. 'Leave off, Ruby. It's a bloody scratch.'

Dodge was staring at him. Eric struck a pose. 'What d'you think of me uniform, Dad? How do I look?' he asked proudly, giving him a demonstration of the fascist salute.

'You look like a bleedin' idiot. Get that tat off your back, I ain't having you wearing it in my house!'

Eric's lips thinned with anger. 'What's wrong with wearing a uniform? Our leader says it shows I'm doing something important, fighting for a better country! At least I'm not on the dole, hanging round street corners cadging fags, nicking stuff off of our own.'

Here he took a swipe at the wireless with his fist and Ruby noticed his knuckles were already grazed. Ambrose's singer warbled a complaint – '*if that isn't love, it'll have to do, until the real thing comes along,*' but was abruptly interrupted as the wireless tumbled to the floor. They all stared at the brown bakelite case, while the voice, accompanied by a fierce crackling, continued to sing into the linoleum floor.

'This uniform is something to be proud of! Not like you and yer bit of schmutter,' he said in a crude imitation of a Jewish voice, fingering the collar of Dodge's suit jacket.

Dodge stood up and lunged for Eric. 'You stupid little git! Haven't you got no respect for your mother.'

'What's she got to do with it, she's dead!' Eric shouted, evading Dodge's wild charge.

'You bloody moron, your own grandad was Jewish!'

Eric froze, gripping Dodge's jacket and holding him at arm's length. Ruby hadn't known her grandfather, but her mother's Bible and her insistence on sending her children to Sunday School was proof that she was Christian.

'You're making that up! If it's true then why didn't we know about it?' Eric said, clearly rattled. He released Dodge, who pulled away. Drawing a hand across his face, he sat down, breathless.

'Your nan was a Christian, brought her kids up Christian. Her old man was dead by the time I met your mum and it didn't seem important to tell you kids, not once your mother was gone.' He put his head in his hands. 'My poor Rachel, she would have told you about him, I daresay. If she'd been spared...' And, being Dodge, the tears came easily.

Which enraged Eric. 'So you choose *now* to tell me? Now I've got something worth fighting for? Well, I don't believe you, you're a lying bastard.'

Dodge's tears of sadness stopped. He grabbed Eric by the seat of his trousers with one hand and his collarless black shirt with the other and hustled him out of the room. 'Get out and don't come back till you've got rid of that uniform! You're no son of mine while you're wearing it!' he shouted.

Ruby ran after them into the passage just as Davey poked his head out of the bedroom. Alarm clouded his sleepy eyes as she drew him in close. 'Will you stop it you two, you're upsetting Davey!' she pleaded. But they were deaf to her pleas and blind to Davey's tears. Dodge launched Eric out of the front door and down the stone steps. After regaining his balance, her brother stood on the pavement, hands clenched.

'I don't want to be no son of yours!' Eric spat out. 'Our leader's more of a father to me than you'll ever be! He's noticed me...I've spoke to him and he says I'll go a long way.'

Dodge made a sound of disgust. 'A long way up the stairs to Jack Ketch if you carry on with that lot!' He slammed the front door, which made Davey jump and cling to Ruby's legs. She would have liked to run after Eric but Davey needed her more at the moment. She took him back into the bedroom and settled him down, sitting on the edge of the small cot bed which had come from the Sally Ann when Eric refused to share with his little brother any longer. She smoothed his hair.

'Don't be upset, Davey. They'll make it up.'

'I don't like it when Dad shouts,' he said, sniffing back tears.

'And why was he saying our grandad was a Jew? Eric don't like them.'

She took in a deep breath. 'Don't you listen to what Eric says. He's not being kind and our mum always taught us to be kind.'

'Was my mum kind? Tell me,' he pleaded with a hungry look in his dark, liquid eyes.

She began again the litany of all the things she remembered about their mother: yes, she was kind, patient, always made sure they had plenty to eat, clean clothes, and took them to the big slide in St James's churchyard. Half the time Ruby suspected the memories were only her own imaginings and desires for a mother who had faded with each passing year to a woman in a photograph.

After settling Davey back to sleep she drew the dividing curtain and lay down on her own bed. She didn't want to talk to Dodge. However much she hated Eric's involvement with the BUF, throwing him out would only send him running into their black-shirted arms and he'd never come home again. She thought, not for the first time, how different it all would have been if her mother had been here. Rachel Scully had loved all her children and she would have been their anchor and their haven, whatever storms surrounded them. She let out a deep sigh, wondering whether her mother would have agreed with Dodge about her marriage to Charles. But then she might never have met Charles if Rachel Scully had lived, for Charles had filled all the empty parts of her life. She rolled over and took the photo of her mother from the little bedside table. She looked into the wide, dark eyes, so unlike her own, and the eyes seemed to tell her that it was she, Ruby Scully, who was holding Charles and not the other way round. Whatever prayers he said or meditations he undertook on his retreat, Ruby knew that, for better or worse, he must inevitably come back to her.

12

Nor Money

Autumn–Winter 1936

Ruby stood at her front door. 'Davey, tea!' she called down the steps to her brother who was sitting on the kerb with two friends, playing alley gobs.

She walked back into the house and began dishing out boiled potatoes, cabbage and scrag-end stew. She was about to call Davey again, when something landed with a thump on the kitchen table. She spun round, ready to tell Davey off for making her jump, but it wasn't him.

'Eric! You frightened the life out of me!'

'I told you I'd be in the papers today,' he said, tapping the rolled up newspaper he'd thrown at her. 'Is the old man about?'

'Where did you stay last night? I've been worried sick.'

'In the Defence Corps barracks at Black House. I'll be staying there from now on,' he said, looking round as if he wished Dodge would come in.

'Oh, Eric. Dad didn't really mean you couldn't come home!'

'Yes, he bloody well did. I'll stay at Black House till I can find somewhere else.'

'But what will you do about getting to work? You can't afford the fares to and from Kensington every day!'

'We've got BUF vans going all over London. I'll get lifts. Anyway, if I carry on getting noticed like this, I'll be promoted to 1 Squad soon. Free bed and board, three quid a week and all I have to do is scare off commies and protect our leader! Better than being an errand boy at the docks.'

He sat down and unfolded the newspaper, then turned it towards her. The front page displayed the bold headline: 'The Battle of Cable Street'. Beneath was a photo showing Blackshirts and communists throwing punches, some tussling on the ground, others running from mounted police.

'Is that you?' she peered at the blurred image of a fair-headed boy wrestling a much bigger man to the ground.

'It is!' he said proudly. 'They tried to stop us marching through the East End. A hundred thousand Reds and Jews against three thousand of us! See what I mean about this country?'

'No, I don't see, Ricky. What good will this do? It's just one great big bundle – you're like a load of big kids. But it's not a game!' She remembered when he'd been a quiet, gentle boy. 'You used to hate a scrap, when you was a kid. The first time I ever saw you go for anyone was that time with the razor at Dad. I don't know what happened to you, Ricky, but you've changed.'

'I grew up! And I found out me dad's no good and no one's gonna make my life better except me!'

She reached for his hand. 'I know you've never been satisfied with this...' She looked hopelessly around the sparse kitchen. 'But there's worse off than us.'

Eric let out a heavy sigh. 'That's no comfort to me. I want everyone to be well off, not everyone poor – like the commies or you Bible-bashers want. I'm telling you, Ruby, we're the future.' He slapped his own chest.

'What sort of future? Like Hitler's promising Germany? No thanks.'

Prodding the paper, he got up. 'Just show that to the old man, will you? I'll go and get me things.'

By the time Eric came back with a tied bundle of clothes, Davey was at the table, eating his stew. He ran to Eric and hugged him. 'Ruby said you wouldn't really leave us!'

'She shouldn't have promised you that, Davey. But you're a big boy now and you've got to start acting like it. Understand?'

Davey straightened up and nodded. 'Yeah,' he said, looking up at Eric before giving him the fascist salute.

Eric grinned. 'Good boy.'

And Ruby suddenly felt glad that her brother was going.

She saw him to the door. 'I'll still give you the extra £1 a week I earn from the BUF,' he said, 'and if I get promoted to 1 squad I can give you more, cos the old man's not going to be any use to you or Davey, is he?'

'I don't want your money, Eric. You'll need it for rent when you find a place. I've got some extra shifts,' she lied. That extra pound suddenly seemed as tainted as the rewards of Dodge's criminal activities.

'Suit yourself,' Eric said, then grinned. 'Look out for me in the papers!'

She watched him walk away and then went inside to Davey, looking for words to explain what the fascist salute really meant. He was pouring over the front page of the newspaper.

'I can see our Ricky here! Look!' Then he gave her his wide grin. 'There's a lot more reds than Blackshirts.' And he jumped up and pumped the air with a closed fist in imitation of the communist salute.

Ruby decided to say nothing. For Davey it was all still a game.

She had agreed to meet Alfie in St James's churchyard. She was to hand over her list of families who were falling between the cracks of all the various charities and council departments and this seemed a neutral enough place, one to which even Charles couldn't object. The temperatures had dropped, but her winter coat was a disgrace, so she wore a sweater beneath her best jacket and pulled on a green woollen hat. Winding a scarf around her neck, she went to check on Davey, who was sound asleep. After asking Aunt Nancy to listen out for Davey while she was gone, she slipped out into the freezing night.

It was only a couple of minutes' walk to the churchyard but when she got there it was empty. There was a light in the bell tower, which stood out black against the charcoal sky. Alfie must be still working on the repairs. She sheltered from the sleet beneath the church portico and soon she heard the side door creak open.

'I'm here!' she called and he waved, reaching her in a couple of long strides.

'You look perished!'

'No, I'm fine.' She pulled down the scarf that swaddled her face, digging into her pocket for the list. 'Here's half a dozen families who need help right away.'

He peered at it. 'This looks really good, Ruby.'

She'd added suggestions for which mission or department could best be of help.

'I'd like to talk about some of my ideas, but you're shivering! Shall we go somewhere warmer? What about the café in Jamaica Road?' Seeing her hesitation, he added, 'No alcohol and not for long. Just so we can talk about some details without freezing you to death.'

Her feet were painful with cold and her fingers numb. 'All right, just for ten minutes. I've left Davey asleep at home.'

As they turned to go she thought she saw a dark shadow moving by the churchyard gate, but a mist had fallen now and visibility was so low she thought it must be a swaying tree branch. Alfie put a steadying hand beneath her elbow as they descended the slick church steps and they hurried toward the café, a small place that stayed open late, catering for evening shift workers. Once inside she was grateful for Alfie's suggestion. All was warmth and glowing light and tonight it was quiet, with a few empty tables by the window. Alfie sat her down before getting them each a hot blackcurrant. No doubt he would have preferred a pub, but she appreciated his nod to her temperance. With her hands clasped around the glass of hot blackcurrant, she felt the steam warm her cheeks.

'Business!' Alfie said, as he placed Ruby's list between them.

'What do you need to know?' Ruby said.

'I think I've already got an idea for this couple.' He pointed to the name of an elderly couple who were about to be evicted from their two rooms. 'There's an almshouse charity that might fit the bill. I just need to get some more details about them – and the others on your list. So, ages, incomes if any, previous occupations, infirmities or illnesses, faiths if any – these almshouses are more exclusive than a flat in Belgravia! But they're lovely little places. I only wish I could get my mum and dad into one of them, but you have to be Christian.' He took a sip of his blackcurrant. 'That's the thing with missions and charities – too picky.' Then hastened to add, 'Not all of them. The Methodists seemed to be more indiscriminate.' He blushed. 'I didn't mean it that way. I seem to be managing to insult you and your faith tonight.'

She laughed. 'It takes a lot to insult me, Alfie. Besides, I just found out I'm part Jewish myself!'

He looked at her. 'With those eyes and that hair! Who says so?'

'Dad. He was having a ding-dong with my brother Eric about wearing his Blackshirt uniform in the house and he let slip our grandad was Jewish. We never knew.'

'I bet Eric was overjoyed,' Alfie said, a hint of acid in his tone. 'Grandad's name?'

'Reubens.'

'Bit of a clue there!'

She felt silly. 'It just never came up; Grandad's been dead thirty years. Anyway, it's what you choose that matters, not what you're born with.'

A half-smile played on his lips. 'That I can agree with, Ruby. Dad's always been a bit liberal, but I think Mum would have liked me and Ocki to keep to our religion. I just couldn't do it.' He cupped the hot glass. 'But for some reason I'm glad your mum was a Reubens. It means we've got something else in common, apart from wanting to improve working people's lives.'

She found herself glad too. 'So, why did you choose to be a socialist?'

'Oh, I reckon Dad put my name down when I was a baby! He's redder than the flag flying over Bermondsey Town Hall! Had me carrying TGWU banners during the General Strike when I was only ten. I was their mascot, went to all the marches, all the meetings. But really, Ruby, it's not that much different to you and the Mission. You just have to feel your life means something, don't you?' His eyes, like dark pools, were suddenly veiled with doubt. 'I hope I'm not just wasting my time with it all...'

She found herself drawn to his odd mixture of certainty and questioning. She understood it. She put an involuntary hand over his, which was warm from holding the hot blackcurrant. 'You *are* making a difference. If you can get this old couple a decent almshouse for the few years they've got left, if you can achieve half of what Dr Salter has – well, that would make your life worthwhile, wouldn't it?'

'I always think I could be doing more.'

'Me too.'

'Really? What would you do, if you had the choice I mean?'

'I'd be a teacher!' she said, surprising even herself with a dream she hardly knew she had. But she remembered those evenings on the Time and Talents roof when her friend had taught her to do 'joined up writing'. At twelve Ruby had lost so much schooling she was still writing like a baby. She'd never forgotten how good that grown up calligraphy had felt, nor her gratitude to her teacher, Ida.

'A teacher? You'd be good at that.'

She pulled a face. 'I'm not sure my reading and writing are up to it.'

'Go to an evening class at the Bermondsey Settlement or Morley College.' He leaned forward and smiled. 'Get better.'

She realized her hand was still resting on his and at that moment, over Alfie's shoulder, she saw someone standing outside the steamed-up café window, his face pressed hard against the glass.

'Oh, dear God in heaven,' she said, whipping her hand away. 'It's Charles and he doesn't look happy. I'd better go.' She felt panic fluttering in her stomach and heard the tremor in her own voice.

'Ruby, you're not scared of him are you?'

'Scared? Why would I be scared?' But she was aware of her heart thumping and her hands clammy and cold now, in spite of all the heat in the café.

'I'll come with you.'

'No! It'll only make things worse.' She glanced at the window. Charles's face was gone, but she knew he would be waiting. She got up, quickly pulling on her hat and scarf .

'Will I see you next week, with another list?'

'I'll be in touch.'

Outside, the air was wet with fog and fine sleet. Trams and car headlights smudged the darkness with golden light.

'Charles!' She hurried up to him and tried to take his hand, but he pulled it away.

'What's going on, Ruby. Why are you doing this to me?' His voice cracked.

'Doing what?'

'Deliberately hurting me with that Diamond chap. You're cruel. When I've been on my knees for days convincing myself you're innocent of anything your father has done – but now I come back to this!'

'For God's sake, Charles,' she said, bewildered, 'I *am* innocent!

Of everything but loving you – and now you're making me think twice about that!'

'You shouldn't blaspheme,' he said in a monotone. He covered his face with trembling hands. 'I don't want you to see me like this. I've been in a turmoil. I thought if I could get guidance on your petty criminal father it would be all right, but I never thought you'd be going behind my back while I was praying about our future!'

'Charles, I've *always* been straight with you. But you've got no respect for me – you can't have, if you think there's anything going on with me and Alfie. Don't you think I care about our future?'

As they walked back past the café she saw, through the steamy window, Alfie still sitting there. 'Come in and ask him for yourself, if you don't believe me!'

Charles stopped dead, blinking his pale hazel eyes. It was the first time she'd seen him paralyzed by indecision. 'No, no, you're right, I'm being unreasonable.'

'Yes, you are,' she said firmly. 'Just let me go in and explain.' She wasn't sure how much Alfie had witnessed of her encounter with Charles, but now she felt ashamed and embarrassed by it. Charles nodded and she pushed open the door and went in.

'I will be seeing you next week, Alfie. Same place, same time,' she said quietly.

He raised his eyes and nodded. 'Bravo. Good luck,' he replied just as softly.

Charles was waiting for her outside and they walked back in silence to her house. At the doorstep he spoke first.

'I'm sorry, Ruby. But I only get upset because I love you.'

His apology left her feeling cold. 'But you don't respect me, Charles. You never even asked why I was meeting Alfie. I was trying to do some good for the poorest people I visit – no different to our missionary work. But you're so jealous you can't see anything else!'

He ducked his head. 'You're right about me being jealous, but I do respect you. You're my Ruby – *Who can find a virtuous woman? For her price is far above rubies*.'

But what she'd once taken as a compliment she now felt as a burden. 'You need to remember the verse that comes before that as well.'

He paused to think. 'Proverbs 31:9? *Plead the cause of the poor and needy*?'

She nodded. 'I'm just an ordinary person, trying to do some good, and so is Alfie. We *all* are.'

'You're not ordinary to me, and I know I was wrong tonight.'

'And you were wrong going off to that retreat without telling me! I was worried,' she said, softening a little.

'It was your father turning up like that; it was a shock. You'll think I'm stupid and weak, but I felt as if my own father had arranged it from the grave just to spite me.'

'Oh, Charles. I don't think you're stupid, but I wish you'd see it's what's between *us* that matters. Not our dads or Ida or Alfie. We're planning to dedicate our lives to something bigger than us and our little concerns.'

He smiled. His smile was rare, but when it came she was always struck by what a boy he still was under all his manly bluster.

'Do you love me?' he asked.

She put a hand to his strong-jawed face. 'Of course I do.'

'More than anything?'

She shook her head. 'Not more than God.' Which was the answer she knew would please him most.

She'd surprised herself with her forcefulness tonight and hoped it had been enough to put an end to Charles's jealousy and disapproval. But as she lay in her bed, looking out at the dark tower of St James's with its silent bells, her thoughts returned to Alfie and how in one short conversation he had uncovered a secret dream of a future that would depend not on Charles, but on herself alone.

*

It was one night in early December, after a late extra shift, that she came home to find a strange man in her kitchen. A flashy ill-fitting suit stretched over bulging arm and chest muscles and long Brylcreemed hair rested on his collar. He was sitting flicking through her mother's Bible.

'Hello, sweetheart! You the Bible-basher daughter I've heard so much about?' he asked with a grin.

She felt a chill of fear creep up her spine.

'Don't have to be scared of me. I used to go to Sunday School meself,' he declared proudly. 'Got chucked out for nickin' the collection and I ain't opened one of these since.' He tossed the Bible aside. 'Sit down, love, I'm waiting for Dodge.'

'Where's me dad?'

He pointed in the direction of the bedrooms. 'Go and see him. He'll want to say his goodbyes.' And the man smiled broadly, revealing a mouth full of brown-stained teeth.

Dodge was packing a small suitcase.

'Dad! Don't tell me you're going away again?'

Since Dodge's return it had often felt as if she had another child to look after, but his presence had also been a comfort. He'd been missing on a few nights, but there had been none of his old long absences and she'd allowed herself to believe he might be reforming.

He looked up, his face flushed, sweat plastering his blond hair to his head. He was stuffing clothes in at random.

'Give it here, you'll get it all creased.' She took a shirt from his hand.

'No gel, I ain't got time for that. Just shove it in.'

'What's happened? You don't like getting your clothes creased.' She was bewildered at his hasty disregard for his precious shirts and ties.

He stopped and bit his knuckle. 'I'm sorry, Ruby love. I've gone and got meself into a bit of trouble.'

She groaned. 'How's that possible? You've not been out of nick five minutes!'

'It's not since I've been out. I did a wrong thing in Dartmoor, got meself mixed up with a right nasty mob. They looked after me in nick in return for a favour when I got out, but something's gone wrong, love. Really bad.'

'How bad?'

Dodge lifted pale blue eyes, clouded with fear. 'Someone got shot.'

She slumped down on the bed.

'Did you kill him?' she whispered.

'What? No! What d'you take me for? The geezer's not dead, but it sounds bad and if he carks it... But I wasn't even there! All they asked me to do was get hold of a key to this place in Hatton Garden from a feller I know. Which I did. Nothing bad in that. But then some idiot shot the security guard.' He paused, dabbing his forehead with a handkerchief. 'Him outside, he's here to collect me. They want me where they can see me, in case I take it into me head to talk – which why would I? I ain't a moron. But if they say I've got to lay low, that's what I do, love.'

'Oh, Dad.' She put her arms around him. 'That poor man could die?'

'I know, love, and if I could do it different I would. But what's done's done. You just have to pray your old man don't end up dead and floating in the Thames. They wouldn't think twice if they thought I was a nark.'

Her world felt like a pack of cards, swept up by a giant hand and thrown to the winds.

'Don't look at me like I shot the poor sod meself. You don't know what it was like inside, they're animals, and someone like me – well, I needed protection.'

He hugged her. 'I've left you a bit of money to help you out. Look after Davey, and if you see that silly sod Eric, talk sense into him. And whatever you do, don't marry Charlie Best while

I'm gone, will you?' He grinned, trying to make light of her disappointment in him. 'Promise?'

'I promise, Dad.' She held on tightly to him, believing, as she always did, that he truly loved her and that, if only he could get past this one little hiccup, he would look after her.

He didn't know where he was actually going, but he promised to send her word from time to time, letting her know he was still all right, which she took to mean still alive.

The large man stood up and greeted Dodge like a long lost pal when they returned to the kitchen. But she knew wherever Dodge was going, it would be as much of a prison as Dartmoor ever was. After they'd left, she felt the heavy weight of responsibility shifting back onto her shoulders. He'd even made her responsible for Eric with that parting promise. It wasn't fair.

She sat feeling sorry for herself for all of five minutes and then went to the kitchen table. She pulled out the cutlery drawer, intending to make something for Davey's dinner, but it stuck. As she put her hand inside to dislodge whatever was impeding it, she pulled out a manilla envelope. Stuffed inside was more money than she'd seen in a lifetime.

A dank, sweaty smell rose from the roll of notes.

'I don't want your bloody money!' she yelled at the empty room, before tossing her dad's pay-off across the kitchen. Fivers and tenners littered the lino like dead leaves and Ruby sat down, leaned her head on the table and wept, reflecting on the two men in her life who had offered her money. Of Eric's pound a week from the BUF and Dodge's hundreds from the robbery, she couldn't decide whose gift she despised most, but she knew she would be using neither.

13

If Thine Eye Offend Thee

Winter 1936

Ruby felt sorry for the King. He looked hunted, haunted. A friend who worked at Hartley's told her that, as Prince of Wales, he'd once visited the jam factory, how kind he'd been to the girls, listening while they explained their jobs; and how he was the handsomest man she'd ever seen. But now he looked gaunt. To love the wrong person was a terrible thing, Ruby knew that. When all your friends and family insisted it was pure foolishness, that it would ruin your whole life, then it was hard to hold on to love. There must have been times the King had been tempted to give in and do what everyone else required of him. Ruby understood that too.

Tonight she and Charles were in the Mission reading room, waiting for others to arrive for the Basutoland prayer meeting. Charles sat with the newspaper spread out on the table and she came up behind him to read over his shoulder how King Edward had decided to give up everything for the woman he loved.

'I think that's the bravest, most noble thing I've ever heard,' she said, resting her hands on Charles's shoulders. She kissed the top of his bronze head but he ducked away.

'Not in here, Ruby!' Then seeing her hurt expression, he reached for her hand.

She couldn't help being upset. For her, damming the flow of her affection – whether for Davey, Dodge or Charles – was like trying to cap a bubbling spring. A hug or a kiss was as automatic and natural to her as breathing.

He shook his head. 'Sometimes your sentimentality blinds you to what's right.' And for a moment she thought he meant the kiss. 'The man's an absolute disgrace!' he went on. 'Calls himself a king? He should be setting an example.'

'But he's following his heart,' she argued. 'Just like we are.'

'No, not like us. We won't be abandoning our duty by marrying. We'll be partners in our work and if there's anything in our lives that ever seems to be hindering that, we'll give it up! Won't we? *If thine eye offend thee, pluck it out*. Well, let's not talk any more about our former king. I've got some good news to tell you.' He gave a secret smile, pulling from his pocket a letter which he gave her to read.

'You've been accepted at Bible College!'

In his excitement, he broke his own rule and stood up to kiss her full on the lips.

'It's the proudest day of my life, Ruby. They still have to interview me, but the selection committee said I was just the sort of candidate they like to take on. I mean, someone from my background – well, it's unusual to rise to the ministry.' He was trembling with emotion. 'And I'll be raising you up with me too, Ruby.'

She didn't care about being raised up. She looked again at the letter, the college was in Derbyshire. 'But you'll be going away next year?'

'Is that all you've got to say? Aren't you proud of me?'

'Of course, I'm proud of you, but I'll miss you.'

'And I'll miss you too, but Ruby, it's a sacrifice we'll both have to make.'

*

Next day at work, when Ruby told Ida that Charles would be leaving for Bible College next year, she couldn't hide her pleasure. 'Thank God for that!' her friend said.

'Well, Charles did thank God when he was accepted, and so did I!' Ruby said defiantly.

'If Charlie was my fiancée, I'd thank God he was going away too!' Ida shot back.

'Ha ha! Very funny. Charles says it's unusual for them to take people like us. It's an honour to be chosen.'

'What do you mean, *people like us*? We're as good as anyone else! Anyway, you'll be able to come and see me without sneaking around now.' Ida grinned and put a strong arm around her. 'I might even come to the odd Pleasant Sunday Afternoon once Lord Charles of Chumpton's gone orf to his country estate.'

'Ida! You wouldn't like me talking about Ocki like that.'

Her friend attempted an apology, but Ida's happiness was irrepressible today, especially as they were back working together. After the fire, Ida had been given the pick of the factory departments and Ruby, more famous now as a heroine than a Bible-basher, was allowed to go with her. Ida had chosen the Paste Kitchen, where they could work the bonus system and bolster their earnings. With Eric and Dodge gone and her determination not to take a penny of their money, Ruby sorely needed the new job.

Every girl on the 'paste flaps', as the lines were known, had one aim in mind: to keep her filling output up to twenty-five jars a minute; any less and the bonus would be lost. The Paste Kitchen produced every variety of paste imaginable, from turkey and pheasant to anchovy and crab. Today they were making bloater and chopped tongue and Ruby's stomach heaved at the cooking smells as grease from stock bubbling in twenty-five-gallon pans rose up and covered every surface. She could feel the slick, oily patina already coating her face and overall as she settled down to filling on a line with six other girls.

'Come on girls, get wired in!' Florrie the forelady encouraged them. 'You was all doing twenty-six jars a minute last week. Keep it up and you'll have a bloody good Christmas!'

Ruby viewed with queasy determination the continuous ooze of paste snaking out of the vertical filler. She and Davey deserved a good Christmas. Grabbing three empty jars in her left hand, she filled each with the sludgy brown contents, careful not to dribble paste down the side of the jars. Gagging at the reek of bloater she shot them down the line to Ida, who was sealing on the caps. Ida grinned at her and mouthed 'Only another twelve thousand to go before we knock off!'

The frenetic pace didn't let up and there was little time for chit chat, so it wasn't until one o' clock, when the hooter sounded for dinner, that she could voice her worries to Ida.

The Crosse's canteen was a good one, mostly stocked with their own produce, and it meant Ruby could get a good cheap meal and only have to worry about feeding Davey during the week. Unfortunately, her morning's work hadn't given her an appetite and she picked at the tinned meat pudding on her plate.

'I'm really worried about Dodge,' she confessed eventually.

'Why, what's he been up to now?' Ida asked. Ruby might have been sworn to secrecy by Dodge, but she'd burst if she had to contain her anxiety any longer. Besides, she could trust Ida with any secret, however dangerous.

'Why didn't you tell me before now? How long's he been gone?'

'About a fortnight and I've not heard a word from him. What if he never comes home? I can't very well go to the police about him, can I?'

'Not really, love. What about Uncle Jim, can't he find out anything?'

Ruby shook her head. 'I shouldn't think so; he's doing three months for assault!'

'I could ask around Dockhead for you – some of the boys work for Sugar Sweeting,' Ida said, naming a local villain.

'No! I don't want you getting involved with him or that Elephant mob, Ida. I just needed to tell someone.'

'And you certainly couldn't tell your beloved, could you?' Ida said.

The meat pudding stuck in her throat. She shook her head.

'Don't worry. Charles won't find out.'

She wished she could share Ida's confidence that Dodge's disappearance wouldn't get back to Charles, but the Mission, with its huge congregation, was a gossip mill; and besides, he had a way of wheedling the truth from her.

When he paid her an unexpected visit that night – as her fiancée, he now allowed himself to come into the house – she made him tea, and as she put the cup on the table before him, her hand shook. She hoped he hadn't noticed. His large, dark-suited figure blocked the light from the gas mantle, so that she couldn't make out his expression or judge his mood.

'I wasn't expecting you, Charles. It's late for you to be visiting.'

He leaned forward so that the glow from the lamp struck one half of his face. Good, she thought. He looked excited, not angry.

'We're going away for a wonderful trip next weekend, Ruby!'

'We are? Where – Margate?'

He laughed at her. 'Why would we be going there?'

She shrugged, embarrassed to believe Margate was a desirable location. She'd been there once with the Methodist young girls; waves silvered the sand and lapped her bare feet and it had seemed like heaven.

'No, we're going to Derbyshire. The College wants to interview you. You'll be half of a team when I'm on the mission field, and they need to be sure my future wife is up to the task!'

She wanted to be sick. 'I don't think I can go, Charles.' She hadn't minded telling Alfie that her reading and writing skills were not much better than Davey's, but she couldn't tell Charles. He would be so disappointed in her.

'Ain't there some way out of it?' she asked, panic-stricken.

'No, there certainly *isn't*,' he said, with emphasis.

She would just have to pray for a minor illness to strike her down before next weekend.

Charles spent every evening of the following week going over the questions Ruby might be asked and the responses she should give. He advised new clothes and when she told him she'd get something from the clothing club, he was horrified. Instead he took her to Chiesmans in Lewisham and chose a new coat and frock for her, which were really not to her taste, but he said it was best to be sober in dress and that she should wear a hat. He insisted on paying for the clothes, though she'd much rather have paid for them herself on the never-never. Every day in the run up to the weekend was an agony and when she spoke to Ida about it, her friend was no help at all.

'Don't go. It's not you getting the benefit of a college qualification, is it?' Ida had reasoned. 'Anyway, they've got an effin' cheek interviewing you! What if they say you're not up to it, what's he going to do then? Dump you?'

Much as she might have wanted to follow Ida's advice, by Friday evening her suitcase was packed and Davey was tucked up in bed with Aunt Nancy's youngest. Ruby sat in her new coat and hat, waiting for Charles's knock on the door. She tried to imagine the Peak District, perhaps there would be mountains, craggy and dusted with frost in the icy weather.

At first, she thought the noise she'd heard was a spattering of hail against the scullery window, but then it came again in a directed burst and louder. She went into the unlit scullery and looked out of the back door, peering down the wooden stairs leading to the garden where a jaundiced sunset illuminated the figure at the bottom. At that moment she also heard behind her the sound she'd been waiting for, a loud, double rap on the front door. Charles had arrived – but so, it seemed, had Dodge.

'Gawd's sake, gel, help us up the stairs!' Dodge pleaded. 'I'm pissed as a puddin' and I've had a bit of a fall. Me legs won't work, darlin'!' Dodge put up both arms to her, an expectant grin on his face and then collapsed in a heap.

Ruby stood like a statue, staring at the dishevelled bundle below. Charles was waiting at the front door. How on earth could she let him in with Dodge in the house? She wasn't conscious of making any decision, but with a slight click she carefully closed the scullery door and turned her back to it. Her father's expletives rolled up behind her. She snatched up her small suitcase and hurried to the front door, where Charles's knocking had become more insistent. Halfway along the darkened passage she stopped dead. What was she *doing?* It was Dodge. Her dad. What unnatural coldness had possessed her to leave him out in the icy yard? He could be running from the oily-haired mobster or even the police. Yes, he was drunk, and he seemed annoyingly cheerful, but he could really be injured.

'Hang on, Charles. I'll be out in a bit!' she called and rushed back to the scullery.

She stumbled down the frosty wooden stairs and misjudged the lower ones, so that she fell over Dodge's hunched figure, scraping both knees in the process.

'Come on, Dad. Get up. You're freezing!' she said, draping his arm over her shoulder. 'Why didn't you come in the front door?'

'Still layin' low, love. But I missed me lovely gel and me boys, so I come home. I thought you was leaving me out all night for a minute there, but me little darlin' wouldn't never do that to her old man, would you?' He gave her a boozy kiss on the cheek as they got to the top step. Then he yelped with pain.

'I've done me ankle in climbing over that bloody fence. Just leave me here, I'll be all right. Go asleep now…' And he curled up in a sozzled ball on the scullery floor.

The knocking had resumed, so, leaving Dodge in the scullery, she finally opened the door and ushered Charles in.

'What did you leave me standing outside for? You were meant to be ready! We'll miss our train if we don't get a move on.'

'Charles...'

She saw his eyes light upon something behind her. When she turned around, she saw that Dodge had crawled from the scullery into the kitchen.

'I told 'er afor I went on the run to get rid of you. Silly little mare,' he mumbled and then toppled unconscious onto the hearth.

'Don't just stand there, Charles, help me get him up,' Ruby ordered.

Between them they carried Dodge to his bed and Ruby inspected his leg.

'Go and get me some hot water and a cloth from the kitchen, his ankle's the size of a football.'

She found some scissors to cut Dodge's laces and had to force the shoe from his swollen foot. Dodge was awake and swearing when Charles returned. She saw him staring at Dodge's bare left foot.

'He's hurt his toe,' Charles said, bringing her the bowl of water.

'He got that in the trenches, a rat gnawed it off.'

'Looks like the rat could hold a rifle, then. A lot of cowards shot their toes off to get home.'

She gave him a long look. 'Perhaps he wasn't brave, but at least he was there; you weren't.'

He said nothing as he handed her the cloth. She made a cold compress and administered Anadin, and soon Dodge fell into a drunken sleep. Closing the bedroom door behind them, they returned to the kitchen for their bags.

'We've missed our train,' Charles said in a dull voice.

'What time's the next one?'

'An hour.'

'We can still catch it. I'll ask Aunt Nancy to look after him over the weekend—'

But Charles didn't respond. He'd sat down in front of the grate, staring at the hearth rug. Dodge had rucked it up and she went to straighten it.

'Leave it!' Charles's shout made her jump. 'What was your father talking about, when he said "before I went on the run?" Why was he on the run, Ruby?'

She sat down and only now did she notice the burning pain in her knees. Her stockings were ripped and caked with blood where she'd stumbled on the stairs. 'I'll need to change these,' she said, rising. But Charles pulled her back down.

'You're not going anywhere till you answer me, *honestly* for once!' His grip was like iron.

'All right! Dad was involved in a crime and someone got shot. He didn't hurt anyone, but he had to lie low.' She was surprised she didn't feel more worried that he was finally finding out the truth. It actually felt a relief. Now Charles knew exactly whose daughter she was and she had nothing left to hide.

His face was ashen. 'So your father's a drunken, violent criminal.' He threw back his head and gave a dry, bitter laugh. 'If I believed in luck, Ruby Scully, I think I'd be cursing mine now. Turns out my future wife's old man's as much of a wrong 'un as mine was!' And for the first time ever she heard Charlie Best's accent, the one that sounded like hers, the one he'd grown up with, not the restrained enunciations he'd practiced so diligently over the past years.

'I told you, my dad's not a violent man.'

He chuckled mirthlessly. 'One look at his toe told me that. But what does it matter if he shot the man himself? Ruby! This could ruin my – *our* – future. If the College board finds out the sort of woman I'm intending to marry, they'll have to question my judgement.' He got up and began pacing across the hearth rug, each step scrunching it up further into a ball. She wanted to yank him off it, but it was mesmerising, watching him walk, listening as he rehearsed every possible way she could ruin his planned ministry.

'There's one way to solve the problem, Ruby,' he said, eventually stopping in front of her. He dropped to his knees and looked into her eyes. His were wide with urgency. 'Ruby, you'll have to cut all ties with your father. Then there'll be no taint on you. *If thine eye offend thee, pluck it out.*'

Ruby rarely felt anger, but when she did it always took her by surprise. Now anger bubbled up like hot lava and burst in a shower.

'What do you mean? Give up seeing me own *dad*!'

'Promise me that and I'll overlook your father's shortcomings. It'll all be the same as before. Remember, we agreed we'd be willing to give up anything that stood in the way of my – our – ministry?'

'But you said "once they see the sort of woman I'm intending to marry". What sort of woman do you think I am, Charles? What sort of woman is Ruby Scully?'

'Ruby, my Ruby, virtuous among women…' He stuttered to a halt, caught in the web of his own illusion.

'See, you don't even believe it yourself. Well, I'll give you another solution. You can stop worrying about *our* future because there won't be one. You can have your precious future all to yourself, I won't be part of it!'

The heat felt good, the fire felt better, the sparks of pent-up emotion rained down on Charles and she didn't care.

'Don't talk like that, Ruby,' he said, looking stunned. 'I don't recognize you.'

She hardly recognized herself. She wondered if she might regret her outburst, but there was no stuffing the lava back in the volcano.

'Well, this *is* me,' she said. 'And there's one virtue I'm certain I've got, Charles. I love my family. For all their faults, I love them. I even love my dead mum and I kiss her photo every day. What I'd give to have her real, live flesh and blood arms round me again! But I've still got one parent alive and you think I'm going to give up my dad? For what? So, you can get into Bible

College? Rise in the ministry? No, Charles, I won't do it. You'll have to go to the college without me.'

'But what will I tell them?'

'Tell them you haven't got a fiancée, tell them she wasn't the virtuous woman you thought she was. Tell them anything you bloody like!' And she turned away from him because she didn't want him to see the tears beginning to pool in her eyes and think they were weakness when they were pure anger.

He surprised her by pulling her into his chest. 'I know it isn't your fault. We can't choose our fathers...but Ruby, I'm afraid that you'll lose your way if you stay under his influence. You're already sheltering a wanted criminal. You're an accessory. Can you really say "it is well with my soul?" after this?'

'Are you worried about my soul,' she spoke into his chest, 'or that I'll drag you down?'

'No, no! I'm offering you a way out! Do you really want to waste your life on him?' He nodded towards the bedroom. 'Does he care if you wear yourself out, smelling of fish paste day in, day out? Does he? *I* care what happens to you.'

But she shook her head and pushed him away. 'No, you care about some girl you've made up in your head. Go to Derbyshire on your own.'

'You'll regret this, Ruby,' he said, his expression hardening. Snatching up his bag he charged out of the kitchen. She heard the front door slam. And then she let herself cry. But she didn't think Charles was right in his prediction. She would never regret her decision to stick by her father.

Her resolve was sorely tested the following morning when, instead of being in the Peak District, Ruby found herself clearing up vomit from Dodge's bedside. It didn't help that he was groaning in exaggerated agony from his swollen foot.

'Don't moan! I thought you'd broken your leg the way you were carrying on last night but it's just a bad sprain and you've only got yourself to blame! Sit up on the edge of the bed; I'll have to strip it all off,' she ordered.

'Don't shout, darlin', there's a vice on me head and a football on the end of me leg, how would you like like it?' He was rocking back and forth as she shoved him out of the way so she could pull off the blanket.

'Ouch! Where's your Christian charity?'

'Just be quiet and let me do this.' She stalked out of the bedroom and stuffed the soiled bedding in the washtub – she'd had to heat the copper specially to fill it. Now she began scrubbing away with Sunlight soap.

Dodge hobbled into the scullery. 'You upset about Charlie? Did I frighten him off?'

She pushed her hair from her face with a wet forearm. 'It doesn't matter.' The soapsuds rose as she worked the sheet against the scrubbing board.

'You would never have been happy with that bloke, Ruby. You could never love a cold-hearted bastard like him, you're too loving a girl. You'll thank me one day.'

'He wanted me to cut you off. Said you're a bad influence,' she said curtly.

'Well, he ain't far wrong there, gel. I *am* a bad influence. But you're too strong-willed for that to make a blind bit of difference! See, Charlie Best never knew my Ruby at all.'

He was right in that. And she shouldn't punish Dodge for her own decision. Relenting, she gave Dodge a soapy embrace. If Charles still wanted her, he could take her as she was, with the accent she was born with and the father she never chose.

14

Dictators

Winter 1936

It was the week before Christmas and the Central Hall was even more packed than usual. Peering over the polished rail of the gallery, Ruby spotted the top of Charles's bronze head far below her. He was making his way to the front. Perhaps he'd be doing the reading? But when he reached the raised platform and turned around she was shocked at his appearance. All the lustre had faded from him. His bright hair had tarnished to rust, his tight mouth and deeply etched frown suggested some hidden pain and she wondered if he'd been ill while he'd been in Derbyshire. He mounted the platform to give the reading and his normally strong, baritone voice barely reached her in the gallery. He returned to his seat and slumped down, looking as if he might be asleep.

It surprised her how bound to him she felt. In spite of all their discord, during those few days without him she had felt as if her life was on hold. He hadn't come to see her after he'd arrived home, but she knew she couldn't be the one to seek him out.

So, after the service, she decided instead to find the person who was the quiet witness to all the dramas that went on in the lives of the congregation.

Sister Evelyn was already making her way to her tiny flat when Ruby stopped her outside the Central Hall.

'Hello, Ruby.' Seeing Ruby's expression she asked, 'Is anything the matter? Is your father all right?'

Ruby nodded. 'He's still at home, says he wants to stay for Christmas. It's not Dodge I'm worried about, it's Charles. He looks so miserable. Do you know what happened at the interview?'

'No, I don't. But I expect he'll soon tell you himself.'

'No.' Ruby shook her head. 'We had a falling out over Dodge and I don't think he wants to see me – or my dad.'

Sister Evelyn raised her eyebrows and looked beyond Ruby towards the church entrance. 'I think he might have changed his mind.' She smiled and whispered, 'Perhaps he's realized how much he needs you. I'll leave you two to have a chat.'

Feeling a hand on her shoulder, Ruby spun round. Charles's face was even more strained close up. He took in a deep breath. 'Ruby, I want to apologize for the way I treated you... It was harsh, unloving...' Swallowing hard, he raised his palm to stop her from interrupting. 'No, let me go on. What I said about your father, it was... unchristian. I need to know – can you forgive me?'

He seemed genuinely contrite. She imagined Ida's voice, urging her to box clever and let him wait, but it wasn't in her nature to torture any creature, let alone someone she loved.

'I *do* forgive you, Charles. But I haven't changed my mind about me dad – you do know he's still at home?'

He lowered his head and stared at his Bible, flicking the gold edged pages as he considered what to say. 'I do know. But I was unreasonable.'

Ruby felt a surge of relief. She'd known, deep inside, that for all his stiffness and insistence on propriety, his love ran deep – deep enough to change his mind when he knew he was wrong.

'He's your father, after all…'

'You don't have to condone him, Charles. Just let me keep my dad.'

'Yes. Yes. Of course you can keep your father.'

She gave a brief nod. 'Well, in that case, I suppose *you* can keep *me*.'

He lifted her hand to his lips, then slipped it through his arm. 'Oh, Ruby, you've made me so happy. Can I walk you home? I've missed you.'

As they walked he brightened, telling her about his interview with the Dean and how impressed the panel seemed to have been with his determination and commitment. 'Do you know the Dean once worked in Bermondsey and he said to me, "You're a fine young man. And to see how you have raised yourself up from such beginnings in Barnham Street Buildings is nothing short of a miracle." That's what he said Ruby, a miracle!'

'So why were you looking so glum today? Was it just because we had a row over Dad? I'm sorry if my not going spoiled things for you.'

'It didn't spoil things, not exactly. But it did cause a little problem.' He gave her a hesitant smile. 'Nothing that we can't work out now we're of the same mind.'

'What problem? They haven't refused you?'

'Not refused.' He shrugged up the shoulders of his jacket. 'But after our – our disagreement, I couldn't tell them in all honesty that I'd be a married man when I left for the mission field. And, of course, they *prefer* to send married men.'

Perhaps the world had stopped moving around her, for she was only conscious now of the doubts rushing through her mind. 'Is that the only reason you asked for my forgiveness, so you could tell them you'll be married by the time you go?' she asked, a cold band around her heart.

'What? No, of course not!' He slipped his arm around her,

ignoring his rule about public displays of affection. Two young boys passed them, sniggering, and one asked the other in a high-pitched voice, 'Oooh, do you love me, my darlin'?' She waited for Charles to reprimand them. But he turned towards her, his eyes brimming with tears. 'It's just that I can't live without you. Not without my Ruby.'

Believing him, she kissed him on the mouth, not caring if he objected, only knowing that whatever difficulties they faced, their future lay together.

'So, it's all back on with Charlie, then?' Ida said, unimpressed, as they hurried out of Crosse's gates. 'That's put paid to my plans. I was going to ask you to our Christmas do at the Labour Institute. Don't suppose you'll chance it now, will you?'

Ruby thought for a moment. 'Why not?'

Ida's eyes widened and she gave an exaggerated step backward. 'Knock me down with a feather duster. Are you sure?'

'Charles has been more understanding since he came back from the College interview.'

'That's only cos you stood up to him, love.'

'Or perhaps he's changing.'

Ida looked unconvinced. 'So, you'll come?'

'Yes, I will!' she said decisively, and was rewarded with one of Ida's broad smiles.

'What are you doing for Christmas Day – are you at the Mission?'

Since joining the Mission, Ruby had always taken her brothers to the free Christmas dinner. Dodge usually protested, but only half-heartedly. It gave him the opportunity to spend Christmas morning in the World Turned Upside Down. He would invariably come home drunk at around the same time as his children were returning from the Central Hall. Later he'd wake from his afternoon stupor and hand out presents – usually whatever knocked-off toys he'd been able to acquire at the pub that morning. After the present-giving he'd fill a bucket of water, drop in a couple of apples and leave them to a game of apple bobbing while he returned to the Upside Down for the night, secure in the knowledge he'd done his Christmas duty by his kids. Ruby thought it strange that, with wet-eyed nostalgia, he regularly reminisced about their Christmasses and she supposed he genuinely believed that they always spent a happy day together.

'Oh, I don't know what I'm doing, Ida, and I don't think I care. I'm not looking forward to it at all.'

'Why not? You've got Dodge home – or is he going back to his minders?'

'Who knows? I can't get a straight answer. I just want us all to have a nice family Christmas for once. But I haven't seen our Ricky for ages and if he knew Dodge was home, he wouldn't come.'

Ruby was feeling guilty about Eric. He'd visited a couple of times, trying to give her money and had eventually given up, insulted. But she'd hoped he would relent and visit before Christmas, so she could invite him to Christmas Day dinner. Perhaps that way she'd get him and Dodge back on speaking terms.

'It don't take much to upset your Eric. He'll be round when he needs something.'

'Seems like he don't need anything, Ida, except his precious jackboots and his blackshirt.'

'He might not be wearing them for long. The government's talking about banning the uniforms.'

'I hope they do. If the BUF made him wear a docker's cap and workman's boots he'd change his tune; he's as vain as Dodge!'

They laughed as they walked arm in arm to the Earl of Derby in Grange Road.

'If you're worried about Eric, perhaps you should just go down the dock office and catch him after work.'

'I might have to. But what shall I do about Charles? He won't go to his mum's. But how can I invite him to ours when Dodge is there?'

'I'd leave well enough alone, see it as a lucky escape, love.' Ida laughed.

She gave Ida a thump on the arm. 'It's not funny. Honestly, Ida, I feel like a Christmas cracker, pulled between all these squabbling men!'

'You sound like you need a stiff bitter lemon, love. Coming in?' Ida pulled open the corner door of the pub. 'Ocki's already here.'

Ruby shook her head. 'I've got the Women's Fellowship tonight.'

'Alfie's coming for a drink too,' Ida said with a mischievous glint in her eye.

'Oh, is he?' Ruby pretended not to know what her friend was doing and gave her a kiss on the cheek. 'Say hello to the boys and see you tomorrow.'

As she set off along Grange Road, Ida called back to Ruby, 'Tatta, love! And I don't want no more talk about not looking forward to Christmas. We might all be dead next year!'

Ruby dipped her head into a biting wind. Sometimes Ida came up with just the right thing to do. She had a native common sense that Ruby did not. She often thought her own practicality had been forced upon her by her mother's early death. Like an ill-fitting garment, her life had never felt her own. Looking after a baby and a family at such a young age was not the future she would have chosen. What if Eric was the same and their mother's death had set him on a course that hadn't felt like his life either? He'd been forced into being the 'man of the house' while Dodge abdicated his responsibilities in drink and gambling. Perhaps the fascists made Eric feel as if he'd found his own life again. Ruby determined to go to Surrey Docks one evening. She'd wait outside the dock gates and force him to speak to her. She would say she was sorry...

*

On her first spare evening she went in search of Eric. She'd run out of money. The Christmas club was already spent, any spare had gone on treats for Davey, and Dodge hadn't given her a penny this week, so instead of getting the bus to Surrey Docks, she walked, or rather trotted, so that she'd be there for the shift end. She knew she'd cut it fine when she heard the ringing of hobnailed boots reverberating along Lower Road and had to fight hard against the tide of jostling dockers pouring into the surrounding streets, but once at the dock gates she planted herself in a position where she could spot Eric amongst the exodus. A fine rain came on, stinging and soaking. She had no umbrella, and her hair was soon plastered to her head. Standing on tiptoe, she attempted to peer over a sea of wet flat caps and noticed a young man break away and begin walking toward her. At first she didn't realize who he was.

'Hello, Ruby!' He gave her a friendly smile.

'Malchy Mongey! What are you doing here?'

'I've got a new job as a messenger. When Ricky found out he was leaving he put in a good word at the dock office and they gave me his job. He's a good mate.'

'Eric's left his job? When?' She felt jolted, almost betrayed. It was the sort of thing her brother would once have sought her advice about.

Malchy flushed. 'I know he's fallen out with you but I don't care if I've put me foot in it, you deserve to know where he is. You was always good to him...and to us.' He looked her full in the eyes as they silently acknowledged little Jenny. 'Ricky's gone full-time in the BUF – he lives at Black House now.'

'Oh, no!'

'What's so wrong with that, Ruby? It's an honour. He's elite – 1 Squad. £3 a week, all found, and he's doing his bit to make this country a better place for ordinary working people like you and me!'

Malchy sounded like one of the BUF recruitment posters. 'Malchy, I read in the *South London Press* that your leader's a millionaire. Do you really think he'd come and live in a Bermondsey slum – like Dr Salter or Sister Evelyn have?'

Malchy wiped rain from his face. 'Maybe not. But Ruby, the system the BUF's planning – it'll be better for us. *We'll* be running the show!'

'Well, I know you believe that, Malchy,' she said, cutting short the argument. 'Will you give Ricky a message for me? Tell him he's welcome to come home for Christmas dinner?'

'Sorry, Ruby. I don't see so much of him. It's hard for him to get time off. He has to apply for a pass if he wants to leave the barracks in the evenings. It's a bit like the army. But Ruby, don't worry about Ricky. He's happy there and he says the grub is great.'

But she couldn't help worrying about Eric. Would her mother simply give up, leave Eric to the life he'd chosen however dangerous and wrong-headed it might seem? He was only sixteen, still a child. She was certain her mother would want her to keep the family together. So, that Saturday afternoon she decided that if Eric wouldn't come to her, she must go to him.

She asked Ida how to get to Chelsea and then memorized the instructions. But first she had to find the fare. She searched Dodge's suit pockets and discovered a surprising amount in silver and coppers which would pay for the tube with a bit over to put in the food tin. She left Davey playing with Aunt Nancy's kids and walked over Tower Bridge. Ida had been a bit vague about the location of Mark Lane station, but she asked a policeman who sent her down some steps and around the sooty walls of the Tower of London. Beefeaters in crimson and gold, with pikes to the ready, guarded the Tower and she allowed herself to enjoy the sight, wondering if they felt ridiculous in their outmoded breeches and pleated hats. If they were anything like Eric, she reflected, they probably loved their uniform.

Emerging at Sloane Square, she felt suddenly out of place. This wasn't her London. It was as foreign as another country. She hurried along the King's Road, not sure what number she was looking for. She passed some Chelsea Pensioners in long scarlet coats and black caps and it seemed her journey had been punctuated by uniforms. Then she spotted the example that was uppermost in her mind. A young man wearing the lightning strike armband over a black collarless shirt walked briskly past her. Following close on his heels, she found herself outside a building that resembled a school. It was only when she saw the sign outside, proclaiming *Fascism is Practical Patriotism* that she realized this must be Black House.

The young man skirted around the side and she followed him into a yard. Ranks of cars and vans, with reinforced armour plating and mesh-covered windows stood at the ready. Dozens of young black-shirted and booted young men were standing with chests puffed out and arms ramrod straight being inspected by an officer. She spotted Eric immediately. His bright blond hair, full on top, shaved at the sides, shone in the pale late afternoon light. His jackboots were immaculate and even his uniform seemed of a better cut than his fellows. She remembered that he'd said 1 Squad was an elite.

He stood to one side of the troops on parade, next to a short, wiry man, who'd obviously modelled his hair and moustache on Herr Hitler. They were bent over a map, spread out on the bonnet of one of the vans. She was about to approach them when something made Eric look up. The only change in his expression was a brief widening of his sky-blue eyes. But then Eric turned his attention back to the officer, who folded the map and gave it to him. The officer laid a hand on Eric's arm, speaking earnestly. He looked almost stunted beside Eric and although his face had a sharp-chinned, unsmiling quality, his gaze as he looked up into her brother's face was almost adoring. She had seen that expression on Charles's face as they stood beneath the gas lamp outside her house...

Ruby stood at the edge of the yard, feeling invisible and irrelevant in Eric's new world. But whatever he was becoming, he was still the boy who'd crept up to be held when his grief at their mother's death had been too raw to bear. She would do what she'd come to do.

Eventually she saw Eric give the fascist salute as the officer let go of his arm, walked away and began ordering the ranks of Blackshirts to muster beside the vehicles. Still ignoring her, Eric stood beside a van, which had three huge trumpet speakers, looking like blossoming black lilies, mounted front and back. There was a rail around the roof and a ladder was hooked on to the side of the van. Obviously, this was a mobile stage of sorts. She ran across the yard, only to be intercepted by the small Hitler lookalike.

'I'm sorry, miss, if you want to sign up, you'll have to go around to the front reception.'

She was about to tell him she wouldn't be seen dead in a black shirt and beret, when Eric hurried over.

'I'm sorry, sir. She's my sister,' he explained, his lips drawn tight in anger.

The officer gave a curt nod. 'Very good, Scully. But our leader is due in five minutes, you be ready to go. Remember, Party over family!' He fixed Eric with his intense, currant-like eyes then strode off.

'What are you doing here, Ruby?' Eric hissed.

'Is that all you've got to say to me? When I've come all this way to see you?'

'*All this way*?' He laughed. 'Perhaps it's a long way in your little world, Ruby. Not in mine. What do you want?'

'At least they look like they're feeding you well,' she said.

'We get everything we need.'

His face seemed harder. Perhaps it was the severe haircut or the fresh bruise on his cheek. She put an involuntary hand to his face. 'Pity you're not looking after yourself a bit better.'

He pulled away. 'They've chose me to go in the van to protect

Mosley. It's an honour! So tell me what you want and be quick about it.'

If he'd been at home she would have clipped him round the ear. But she restrained herself. 'I've only come to invite you for Christmas Day. Dodge wants to see you.' The lie burned on her lips. 'Just come for dinner. I won't go on at you. I promise. And then there's Davey—'

'What about him – he's not ill nor nothing, is he?' Eric's forehead creased with concern.

'No, nothing like that. He misses you. Keeps asking when you're coming home.'

She saw him hesitate. He glanced toward the building's side entrance and Ruby saw an imposing, black-uniformed figure wearing a cap and highly polished jackboots. Flanked by others in similar uniforms, he stood out among them, exuding a sort of fizzing energy that felt attractive and repellent at the same time.

'Our leader's here!' Eric turned as one with everyone else in the yard and flung up his arm in the fascist salute.

She was invisible again. But when Eric lowered his arm and went to walk away, she put a hand on his chest. 'Mum always loved this time of year; remember our Christmases before she died, Ricky?'

'All right, all right, I'll try to come,' he muttered As he strained loose of her hold she felt an object beneath his black shirt. She hoped she was mistaken, but the shape resembled a holster and she was fairly certain there was a gun in it. He saw her look of shock.

'I told you, it's my job to protect him! You just make sure you don't you say nothing to no one.' He gripped her arm so that it hurt and then turned abruptly away and hurried back to the speaker van. Mosley and his entourage leapt inside it and she saw Eric follow. He was in the presence of his hero, and would obviously do anything for him. No wonder he had no time for her. She remembered how often he'd accused her of thinking more of the Mission than she did of her family. He had been right once, but not now. Eric was her family and she wouldn't rest until she'd got him far, far away from his beloved hero.

Ruby was surprised that Ida had invited her to the Labour League of Youth Christmas party but she was glad of an excuse to go out for a night to a place which had nothing to do with Charles or Eric or Dodge. She'd done her best to reconcile the men in her life and all she could do was wait until Christmas Day to see if she'd been successful. For now, she was doing a rare thing: going out to enjoy herself.

The Labour Institute in Fort Road usually had a worthy, serious look about it to Ruby's eyes, but tonight it wore a festive gloss that lifted her spirits. She felt slightly ill at ease in her frock of dark green satin. She'd added a contrasting wide sash to give the illusion of a waist and hips, but she knew her straight, slim figure would never be curvaceous. Still, her legs were shapely and she had bought, from the Tower Bridge old clo', a pair of second-hand black court shoes which were classic enough never to be out of fashion. She wished now she'd come with Ida, but her friend was helping to prepare things behind the scenes. After depositing her coat, Ruby went back upstairs and she was relieved to see a familiar face.

'Ruby, you're here!' Alfie Diamond seemed surprised and pleased.

'Didn't Ida tell you I was coming?'

He nodded. 'But I didn't believe her – you wouldn't even step inside the place for a meeting before now!' He made a cross with two slender fingers as if warding off the evil eye and then burst out laughing.

'Ha, very funny. But I ain't scared of demons *nor* socialists!'

He gave her a curious look, but she was grateful he didn't ask her what had changed her mind about entering the Institute. If he had, she wouldn't have known what to tell him. She only felt that somehow the balance had changed with Charles and that now there were things she could choose to do without consulting him.

He took in her dress and the home waves she'd manage to put in her straight hair.

'Lovely!' he said, and flashed a sudden smile. 'Come with me.' Taking hold of her elbow, he steered her into the large hall which had been transformed from the workaday place she remembered from her one and only visit, into a winter wonderland. She gasped with delight, which seemed to please him.

'Like it?'

'I love it!'

A glitter ball hung from the ceiling and spun like a great star above them, dappling the darkened room with magical light. On the stage a band was playing a jazz song and a few couples were already dancing. Long tables ranged against the walls were laden with a buffet of sausage rolls, sandwiches and cakes; on another table, champagne flutes, light glancing off them, were being filled with bubbling, golden liquid. Ruby had never been anywhere so elegant.

He grinned. 'We may be a political movement but there's a line from a speech I love: "The worker must have bread, but she must have roses, too." This is our attempt at the roses!'

'It's magical,' she whispered.

He'd made some effort to tame his usually wayward curls, but he was wearing a slightly ill-fitting jacket and dark trousers which didn't quite match. His broad shoulders, coupled with such long arms and legs, needed a tailor-made suit to make them look elegant, but on Crosse's wages he'd have had to save for a year to achieve that. Still, his rangy figure wasn't ungraceful and she appreciated how smoothly he drew out a chair for her and made sure she was comfortable before going off to get them drinks.

While he was gone, she looked around. The crowd was predominantly young but there were some who looked to be approaching thirty – she wondered how long they would qualify for the League of Youth. There wasn't the same uniformity of dress or look that she'd seen at the Pleasant Sunday Afternoons or the Crosse's dance she'd been to. Some women wore heavy make-up, others looked like nuns. A few of the men had dressed with deliberate casualness, wearing v-neck jumpers and baggy trousers. Others were as svelte and chic as the clientele of a Mayfair night club. She smiled to herself, feeling oddly excited.

Alfie came back with drinks: champagne for him and bitter lemon for her.

'Oh, you got me a champagne glass too!' she said, childishly delighted.

'Why should you miss out, just because you're teetotal!'

They clinked glasses as the band began playing 'The Way You Look Tonight' and she put her head to one side, listening.

'Did you see the film?' he asked.

She shook her head. 'I heard it on the wireless,' she explained, remembering the guilty pleasure of Dodge's knocked-off set. 'Charles doesn't approve of the cinema.'

'Doesn't approve of us lot either, but you're here just the same.' He lifted the champagne flute to his lips, looking at her over its rim.

'Things have changed.'

'Tell me.' He leaned forward and she suddenly found herself relaxed and unguarded, as if she could tell him anything.

'He asked me to give up my dad – for appearance's sake. I said no.'

He clapped his slender, long-fingered hands together in silent applause. 'Well done, Ruby. No wonder you don't mind joining the revolutionaries tonight. Word of warning, though, dictators are everywhere, not just Hitler or Mussolini, and they're all the same; once they're in power, they don't let go easily. They'll rob you of your people, rob you of your power – and if you're not careful they'll rob you of yourself. One day you might turn around and find there's nothing left of Ruby Scully...'

'What do you mean? Charles is my fiancé, not a dictator!' She flushed with a moment's anger that he had mistaken her rebellion for disloyalty to Charles.

'Sorry.' He paused. Then, 'Want to dance?' It was almost a challenge. As if he wanted her to prove just how free she really was.

'Yes!' And she jumped to her feet.

Laughing, he led her to the dance floor. The song was being played as a slow foxtrot and again she was surprised at how smooth his movements were. He made her feel like a good dancer as they glided around the small dance floor. His trade as a cooper had given him strong hands, but he held hers lightly and she was only aware of his palm on her back when they needed to turn or sidestep out of the way of another couple. She felt there was air beneath her feet instead of the polished parquet of the Labour Institute hall.

'Where did you learn to dance like this?' He leaned in so she could hear him above the band, a look of delight on his face.

'I didn't know I *could* dance – until now!' She smiled up at him, trying to remember what it was like to dance with Charles before realizing that she never had. Suddenly a wave of guilt hit her. This was wrong. It wasn't so much that she was dancing – Charles had never said she couldn't, he simply disapproved of dance halls – no, it was that she was in the arms of another man and, what's more, she was enjoying it. She realized it wasn't the first time she'd been in Alfie's arms. She remembered the last night of the Crusade, almost a year ago. How she'd been sent flying across the floor of the John Bull Arms and Alfie had caught her. Back then she had gazed up into irreverent dark eyes and been mortified, but his expression now was anything but mocking and his dark eyes seemed lit from within, fixing her with their bright intensity. It wasn't until the band struck up a furious-paced quickstep that the spell was broken.

She was glad that when they returned to the table Ida had

arrived with Ocki and she could hide in her friend's enveloping, bony embrace.

'Look at you!' Ida said, and turning to Alfie, 'Don't she look lovely?'

'I've already told her that,' he replied and Ruby avoided looking into his eyes.

'Well, *you* look beautiful,' Ruby said to her friend, who wore a scarlet silk frock and lipstick to match, her curls contained by a sparkling bandana.

Ocki gazed at Ida with undisguised admiration and said to his brother, 'I'd say we've landed ourselves with the best-looking girls in the place!'

And Ruby blushed, beginning to think it had been a mistake to come. If she and Alfie could be mistaken by someone for a couple, Charles would see it as a betrayal.

'Ida, come to the cloakroom with me?' she asked, feeling rising panic.

Ida followed her downstairs where she stopped outside the lavatories. 'I think I've got to go home, Ida. I shouldn't have come, it's not where I belong.'

'Rubbish, you're with your friends. It's no different to a Pleasant Sunday Afternoon…' Ida looked genuinely perplexed and then suddenly she raised her eyes. 'It's Charlie, ain't it? You're scared he'll find out you've come and have a go at you.'

'I'm not *scared*! Everyone seems to think he's a monster.'

'Everyone?' Ida gave her a sharp look. 'Did Alfie say anything?'

'What do you mean?'

'When I told him you were coming tonight he said you'd bottle out 'cos you're scared of Charlie—'

'Well, Alfie doesn't know me at all then!' But she'd got used to believing she was honest, and she could hear the empty sound of a lie on her own lips. The truth was she *had* been enjoying herself, and now she was running away. What was this if not fear? 'It's Charles I'll be marrying and him I should be considering. I just don't want to upset him over a dance.'

She walked towards the coat rails, but felt Ida's large hand restraining her. 'I should think it's your own conscience you should be worrying about. You're out for an innocent night dancing – which you deserve. If there's something you're ashamed of then it's down to you, love, not to having strong drink on the premises or getting up close to a handsome feller. What you got to feel guilty about?'

Ruby took in a deep breath and exhaled. 'Nothing.'

'Well, stop being such a silly mare and just have a good time. You can dance with me if it'll make you feel better. I ain't got no chance of a spin round the room from my Ocki, have I? But I'm leading!'

Ida put her arm around Ruby and ran her up the stairs, so that at the top they were stumbling and breathless with laughter. As they crossed the room, Alfie was returning to the table with a plate of food.

'Thought we could share.' He lifted his eyes to Ruby. 'Can I claim the next dance?'

'No, you can't, she's all mine,' Ida said, grabbing her hand. 'And don't you two eat all the sandwiches!'

As Ida dragged her onto the dance floor for the next quickstep, Ruby called back to Alfie, 'You can have the next dance if you don't mind waiting!'

And for some reason she felt a surge of that earlier excitement as he called back, 'Don't worry. I can wait.'

15

Peace, Goodwill Toward Men

Christmas 1936

Ruby could hardly credit it, but she'd managed to persuade Charles to spend Christmas Day with her and Dodge and Davey. She didn't believe she was a persuasive person, so she had to put it down to a genuine change in Charles since his Bible College interview. She'd heard nothing from Eric, but had set a place for him and prayed he would come. After the miracle of Charles's acceptance, she had faith that this day really would bring goodwill toward *all* men.

When she came back into the kitchen, Dodge was combing his hair in front of the mirror above the fireplace.

'Dad, do you really *have* to go to the Upside Down this morning? Couldn't you just leave it till tonight?'

'Ain't it enough I'm sitting down to dinner with that stuck-up git you want to marry? I don't see why I should give up my Christmas drink for him as well,' he said, a flash of irritation in his eyes.

'But you say the mob wants you back where they can keep an eye on you after the holiday, so who knows when we'll see you again? Do it for Davey, if not for me. He deserves a nice Christmas with you.'

Dodge glanced at the table where Davey was playing quietly with a small red fire engine Ruby had bought for him at Woolworth's.

'It's for his sake I'm going there,' Dodge went on, his voice hushed. 'They're getting in some bloody good toys in the pub today. Someone's had a Gamages' lorry away. I'll bring him back something nice, eh?'

'Well, at least you'll make one of your sons happy this Christmas.' She sighed. 'What do you think Mum would have thought of our Eric not being welcome today?'

'Well, I know what she'd have thought of him dressed up in that fascist fancy dress! Besides, your mum's not here. It's me has to deal with the lot of you on me own! The only one's not disappointed me is that lovely boy.' He nodded towards Davey.

She ignored the allusion to her own choices.

'I think Ricky's just in it for the uniform and Ida says they'll ban that soon. He's not a bad boy – it's just like the Boy's Brigade to him. If you'd only asked him over today, I reckon he'd have come.'

Dodge sighed. 'Maybe I was a bit hasty. But it's too late now.'

'If – if he turned up, you wouldn't send him away, would you?'

'Gawd sake, you're as bad as your poor mother for going on at me! No, I wouldn't turn me own son away, not if it come to it. Now I'm going to the pub.'

Ruby put a hand on his arm. 'Just promise me you won't get drunk.'

'I'll be on me best behaviour, promise.'

He ruffled Davey's hair and gave her a kiss and left, whistling. She wondered at how nothing ever seemed to get him down. Not even the prospect of being taken into custody again by his mob minders. They had come knocking for him one night last week and, whatever promise he'd made them, they'd agreed to let him stay with his family until the New Year, so long as he didn't do anything to attract the attention of the police. Ruby thought they were taking a lot on faith.

After he'd gone, she went to the scullery and looked around with satisfaction. The turkey and roast potatoes were in the oven, the brussels peeled and ready to boil, the Christmas pudding steaming away. She felt that she was finally about to recreate the long remembered Christmases that her mother used to preside over. Ones which Dodge would never have missed.

Back in the kitchen she laid out the remnants of Mum's good china and then stood beside Davey, smoothing down hair that Dodge had ruffled.

'Do you like your fire engine?'

He nodded. 'Will Eric be coming?'

'Perhaps. It's hard for him to get a pass out.'

'But *if* he does, do you think he'll bring me something?'

'Maybe.'

'Dad didn't get me nothing,' Davey said.

'Maybe he'll get you a surprise.'

His face lit up. 'A surprise?' Then he seemed to sober. 'If he's got the money – but this is me best present, Ruby.' He made the clanging sound of an imaginary bell.

She bent down to give him a hug, wishing that she could have given him more. Not just more toys, but more security, more love. She'd done her best, but hers had only ever been a substitute for a mother's love. Today she'd felt her mother's absence keenly and she pulled Davey into an embrace that he'd soon had enough of.

It was Charles who arrived first, with typical punctuality, yet she had suspected that if anyone let her down today, it would be him.

He kissed her in the passage. 'Don't look so surprised. I promised I'd be here.'

She smiled and put a hand on his chest, 'It means a lot to me.'

Dressed in the suit he'd bought for his dad's funeral, he stood like a black shadow in the corner of the warm kitchen she and Davey had decorated with paper chains. Charles handed her a bottle of ginger cordial and a box of dried figs, which Davey eyed hungrily. She took the gifts and then his trilby.

'Go and sit with Davey, while I put the Brussels on.'

'Where's your father?'

'Oh, just popped out to see a few friends.'

He raised an eyebrow. 'He's at the pub, then?'

'He'll be here for dinner. And when he comes back, remember—'

'I'm not going to do any preaching today, I promise!' he said laughing and began admiring Davey's fire engine. She thought that the new Charles was so much easier to love than the old one.

There was certainly no room at their small kitchen table for a turkey or tureens, so she set about dishing the dinner onto plates in the scullery, contentedly singing:

All glory be to God on high, And on the earth be peace,
Goodwill henceforth from heaven to men
Begin and never cease.

A knock interrupted the angels' chorus and she dropped the serving spoon.

'Shall I answer the door for you?' Charles called.

But Ruby was already dashing through the kitchen. 'No need!'

Dodge had only been gone a couple of hours, so it must be Eric! She flung open the door, ready to greet her brother with a hug.

'Oh, it's you? Why didn't you use your key?'

'Sod me, what a face to greet your old man with, I thought you'd be pleased.' Dodge had a couple of parcels underneath each arm and both hands deep in his trouser pockets. 'Can't find it. I thought to meself, I'll get home early, show willing… Hang on, here it is.' He held up the key and dropped the parcels.

'Of course I'm pleased! Dinner's nearly ready.'

She helped him retrieve the parcels and then caught him as he stumbled over the door step.

He waved her away. 'I'm not pissed. I've only had a couple.'

'Charles's here, behave yourself,' she whispered, and Dodge held up a palm.

'Boy Scout's honour, darlin'.'

She was pleased to see Dodge stretch out his hand to Charles, but her heart gave a lurch as he swayed, tripped and landed in Charles's lap.

'Apologies,' he said and Ruby gave him credit; he might be tipsy but he was at least being very polite. Then her father turned to Davey.

'Here y'are, son. Christmas present.' He put the largest of the parcels onto the table and watched, with a smile, as Davey pulled out the flat box, his eyes widening.

'A train set! I got a train set! Is it a real one?'

'Go on, open it. It's all there.'

Ruby stood back as Dodge, Charles and Davey, united in boyish delight, began unpacking the train set.

'For goodness' sake, do that on the floor. I'm bringing in the dinners.' For once, she didn't care that the toy was knocked off, it just made her happy to see the three of them occupied together, like a normal family. The only thing that could complete her happiness was Eric and it was while they were sitting at the table in the middle of grace – a concession to Charles – that the longed-for knock came.

'Who the bleedin' 'ell's that of a Christmas dinner time?' Dodge said, interrupting Charles's prayer. 'Scuse me, Charlie – sorry, *Charles*,' Dodge said, getting up.

'No! Sit down, Dad. I'll go.' She dashed to the front door.

'Am I late?' Her brother looked almost as if he feared being in trouble.

'Oh, Ricky, I'm so happy.' She squeezed him tightly, thanking the Lord he wasn't wearing the uniform.

'What you crying for then?' he said, laughing.

He looked more like himself today; the only tell-tale evidence of his job with the BUF was the severe haircut and a set of newly grazed knuckles.

'Ricky, just to warn you, Dad might be a bit surprised you're here...'

His smile faded. 'Oh Chrissake, Ruby. You've fuckin' ambushed me!'

'No, no. He wants to see you; I just thought it was better not to say anything in case you never turned up. Charles is here too.'

He rolled his eyes. 'Charles? In the same room with Dad? You're a nutter, Ruby Scully.'

'Don't start. They're getting on like a house on fire. Let me go in first.' He followed her as she pushed open the kitchen door. 'Dad, guess who's come to see us?'

Davey leaped out of his seat, which at least made Eric's entrance less awkward. She had time to fix her father with a stare and a nod toward the photo of her mother on the mantelpiece. Dodge didn't get up. 'Hello, son. You've missed grace,' he said dryly and Ruby beamed at him.

'Sit down, Ricky. I'll get your dinner.'

Throughout the meal she was careful to steer the conversation away from religion and politics and after she'd cleared away they sat around the fire with cups of tea. Their meal had been teetotal, but when she went to fetch the mince pies, Ruby caught Dodge in the scullery, adding a nip from his hip flask into the tea. 'Dad, don't spoil it!' she pleaded. 'It's all been so lovely.'

'Just the one!' Dodge grinned, but there was such a rummy smell in the scullery she guessed he'd lost count. Still, the meal was over and that had been the most dangerous part of the day. Now they could all relax and listen to the king's speech on the radio. And then she remembered that this Christmas there was no speech. There was no king. The abdication seemed to have derailed the country in every way.

'What, no speech?' Dodge asked, scandalized. 'That man's a bloody disgrace, pissing off and leaving the country in the lurch!'

'He's not a disgrace, Dad. He just fell in love – and he's stuck by the woman he wants to marry,' Ruby ventured, and then wished she hadn't, for Charles shifted uneasily in his seat. Thankfully he kept his opinions to himself.

'It's a known fact he's been pushed out because he's a big supporter of the BUF. He's a good friend of Mosley,' Eric said, calmly.

'Cobblers!' Dodge sat up in his chair, red-faced. 'He might have been a useless king, but he wasn't a soddin' fascist!'

'Dad…' Ruby tried to intervene, but Eric had already started laughing at his father.

'What do you know? I was there, outside Buckingham Palace the night of the abdication and I can tell you for a fact that if the king had kept his nerve we would have been a fascist state by the end of the year!'

'Well, thank gawd he's gone and good riddance to the lot of you!' Dodge shot back. 'You might not have your black shirt on, but you're as rotten as the lot of them. Now piss off out of it!' Dodge was on his feet and had begun to manhandle Eric out of his chair. In the struggle, the teacup her brother had been holding tumbled to the floor.

'That's Mum's best china!' Ruby dived to catch it, but it smashed in pieces at Dodge's feet.

Before she could understand what was happening, she saw a flash of steel in Eric's hand and rushed to intervene.

'Ricky, no!' Now she could see it wasn't a knife. He'd somehow slipped on a vicious-looking knuckleduster which he drove into Dodge's cheekbone. She heard a crack and Dodge yelped.

'I'll fuckin' 'ave him! I'll kill him!' her father yelled.

By now, father and son's battleground had moved to the centre of the railway set and one of the dark green carriages gave a crack as Dodge's foot crushed it. Davey began to cry. Ruby attempted to pull Dodge away from Eric just as her father took a swing, catching her a heavy blow to her forehead and she sank to her knees, pain bringing tears to her eyes.

She was too busy nursing her own wound to see what happened next, but she heard Eric's deep groan as his father's fist caught him in the stomach and then she heard him gasping for breath. When she looked up she saw a knife appear above her and from her position on the floor stretched out a hand to grab her brother's ankle.

'No, Ricky, no!'

But he shook her off like an annoying puppy and, with a cold smile curling the corner of his mouth, moved steadily forward. Her father's bloodshot eyes clouded with fear. But Charles, who had stood back until now, made a swift leap forward, chopping a hand down on Eric's wrist. The knife fell and Charles kicked it out of the way, tripping Eric in the process. Her brother had bulked out, but Charles was stronger and pinned him to the floor with one knee in his back.

'Oh, Eric,' she moaned, as she sat slumped in the midst of poor Davey's train set. 'Eric, you idiot.'

Only then did Dodge realize Ruby was injured. Blood oozed from a graze on her temple and he looked at her, horrified. 'Oh, darlin', did I do that? Did I? Gawd forgive me, did I?' Then, looking down at Eric, he said, 'See what you made me do to your sister? You're a disgrace to your family. I'm ashamed to be your father!'

Eric's rage calmed and an icy look of hatred replaced it. 'Our leader's the only father I've got. And my family's at Black

House, 'cos it ain't bloody here!' His final words were almost a sob.

'Let him go, Charles,' she said. 'Let him go if he doesn't want us.'

As Charles released him, Eric leaped up and, as he passed her, he muttered, 'Sorry, Ruby. You should go too – Dad's just not worth it.'

When Eric had gone, Charles helped her up. 'Come on, Ruby, I'm getting you out of here. Davey, leave the train set, where's your coat?' he said, dragging the little boy away from his broken toy. Before she knew it, they were making their way along St James's Road, Davey's sobs reaching Ruby through the cloud of misery that shrouded her.

'I'm sorry your father's proved me right, Ruby,' Charles said. 'He couldn't stay sober for one day, even when he knew how much it meant to you! Well, at least your eyes have been opened.'

In fact, her eyes were still half closed and the pain in her head was too insistent to even attempt an argument with him now. She asked where they were going.

'To the Mission, where else? It's the only place where we can be happy, Ruby. It's where we belong, not back there in that den of *degradation*!' He almost spat the word, but she sensed in his slightly breathless voice, not so much anger as exhilaration.

At the Central Hall the Christmas tea was in full swing, but Charles took her to a small office and sat her down. 'I'll get you some hot sweet tea. You're trembling. If I'd had my way I'd have joined Eric and given your father the trouncing he deserved...'

When he came back, he wasn't alone. Sister Evelyn came to her, immediately examining the growing egg on the side of her forehead. Ruby winced.

'I'm sorry, my dear. It's coming out in a bruise now, but that's good.' She was dabbing at the graze with an antiseptic cloth grabbed from the clinic. 'I'll leave it without a dressing, best for it to dry out.' She took both Ruby's hands and gave them a squeeze. 'You'll live.'

'Charles,' Ruby said, in a dull voice, 'perhaps you could take Davey to the children's table, get him some tea?'

Charles nodded. 'Come on, Davey, your sister needs some peace and quiet.'

But Davey cringed against her, shaking his head mutely. Charles grasped for his hand and Davey pulled away, scratching his hand.

'Little devil!'

'Leave him, then. He's just upset.'

'Charles, perhaps it would be best if I take them to my flat.' Sister Evelyn laid a hand on his arm.

'I'm not leaving her. Who knows if that man might come and find her here?'

'Stop it! He's me dad, it was an accident. Thanks for bringing us, Charles, but I think Sister Evelyn's right, me and Davey'll be fine now.'

He looked hurt and for a moment she thought he'd argue. But Sister Evelyn intervened. 'It's better she's with a woman right now, you do see, Charles?'

He nodded mutely and bent to kiss Ruby on the forehead, but the site of the bruise was so tender she flinched. 'You've no need to be frightened of me, Ruby. I would never harm a woman.'

'No, I didn't mean… It's just it hurts.' She put a hand to her head and he seemed satisfied. But when he left the little room she bent over her knees and let out a deep, wrenching sob.

'I hate all men!' she said into her lap and then reached out a hand to the slight figure, still pressed against her legs. 'All except this one.' She looked up to see silent tears rolling down Davey's face.

Sister Evelyn's flat proved to be the haven of calm Ruby needed, away from the men who'd disappointed her. True, Charles had been blameless, but she resented his belief that the drunken accident had somehow proved Dodge a monster.

To her mind, it was Eric who'd been turned into a monster by the BUF and she feared that the influence they had over him would not end well for her brother. He'd proved even more evangelical about his beliefs than she was about hers; the perfect recruit.

Perhaps they had all been the perfect recruits in their different ways, she thought: herself, Charles, Alfie, Ocki and Ida. She saw them all, being moved about on some giant chessboard, and always it was a hand from far outside of Bermondsey that moved them. Even dearest Sister Evelyn had come in from outside and much as she loved the local people she served, her allegiance would always be to the Mission. One day she would leave, but, Ruby reflected, one day, so would she...

The following morning Ruby woke from a dream of Christmas Day – before Davey or Eric was born – when her mum and dad had been happy and she was their most treasured only child. But within seconds the memory of yesterday's reality crushed the dream. She got up and tried to make something respectable out of her dishevelled Christmas day outfit. She knew Charles wouldn't be able to resist coming to see her. And shortly after eight o' clock, as the three of them sat drinking tea in front of the fire, a knock came at the door.

'It'll be Charles,' Ruby said, simply. 'Davey, will you be all right here while I go for a walk with him?'

The boy nodded, his mouth full of toast and jam, and she threw on her coat.

Outside, they walked briskly to keep warm.

'Ruby, I've thought long and hard about this – I can't protect you if you stay in that house with your father. I think you should come with me to Derbyshire when I go to college in the New Year.'

Ruby shook her head. 'I know I'm eighteen and we don't need Dodge's signature now, but—'

'I'm not saying we should get married right away. There are places near the college where you could find respectable work and decent lodgings. You don't *have* to stay in Bermondsey – what's here for you?'

'What about Davey? Dodge is going away again soon.'

'Perhaps he could stay with Aunt Nancy?'

'No! How can you think I'd leave him behind? He's only eight!' Gripped by a sudden fear, she remembered Alfie's warning about dictators. What had he said? *They'll rob you of your people.* Well he'd certainly been right in Eric's case, the BUF had robbed her brother of all his family. So, could this be Charles's way of separating her from them?

'Bring him too, then. Whatever you want to do.'

She felt foolish to have doubted him.

'Ruby, I want us to be married before I finish college and sooner or later you'll have to decide what happens to Davey.'

'I suppose I just thought he'd live with us. I knew I'd have to leave him when we left for the mission field, but he'll be fourteen or fifteen by then and he'll be working… It – it's just everything seems to be happening so quickly. I need to talk to Davey so I think I'd like to go back now.'

'All right, but say you'll pray about what I've asked. I'm only thinking of what's best for you.'

She nodded vaguely. 'I will, Charles.' But she felt more beleaguered than comforted by Charles's concern.

Sister Evelyn would have let them stay in her flat longer, but later that day she was due to visit her family in Surrey. Before they left, the deaconess said a prayer for them, but Ruby was too distracted by the thought of what she would find at home to be much comforted. It had been a miserable Christmas for Davey as well as for her, and as they neared Fort Road her thoughts turned to Ida. Ida, who, whatever the circumstances, could always make her smile, who would cut through her self-pity like a sharp knife.

'Shall we got to see Aunt Ida?' she asked Davey and he nodded, brightening.

She was surprised that Alfie opened the door. 'Oh, I've come to see Ida,' she explained.

'Ruby!' Surprise and pleasure were mixed in his greeting. Then he pointed to the purple swelling above her eye. 'What happened?'

She glanced at Davey and shook her head. 'Tell you later.'

'Come in, come in.'

She followed him to the small sitting room, but he was obviously alone. The table was spread with newspaper covered in small pieces of carved wood and there was a pot of pungent glue open. It looked like he was making some sort of model.

'Ida's not here at the moment, she's taken Ocki to her mum's.'

'Oh, sorry, you should have said. I'll leave you to your...' She waved vaguely at the wooden collection.

'Model of a Viking longship. Want to see?' he asked Davey, whose sad face brightened. 'No need to go, Ruby. They'll be back soon. It's a sort of peace offering – a not-quite-Christmas dinner for the Jewish son-without-law!' He grinned.

'Ida didn't tell me her mum and dad had a change of heart! But it's good. Didn't you want to go to your parents?' she asked, feeling sorry that he'd been left alone on Boxing Day.

'We don't celebrate Christmas.'

'Oh, of course not.' She blushed, feeling stupid.

'I like the carols!' he added quickly, covering her embarrassment.

'Do you? Me too.'

Alfie began showing Davey a series of small shields he was making. 'You see, they hung them over the hull of the ship, like this, so they were ready to grab when they landed. ' His slender fingers handled the shields with a surprising delicacy considering the tough coopering that was his trade. 'Want to stick one on for me?'

'Can I?' Davey asked and Ruby's heart contracted at his smile. It was so easy to make Davey happy.

'When it's finished, I'll paint it and put it with those and you can come and see it.'

There was a small glass cabinet filled with wooden models. Everything from biplanes to sailing ships.

'Did you make them all?' Davey asked.

Alfie nodded and went to open the cabinet. Taking down a couple of models, he placed them on the table. 'You can play with these if you like.'

'Careful with them!' Ruby warned.

'He's all right. I made those to be played with. See Davey, the wheels of this cart go around!' he said, pointing to the model of a cart.

While Davey played, Alfie made tea for Ruby and she felt herself relaxing for the first time since yesterday morning.

'Are you all right, how did it happen?' he asked softly, and in hushed tones she recounted the story of her Christmas Day. 'Charles came to see me this morning and he's decided it's best for me to go up to Derbyshire with him when he goes to Bible College in February.'

Alfie blew out a slow breath. 'And what did you say?'

She smiled, awkwardly. 'It's funny, Alfie, but I thought of you and what you said about—'

'Dictators?'

She nodded, wondering how he'd read her mind.

'Then I felt bad, because Charles behaved the best out of all of them and he said there was no pressure…'

'Except there was.'

She remembered the tight feeling in her chest as Charles had outlined his plan. 'I thought it was just me, being silly.'

'No. You're far from silly.' He paused. 'Are we friends, Ruby?'

She nodded and he went on. 'So, I'll be a real friend and tell you what you might not want to hear. I think Charlie's always been the sort of feller that likes to be in charge, whether it's his mum, church or you. I don't think it's that your dad's a villain that he doesn't like, it's that you're loyal to him. Imagine what it'll be like when you're up in Derbyshire: no friends, no family. Charlie's the big man up at the college, the only person you know – who's in charge then?'

They looked at each other in silence for a short minute before laughter reached them from the stairs and the door burst open.

Ida came in, fresh with cold. 'Ruby, darlin'! Come 'ere!' She found herself wound in a damp embrace. 'This is a nice surprise! I thought you'd still be looking after yer menfolk!'

And then her friend saw the evidence of Christmas Day on Ruby's forehead and her face darkened. 'Who done it? I'll kill 'em,' she said in a steely voice.

Ocki stepped forward to put a restraining hand on her arm. 'Just wait, Ida, before you go off the deep end.'

And Ida, who would listen to no one else on earth, all at once reined in her anger.

'It was an accident.' Ruby shot a look at Davey and put a finger to her lips. 'Bust up between Dodge and Eric. I got in the way,' she whispered.

'Why didn't you come straight here? Let's go in the scullery.' With the scullery door closed, Ruby gave Ida the full story. 'I'm so sorry, darlin'. I know how much you want to keep the family together, but you should start doing what's best for you, not always try to please your dead mum. I know you loved her, but you need to live your own life!'

'Well, that's exactly what Charles thinks. Oh, Ida, I didn't think I'd ever say I've had enough of my family, but I have. So maybe it's best if I go with Charles to Derbyshire – after all, he's going to be my family when we're married.'

'I didn't mean that! You're not seriously thinking of upping sticks and taking your Davey miles away? And even if you've give up on your family, what about your friends? What about me?'

'But he'll be my husband, Ida.'

Ida shook her head vigorously. 'He'll be your keeper! Ruby, you mark my words, you'll regret it if you go.'

16

A Dark Wood

January–March 1937

Ruby might have given up on her family, but that didn't stop her from worrying.

She worried about Dodge. She'd asked for no apologies from her father after the disastrous Christmas, but Dodge was abject. Over and over he would tell her how sorry he was, that he'd be turning over a new leaf, giving up the booze. She told him she forgave him for the crack on the head. What was more difficult to forgive was how he'd let her down, sabotaging her attempt to pull the strands of her unravelling family together.

She ignored his empty promises to reform, and almost wished she could stop loving him – but that she couldn't do, so it was with a surprising sense of relief that one day, early in the new year, she came home to find Dodge gone. He'd left a scrawled note. *Dear Ruby, that security guard's died, poor sod. Police sniffing around again and me minders don't trust me not to talk. Got to go with them. Be in touch. Love, Dad.*

She worried about Eric. As the weeks passed, she resigned herself to never hearing from Eric again. He seemed to have chosen the Black House over his family. Then one evening in late January, as she and Ida were leaving Crosse's, Ruby found

Malchy Mongey waiting at the gates. Heart racing, she rushed over.

'Is it Ricky?' she asked. 'Has something happened? Is he hurt?'

'No! He's happy as a sandboy, he's in nick!'

'What's he done wrong?'

'Your brother likes a bit of attention, and now he's gone and got it. You know the government banned the BUF uniform?'

'I told her they would!' Ida butted in.

'Well, Ricky's got himself locked up for wearing the black shirt in a public place. He's like a bloody war hero up at Black House.'

'They locked him up for that? Do you know where?' Ruby asked.

'Brixton. He could have got off with a fine but he would have to make a speech from the dock, wouldn't he? Spouting off about how the BUF would clear out all the corrupt judges and bankers. So that did it.' Malchy's disapproval was obvious.

'You sound like you've had enough of the BUF, Malchy?' Ruby ventured.

He pulled a face. 'I've packed it in. Jews ain't done nothing wrong to me. I thought the BUF would change things for the better, but half the time it's all about punch-ups with commies or running round Whitechapel scaring Jewish women and kids. I got better things to be doing with meself.' Then he grinned. 'I'm engaged, Ruby!'

'Ah, the love of a good woman always works wonders!' Ida said and patted his smooth cheek.

'I'm happy for you, Malchy. Who is she?' Ruby asked.

'She works here – Betty in labelling. I'm waiting for her to come off shift.'

'I know Betty! She's lovely. So, did Ricky ask you to come and see me?'

Malchy shook his head. 'Sorry, he didn't, but I thought you ought to know what's happened. And there's another thing, his officer in 1 Squad? He's a nutter. Got his claws stuck into Ricky and been stirring him up. I tell you, he'll load the gun but it'll be Ricky firing the bullets and if he does what I think they want him to do, he'll be up the stairs to Jack Ketch…'

Malchy pulled up an imaginary noose around his neck, frightening Ruby, who was about to ask him what on earth he meant, when the young man's eyes lit up, his attention claimed by the pretty dark-haired girl who ran up and put her arm through his.

As she and Ida walked home, Ruby felt sick with anxiety. 'Ida, what do you think Malchy was getting at when he said that officer was setting Eric up to fire the bullets?'

'I don't know, love. But listen, Rube, there's so much hot air and bluster in the BUF, it's probably nothing. I don't think Malchy meant *real* bullets.'

'Then why did he say that about Jack Ketch? It's only a *real* bullet and a *real* gun that can get you hung, ain't it, Ida?' Ruby shivered, remembering the feel of the gun hidden beneath Eric's black shirt. She was sure Malchy had meant a real gun and she told Ida why.

'You can't go worrying yourself sick over something Malchy Mongey's said. But I'll have a word with Ocki. Him and Alfie's started going along to BUF meetings, pretending to be Blackshirts. They're finding out the meetings Mosley's planning to be at, dates of all the street marches and speeches – then they go along and try to stop 'em! They got into big trouble with Dr Salter over it – he says we should allow them their free speech. But the boys ain't stopping. I'll see if they've heard about the BUF using guns. Not that you could do anything about it – Eric's made his choice.'

Well, while Eric was locked up he couldn't get himself into any worse trouble. And with Dodge in hiding, at least Charles couldn't argue that she was being endangered by his presence or his immoral influence.

But most of all she worried about Davey, who, given the news of their move to Derbyshire, had responded, 'Live with Charles?

I don't want to!' Then, seeing her face fall, he'd gripped her hand tightly, and pleaded, 'Don't go without me, though, will you, Ruby?'

She would have preferred to see resistance in his eyes rather than the fear of being left alone reflected there.

Well into the new year Charles continued to display the same restraint and consideration that he had since his return from his college interview. He was going up before term began to organize lodgings for Ruby and school for Davey. They'd agreed she would join him the following month. She was glad he was going before her – focussing on his plans was easier than considering her own. Sse helped prepare his clothes, mending the ones he already had, and choosing a new suit; he couldn't wear his funeral suit every day. There were books to be bought and she went with him to Charing Cross Road to search out the second-hand bookshops. She liked poking around in the dusty, rackety old places and he was delighted when she came down from the top floor of one narrow old shop in Cecil Court, covered in dust, with a Hebrew Old Testament and a Greek New Testament. She felt almost sad to hand them over, knowing that it would never be she who learned how to read the intriguing cyphers that covered their pages.

After their book hunt Charles took her to Lyons Corner House and bought them hot chocolate and Chelsea buns. He was happy. 'This is how it will be, Ruby. When you join me in Derbyshire, you'll be my helpmeet. Haven't you enjoyed yourself today?' He smiled and she reached over to wipe chocolate foam from his upper lip. He flinched, and she gave an irritated sigh.

'I'm sorry, Ruby, but that's not the way to behave in public,' he said.

'Oh, I just wish—'

He set his jaw. 'I can't be any different,' he said. 'Don't ask me to.'

She was silent for a moment. There seemed to be one rule for him and another for her.

'You can't change, but you want *me* to,' she said, finally.

'No, I don't! I love you just as you are, you're perfect!' He seemed genuinely shocked.

'Am I? But you want me to change how I feel about me dad; you don't want me seeing Ida or working with the Labour Party; you want me to behave a certain way in public and you want me to let you make all the decisions, when I've been making all my own decisions since I was ten!'

'Of course. *I'll* be head of the house when we're married, that's the way God has ordained it. You can't blame *me* for that.'

And perhaps she couldn't, but she began to ask herself if that was really what God thought – the one who had all those years ago borne her up on waves of love in the decision room. Did *he* think her decisions were second-rate? But she didn't want to get into a theological argument. Charles would always win.

'We'd better go. It's getting late and I'm going to see Ida tonight.' She didn't feel like sparing his feelings. He'd only reluctantly accepted her renewed contact with Ida. 'She says Ocki's had some news about Eric.'

She'd already told him Eric was in prison and that Ida was enlisting Ocki's help in finding out what her brother might be getting himself involved in, but she'd almost immediately regretted it. Now the muscle of Charles's jaw tightened. If Ocki was going to be there, Alfie would be too.

'Are you your brother's keeper? You should stay out of it, Ruby,' was his only response

That evening, with Aunt Nancy keeping an eye on Davey, she hurried to Ida's. She knew that the Diamond brothers had infiltrated several BUF meetings over the past weeks. There was no BUF branch in Bermondsey, so they had to travel further afield. In the Lewisham branch meeting they'd posed as new recruits, but were discovered and had to run for it, which was no mean feat for Ocki. Ruby hoped they hadn't endangered themselves again trying to uncover information about Eric.

When she arrived, Ida's normally bright greeting was muted. It was only when she followed her friend into the small sitting room, that she saw the cause.

Ocki was sitting with his calipered leg up on a stool, his face grey and strained.

'Wounded hero!' he said, giving her his shy smile.

Alfie got up to greet her. His left eye was bloodshot and surrounded by a purple bruise. 'We had a run in with a few Blackshirts at the Streatham meeting,' he explained. 'They didn't take kindly to us spying on them.'

'Alfie, are you OK? Why did you take that risk?'

'My brother's tougher than he looks,' Ocki said. 'It wasn't any riskier than usual, it's just that our luck ran out.'

'They're both black and blue! Those fascist cowards, I'd like to have a go at them meself,' Ida said fiercely.

'Ah, my warrior woman!' Ocki joked. He patted his leg. 'This let me down. Alfie would have got away if he hadn't come back for me.'

'But I didn't want you putting yourself in danger just to find out about my brother!' Ruby said.

'We would have gone anyway. And we heard something about I Squad that we shouldn't have. That's probably why we got such a good hiding,' Alfie said, sitting opposite her.

Ruby put down her cup. 'What did you hear?'

His straight eyebrows knitted together as he recalled the details. 'You might wish we hadn't told you, Ruby.'

But she waved his warning aside, feeling suddenly cold in the cozy room.

'They *are* being issued with guns. Pistols, machine guns—'

'Machine guns! But they're not an army.'

'*They* think they are,' Ocki said.

'They're doing weapons training at Black House – which would explain Eric's gun. What Malchy said about the 1 Squad officer, that's the more worrying thing…' Alfie glanced towards Ida.

'Tell her,' she said.

Ruby said, as firmly as she could, 'Yes, tell me.'

'He's definitely out for blood. You remember the Battle of Cable Street last year?'

'Of course; Eric was proud of being there.'

'Well, they're planning another big march through a working-class borough and this time they don't intend to be stopped. There was a group of toughs boasting about how the Reds and Jews'll have more than knuckledusters to worry about this time.'

'And we heard talk that 1 Squad were preparing sharpshooters. Some of them actually sang a vile little song: "A bullet in the head'll stop any Jew or Red",' Ocki added.

'My God. But surely the police won't allow it?'

'Some of the police are on their side, Ruby – they could look the other way.' Ocki's grey face was deadly serious.

She put a hand to her face, feeling all the fight drain from her. 'I've lost him, haven't I?' She saw the hangman's noose swinging and her brother walking up the steps as Malchy had predicted.

Alfie leaned forward, his dark eyes burning with conviction. 'Not if we can stop them first.'

'But where are they planning to march?' she asked.

'Bermondsey. They're coming to Bermondsey.'

'They can't!' Ruby said, suddenly full of rage that the bullies who were duping her brother and so many others should dare to come marching through her home. 'How can we stop them?'

Ida's throaty laugh filled the room and Alfie's straight mouth curled into a slow smile. 'We've got a few ideas – want to hear them?'

Ruby stayed late into the night, listening intently as the ideas flew back and forth between the three young socialists.

'We've got to put all our efforts into convincing the Home Secretary,' Alfie explained. 'I'm pretty sure he won't want another Cable Street on his hands!'

Ocki suggested challenging any gangs of blackshirts leafleting or trying to set up a Bermondsey branch. 'If we let them get a foothold here before the march we'll never be able to stop it.'

'Good idea, Ocki,' Alfie said. 'There'll be hell to pay from Dr Salter about their free speech and right to assemble, but the BUF say they want to end democracy! I don't see why they should take advantage of a system they want to overthrow, do you?' For a moment she didn't register that he was speaking to her. But he'd asked with an intensity that demanded a true answer.

'Everyone should be able to speak their mind, but we shouldn't let them turn boys into killers. Perhaps I'm being selfish – I just want to save Ricky from them...'

'Good enough reason,' he said.

It was almost midnight when Ida insisted Ocki needed to get to bed and Alfie offered to walk her home.

'Oh, I'm used to walking the streets at all hours,' she said, and she thought he looked disappointed.

'Take no notice of her, Alfie,' Ida ordered, putting two hands under Ocki's armpits and lifting him effortlessly out of the chair.

Once outside she was grateful for Alfie's presence, for the road ahead was cloaked in fog. Enveloped by damp, she drew thick, sooty vapour into her lungs. They walked hesitantly, silently for a while, their shoulders occasionally brushing, but then as they crossed Thorburn Square a smudgy moon made its way through the fog and lit their path. They skirted the church yard.

'I'm grateful for your help with Eric...' she said, her breath a pale plume in the dirty yellow air. 'I felt so helpless about him, but now...I think there's hope.'

'I couldn't imagine you ever feeling hopeless!'

'I have my doubts, same as any one. I've decided to go to Derbyshire with Charles, but since the bust up at Christmas, I've just felt a bit...lost.'

'*Midway through the journey of this life I came to a dark wood...*'

'Is that from the Bible?'

'No, it's poetry – *The Inferno* by Dante.'

'Alfie, where do you manage to find all this stuff!' she said, with a tinge of envy.

'Well, Dad's bookshelves, and Spa Road Library of course!' he laughed. 'I've practically lived there since I was a kid.'

'What does it mean?'

He shrugged. 'It's what you're feeling...sometimes you get lost, and can't work out the best way forward, but there's always hope you'll get back on the path – hope for you, hope for Eric... hope for all of us.'

She felt a sudden rush of joy and, hardly knowing why, laughed. It must have infected him, because he joined her and she felt there was a giddy quality to their laughter, which she didn't understand. Their conversation throughout the night had been so serious, but here and now felt like the most fun she'd had in a very long time.

She wanted to go straight to Eric, to warn him he must get himself out of the BUF, but meetings with Alfie and the others in the Labour Institute convinced her she could not. Though the march would eventually become public, what they had found out about the weapons had to be kept to a small group of people until they could put their case to the Home Secretary, get him to have the Black House raided and the march banned. Going to Eric would tip off the BUF that their plans had been discovered. It meant she couldn't tell Charles either, which played on her conscience.

The weekend before he was due to leave, there was a farewell service for Charles at the Central Hall. Ruby watched from the front row as he stood on the platform next to the pastor and she couldn't help feel some reflected glory as the congregation of over a thousand followed in the prayers for him. But she listened to the fulsome tribute the pastor gave and tried to recognize her Charles in the words. Since the day of his conversion, Charles had been, the pastor said, shot straight as an arrow in the service of God, his dedication and self-sacrifice never deviating. God had lifted him from humble, difficult circumstances, and Charles had proved himself worthy. His heart, captured by God, had felt the burden of the call to Africa and he had answered it without regard for self. Upright in all his ways, he was a shining example of Christian manliness.

But the words rang hollow to her. How could the minister not see the straining muscles that pulled the bow, the bowstring sometimes taut to breaking, the wildly spiralling course of Charles's arrow? Not shot straight at all, but fired with such effort of will that it could not help but fly off course?

She became aware of Charles staring at her from the podium and felt that he'd read her mind. She blushed. She had to stop it, to quell the dizzy, queasy feeling her train of thought had caused in her. She wanted to run from the hall. But instead, she sat rigid, grateful when everyone closed their eyes and she could pray with the others, that he would be guided aright in all his ways. And perhaps hers was the most fervent prayer amongst the thousands.

After the service, Sister Evelyn sought Ruby out. There was a new family in urgent need of a visit, she said, and did Ruby have an hour to come with her to deliver emergency parcels? Ruby saw Charles hovering nearby, as did Sister Evelyn, who said, 'Oh, I'm sorry, my dear. You should go to Charles; it's a very proud day for him, for you both. This can wait.'

'Oh, no, Sister Evelyn, it's all right. Just a minute...' She quickly ran to Charles.

'There's a family in need and I have to go with Sister Evelyn.' Seeing his disappointment, she added, 'I'll see you when we get back. We'll have a chat then, eh?'

He nodded. 'You're right, Ruby, the Lord's work is more important, go.'

She and Sister Evelyn walked briskly to the family in Alice Street, which was only a short distance from the Mission. They had gathered together a couple of parcels for the eight children and their widowed mother.

'The husband died three months ago and they've had no help from the Assistance Board; the mother's been ill, so it's fallen to the eleven-year-old daughter to look after them all and the poor girl is exhausted.' Sister Evelyn glanced Ruby's way. 'You would know what that's like; it was one of the reasons I wanted you to come. I hope Charles wasn't too upset that I dragged you away?'

'He said he'd rather I be doing the Lord's work.'

The deaconess gave her a sidelong glance.

'You seem a little subdued, Ruby. Is it because you'll miss Bermondsey? Or do you feel pressured about the future, marriage?'

Ruby shook her head vigorously. 'Oh, no. Charles has been really understanding since his interview, says there's no pressure for me to go, but...'

'What, Ruby?'

'It's not always words, is it? That make you feel you ought to do something? Sometimes I think I should just marry him tomorrow! It would make him so happy.'

'Of course it would; he'd have no worries about being chosen for the mission field then,' Sister Evelyn said quickly.

'What do you mean?'

'Apparently, so the minister told me, the interview panel returned a very favourable report on Charles, but said he wasn't mature enough for the mission field, not as a single man. They felt he wouldn't be able to do a good job as a missionary without the support of a wife. Didn't he tell you all this?'

'No,' she said in a small voice. 'He said they *preferred* married men, but not that he wouldn't be accepted without me!'

'He should have!' Sister Evelyn showed a rare flash of anger.

Ruby's heart was in turmoil. Had he really been so understanding because he loved her? Or was it only his own missionary career he loved?

'Perhaps he thought that if he told me I'd get myself all worried about it?'

Sister Evelyn sniffed. 'Ruby, you're an angel. You doubt no one, forgive everyone, and that is your God-given gift, but in this case I can tell you that Charles was wrong not to discuss it with you honestly. Promise me you'll ask him about it before he leaves?'

Ruby nodded, grateful that they had come to Alice Street, though all inside was as upsetting as anything she'd seen in all her home visits. Her heart went out to the emaciated and unkempt eleven-year-old Maggie. Her stick-like arms and legs, protruding from a tattered, thin frock, were blue with cold, and the house was perishing. The younger children looked marginally better, their clothes more suited to winter. Ruby guessed that the eldest had concentrated all her energies on caring for them and had neglected herself. While Sister Evelyn went to talk to the mother, Ruby set about making a fire with the coal they'd brought.

Maggie came to help and Ruby waived her away. 'You just go and sit down, you need a rest!' she said, but when she looked around, she realized there were no chairs.

'We used 'em all for firewood,' Maggie said, following her gaze. 'But without no coal, it don't last long. It'll be lovely to have a proper fire.' She gave a little shiver.

'Haven't you got anything warmer than that?' Ruby asked and the girl looked down at her frock. 'Oh, all me clothes is in the pawnshop, but this does me.'

'Hang on a minute,' Ruby said, opening a parcel. 'Will this fit you?' It was a woman's cardigan, handknitted from donated scraps of wool by one of the Mission's knitting circle. Maggie grabbed it eagerly and put it on. It would have gone around her twice, but she beamed with gratitude and grabbed one of the toddlers to come inside the warm folds of her new cardigan. 'Room enough for two in 'ere!' she grinned.

By the time they had doled out the rest of the clothes and food and Ruby had helped to wash the little ones, it was far too late to expect Charles to be waiting for her. And although she barely admitted it to herself, she was glad not to have to put her questions to him tonight.

It was as she stopped to light the gas mantle in the passage that she heard noises coming from the bedroom. She softly pushed open the door and went in, drawing aside the dividing curtain. Davey was lying on his back, his pale face screwed up and his chest heaving as he tried to stifle his sobs. She rushed to him and he turned over into her arms.

'Oh, Ruby I don't want to go, don't make me go. I want to stay here with me friends, and I want to be here for Dad when he gets back – and I don't want you to go neither! Why can't it stay like it's always been?' He sniffed in a long, shuddering sob.

She held him tightly, remembering that she'd been the only mother he'd ever known.

'Don't cry, Davey, don't cry. We won't go if you don't want to,' she promised, trying not visualize the scene with Charles when she came to break the news.

When she told Charles the following evening, he looked at her with wordless astonishment.

'I can't come! Davey was making himself sick last night, crying about leaving his school and his friends and Dodge. I can't drag him away from everything he's ever known.'

His lips tightened. 'It's a bit late to be changing the plans!'

She went to him, putting her arms around him and leaning her head on his hard-muscled chest. 'Please, Charles, don't force me to choose between the two of you. Davey's like my own child. I just can't do this to him now!'

She felt his chest heaving and then he seemed to calm himself.

'Then I'll wait, Ruby.'

'Oh, thank you, Charles!' She kissed him, feeling a heady lightness that was a mixture of relief and fear that he would change his mind. But they sat and talked about the farewell service and a monthly prayer letter that Charles planned to send home to the church and he was as attentive as he'd ever been, holding her hand, not wanting to take his eyes from hers.

When it was time to see him out, she still hadn't mentioned Sister Evelyn's revelation about the marriage condition on his college offer. She was a coward, she told herself. She must say something now or end up loathing herself until she did. He drew her down the outside steps, so that they could say goodbye in their familiar place, beneath the gaslight in St James's Road.

She was cold and he held her and kissed her in the shadows as he asked, 'Do you love me, Ruby?'

She trembled, shivering because she was frightened to even look into her heart. He felt too bound up with her love of God to find the place where her feelings for him began or ended.

'Yes, yes of course I do. I wouldn't be marrying you otherwise!' she said, a band tightening around her chest.

'So, you will definitely be marrying me?' he asked, smiling. He threw his head back and looked to the star strewn sky. 'Thank God!' he laughed. 'That's all I needed to know. I can go off with an easy mind now. I know I can do great things, Ruby, with you to help me.'

'About that, Charles, me helping you. Sister Evelyn mentioned that the college laid down a condition, that you definitely had to be married.'

'Yes, yes. Surely I told you that, didn't I?'

She shook her head. 'No, Charles, you said they preferred married men, not that you *had* to be one.'

He held her at arm's length. 'I'm sure that's what I meant, Ruby. But it wouldn't have made any difference, would it? You're marrying me and I'm happier than I can say. Kiss me goodbye.'

She let him kiss her and then she watched him go. They'd agreed that she wouldn't see him off at the station tomorrow and she waited for him to look back, but he didn't. He had a spring in his step and she felt left behind, as if her imagined future was walking away with him. And yet, as she mounted the front steps and swung open the door, she also felt the great relief of being left alone; it flooded her, warming her in spite of the chill night. And when she sat in the tiny kitchen, as the embers of the fire died, she took down Rachel Scully's photograph. She traced the familiar face with her finger and looked into her mother's kind, dark eyes.

'I did the right thing, didn't I, Mum?'

17

The Battle of Bermondsey

March–October 1937

In spring, when the cherry trees planted by Bermondsey's Beautification Committee were in full bloom, Ruby met Alfie in St James's churchyard. They still kept to their routine of meeting here once a week, even though now that Charles was not here to be upset, they could have met anywhere. Ruby didn't have any new families to recommend this week, but she waited at the church steps anyway. She liked talking to Alfie; he had such a different way of looking at things and always made her feel as if he was interested in her opinion. He was coming to the end of his task of patching up the rotting frames for the great bells.

'Want to go up to the tower?' he asked. 'We won't have the excuse for much longer.'

As it was a warm evening and she'd left Davey playing happily with Aunt Nancy's youngest boys, she agreed. Only when they had climbed the steep wooden stairs to the ringing room did he break the bad news.

'Ruby, they've announced the march in the Blackshirt rag.'

She'd been peering through the circular tower window onto a foaming sea of cherry trees and sunny daffodils in the churchyard below. He joined her at the window and she turned to face him. 'Why did you wait till we were up here to tell me?' she asked.

'I thought you'd be upset – it's more private here.'

She slumped to the dusty floor and he sat beside her.

'Eric's done for now,' she said, feeling hopeless. 'Perhaps I should just take Charles's advice and stay out of my brother's business.'

'Don't give up at the first hurdle. They've just proposed a route.'

'What is it?' she asked.

'Starting at Parliament Square, crossing the river to Southwark Street and through Bermondsey to Mill Pond. They'll try to hold a rally in West Lane. Mosley will speak.'

She remembered the armour-plated speaker van and pictured Eric inside with his gun. She gave a groan. 'Did I tell you they let Eric out of prison?'

'Yes.' He laid a reassuring hand on her arm. 'Listen, it'll take months to organize this thing and, meanwhile, we'll be lobbying the Home Secretary.'

'Why haven't you got on with doing that already?' she asked, testily.

'Too many cooks. We all want something different. There's the League of Youth, the Labour Party Executive, the Trade Unions, the MPs, the Mayor, the Communists, the—'

'All right, Alfie, I get the picture!'

He took no offense. She had noticed how unprickly he was compared to Charles – but then, he didn't love her as Charles did.

'And what about the Blackshirts' guns; do all those committees know about them now?'

'Oh no. We've only told a few others in the League – and Dr Salter, of course. And I know you think he's a saint, but he can be stubborn as a mule when it comes to his pacifist principles.'

She looked at him. 'So?'

'He said all we need to do is stay at home and just let the fascists march through. He says if we allow them their free speech, they'll have no audience and there'll be no one to shoot – so no one gets hurt. Simple.' Alfie took in a deep breath and pounded his fist on the ringing room floor so that soft puffs of dust rose up around them where they sat.

'It *is* simple, ain't it?' she replied, thinking it was probably what Jesus would do.

'No, Ruby, it's never simple. If we let them pass through without a fight, we're saying we agree. And how can me and Ocki agree? How can anyone who sees what's going on in Spain and Germany agree? They want their free speech now, but when they're in power no one else will be allowed it! Especially not Jews.'

'So, what will you do now?' she asked, feeling justly rebuked.

'We'll go to Westminster, lobby the Home Secretary to ban the march. They can't afford another Cable Street.' He got up, stretching his long arms and arching his back, like a supple tree in the wind.

'And what about the guns?'

'Dr Salter's sending a report to the police. They'll raid Black House, but something tells me they won't find anything because there's a lot of Blackshirts wearing blue these days – if you see what I mean.'

'Can't he send the report higher up?'

Alfie shook his head. 'It's them that are most sympathetic to Mosley.'

He held out a hand to help her up and they took one last look out at the Bermondsey skyline in the setting sun. Red, orange and gold bands of light illuminated the river and gilded Tower Bridge to the west. Alfie pointed to Dockhead, then traced the route the fascists would take, up to where the spire of the Norwegian church split the sky by West Lane. It seemed an out-of-the-way place to gather and she asked Alfie why there.

'To stir people up. Mosley will be giving his speech right next to the Bermondsey war memorial, prancing around, pretending he's some great military hero fighting for Britain, as if his rabble's got anything to do with the real heroes who didn't come back.' His voice shook with emotion.

'Did your family lose someone in the war?'

'Dad's brother; I was named after him.'

'You'll stop them. I know you will,' she said, with all the conviction she could muster.

Now and then Uncle Jim visited her with news that her father was 'alive and kicking and not to worry about him'. And once he turned up with a crisp white fiver from Dodge, but when she asked him if her dad was coming home, he patted her hand and said, 'Don't you worry about your dad, the main thing is he's staying out of trouble, gel.' But that she doubted. And when she went to Dodge's wardrobe to put the fiver with the stash of money her father had left for them, she found that it was gone. Dodge had obviously found a use for it. She wasn't sorry, for there'd been times over the winter, when the coal had run out or there was no bread left to give Davey, that she'd been sorely tempted to break her vow not to use his blood money. But when that happened, she'd swallowed her pride and put herself on the emergency parcel list at the Mission.

She continued to attend the Basutoland prayer meeting, but it seemed to have lost some of its impetus since Charles's departure for college. Still, the little group continued to pray for the work and now they included Charles and Ruby in their prayers as future missionaries to the far-off kingdom. Sometimes it crossed her mind that the salvation of untold African children might depend on Charles and that he could only fulfil his mission if she married him. How would all her fellow supplicants feel if ever she decided not to go ahead with it? Would they condemn her for thwarting God's plan? It was stupid thinking; she *was* going to marry him. And she would shake her head to rid herself of thoughts that felt almost heretical.

It was after one such meeting that she came home to find Dodge sitting at the kitchen table eating fish and chips out of a newspaper.

'Hello, Ruby, love. Want some?' he asked.

She went for a plate. 'You're getting all grease on me scrubbed table.'

He picked up the parcel and tipped the contents onto the plate.

'Sorry, I was starving. Come all the way down from Derby today.'

'Derby? That's where Charles is at Bible college.'

'Well, the Lord didn't see fit for our paths to cross,' he said, licking his fingers. 'Thank gawd!'

'It's where me and Davey'll be living after I'm married.'

He ignored her. 'Make us a cuppa, Ruby, there's a good girl. And where's me kiss?' He opened his arms and she gave him a brief peck on the cheek.

'Oh, bit chilly in 'ere,' he said sarcastically, lighting up a Woodbine.

'I don't see you for months and you want me to be all over you? No, Dad. You left me in the lurch again after ruining our Christmas. All that talk about turning over a new leaf? That's all it was – *talk*!'

'I didn't have no choice! You can't piss about with these hard bastards, Ruby, you do as you're told. I sent Uncle Jim to make sure you was all right, did you get the money?'

She nodded.

'Well, I'm back for good. And I tell you what, you can go to Derbyshire with Charlie if you like, but you ain't taking my boy up there!'

'No? Who's going to look after him then?'

'I'll pay Aunt Nancy.'

'Don't talk silly, Dad. She couldn't look after him full-time, not unless you give her some keep, which we both know won't happen. And you can't look after him, can you? You'll be on the run the rest of your life.'

He took a long gulp of tea and then an equally long drag of his Woodbine.

'No, I won't, actually. It needed a good few bungs, but the police ain't on anyone's tail no more. Only thing is, I'm in the firm now, whether I like it or not. So, if they say jump, Ruby, I jump.'

He'd only been back a week before they said jump and he was gone again.

Alfie's belief that Mr Samuel Hoare would not risk another Cable Street turned out to be mistaken. After months of lobbying parliament to ban the BUF march, the Home Secretary informed them that he couldn't see any problem with fascists marching through their borough, because, he explained, 'There are so few Jews living in Bermondsey, the threat to individuals is negligible.'

Ruby's conscience told her to follow Dr Salter's advice and simply stay at home, but when Alfie came back from Westminster, more dejected than she'd ever seen him, her heart told her something different. How could she not stand shoulder to shoulder with Alfie and Ocki?

Through that summer, the only contact she had with Charles was his letters. He wrote describing how well he was doing at college, passing his first exams, leading prayer groups and running societies. He'd already found lodgings that they could move into once they were married and there was a place for Davey at the nearby school. She wrote and told him about her trips with Ida to choose a wedding dress – leaving out the part about Ida, near to tears, telling her she looked beautiful but begging her not to waste her life on Charlie Best.

She felt the gap widening between his world and hers. She never missed a home visit with Sister Evelyn or her stints at the Welfare Clinic, but the Mission was not her whole life as it had once been. She spent more and more time with her friends at Fort Road and when the date for the BUF march was announced as Sunday the third of October, she began to attend meetings at the Labour Institute.

Then, almost as if he knew of her wavering allegiance, she received a letter from Charles announcing that he was coming home on a visit to finalize their wedding plans. They'd decided on a Christmas wedding at the Central Hall, and so, he said, it was time for them both to see the minister and talk about the service. But Ruby couldn't help feeling there was more behind his sudden visit than wedding plans. For he was to arrive only a week before Mosley's march through Bermondsey. She'd mentioned in her letters, as casually as she could, that she'd been helping with the campaign to have the march banned, and so far he'd voiced no objections, but now the timing of his return made her feel uneasy.

When she first saw him, she was shocked at how quickly she'd forgotten what he looked like. The bronze hair she remembered, but had his face always looked so full and ruddy? And she'd forgotten the sharp, almost antiseptic, scrubbed smell of his skin and the way his pale eyes seemed to pierce through to her heart so that she felt always uncertain in his presence.

They sat in her kitchen. He'd come straight from the station and his small black bag sat on the floor, his black hat perched like a raven on top of it.

'So, Ruby, my love, I've read all about this BUF march you've been so concerned about stopping. What has the Lord told you to do? I hope you've received guidance to stay away and leave your brother to follow his conscience. He obviously is doing what he thinks is right.'

'Well, he is.' Ruby hesitated, then said, 'But I don't think the Lord would think fascism is right, do you?'

He frowned. 'You do understand that it was the Jews who crucified our Lord?' he asked as if he was talking to an idiot. He sat back as if he had said all that was needed.

'But Jesus forgave his persecutors,' she said in a small voice, 'Romans and Jews. And he said that if we forgive, so we'll be forgiven…'

He shook his head impatiently. 'I've studied biblical history and theory and it's clear the Jewish race is cursed.'

She couldn't believe what she was hearing. She knew it was not right, and yet it wasn't she who was studying for the ministry so she kept her peace, only saying softly, 'Well, Dr Salter says we should just boycott the march, turn the other cheek.'

Charles made a disparaging gesture; Dr Salter's Christian Socialism did not appeal to him either. 'All that aside, I want to be clear: you're not to go anywhere near that march. Do you understand, Ruby? It would be very bad for my position at the college if you were seen making an exhibition of yourself. I can't have my future wife standing on the street with that immoral, communist rabble. It's just as well I've come home now, I think. Don't you?'

Thousands upon thousands of Blackshirts were marching through Bermondsey; she could hear the pounding of their feet all the way up in her scullery in St James's Road. She opened the window and stuck her head out. They were getting closer!

Dr Salter had written in the paper that boycotting the march would prevent destruction and uphold free speech, so it seemed the right thing to do and Ruby had stayed at home. But now they were coming, marching right past her home, and something in Ruby rebelled.

Her dear friends had gone out early on this Sunday morning to build the barricades which by now should have prevented those endless, pounding feet from passing through the borough. They should never have got this far! Her house was ten minutes away from the BUF rallying point at West Lane. *Her friends had failed!*

She ran downstairs to Aunt Nancy's. They'd already heeded the Labour Party's official advice and decided to keep the children inside today.

Aunt Nancy answered her knock. 'Come in, love. Can you hear them? Good job we kept the kids out of it!'

'Nancy, can you look after Davey for me till I come home?'

'You ain't thinking of going up to West Lane? You silly mare, you'll get yourself hurt. Think of him!' Aunt Nancy dropped her voice and nodded her head towards Davey and her youngest son Harry as they played Snakes and Ladders at her kitchen table.

'But I've got *two* brothers – and one of them's out there.'

'On the wrong bleedin' side, and whose fault's that!'

'I know. That's why I want to be on the right side.'

Aunt Nancy shook her head. 'That's your trouble, Ruby, you're always too worried about doing the right thing – sometimes you got to be selfish. Have a bit of nous and leave well alone.'

'So, you can't look after him for me?' she said, feeling like a caged bird, desperate to fly.

'Course I will, you silly mare. But there's police horses, I can hear them – you could get trampled underfoot – you be careful!'

Almost before the words were out of Aunt Nancy's mouth Ruby had dashed to the basement front door, flung it open and rushed up the steps. The roar of a thousand voices assaulted her and, borne on the wind, came the clash of metal on wood and brick on stone, punctuated by the shattering of glass shopfronts and windows. And then she heard high-pitched women's screams. Could it be Ida? There were yelps from men in pain. Could it be Alfie? How could she stay away?

She ran towards the noise and at the junction with Jamaica Road she stopped. It was jammed with thousands of men, dressed in flat caps and jackets or overcoats, charging headlong like a frightened herd, pursued by dozens of mounted police horses, flank to flank across the entire width of the road. The anti-fascist demonstrators were being corralled, the police forming a protective phalanx around Mosley's men. She caught hold of a young man's raincoat. His face was red and shining with sweat, his eyes bulging with excitement.

'Have the Blackshirts got through?' she shouted at him above the cacophony of voices and the cries of those caught by batons or hooves.

'Yes! The coppers have been pulling down all the barricades!' But flinging up his fist in the communist salute he shouted, '*They Shall Not Pass!*'

He tore away and she looked back down Jamaica Road to the sea of horses and lines of foot police, six deep, surrounding the advancing Blackshirts. Though the anti-fascist demonstrators had turned up in their thousands, they were being forced into a run by police using batons to buffet them on all sides.

Ruby was inexorably borne along by the panicked, jostling bodies. Sparks flew from horses' hooves on cobbles, and screams and shouts exploded around her as she saw men beaten about the head with batons till they fell writhing to the ground. If only she could find Ida and Alfie! Looking wildly around, she spotted up ahead an unending wave of demonstrators concentrating into a wall of bodies that seemed to be slowly repelling the police onslaught.

Then she saw the barricade. It was being thrown up at astonishing speed. Men and boys tossed fences, barbed wire, lumps of timber into high piles, and like the dilapidated towers of some ancient fort, each lofty pile had a red flag planted atop it. Between the towers, bull-like men were dragging into place coster barrows, handcarts, corrugated iron, wooden crates, even a disused water tank to form a long mound that blocked the entire width of the road. A tall figure, with light feet and perfect balance, was traversing the precarious barricade as if it were the knife edge of a mountain peak. He carried loops of chain and was linking the assorted objects together to form a bulwark against the oncoming tide.

She could not mistake the slim, broad-shouldered figure and screamed at the top of her voice: 'Alfie!'

Carried along by the thudding hooves behind her and the mass of humanity around her, she found herself heading inexorably toward the heart of the barricade. She couldn't deviate from her course and it was only a matter of time before she stumbled. Squashed between a roll of barbed wire and the gushing flood of humanity, she felt a strong hand lift her up.

'Get out the way, love, or they'll trample you to a pulp!' her rescuer yelled. It was one of the bull-like dockers who'd been building the barricade and now he tossed her to one side as if she were a feather pillow. Falling to her hands and knees, she looked up to see hooves rearing just inches from her face. Ruby covered her head with ineffectual hands and scrabbled her way to the pavement, chest heaving, knees bleeding, staggering to her feet only to be grabbed by an ungentle policeman who shoved her behind him into a throng of bodies being contained by the lines of blue uniforms. She immediately began worming her way out, squeezing under armpits and between sweaty muscled bodies that smelled of Woodbines. When she reached the pavement edge, she craned her neck to get another glimpse of Alfie on top of the barricade, but he had gone.

Farther back down the road the fascists were advancing steadily. Four thousand, four abreast, not in uniform, but many wearing black shirts beneath their jackets, they marched like the military machine they aspired to be. At their head was the unmistakable figure of Mosley, his normally arrogant face marked by something very like fear. And now there was another face she looked for but dreaded to see. To one side of Mosley she saw the speaker van, with its three trumpets front and back, like unholy bunches of huge black lilies. The van was crawling along and there, crouched on the roof, holding onto the guard rail, was her brother. His pale hair, perfectly in place, he wore an immaculate black shirt, his right hand thrust inside a grey jacket. She knew the gun would be hidden there and a flash of chill anger at the Blackshirts who'd manipulated her lost brother lit a fuse inside her. For the first time she understood Jesus's anger as he'd turfed out the moneylenders from the temple.

She burst out from the police cordon and into the Blackshirt ranks, beating against the black tide until eventually she stood in front of the van.

It was forced to halt and the driver shouted at her to get out of the road. Eric removed the hand from inside his jacket and leaned over the railing, waving her back. 'Get out of it, Ruby! You'll get hurt! Go home!'

'Only if you come with me! You don't belong with this lot.'

His sky-blue eyes fixed on hers and there was a flicker of doubt, she thought, then almost immediately his hand went back inside his jacket as he compressed his lips and shook his head. And the sheer force of bodies swept her away from Eric and back to the barricade, which was now being torn down by the police. The confined crowd of demonstrators jeered at them and then a brick whizzed past her head. She ducked. But it hit its mark and a young constable's helmet skittered across the road. As he picked it up, what looked like a lump of concrete hurtled over her, catching the policeman full in the face. Then, from the roof of the flats behind them, came a steady rain of eggs, rotten fruit and stones, pelting police and advancing fascists alike. High above her, people in the flats were hanging a huge banner from a balcony. Painted in blood-red, bold lettering was the defiant message: *SOCIALISM BUILDS, FASCISM DESTROYS. BERMONDSEY AGAINST FASCISM*. Alfie had told her it would be the BUF's biggest mistake to try marching through any of the new flats the Labour council had built to replace the decaying Victorian slums. He said it would seem as if Mosley's men were marching in to pull down the flats brick by brick. It seemed he had been right.

A firework thrown from a balcony startled one of the horses. It reared in terror, sending its rider flying into the crowd. Now the police turned their attention from pulling down the barricade to cutting down the crowd. A dozen policemen were coming her way, all with batons raised. Suddenly instinct took hold of her and she ran. A policeman made a grab for her but she stuck out a bony elbow, shoving him aside. Steadying herself on a jagged corner of the rusty water tank, she brought her hand away bloody and then she heard her name called.

'Ruby! Ruby Scully!'

Up on top of the barricade was Alfie Diamond, silhouetted against a pewter sky, a red flag flying beside him. Further along was Ida, her red beret pulled down low, brandishing a piece of paling like a spear. Alfie, his dark curls even more dishevelled than usual, ran nimbly down a huge beam, balancing like a tightrope walker, till he stopped and reached down a hand.

'Up here!' he urged her. 'Grab my hand!'

But there was an obstacle. A policeman, beefy and smirking, stood square in her path. 'Go home where you belong, little girl!' he warned.

Skinny she might be, but she hadn't been a little girl since she was nine. She charged, shouting in a hoarse voice she hardly recognized, 'Why don't you pick on someone your own size, you big bully?' and to her amazement the policeman stood aside.

She leaped onto the barricade and took Alfie's hand. Hauling her up onto the beam, he helped her clamber to the top. On their high perch, beside the flapping red flag, they swayed perilously as he flung his arms around her, holding her tightly to him.

'Ruby Scully! I always guessed you were a rebel at heart,' he said, laughing, exhilarated. His dark eyes shone. 'I knew you'd come!'

And then they tumbled ignominiously down the far side of the barricade, landing in a heap at the bottom.

'Can't you two never stay upright?' Ida said, jumping down to join them.

Ruby and Alfie scrambled to their feet as Ocki hobbled painfully towards them.

'Ocki,' Ida scolded, 'you was meant to stay back and be the bloody general giving the orders!' But Ocki ignored her.

'We'll have to build another barricade across West Lane. Coppers are trying to drive the Blackshirts into Southwark Park Road – but they're getting around them.' He grinned. 'Good to see you, Ruby.' He was shaking her hand, breathless and excited, as exhilarated as Alfie. 'Got to go!'

Alfie grabbed Ruby's hand and they ran with Ida to the next muster point. But when they stopped to look back, Ida cried out, 'Oh no, they've got Ocki!' and Ruby looked back to see his hobbling figure being frog-marched off by the well-built copper she'd evaded.

Ida shot off like a loping greyhound and jumped onto the policeman's back, gripping him round the neck till he was forced to let go of Ocki. Ruby was about to run to their aid but Alfie held her back.

'No, leave it to Ida. We're needed here. Come on!'

Soon she was part of a human chain, passing debris and timber and broken fencing to build up the new defences. She waited with Alfie, peering over the top of a large orange crate, at the BUF marchers who'd escaped the police cordon. They were now piling through the demolished first barricade. Ruby felt fear grip her for the first time as a swarm of Blackshirts thundered towards them. Alfie turned to her.

'Time for you to go now, Ruby.' He took her by the shoulders and gave her a little shove. 'Run!'

'You must be joking!' she said. 'I've not come here to run away.'

As the Blackshirts reached them, she was shocked to see that the police seemed to be concentrating their efforts on pulling down the ill-made barrier across West Lane, rather than deterring the Blackshirts. She wasn't sure how it happened but she found herself on the wrong side of the diminishing blockade and within minutes was surrounded by hundreds of police and fascists. The thick-set policeman she'd escaped earlier grabbed her by the arm and dragged her toward a side street. She screamed Alfie's name, but the mayhem and the descending gloom of evening had hidden him from view. She kicked and wriggled, but he gripped her tight all the way to St Crispin's church. On the church noticeboard she saw a sign advertising the harvest festival. Of course, it was today, and by now she'd missed the service at the Central Hall. The church garden had been turned into what looked like a holding pen, guarded by a mounted policemen. Ruby could see prisoners being ferried out to a Black Maria in a nearby side street.

The church garden was crammed with handcuffed prisoners and the vicar was pacing up and down in his long black cassock, begging the police to choose another jail for fear his harvest festival would be a washout and his perishable display ruined. 'We've been preparing for weeks! People won't want to walk through this lot!'

Ignoring him, the officer snapped handcuffs on Ruby's wrists and threw her past the vicar like so much rubbish. As her face smashed against the gravel path, someone yelled, 'Oi you bloody big-brick shithouse, she ain't half the size of you!' Ruby looked up into the bloodied face of Ida. 'Hello, love, y'all right?' her friend asked gently, reaching handcuffed hands to lift Ruby into a sitting position.

Pain shot up Ruby's arm and she looked at her gashed hand. Blood dripped off the ends of her fingers. Ida tore off her blouse sleeve and wrapped it tight around Ruby's hand.

'Got someone wounded here!' she called to a mounted policeman. 'She needs a doctor!' But he stared above their heads and patted his horse's neck as two policemen dragged along another bloodied demonstrator between them and dumped him head first into the vicarage garden.

'Did they get Alfie?' Ruby heard Ocki's voice coming from somewhere behind Ida.

'No, don't think so,' Ruby replied hoarsely.

'Oh, yes, they did,' said the man on the floor.

Alfie hauled himself up to sit beside Ruby, and for some reason began to laugh.

'Alfie! What are you laughing at?' she asked. There was nothing going on that seemed remotely funny.

He pointed to the board proclaiming the name of the church. 'St Crispin's! Ha! That's rich.'

'Why?' Ruby asked bewildered.

He shook his head. 'It's the date of a famous battle, Agincourt. Shakespeare wrote about it. Just seems funny to me – whether we won or not, perhaps our little battle will go down in history one day? Give us some, brother,' Alfie called into the gloom and Ocki's voice emerged from the shadowed garden.

We few, we happy few, we band of brothers;
For he to-day that sheds his blood with me
Shall be my brother; be he ne'er so vile,
This day shall gentle his condition;
And gentlemen in England now a-bed
Shall think themselves accursed they were not here,
And hold their manhoods cheap whiles any speaks
That fought with us upon Saint Crispin's day.

The words sent a chill up Ruby's spine and brought a hush among the rest of the prisoners. Even the vicar of St Crispin's was silenced.

18

Insulting Behaviour

October 1937

She spent the night in the cells beneath Tower Bridge Police Station, along with her friends. There had been over a hundred arrests and it wasn't until early next morning that she was given a dressing for her hand and shown before the magistrate. They were paraded into the courtroom and Ruby was astonished to find the public gallery crammed to bursting. From outside she could hear an angry crowd shouting, 'Down with blue-uniformed fascists! We demand justice!' The magistrate seemed unperturbed.

Ruby had been charged with insulting behaviour, presumably for telling the copper to pick on someone his own size, and she was remanded on bail – which Alfie had assured her the night before that the Labour League of Youth would pay.

Ida had also been charged with insulting behaviour and was remanded with Ruby, but Alfie and Ocki's charges were more serious. They were accused of inciting a violent crowd and their bail was set at ten pounds with a ten-pound surety.

Outside, a demonstration was going on and they were greeted like heroes. Ruby felt hands clapping her on the back and there was even applause for them and the others released on bail that morning.

As the four friends walked home, they felt that same exhilaration which had carried them through yesterday. Bermondsey looked like a battlefield, with streets of boarded-up shops and houses. Debris from countless barricades was strewn far and wide; windows had been smashed and there were dark brown stains – evidence of bloodshed. Ocki put his arm across Ida's shoulders and hobbled on his painful leg; the caliper had been twisted in his arrest and was doing more harm than good. Alfie put his arm around Ruby, supporting her as she strove to keep upright. Every bone in her body felt battered and at some point she'd twisted an ankle. They stumbled like wounded soldiers across the battlefield the day after a great victory.

And it *had* been a victory. For when they came to a newspaper stand, they read the billboard declaring: *THEY DID NOT PASS! BERMONDSEY SAYS 'NO' TO FASCISM!* Alfie bought a copy and they went into a café to read the reports. With the paper spread open on the table for them all to read, Ruby scanned the headlines and offered a silent prayer of thanks that there was no report of guns being fired. It seemed that their final barricade had done its job. The report said it had been a decisive defeat for Mosley, leaving him addressing no one but his own supporters, penned into a side road. And in West Lane, instead of the Blackshirts, it was the anti-fascist demonstrators who had held a rally of their own. They read how the communist speaker had praised Bermondsey for giving the same answer to Mosley as Stepney had twelve months before. It was when Alfie turned the page so that they could read the in-depth report that they saw the dramatic photograph of the high barricade. Atop it, beside a red flag, a man and woman were locked in a triumphant embrace. And it was Ida who stated the obvious.

'Stone me, Ruby. That's you and Alfie!'

Ruby let out a long groan. 'Oh, no, please God Charles never sees this!' She felt sick.

'He can't blame you for following your conscience,' Ocki said, earnestly.

'Don't be a clot, Ocki, darlin'. It's not her conscience Charlie's worried about, it's the feller that's got his arms round her!' Ida tipped her head to one side to better see the photo. 'They do make a lovely couple though, don't they?' She grinned.

'You're the one who's a clot, Ida!' Ruby said, her face hot with embarrassment.

Alfie pushed back his curls. 'Doesn't matter what the cause is, either way Ruby'll be in trouble. It's no joke.'

'Sorry, Ruby,' Ida said, chastened. 'And I'm sorry if we dragged you into this.'

'You didn't! It was the right thing to do and I'd do it all over again. It was my choice to go against Charles, no one forced me.

Ida put a hand over hers. 'Well, what's he gonna do, call off the wedding?'

'He won't call off the wedding,' she said with certainty. Without her, he couldn't go to the mission field.

There was no hope of any of them making it into work that day. So, while Ida and Ocki went back to Fort Road, Alfie walked her all the way home. And all the way home he had his arm around her waist and she didn't suggest he let go. They rehearsed every detail of the day before, laughing at themselves over the beefy policeman she'd challenged and Alfie's ignominious dumping in the vicarage garden. He asked her to describe again how she'd stood in front of Mosley's van.

'Ruby, that was such a brave thing to do. You ought to feel proud of yourself.' She could hear the admiration in his voice.

'But I never persuaded Eric to get off that van, did I?'

'No, but who knows, if it hadn't been for you, he might just have pulled out that gun when things got rough.'

As they turned into St James's Road, he asked, 'What will you say to Charles?'

'I don't know, I'll think about it,'

'Well, you'd better think fast, Ruby...' he said, his voice faltering slightly as his arm dropped from around her waist.

But it was too late, Charles had been standing outside her front door. Now he bolted down the stone steps and strode rapidly towards them. He held a rolled-up newspaper in his hand. Raising it, he launched himself at Alfie, beating him around the head with it.

'Get your filthy hands off my fiancée!' he almost screamed.

Alfie ducked to evade another blow and stepped nimbly back. He threw his hands wide. 'Charlie, you're making a mistake! I was only helping her, she's twisted her ankle.'

'Oh, and were you only *helping* her yesterday?' Charles said, his voice full of sarcasm. 'Helping her to make a disgrace of herself and a laughing stock out of me, were you?' And Alfie was swatted again and again.

'Stop doing that and let us explain, will you?' Alfie said, in a reasonable voice which incensed Charles even further.

'*She* can explain!' Charles said, grabbing Ruby's arm and yanking her to his side. 'You can clear off back to the slum you crawled out of and leave her alone!'

But Alfie stepped forward, reaching out a hand to help Ruby as, wincing, she was forced to put weight on her injured foot. It was a step too far for Charles, who lashed out with a balled fist, catching Alfie a glancing blow to the temple. Furious, Ruby tore herself out of Charles's grasp and rounded on him.

'Now who's making a disgrace of themselves? Here you are, scrapping like a kid in the street, and you're worried about me making a laughing stock of you? Just stop it, Charles!'

The old man next door had stuck his head out of a top-floor window to enjoy the commotion and a delivery boy was leaning against his handcart, grinning at the unexpected entertainment. Charles halted in his tracks and drew a hand across his red, sweaty face.

'Go home, Alfie,' she said, desperate that he should receive no more undeserved blows.

'Will you be all right with him?' Alfie asked, ignoring Charles.

She nodded. 'Please go,' she pleaded and his eyes locked onto hers for an instant before he nodded and walked away.

She walked past Charles and, without a word, limped up the steps to her front door, pulled out the key hanging on a string behind the letter box, and let herself in. She left the door open behind her, not wanting to look back, not caring if Charles followed. She had never seen him so out of control and, as she hobbled along to the kitchen, she dreaded the confrontation that would follow. She eased herself onto a chair and looked up as he followed her in.

'You shouldn't have attacked Alfie like that.' She rubbed her ankle and stared at the bruises patterning her legs. 'It wasn't his fault that I climbed up on the barricade. It's me you should be angry with, not him.'

'I *am* angry at you!' he spat out with a sudden venom that made her jump. He flung the newspaper aside and crossed the room in two strides. Planting his hands on the arms of her chair, he fixed her with eyes like pale stones. With his face inches from her, she could see spittle gathered at the corners of his mouth. 'I'm angry that you disobeyed me. I'm angry that you cared so little for my reputation that you've made an exhibition of yourself and me! But most of all, I'm angry I've been duped by a *whore*! Ruby, virtuous among women? What a joke! To think I've let myself be made a fool of by a slut like you! Has it been going on all this time?' He prodded her chest. 'No wonder you couldn't wait to get rid of me to Derbyshire! No wonder you never wanted to come with me!'

He was bellowing into her face and she leaned back in the chair, desperate to escape the intimacy of his burning rage.

Suddenly he broke away, a look of disgust on his face. 'I can't even look at you. Letting that little yid paw you!'

Ignoring her painful ankle, she jumped up from the chair. He'd turned his back on her and now she grabbed his shoulder, trying to make him face her.

'Don't talk about my friend like that! You're vile!'

He turned a face to her that was creased with hurt and she realized that he was crying. 'Me? Vile? I'm the Christian man you're marrying, I'm the one who's worked night and day to lift myself – and you – up out of this dung heap. How could you put him over me, Ruby? How can you call *me* vile?'

'And how can you call me a whore? All I did was follow my conscience and try to help my brother.'

All his venom had been spent and he took a step towards her, his mouth trembling. He grasped both of her hands. 'Ruby, can you promise me there's nothing between you and that scum? Can you tell me truthfully it's me you love?'

Into her mind, like a surge of light, came the memory of a walk home with Alfie, when she had felt pure joy in someone else's presence. A feeling she had never experienced with Charles. She hesitated.

He dropped her hands as if they had burned him and his mouth curled in disgust. 'You bitch,' he snarled. 'You common, filthy bitch. What have you been doing with him?' He gripped her wrist and twisted it till it burned.

'Nothing! Talking, that's all, just talking. Let me go, Charles, you're hurting me.'

'Oh, I'll let you go. I don't want anything more to do with you, ever!' His face was contorted now into what looked very much like hatred. 'I wanted a worthy Christian helpmeet, but you've turned your back on God to side with these immoral Reds. I wanted a virtuous woman, but *you*!' He flung her hand away from him. 'If I'd wanted a prostitute I'd have gone under the arches at Waterloo.'

The force of his revulsion rocked her. 'Charles! Why are you tormenting yourself? I wouldn't lie to you.'

'You already have! You promised me you wouldn't go to that march! You lie all the time. Well, I'm finished with you, and by the time I've told them at the Mission what sort of woman you are, they'll be finished with you too!'

He snatched the rolled-up newspaper and struck her around the face with it before grabbing his hat and charging out. For an instant she stood, immobile with shock, and then she ran after him. 'Charles, don't go like this, come back!'

But he was already out in the street.

Only when he'd disappeared did she begin to register what he'd done. She put a hand to her smarting face. Of all the wounds she'd suffered over the past two days, this was the hardest to bear, because it was the least deserved. She staggered to her bedroom and, falling onto the bed, rolled herself up into a ball, trying to stifle the racking sobs that erupted from deep inside her. She'd been so certain that having a wife – even one that disobeyed him – was the most important thing to him, that she'd forgotten his irrational jealousy, a jealousy so consuming he'd sabotage his own future because of it. Her sobs would not be suppressed and soon the pillow was stained with tears.

She tried to pray, but how could she expect to be heard, when she'd let God down so badly? Her romance with Charles had always been so tied up with God's plan for her, that now it was as if she'd fallen from a boat in mid-ocean, with no one to pull her on board and reassure her that she would get to her destination. Without Charles, it seemed impossible. She hadn't only failed as his fiancée, she'd failed as a Christian. And soon all the staff and her friends at the Mission would know it.

She must have dozed, for she woke with a start to the rattling of the door handle.

'It's only me, Ruby love.' Aunt Nancy came and sat on the bed. 'I heard the barney. Did he give you a wallop?'

Ruby shook her head. 'Not much of one.'

'A wallop's a wallop, gel, and once they start that old lark you know you're in for a life of it.' She was staring at Ruby's bruised arms and legs. 'By the state of you, it looks like he's kicked you from here to next week!'

'The coppers did that at the march. I got arrested. I'm so sorry I couldn't let you know. Is Davey all right?'

'He's been good as gold and I sent him off to school with me own. I was worried when you didn't come home, but my friend Mrs Nazer in Jamaica Road, her son got arrested and she told me the coppers was collaring everyone they could get their hands on. I guessed you'd be one of 'em. Silly as a sackload, ain't ya?' she said, not unkindly. 'I couldn't help hearing what he was accusing you of, darlin', and you're better off without him. The bastard! Talking like that about our Ruby.' Aunt Nancy reached out a hand to straighten Ruby's tousled hair. 'Now, you stay where you are. I'll get you a cuppa and then you can have a nice little sleep.'

Ruby felt the tears threaten again at her kindness. 'I don't know what I'm going to do, Aunt Nancy. I thought God had a plan for me. Charles always said that I was…' her voice caught on a sob, 'special, but I'm not.'

She felt herself drawn into Aunt Nancy's bony embrace. She smelled of flour and margarine. She must have been baking. 'Don't talk silly, Ruby. That Charlie Best, he's a bully. So good riddance. And as they always say, darlin', there's more churches than Christchurch. You'll be all right. Let me go and get your tea.'

While she was away, Ruby battled to block out the memory of Charles's hate-fuelled rant, but certain phrases played in a loop, piercing her heart. It was a relief when Aunt Nancy came back and interrupted Ruby's tormenting thoughts with hot tea and a warm jam tart.

'Eat it all up. I've brought one for Davey too,' Aunt Nancy added, knowing Ruby would save hers for her brother. 'Let's have a look at this ankle, it's come up like a bleedin' balloon!'

She got a bowl of cold water and made a compress, wrapping it firmly around Ruby's ankle. 'Now keep your foot up and stay off it!'

After Aunt Nancy had covered her up and crept out, Ruby lay staring at the ceiling. What had she done? Ruined her life for a futile moment of rebellion – or even worse, for a man who, however much he might enjoy her friendship, certainly didn't love her as Charles had. Eventually her eyes drooped and she lost herself in topsy-turvy dreams of sailing to Africa with Alfie in a boat made of an abandoned water tank and a corrugated iron fence, with a red flag for a sail.

Ruby wasn't often glad that she had to go to work, but the following day the Paste Kitchen beckoned like a haven in a storm. She'd woken feeling sick with confusion. Should she go to Charles and make him see reason? It was a question she'd been wrestling with all night, but every time she pictured it a wave of nausea overcame her. She must get out of bed now if she wanted to clock on in time. She'd already lost one day's pay and she couldn't afford any more. It would be much easier just to go to work and decide what to do about Charles later.

Easing herself out of bed with every muscle protesting, she woke Davey then limped to the kitchen to get him some breakfast. All she had to give him was one last stale slice of bread and a spoonful of jam. He'd just left for school, when she heard a knock at the door. He'd forgotten something! She hobbled resentfully along the passage, shouting 'Davey, why couldn't you just pull up the key!' before opening the door to a white-faced Ida.

'Alfie told me what happened.' She pulled Ruby into her arms. 'He would have come himself, but he didn't want to get you in no more trouble with that git Charlie Best!'

She let Ida in and waited for her to launch an attack on Charles, but instead her friend poured them tea while she coaxed from Ruby the whole story of Charles's attack on her. Ida made no comment until the point where Ruby confided that he'd finished with her.

'So, you've finally got your way, Ida. He's slung his hook. I know you never liked him, but he did love me, Ida, he did. He made me feel worth something, now I just feel empty...'

Ida said firmly, 'Ruby Scully, you never needed no Charlie Best to make you worth something! I'm not going to say I told you so, but you just had to find out for yourself that he's a wrong un'.' She paused and looked at Ruby uncertainly. 'You have found it out, haven't you?'

Ida was forcing her to answer the question she had been avoiding all night. She nodded. And Ida sighed. 'Thank gawd for that.'

But Ruby couldn't thank God. For if Charles was a wrong'un, it followed that God must be a wrong'un too. They were linked in Ruby's heart like night and day. But she couldn't even begin to explain that to Ida.

'Oh, love, one day you'll see you've had a bloody lucky escape. Come on, let's get to work.' Ida looped Ruby's arm through her own and helped her down the front steps. But they hadn't gone far before it became obvious that Ruby couldn't walk all the way to the factory.

'We'll have to get the bus from The Blue,' Ida said. 'Lean on me till we get there.'

'No, I'll be fine,' Ruby replied, even though each step was agony.

'You're not fine. You ain't got the fare, have you?'

Ruby sighed. 'Our landlady's daughter's come home to look after her mum and made her put up the rent! I've been cutting back on everything else just to keep a roof over us.'

Mrs Nash's daughter had only ever made infrequent visits until the old lady had become bedridden and Ruby suspected she'd sniffed out her inheritance was near and that it wouldn't be the last rent increase now she was in charge of the house.

'I'll pay the fare,' Ida insisted.

The Blue Market was already bustling with women buying their early morning shopping from the hundred-odd stalls lining the road, and the two friends had to push their way through to the bus stop. 'And, Ruby, you shouldn't need to worry about tuppence for a fare; you'll have to ask Dodge to stump up a bit more.'

'He's trying, Ida, he's got a proper job – driving. It don't pay much at the moment and he needs his money for work clothes and lunches and I'd rather he spend it on that and make an honest living.'

Ida looked doubtful. 'Is it full-time, this job?'

'Not yet. But he's hoping to get more hours. He says the firm's very pleased with him.'

'I bet he's still selling bent stuff on the side. Can't you turn a blind eye and ask him for some of the proceeds?'

'No! Anyway, he's promised me he's gone straight because that business with the mob really scared him. He's a different man.'

'Miracles do happen,' Ida said sourly, and added under her breath, 'Or so you say.'

As Ruby lowered herself gratefully on to the bus seat, she asked Ida about Ocki.

'He couldn't go to work today. He can hardly walk without that caliper, so he's gone to the doctors about a new one. Alfie went with him.'

'How is Alfie?' Ruby asked as casually as she could.

'Charlie probably did more damage to him than the Blackshirts and the coppers put together! But he was fuming about Charlie when he come home. He told us Charlie was raving like a madman, said he'd have landed him one, but it would only make things worse for you.'

Ruby put an unconscious hand to her cheek and turned her face to the window. For the rest of the journey she let Ida talk; she was now worrying about the sentences they might all receive. With over a hundred arrests, there were whispers that the judges were deliberately handing out tough sentences in an attempt to avoid any more street battles.

'Do you think they'll put us away?' Ruby said, fearing for Davey if left to Dodge's inept care.

'Ocki reckons you and me should get off with a fine, but him and Alfie could get prison.'

'Prison! But they didn't hurt anyone.'

'I'm not sure any of us are safe, but there's no point worrying till we're certain,' Ida said, trying for her usual optimism, but falling short.

Ruby spent the day trying to hide the pain in her heart behind the unending, ever moving jars, but when they finally hung up their smelly overalls and walked out of the factory arm in arm she knew from the look on Ida's face that she'd failed.

'I'd ask you to come out to the pub tonight, love, and drown your sorrows,' Ida offered, 'but I know it won't do 'apporth of good. You know what you should do?'

Ruby shook her head miserably.

'Go and see Sister Evelyn.'

Ruby leaned her head on Ida's shoulder. 'You're the best of friends, Ida.'

Ida smiled and put two pennies in Ruby's hand. 'I know. Here's the fare, love.'

Sister Evelyn answered the door wearing a floral apron. She didn't seem too surprised to see Ruby.

'Working attire!' She patted the apron. 'I was about to wash up my tea things! Come into the kitchen, Ruby.'

It had obviously been a meagre meal. There was only a saucepan, an egg cup and a tea plate to wash up.

Ruby picked up the tea towel. 'Have you seen Charles?'

'Oh, my dear.' Sister Evelyn looked at her with compassionate eyes. 'I haven't *seen* him, but I've heard. Let's have a cup of tea and you can tell me your side of things.'

They sat in the cosy sitting room, while the fire crackled and

Ruby recounted what had happened. When she'd finished, the woman shifted uneasily in her seat. 'Charles has told a different tale, Ruby. One that reflects rather better on himself.'

'What's he said about me?' she asked.

'He went to the minister, in tears apparently, saying he'd been forced to call off your wedding, that you'd ruined his chances of his ministry *and* his happiness – accusing you of inappropriate behaviour with another man.'

'Inappropriate?' Ruby sat forward on her chair. 'Why, because of that stupid photo of me and Alfie on the barricade?'

'Not just that, he also said you were untrustworthy because you'd lied to him about joining in the demonstration.'

'I changed my mind! I had to try and stop it, Sister Evelyn, especially when I knew Eric would be there with Mosley.'

'Eric was there? Oh, I see.'

'But Eric wasn't the only reason. I wanted to stand up against fascism. If we'd let them march through Bermondsey it wouldn't have stopped till they'd marched through the whole country and then we'd end up like Germany!'

'I can quite understand that. Just last week we sent parcels to a family of German Jewish refugees living in Wild's Rents; they'd fled with nothing but the clothes they stood up in…But Ruby, it wasn't just your behaviour at the march Charles was complaining about. He says that you've been having relations with a man – out of wedlock.'

'He's a liar!' Ruby's anger flared. 'I've got to see him and make him take it back. He can't spread lies about me and get away with it!'

'I'm afraid you can't, my dear. He returned to Derbyshire this morning.'

Ruby slumped in her chair. 'Sister Evelyn, you do believe me, don't you?'

The deaconess took her hand. 'Ruby, I don't think Charles has made up deliberate lies about you.' Ruby's heart sank and then Sister Evelyn went on, 'He believes what he says but I am sure he is absolutely mistaken. Ruby, of course I believe you and so will everyone else.'

It was at the next Basutoland prayer meeting that Ruby discovered not everyone had Sister Evelyn's belief in her. She'd been debating not going to the prayer meeting. She wouldn't be going to Basutoland, and neither perhaps would Charles, not if his being married was a condition. But she told herself that the children of Basutoland still needed saving and so she went. She walked in on a heated discussion between the new leader of the group and the others. It was only when every voice fell silent that she realized they had been talking about her. Some looked shamefaced, two of the girls sniggered. But as she said a nervous hello and took her seat, she noticed that everyone avoided looking at her. The young man who'd taken over the group asked them to be seated and people hid their awkwardness behind closed eyes. Ruby's face burned as she sat through prayers that felt increasingly meaningless to her. When Charles's name was mentioned there were references to 'his trials of faith' and the need 'for the Lord to strengthen his heart,' but there was no mention of *her* heart. Each prayer for him felt like a blow from that rolled-up newspaper Charles had beaten her with, but it was her heart taking the battering this time. Tears squeezed their way through her closed eyes and when the final prayer was said, she dabbed her damp cheeks with a sleeve and was about to scuttle away when the young leader called her over. Perhaps he would now offer her a word of sympathy.

He smiled awkwardly. 'Ruby, I didn't expect to see you tonight, after…' He trailed off, not meeting her eye.

'I don't know what Charles told you, but I still care about the mission work,' she said.

He sighed. 'I'm sorry, then, to have to tell you, that I've prayed earnestly and the Lord has shown me it would be disruptive for you to carry on in this prayer group.'

'But why? I might not be marrying Charles, but I can still pray! Can't I?'

'Ruby, your prayers won't reach God's ears. You've sinned.'

'We've all sinned. But I haven't done what Charles accused me of.'

He looked unconvinced. 'I see. But still, I think it's best if you stay away. This is, after all, Charles's prayer group…'

She stared at him for a long time, till his nervous smile faded. 'Oh, and there was I thinking it was God's prayer group – my mistake.'

She walked out as slowly as she could, under the stares of the other members who had obviously heard every word. Only one followed her: her old friend Molly. She caught up with her on the steps of the Central Hall.

'Ruby! Wait for me,' she called, breathless. 'That was *terrible*, what he just did to you! Terrible! I won't be going back to pray with that lot, Ruby. And for what it's worth, I don't believe a word Charles said about you.'

'Thanks, Molly. And you're right, it's all lies. But it's pointless trying to convince anyone. I reckon I'll have to leave the Mission.'

'No! Don't let them chase you off, you'll just look guilty.'

'I don't think I care,' Ruby said, feeling the sorrow, as if she'd already been bereaved, robbed of the place that had been her second home for so long. 'But, Molly, you shouldn't give up the prayer group for my sake.'

'I'll do it for my sake, then,' Molly said decisively and squeezed Ruby's hand. 'Charles did it out of spite – jealousy, wasn't it? Tell you the truth, Ruby, I never did like him!'

But those like Molly were too few and too uninfluential to stem the tide of judgement against her. After all, Charles was a man, and one of standing in the church – his word counted for more than Ruby's. Looks and tones and avoidances combined to make her feel that her presence at the Mission was making people feel uncomfortable. The only place she still felt at ease was the Welfare Clinic, where the mothers, whose only concern was keeping their children healthy and supplied with free milk and medicines, had no idea who Charles was and the doctors and volunteer nurses were so run off their feet they were grateful for any help they could get. Sister Evelyn begged Ruby not to act hastily, to give herself time to pray and reflect before she cut ties with the Mission, and Ruby could not desert her.

Ruby wasn't sure Alfie would want to see her and she'd half expected him not to be waiting outside St James's. Still, she'd promised Sister Evelyn that she'd pass on the name of a Jewish refugee family to the cross-charity group and so, one evening after work, she made her way to the churchyard.

He was there, sitting on the base of the wide granite slab that edged the church steps. She and hundreds of other Bermondsey children had used it as their slide before the magnificent 'Joy Slide' had been built in the churchyard. He shifted over and patted the smooth granite block for her to join him.

'You look sad, Ruby. I'm sorry about Charles. Ida told me he hit you.'

She gave a small nod.

'Sorry if I was the cause – I'm bloody angry with myself that I left you with him.'

'It's not your fault, Alfie. It's just – just *him*. The way he sees things – it's as if we're *all* guilty.'

He nodded and said, 'Born guilty.'

'That's it.'

'I'm glad you came, Ruby.'

'I'm glad you did too.'

He rested his elbows on his rangy legs. 'So, it's definitely all over between you two?'

She nodded. 'And I'm beginning to think I'm finished with the Mission too.'

He turned a shocked face towards her. 'But why? You love it there!'

'Why? I've been going since I was twelve, Alfie. Volunteered for everything under the sun – poor men's suppers, flower arranging, Sunday School. Eric used to shout at me for neglecting the family while I was doing stuff for the Mission. And now Charles tells them I'm a whore and straight away they believe him.'

It was hard to say the words, hard to acknowledge that even Charles's betrayal hadn't stung half so much as that of the people she'd loved and respected, prayed and served with for the past seven years. Her heart felt too damaged to beat.

'Don't feel sorry for me,' she answered his look of sympathy. 'Feel sorry for them,' she said as she stood up and tipped her head back to gaze at the bell tower of St James's, where the golden dragon rode high above all the small and large troubles that plagued the hearts of the frail humans below.

19

A Different Man

Autumn–Winter 1937

It still felt strange to think of Dodge in a proper job, even if it was one that took him away from home at the drop of a hat. He wasn't a delivery man, he stressed, he chauffeured the bosses of an import firm around London, sometimes to other branches in Liverpool or Southampton. She hadn't seen much increase in the housekeeping money, but it was a part of her life she could be happy about.

She walked home from the churchyard meeting with Alfie and found Dodge getting ready for a night's work. She was surprised he'd only just returned from the Liverpool office. He paused as he straightened his tie in the mirror.

'Look at that face.' He pointed at his own reflection and smoothed back the sides of his blond hair. 'Handsome or what?'

Her father might be lacking in many things, but self-confidence was not one of them. 'Very. Do you know where you're driving tonight?'

'Won't know till I get to the firm,' he said and grinned. 'I like a surprise.'

She was about to ask him if he'd be back tomorrow, when

there was a knock on their kitchen door. Dodge carried on getting ready, while Ruby answered.

It was Mrs Nash's daughter. 'Oh, I wanted to see your father,' she said. 'Is he at home?'

'Yes, come in,' Ruby said, standing aside.

Alice Nash was an unsmiling woman in her late thirties, with what Dodge described as a face like a potato. Ruby thought that her features would certainly have been brightened by the occasional smile.

Dodge was no longer in the kitchen. 'I'll get him,' she said to Alice. She went into the scullery and found the back door to the outside stairs swinging open. 'Oh, Dad, what you done now?' she muttered under her breath.

She went back to the woman.

'I'm sorry, Alice, he's gone to work.'

'Work? Is that what you call it? Well, you can tell him when he comes home that I'm due three weeks' rent, and if he can't pay me this week you'll be out on your ears, the lot of you!'

'Three weeks? That can't be right; I've got it down as paid in the rent book, I'm sure. Please come in.'

With a sinking feeling Ruby rushed to the drawer in the kitchen cabinet where the rent book was kept and flicked it open. She jumped as Alice Nash leaned over her shoulder. The woman put a stubby finger on the date column.

'See! Not a farthing's rent has he paid me. All he's given me's been promises – and I'll tell you something for nothing, he's picked the wrong one to try and sweet talk. I'm not one of his tarts!'

'I'm sorry, Alice. He told me he was taking care of it. You know I've always paid the rent...'

'Well, more fool you for believing him. He's taken advantage of my mother long enough. I could get twice what I'm charging you.' She folded her arms, waiting, as if she expected to be paid there and then.

'I'll get you the rent, I promise.'

'I'll give you till next week. No longer!'

When she'd gone, Ruby sat with a thumping heart. Alice Nash was right. More fool her for believing Dodge when he'd insisted he was now a 'different man'. Where could she find four weeks' rent money! She'd never been so much in arrears. Whatever she'd had to go without, she'd always made sure the rent was paid. Why hadn't Dodge just told her he couldn't afford it?

She went to Dodge's bedroom, not even bothering to look in his hiding place above the wardrobe; instead she looked inside it. He'd bought two suits, saying he needed to be dressed smartly for his work. The second best one and a woollen overcoat were hanging there. She threw them on the bed. They were going to the pawnshop. He wouldn't be happy, but he'd got them into the mess, he could get them out of it!

Before she began folding the clothes, ready to wrap in a bundle, she went through the pockets for small change. She found half a crown and some coppers in the suit. But in the deep overcoat pockets she found nothing but a train ticket. It must be very old; she couldn't remember the last time Dodge had been on a train. She examined the ticket stub. It was a return ticket to Coulsdon and the smudged date on the ticket was for the previous week. But that was impossible. Last week he'd been driving his employers around Liverpool. Unless he'd been lying to her about his 'job' all along.

She rummaged through every drawer, nook and cranny in his bedroom, taking every penny of spare cash she could find and anything that could be pawned: a pair of cufflinks, a tiepin, ties and shirts. The last thing she debated over was his wedding ring, which he'd stopped wearing years before. Her mother had given it to him, which made it sacred to Ruby. She held it in the palm of her hand, asking permission, and she heard her mother's voice warning her: 'Always make sure you pay the rent. Don't matter if you go hungry, don't matter if you're freezing, you've got to keep a roof over your head – always.'

'Thanks, Mum,' she whispered, and put the wedding ring in with the bundle.

Very early next morning she joined the queue outside the pawnshop. Women and children, each with their carefully wrapped bundles, stood stamping in the misty post-dawn light, eager to get a few shillings before work or school to get them through the day. Some of the children were barefoot and she wondered how many had been forced to put their shoes into pawn so their families could eat.

Once inside, and in the privacy of the screened-off booth, the young assistant shook his head before he'd even examined the bundle. He always did it, but today she wanted to take the greasy head in her hands and screw it off his skinny neck. He kept her waiting while he picked through her father's belongings and peered at the wedding ring under an eyeglass then told her she could have three pounds for the lot. It was just enough to cover four weeks' rent with a bit over to buy a bucket of coal.

Dodge was away for two days. He came home in the evening, after Davey had gone to bed, giving her a cheery kiss on the cheek. 'You been, all right, Ruby?' he asked and emptied his suit pockets, flinging a pound note and some change down. 'Here y'are, love, a few bob for the housekeeping,' he said, and stuffed the rest of the notes back into his pocket. 'Got paid a bit more this time, 'cos I ended up taking 'em to Liverpool again.'

'That's where you went last week, wasn't it?'

'Yes, gel. I'll just change me shirt. I'm going down the Upside Down.'

She let him go.

Two seconds later he was back. 'Ruby! All me bleedin' clothes has gone!' He stood at the kitchen door in his vest, looking bemused.

'I know.'

'Where are they?'

'They've gone to pay Alice Nash. What did you think she come knocking for? You run away because you knew she'd come for the rent! And you knew I didn't have a penny to pay it! Your clothes are in the pawnshop – otherwise me and Davey would have been out on the streets next week.' She looked into his wide blue eyes and saw him calculating which lie would be the most effective. 'Don't even bother to explain.'

She turned away and took down the train ticket she'd tucked behind the clock.

'But there's something I do want an explanation for. Why've you been lying to me about this so-called job of yours?' She handed him the ticket. 'What was you doing in Coulsdon when you was meant to be in Liverpool? And where've you've been the last two days, because I'll bet it wasn't Liverpool this time either! What's going on?'

He screwed up the ticket and threw it into the meagre fire. 'That ain't mine.'

'Well, it was in *your* overcoat. I took all your change, by the way, and your wedding ring.'

'You had no right to touch that! My Rachel give me that.'

'And *your* Rachel told me I could take it!'

'What are you talking about, you silly mare? Are you hearing voices from the dead now you've give up God?'

She clamped her lips together so that she didn't swear at him. 'Just because I don't go to meetings every week don't mean I've given up God! And you haven't told me why you're lying about your "job". You've been working for that mob all this time, haven't you?'

'No! No, I ain't gel. You got that wrong.'

But she knew too well the signs of his guilt. 'Dad! You *promised* me you was a different man, but you're not. You're the same lying bastard you always was!'

'Ruby! That ain't like you. Swearing! What's got into you? I think I preferred you when you was holy!'

'Oh, go to the pub, Dad. I don't even care what you've been doing, just don't pretend you can help me with the rent – or anything else.'

Dodge stood in front of her like a shame-faced schoolboy. 'Ruby, it's not too bad, what I'm doing. They just call me in when they need someone to turn up, looking smart, distract the shop assistants, while a couple of the boys steam in and lift whatever they can. It's easy money. No violence or nothing. Truth is, Ruby, I'm always gonna be in their pocket now. I thought it'd be easier if I said it was an honest job, and then you wouldn't turn your nose up at the money I was bringing home...' He patted her shoulder warily. 'I suppose that don't matter now that Charlie's slung his hook and you've given up the meetings.'

She walked out, leaving him standing there in his vest.

'I'll just wear the shirt I had on, then, shall I?' he called after her.

The autumn days turned into a chilly winter and she heard nothing from Charles. There were times when she was grateful for his disappearance from her life, but the break had been so unexpected, so final, that she found herself searching for more reasons for it than the ones he'd given her. Was it really because he believed she'd been unfaithful with Alfie, or was that just an excuse? Wasn't it rather her lack of schooling and her parentage? She was too common, too tainted. There were moments when she accepted that he'd simply been mad with jealousy. But when she thought of his accusations and her feelings about Alfie, she doubted herself again. Perhaps Charles had seen into her heart, had known, long before she had, that, for her at least, Alfie was becoming something more than a friend.

When she'd last met him in the churchyard, Alfie had suggested there was no longer any need for them to meet there. Without Charles to object, he said it seemed only sensible for her to come to the Labour Institute and join them for the cross-charity meetings. Ruby felt an instant unsettling pang of disloyalty to Charles. It was oddly disorienting, to feel allegiance to someone who'd abandoned her. But she supposed all those connections between them wouldn't unravel in a day, and no doubt it would do her good to concentrate on helping those who were suffering from much more than a broken heart.

On the night that she would normally have been praying for Basutoland, she walked to Fort Road and made a nervous entrance into the Labour Institute. Alfie was already calling the meeting to order when she crept in and sat at the back. She saw him smile and beckon her forward.

'Plenty of room up the front here, Ruby.'

As she got out of the seat and walked forward, several people turned to stare.

'Ruby's been our valued representative at the Methodist Mission for some time, but she'll be working much more closely with us from now on,' he said, answering the questioning stares.

People smiled encouragingly and one girl gave her a solitary round of applause. She felt herself longing for the familiarity of the Mission and then she saw Ida at the far side of the front row, flapping a hand at her.

'Spare seat over here, love!' she called and Ruby put her head down and hurried over.

'So embarrassing!' she hissed at her friend. 'He couldn't have made me feel more awkward if he'd tried.'

'He's a bloke, what do you expect?'

Alfie began with the first topic on the agenda: the Jewish refugees who'd fled Nazi Germany and had ended up in Bermondsey.

'Ruby, could you tell us about the refugee family you've referred to us. What are their living conditions? Have they got work, school?'

She felt Ida's hand in her back. 'Stand up and speak up,' she ordered.

Ruby stood, her legs trembling slightly. In the Mission's mixed meetings the men generally did all the talking; only in the Sisterhood or Mother's Meetings did the women have free rein.

She clenched her fists and looked at Alfie's expectant face. He obviously had no qualms about asking her opinion, and if he didn't doubt her, then she felt bold enough not to doubt herself.

'The father was arrested before they could get out of Germany. They accused him of being a communist, but his wife says all he'd done was upset their next-door neighbour who went and informed on her husband to the Nazis. The family had to leave without him. They're living in a boarding house in Wild's Rents, but their money's run out. The mother's a qualified teacher, but she's looking for cleaning jobs, anything really. The three children should be in school, but they can't speak English.'

'Why did they come to Bermondsey? the girl who'd clapped asked.

'No family,' Ruby said, finding her mouth was too dry to swallow. She licked her lips. 'Just the Mission. They're standing as guarantors for some German-Jewish families.'

'What does that involve?'

'Well, our government says to come here they have to have at least fifty pounds in the bank—'

'Typical!' Ida chipped in. 'If you're poor you don't get a chance.'

'Not unless someone guarantees the fifty pounds for them. We've done it for a few families and they've mostly settled in Bermondsey because of that. But it's not that they actually get the money to spend. It's more like a deposit in the pawnshop – they're your clothes but you can't wear them.' This caused a ripple of laughter and Ruby wondered if she'd shown her ignorance.

'And we all know what that feels like!' Alfie grinned and then looked around the hall. 'Suggestions for which local charities could help out this family?'

Several people called out at once and Ruby sat down, grateful to be out of the limelight.

'Well done, darlin'. Cracked 'em up your first meeting. Not bad!'

Afterwards, at Ida's flat, they all quizzed her on her experience at the meeting.

'I could've done without Alfie dragging me up the front! But I was surprised how much everyone knew!'

'You mean they're a load of clever dicks!' Ida quipped, 'Like my brain box here.' And she ruffled Ocki's hair, which he pretended to be irritated by.

Ruby laughed. 'No, I mean all the suggestions for helping the refugee families. I'd never have thought of the Quakers.'

There had been half a dozen charities mentioned but the Quakers seemed the most promising. One of the young men mentioned that their Labour Councillor, Ada Salter, had contacts at the Peckham Meeting House who had sent a mercy mission out to Germany and got several Jewish families out of the country. They had funds set aside for clothing and housing, would even take children into a Quaker school if the parents wanted.

'It did give me hope for our refugee family in Wild's Rents.' She smiled, feeling somehow more hopeful for herself as well. Her friends were looking at her with undisguised pleasure.

'I knew you'd like us if you'd just give us a try,' Alfie said.

'Oh, I always liked you...' she replied and Alfie held her gaze before she blushed and added, 'all.'

They talked for another hour but when the conversation moved to their court dates the following week, she grew a little less hopeful. The more Ocki insisted she and Ida would get off with fines, the less confident Ruby became, and she got up to go.

'I can't believe I'm hoping for a fine. I won't be able to pay it and they'll lock me up anyway!' she said, shrugging on her coat.

'There's a fund for people that can't afford the fines. Don't worry.' Alfie had jumped up. 'I'll walk you home.'

Outside, the night was icy but crystal clear.

'Glad we didn't meet in the churchyard?' he asked.

'We would have been frozen!' She had no gloves, so she stuffed her hands deep into her jacket pockets. It was thin, but she had no money to get her woollen coat out of pawn.

'You look frozen right now!' he said. He slipped off his trench coat and draped it over her before she had a chance to protest.

'Yes, you can,' he said, settling the coat on her shoulders. It was only now she realized how tall he was and how broad his shoulders were.

'Now *you'll* get cold.'

'Me? No!' He puffed out his chest and struck a mock pose. 'I'm a man!'

She laughed. 'I have got a warm coat,' she said, defensively.

'Hmm, and I know why you're not wearing it. Ida told me about your rent going up.' She liked that he hadn't put the blame on Dodge; it was only she who could criticise her father.

'You were great tonight, Ruby. Sorry I made you feel awkward.'

'Oh, I just ain't got much confidence, Alfie.'

He pushed back his wayward curls, put an arm around her and gave her an encouraging squeeze. 'Is it any wonder? Between Charles and the church you've been in a cocoon – but those butterfly wings...' He looked down at her, his straight mouth curving into a slow smile, 'I can see they're just about to open.'

If words alone could make her fall in love with someone, these were the ones. Just hearing them gave her a sense of freedom, an inkling that there was a different Ruby waiting to wake up.

'Do you really think so?'

He nodded.

'Charles used to say I was like a precious stone – a ruby. But I always disappointed him.'

'You know what they say about gemstones? The most interesting ones have a flaw, it's what makes them unique. Maybe you shouldn't try to be perfect any more, just be yourself. And what about that dream you had, to be a teacher?'

They approached the gas lamp where she'd so often said goodnight to Charles.

'A teacher? That'll never happen now.'

'Ruby! We want to change the world, don't we? Well, let's start with ourselves – we're young enough to do it. Don't give up on yourself just because Charlie Best did.'

'He used to promise he'd raise me up out of all this. ' She flung an arm out towards her home.

'Go to night school. Get your matriculation. Then apply to Goldsmiths to train as a teacher. You can do it, Ruby.' He spoke as if these were the easiest things in the world to accomplish at the same time as working all the shifts she could in Crosse's while struggling to keep Davey fed and clothed. But it was as if his confidence in her was like the small breath that lights a kindling fire.

'I could do it…' she mused.

'You could.'

She was glad when he walked her past the gas lamp and insisted on seeing her right to her door. On the top step, she handed him his coat then realized she didn't want him to go and it seemed that neither did he, for they spent what seemed an eternity just smiling at each other, before he forced out a 'Goodnight, Ruby,' turned, leaped down the steps two at a time and strode off with his coat slung over his shoulder.

'Don't go,' she whispered and clamped her hand over her mouth, realizing she'd spoken a thought that had bubbled up in spite of herself. 'Stupid, Ruby. Stupid,' she muttered, watching his receding figure, noting his easy, long stride, the head of curly hair. How different he was to Charles: the tight band around her chest that had been there in all her dealings with Charles was entirely absent. Perhaps, she told herself, that constriction hadn't been love or longing after all...

She grudgingly admitted that Dodge had his uses. He had been going through with her everything that would happen in court, even down to the way she should dress. He'd already voluntarily surrendered the money to get her best woollen coat out of pawn.

'Now, when you're in front of the magistrate you mustn't look shifty,' he said the day before the hearing. 'Don't look at your feet the way you do when you get shy, look the beak in the eyes, but not too bold either. If he stares at you for too long, just look down a second, demure. Be natural! Like this.' And Dodge gave an impersonation of a young girl fluttering her eyelashes, which at least gave Ruby a laugh.

'And when you say your name and plead guilty, don't mumble. Say it.'

She repeated her name and the guilty plea.

'Louder! I know you're nervous, but these judges is always Mutt and Jeff and it drives 'em up the wall if they can't hear what you're saying.'

He offered to come with her, but she didn't think that would do her cause much good.

'I'm going with Ida and the Diamond boys.'

'Oh.' Dodge narrowed his eyes. 'You been seeing a lot of them? One of 'em's your mate's chap, ain't he?'

She nodded. 'Ocki.'

'What about the other one, the curly-haired geezer. He's seen you home a couple of times, eh?' And he grinned.

'There's nothing going on, we're just friends.'

'Well, I reckon your *friend* might be going down.' His grin vanished. 'And love, you got to be prepared yourself.'

'Ocki thinks me and Ida might get off with fines.'

'I hope he's right, darlin'. I heard from a bent bobby I know that the judges are making examples of people who wallop coppers.'

'None of us walloped a copper!'

'Well, quite a few of 'em ended up with blood on their faces, so it stands to reason some of your lot are ending up in nick! We just got to hope it ain't you, Ruby love.'

Next day as they were sitting on the hard bench in the gloomy waiting area outside the courtroom, she relayed Dodge's instructions to Ida, with an additional warning of her own for her friend not to lose her temper and swear at the magistrate.

'Don't worry, Ruby, I'll have that judge believing I'm a bleedin' nun by the time I'm finished! Mum's got the priest to speak for me!'

Ruby laughed. 'Your mum must have said a few Hail Marys to get him to agree to that! Still, why not? I've got a character reference from Sister Evelyn.'

'I'm not really worried about meself, it's my Ocki,' Ida said in a low voice, glancing over at the two brothers who were reading the court room schedule posted on a notice board. 'They'll eat him alive in nick.'

Ruby squeezed Ida's hand hard. 'He'll be fine,' she reassured her, but as Ocki walked towards them, wincing occasionally, she began to worry for him herself. Not many people saw past the limp and the lopsided body. But Ruby had come to know that his sweet features were a reflection of his nature. He'd always had pain, but since the rough and tumble of the march it had got worse. They wouldn't be gentle with him in jail, she knew that much. If even Dodge had needed protecting, how would Ocki fare?

The court was running late, but when finally the clerk beckoned Ruby and Ida forward, Alfie helped her up. 'You'll be all right, Ruby,' he said earnestly, his white face suddenly more frightening than reassuring.

Ida gave Ocki a kiss. 'If they put me away, Ruby'll come and cook your dinner, won't you Rube?' she laughed, and the two friends walked the short distance to the court room. It felt to her as if they were Christians being led to the lions.

Ruby followed Dodge's instructions to the letter. The steely-eyed magistrate listened as Sister Evelyn's reference was read out and the beefy policeman gave evidence. He sniffed as he regarded first Ruby and then the constable. 'This young Christian woman has obviously been led astray by undesirable Bolshevik elements and her own youthful enthusiasm, and I hardly think she could have inflicted any physical damage on the constable here. But she was certainly *most* insulting. I hereby fine you one pound, young lady, and I suggest you keep to your church fellowship in future. There is a Bible verse to the effect that: *Bad company corrupts good character*!'

He would have to quote Charles at her. She was about to break the golden rule and be rude to the beak, when Ida saved her. She pushed Ruby down as she stood up herself. Now Ida's long-abandoned church came to her aid too. The priest spoke for her in glowing terms and she too was given a one-pound fine. 'Me mum must have promised our Bridget to the nunnery!' she muttered when she sat down. 'I hope it don't mean I'll have to start going to mass again.'

When they both walked out, Ruby saw relief on the boys' faces. Ocki kissed Ida and, to Ruby's great embarrassment, Alfie gave her a kiss on the cheek. He whispered, 'Ruby, I think I might get put away. If I do, will you try to visit me – just once before they send me down?'

She tried not to read too much into his request. 'Of course I will, but you and Ocki said it'd be a fine.'

'We said anything we could think of not to worry Ida – or you. But I was too visible on the march.'

'But you didn't hit a policeman.'

He pulled a face. 'I did give one a bit of a tap after they dragged you away. Well, they shouldn't have manhandled you like that!'

She thought of Dodge's warning that the judges would be harsh on those who'd attacked the police. What if he was right?

20

Waiting

Winter 1937

When Ocki walked free from the courtroom, Ida ran to him and lifted him clear off the ground. 'Crack a smile, for gawd's sake! You got off!' Ida said, but he straightened his suit jacket and began walking awkwardly towards Ruby. She could see that his expression wasn't simply unhappy, it was one of tight-lipped rage.

'Where's Alfie?' Ruby said, with a sinking feeling.

Ocki shook his head. 'He got two months.'

Ruby felt as if all the air had been knocked from her lungs. 'Two months! Well, at least the judge let you off,' she said, through dry lips.

'I'd rather have gone down with him.' Ocki's misery was palpable.

'But why only him?'

'Judge said he wouldn't lock up a cripple and I hadn't actually assaulted anyone. Doesn't matter that I was the bloody ringleader! Even the judge only sees this,' he said bitterly, thumping his twisted leg

'Who cares if he did? Just be thankful it's not you going to Brixton.' Ida put a hand to his pallid cheek. 'You wouldn't have lasted five minutes, love.'

But Ocki brushed her hand away. 'I'm going for a walk. Need to clear my head.'

Ida was about to follow, but Ruby put out a restraining hand.

'He needs me, Ruby!'

Ruby shook her head. 'Leave him be, Ida. He wants to be on his own.' She had seen how the young man was near to tears and, though he mostly made fun of his own infirmities, she thought perhaps tears were a weakness too far for him to show today.

'S'pose you're right.' Ida looked uncharacteristically teary herself. 'He'll be feeling so bad that he's got away with it and Alfie's not.'

Ruby nodded silently. 'Ida, listen. I promised Alfie if this happened I'd go and see him before he got put away. Will you come with me and find out what I have to do?'

'We'll ask the clerk. You'll have to pretend to be his sister or his fiancée.' She nodded. 'We'll say that, shall we? Never know, might be true one day.' She winked at Ruby who was just relieved to see a glimmer of her friend's usual robust optimism return.

There was no need for subterfuge, the clerk simply assumed that Alfie was her 'young man' and waved her and Ida down to the basement. Alfie's holding cell smelled strongly of carbolic, masking vomit. No doubt a sentence would cause nausea in many people, but Alfie looked almost relaxed.

'How's my brother?' he asked as she sat opposite him.

'Upset that he's not here with you.'

'Well, I'm happy he's not.'

'That's what Ida told him, but he went off.'

Alfie nodded. 'Ida'll bring him round. Listen, Ruby, the reason I asked you to come is... Well, Ida's a brick, but she'll need help. He can get a bit difficult when he's really upset, stops talking. Can you go round and check on them sometimes, make sure Ida's getting out and tell her not to fuss too much? That only makes him worse.'

'I won't leave them on their own. But Alfie, what about you? What can we do for you?'

'I want to ask you to wait.' His eyes held hers, until she looked down, blushing. 'I'll miss you. All this time we've been friends and I've grown... fond of you.' He stopped short, and licked dry lips, clearly embarrassed that the constable guarding him had developed a snigger. He dropped his voice even further. '*Can* you wait?'

'It's eight weeks, Alfie. I think I can manage that.' She ventured a small smile, understanding that he wasn't referring just to the length of time involved but to the belief she would have to hold on to. A belief in an unspoken feeling. Surprised that she didn't feel more devastated that she wouldn't see him for two months, she realized that her mind had honed in on one thing alone: he'd said he was fond of her. Love was ruthless sometimes, caring only that it should be returned, no matter what the circumstances.

Ruby walked home with Ida and she stayed until Ocki returned to Fort Road. Ocki would speak to neither of them. He sat in the small sitting room, staring into empty space. Eventually Ida got up and gave Ruby a wink. 'You'd better be getting back to your Davey, hadn't you?'

Ruby took the hint. Ida saw her to the door and kissed her. 'Thanks for coming back with me, love, but I might be able to bring him out of it once I've got him on his own.'

'Was it worth it, Ida?'

'The march?'

'Yes.'

Her friend considered for a while. 'Too bloody right it was! See you tomorrow, darlin.'

It was still early afternoon and she didn't in fact need to be back for Davey for another hour. She decided to go and see Sister Evelyn, who would have just finished overseeing the mid-week Sisterhood meeting. The women were emerging from the Central Hall as she arrived, most dressed in respectable brown and black coats and squashed pudding-basin hats, flat shoes and thick stockings. There was a definite Sisterhood look. They were women who could spare an afternoon during the working week. Some of them she'd been on familiar terms with since she was a youngster and many now deliberately looked the other way. But Mrs Mongey, who'd found her faith while grieving for little Jenny, stopped to take her hand.

'Hello, me darlin'. We ain't seen you for a while.' Kind eyes in her careworn face searched Ruby's. 'I don't care what no one says, love. I don't believe the lies that Best boy's been spreading about you. You're a bleedin' angel. As much of an angel as my lovely Jenny is.' And Mrs Mongey gave Ruby's cheek a gentle pinch, a gesture which brought tears of gratitude and sadness to Ruby's eyes.

Sister Evelyn joined them. 'Have you come to see me?' she asked eagerly and Ruby felt a heavy guilt rest on her, for what she must tell her dear champion and friend.

She had promised Sister Evelyn she would try, and she had. But she knew in her heart that this place was no longer hers.

'I know you've found it hard to put up with gossip and stares, my dear, but there are many people who realize the truth. No, Ruby, no, you mustn't give up the Mission! Not before I've gone to the minister and made him see that your name needs to be cleared.'

Ruby doubted even Sister Evelyn's voice would count against Charles's. She shook her head.

'I'm grateful, Sister Evelyn, but it just doesn't feel like home any more.'

'All right, then,' Sister Evelyn went on, undeterred. 'For the time being, you *must* go to services at the Manor Methodist's. *Not forsaking the assembling of ourselves together,* Ruby! Hebrews 10:25.'

Ruby knew of the smaller Methodist church at the end of The Blue and she left, promising that she would try to go, but she knew it wouldn't feel like home there either.

When she arrived back at St James's Road, she was surprised at how overwhelmingly grateful she was for Dodge's presence. For once he had no irritating quip or selfish concern to voice. He put his arms round her and held her for a long time in a strong, silent embrace.

'Thank Christ you're home,' he said eventually. 'I even said a bloody prayer!' And she forgave him the blasphemy.

Ruby couldn't go to Brixton prison – the fares alone would cripple her fragile domestic economy and Alfie knew that. So, she wrote to him every week; carefully, checking her grammar in a book borrowed from Spa Road library, and slowly, so as not to blot the notepaper, which was a luxury she could ill afford. Every letter had to be worthy of its stamp and she filled each one with the goings on in the League of Youth, the successes with the Jewish refugee families and even the truth about Ocki's continuing bout of depression. She confessed to him her loneliness. That bottomless chasm that opened up each Sunday morning when her first impulse to jump out of bed in time for the service was replaced by the knowledge that she no longer had a place to go. She always signed off in the same way, 'With fond regards'. It sounded so oddly formal, and yet she trusted he would decipher the code. It was the word he'd used himself, 'fond', and so she was happy to commit herself to this fondness. But, sometimes, before she drifted off to sleep, she would practice another word. Love.

By the end of those two months she felt that Alfie knew her better than anyone else in the world, apart from Ida. But she didn't feel as if she knew him half so well as Charles, whose pent-up emotions, bashed down like a blacksmith's hammer on hot iron, were always bursting forth in sparks and fire. Yet she felt that Alfie had emotions that ran much deeper than Charles's, emotions that Ruby had only ever glimpsed, like an underground spring that surfaced tantalizingly, only to disappear beneath the ground again. She felt he was holding something in reserve, as if he was waiting, just as he'd asked her to wait.

On the day of Alfie's release, Ida and Ocki were throwing a little party for him at the Fort Road flat. Ruby had been through the old clo' market with a fine-tooth comb and eventually found a ruffle-fronted white blouse and a silky blue skirt. She'd saved up for a new pair of rayon stockings and had asked Ida to trim her straight, blonde bob. When she was ready she looked in the mirror and was appalled at the green tinge in her face. She felt literally sick with excitement.

It was Alfie, she kept telling herself, only Alfie. And yet she trembled just because it was Alfie. When she arrived, Ida took her coat.

'What's the matter with you? Had a barney with Dodge?'

'No – and why would there be anything the matter with me?'

'Because you look sick as a dog.'

Ruby drew in another long breath.

'Sorry, love. I forgot to say you look beautiful too!' Ida said, stepping back to look at her. 'He's in his bedroom. Tittivating. Come to think of it, he's got the same look on his face you have. Terrified!' Ida gave a wicked chuckle and guided her into the small sitting room, where a number of Labour Youth were already gathered. 'I'll tell him you're here.'

'No, Ida! Don't draw attention,' Ruby hissed, but Ida ignored her and hurried to find Alfie. Within minutes she appeared in the doorway, followed by a tall beanpole with a shaved head. She was so used to seeing him with an abundance of hair she was surprised by the neat, almost delicate and somehow fragile-looking head. His dark eyes – looking larger than ever in a sharp-featured, shockingly thin face – locked on to hers and, not caring if she drew attention to herself now, she ran to him.

'Alfie, what have they done to you?'

He took both her hands in his and said in a low voice, 'Nothing that matters now.'

'They've starved you! And your hair!' She touched the harsh bristles. 'Why didn't you tell me anything about this?'

He took hold of her hand. 'Wouldn't have done any good. We'll have plenty of time to talk later.' He drew her forward into the room and only then did she realize that everyone was looking at them in amused silence. Ida, as usual, came to her rescue. She grabbed Alfie's hand and raised it like a prize fighter's in a ring.

'Hip hip hooray! Bermondsey said no to fascism!'

A cheer followed from the guests and Alfie was lost to her as everyone came forward to greet the conquering hero. Except, Ruby thought, that what she'd seen in his eyes had been far from conquering. She eased herself out of the crush and found herself standing next to Ocki, who was staring grimly at Alfie.

'He wrote to me every week and never said a word about – that. Do you know what went on?' Ruby asked.

Ocki shook his head. 'He didn't tell me either. I only found out when he got home. Turned out some of the prison officers were Mosley men. They singled out anti-fascists, especially the Jews, spat in their food, kept them out of the showers unless they wanted to give them a beating. I'm glad I didn't go in with him now. I'd have only been a hindrance.'

'Why didn't he say? We could have complained, gone to the Governor!'

'Ruby, they don't run Brixton prison the same way as they do Bermondsey Central Hall!'

'Oh, you'd be surprised, Ocki: when people get a bit of power over others, the same old things go on.'

He gave her an appreciative look. 'You're waking up, Ruby.'

She sighed and said sadly, 'Someone shook me.'

Ocki laughed. 'That's the sort of thing Alfie would say! You and my brother really are a pair, Ruby. Go and rescue him, I'm going to get drunk.'

She wasn't sure if Ocki had paid her a compliment. But she knew herself how Alfie's letters had influenced her. She found herself admiring the way he thought about things, how he could turn something on its head and make her look at it in a different way. She waited for an opportunity and, when Ida announced the sandwiches were coming out, she went to Alfie.

'Do you want something to eat?' he asked and she shook her head. 'Walk?'

They stole out while everyone was occupied at the food table, Alfie linking arms with her as they walked towards Thorburn Square without speaking. With its Victorian church in the centre and once-grand houses, the square gave a false impression of prosperity in the darkness. But Ruby knew that every house was occupied by at least three families sharing one outside toilet and with no bathrooms. Still, it looked pretty, with the bare-branched old chestnuts surrounding the churchyard. Alfie sat on the low wall of one of the houses.

'It wouldn't have done any good to tell you what it was like inside, Ruby,' he said before she'd even asked. 'It would only have worried you all, and besides, I could put up with it for two months. It was the ones with longer sentences I felt sorry for.'

'But I could have brought you food!' He was holding her hand and she traced his bony knuckles with her forefinger. 'There's nothing left of you! I'm so sorry, Alfie, that I couldn't help you.'

'You've made my point. See how miserable you are, even now, when I'm out? It would have been twice as hard when I was inside. I know you'd have gone without so you could get me food and soap and all the things you can't even afford for yourself and Davey.'

'I *knew* you wasn't telling me everything, I just knew it.'

He intertwined his fingers with hers, stuck out his chin and said, 'You were right.' And she saw there was to be no more argument about his silence.

She waited until a lone constable on his beat had passed them, before she asked, 'How are you feeling now?'

He scratched at his stubbly scalp beneath his cap. 'Cold, without my hair!'

'Ah, your lovely curls,' she said, looking up at him, held by his warm, brown eyes.

A solitary car coughed and chugged around the square, but its engine noise seemed to come from far off, as the silence built between them. He dipped his head and it seemed as if time slowed as she felt his lips on hers. His kiss was tender, familiar and strange at the same time, with none of the hard insistence she'd felt from Charles. Instead her lips seemed to melt into his. But though the kiss was gentle, her heart thudded violently as if it might burst through her chest. And when his mouth left hers, she felt a completeness, knowing that there would be more. She was astonished. How could she not have known that those feelings of emptiness she'd experienced with Charles had been a warning? When Charles had held her, she'd felt herself a weak and ignorant girl, but in Alfie's arms, she felt strong and alive.

'Can we stay here forever?' she whispered.

'Yes.' A slow smile spread across his emaciated face. 'Here, we'll stay here...' he put a hand on his heart, 'but not on this wall. We must get back or Ida'll send out the search parties!'

He stood up and put his arms around her and held her tightly against his chest. 'I've imagined this every night.'

'Every night for two months, really?'

He laughed. 'No. Every night for two years.'

'What?'

'Oh, yes, Ruby Scully. Don't you remember the first time we met?'

'In Barnham Street?' she replied, wonderingly.

'And I fell head over heels.'

'On the cobbles. Yes, I remember.'

He shook his head and a thumping, riotous kind of joy she'd never known caught her throat, so that she could barely speak. 'All this time?'

He nodded. 'From the first minute I saw you.'

'You never told me...'

'You knew.'

She thought for a minute. He was right. 'Yes, I suppose I did. But there was Charles and—'

'Yes, there was Charlie. But, Ruby, you don't need to explain anything! I just want to ask one thing – can you love me too?'

'I've loved you for a long time, Alfie.'

'You never told me!'

She took in a deep breath, revelling in the simplicity of it all. 'You knew.'

He put his hands around her waist and lifted her high into the air, so that she had to grip his wide shoulders to anchor herself. When she came down to earth, they kissed again and walked back to Fort Road, stopping every few yards to look at each other and exchange eloquent, wordless smiles.

The Christmas of 1937 proved much happier than the previous one. Alfie had no faith but socialism, so he didn't object to sitting down for Christmas dinner with Ruby's family. She might not have been to Christmas service this year, but when Ruby reflected back on the violence of last year's festivities, she counted herself blessed.

Ida had been ecstatic that Ruby and Alfie had finally, as she said, 'come to their senses and bowed to the bleedin' obvious.'

The two couples spent more time together and Ruby found her love for Alfie beginning to heal the emptiness left by the loss of her old life at the Mission. Dodge was surprisingly supportive of her new romance, giving Alfie the dubious compliment of being 'better than the last one.'

Alfie had taken the Christmas fortnight to recuperate at home, before returning to Crosse & Blackwell's. George, his foreman and a staunch Labour man, had told him there would be a job waiting for him and to take his time getting back to full health.

Coopering was not for the frail. During that fortnight they made the most of every minute together. They took chilly walks along the river, and he warmed her in his arms, catching the mist of her breath in his mouth as they kissed. He took her to Barnham Street Buildings to meet his parents, who took in her blonde hair and blue eyes with good grace and made her welcome.

Ruby most loved walking with Alfie beneath frosted, bare-branched trees in Southwark Park, crunching over ice-stiff grass to hidden benches where they could hide their love from the world. The cold weather felt like her friend, for every minute outside he had his arm around her, keeping her warm and, more importantly, close.

After the fortnight was up Alfie said he would report to George, the Cooperage foreman, on Monday morning, and meet her outside at lunchtime.

As the lunchtime hooter screeched its welcome signal, she dashed out of the Paste Kitchen and down the four flights of stone stairs into the yard below. Girls streamed around her, filling the yard and obscuring her view. Eventually she saw his shaven head above the crowd and her heart lurched as she followed his agonizing progress through the tide of workers pushing in the opposite direction until all at once he was in front of her. He put an arm around her waist and they walked out of the factory together.

She noticed he'd not stopped smiling during their walk to the café. She suspected it was the same dreamy, unconscious smile she'd caught on her own face the other day. She'd been brushing her hair in front of the kitchen mirror, thinking of Alfie and there it was, the evidence of love, plain to her sight. A smile that betrayed her and betrayed him now. He took her to a café in Grange Road and she asked him how his first morning back at work had gone.

Only then did his smile disappear. 'It didn't,' he said. 'My foreman said he couldn't take me back on. I've got the sack, Ruby.'

'But I thought George was a Labour man?'

'Oh, yes, *he* is. He said if it was up to him he'd take me back in a shot. But the high-ups told him I wasn't to be let back on the premises. When I said I was meeting you, he turned a blind eye. He's a decent feller. Thing is, some of the management are BUF themselves. And to be honest, Ruby, I'm grateful to them. It might help me with a decision I've been thinking about for a long time. But I want to talk to you about it first.'

'What decision?' she asked.

'About Spain.'

She was silent, failing to see what Spain had to do with her. He began to stir his tea slowly, staring into the thick, mahogany brew.

'Spain?' Her eyes followed his, as if she could find clarification in the swirling liquid.

When he looked up, there was sadness in his eyes. 'I think I need to go, Ruby.'

'No!' She clapped a hand over her mouth, for she'd drawn stares in the crowded café.

'No. Please, Alfie, don't. We've only just found each other,' she pleaded. 'You can't go. Why would you go?'

'Same reason as I built a barricade in Bermondsey. If we don't stop the fascists in Spain, they'll be running all of Europe before long – and us too. Our little Battle of Bermondsey will mean nothing. If I thought I could live with myself, I'd stay. But Ruby, I'd hate myself forever and that would be the finish of us, before we'd even started. I'd end up blaming you for my cowardice, tell myself I did it to spare you.'

She grabbed both his hands. 'And if you die? We'll be over before we started too!' She licked dry lips, wishing she was half as eloquent as he was, wishing she knew more about the Spanish Civil War, more about everything.

'I won't go if you say no.'

She saw the effort it had taken for him to say that. She sat back, looking at him, knowing he'd played his trump card. 'But you'll hate me – and yourself – if I do.'

She rose, swallowing back tears, and stumbled out of the café, conscious that he was following her. All the way back to Crosse's she could not speak, knowing that if she did she would choke on the tears that she fought so fiercely to stem.

Back at the factory gates, she didn't know whether to slap him or kiss him. Instead she said, 'Oh, Alfie. Why did you make me love you?' It sounded bitter, but it was only sad.

'I didn't mean to,' he answered, hanging his head. 'And I can't help being glad that you do. But Ruby, I can't expect you to wait for me, not again.'

'I've got used to waiting.' She took in a shuddering breath. 'Go then, but promise me you'll come back.'

And, looking deep into her eyes, he made the meaningless promise and kissed her gently, watching all the while as she threaded her way back through the barrel-strewn yard.

21

A Perfect Hatred

January–February 1938

'So soon!' Shock propelled Ruby out of Alfie's arms. They had been curled up together in the armchair beside the fire. Davey was in bed and Dodge away, but she felt no qualms about being alone with Alfie in her home. The only thing that felt important to her was to be in Alfie's arms as often as possible. And this was her favourite place, her legs draped over his, her head on his shoulder, the fire glowing. It felt so right, she was certain there was no wrong in it.

Now she stood in front of him. 'But you said it would be at least a month before you'd go, what with all the paperwork.'

'I was wrong. The Republicans are losing, Ruby, running out of ammunition, supplies, men. All of us new volunteers are being waved through. They need us *now*!'

She dropped to the floor and twined her arms about his long legs. *But I need you now!* she thought. Forcing herself to look steadily into his eyes, she asked softly, 'So, when exactly are you leaving?'

'I'm reporting to the transit camp next week.'

She had known their time together would be brief. But she had hoped for months, not weeks. This was cruel. He lifted her up.

'Sweetheart, I'm sorry. Tell me you understand, Ruby. I know you do. You would have gone to Africa for your beliefs and Africa's a lot farther away than Spain!' He smiled, trying to make light of it. But she couldn't smile back. He tipped up her chin and kissed her. And she pulled him close, trying to prolong the sweet sensation of his mouth on hers. As long as the kiss lasted, she knew he couldn't leave her. But eventually he pulled away, and from that moment she began to practice letting him go. There would be no tears, no blame. She would send him off cheerfully, she told herself. She'd promised to let him go and he'd promised to return. It seemed imperative that she keep her side of the bargain now, if Alfie were to keep his.

She insisted she see him off from Waterloo, partly because she knew she would have to be braver there than if their goodbyes were said in private. Alfie took his leave of Ocki and Ida at Fort Road and then came to collect her.

'There's no need for you to come,' he said, as she handed Davey his toast and dripping. The boy was just as much in awe of Alfie as he had once been of Eric. It helped that Alfie always took the time to ask Davey about his football cards or to help him with his balsa wood models. Davey knew where Alfie was going, and though the cause was in direct opposition to Eric's, with the fickleness of boyhood hero worship, Davey was now firmly on the side of the anti-fascists. Perhaps it was just that Spain seemed more exotic a location than the Kings Road Barracks of the BUF.

Ignoring Alfie's comment, she hustled Davey off to school. 'Quick, then, or you'll be late.'

Davey gave her a kiss as he dashed out, stopping only to give the communist, clenched-fist salute to Alfie. 'Good luck, comrade!'

Alfie smiled as the boy left the kitchen and then caught Ruby's disapproving look. 'He's just a normal boy, Ruby. Don't start worrying about him running off to Spain too.'

'Well, if you could see him in his Life Boys' uniform you'd think he was already a soldier!'

'He's a good boy.'

'I know – and I want him to stay good *and* alive.' Ruby knew she was heaping all her fears for Alfie onto Davey. At ten, he was hardly army material – not yet.

'I'm ready,' she said, pulling on her coat.

The day was as dull as her heart and the tram journey to Waterloo was an endurance test of suppressed anxiety. She tried hard to concentrate on what Alfie was saying to her, but her brain was a fog. He explained how he'd be travelling first to the International Brigade HQ in Albacete in south-eastern Spain and then moving on for a short spell of training with the British Battalion in the nearby village of Madrigueras. It might as well have been the moon. If he'd been going to Africa she could have pinpointed his exact location on a map. But she'd had no chance to research his destination in Spa Road Library.

'How long will the training take?' she asked, reasoning that at least during training he'd be relatively safe.

'A week, maybe two?'

'How can they train you in two weeks!' She'd assumed it would take months to make a soldier out of Alfie, whose only combat experience had been at the The Battle of Bermondsey, as far as she knew. She tried to mask her concern. 'Will it be hot?'

'Cold, so I hear.'

'I thought Spain was hot.'

'Not where I'll be going.'

'Where will that be?

'Once I'm kitted out, they'll send me to Teruel – up in the mountains.'

'Is that a big place?'

He shook his head and she thought for the first time that he looked as if he didn't want to go. 'Small. Very small.'

And she felt sick. He might be risking his life for a very small, cold, mountainous place that she couldn't even begin to picture.

Her mask must have slipped, for immediately he said, 'Small, but important. Really important.'

He guided her off the tram and they walked towards the station entrance. Waterloo was a haze of fog and steam and cigarette smoke swirling above the platforms and around the concourse. He stopped to peer at the departure board and then they wove their way through the crowd to the platform.

'You will write to me?'

'I think I can send letters from the British Battalion HQ, but Ruby, there's no post office up there in the mountains.'

He bought her a platform ticket and hefted his bag over one shoulder. She peered along the length of the train, cursing it for being on time. The fireman was already stoking up the engine and steam escaped the funnel as a long, haunting blast came from the train's whistle. They stood together, smut and smoke stinging her eyes.

'So, once you're in the mountains, how will I know if you're safe?' she asked with a break in her voice.

He dropped his bag and took her into his arms. 'Remember when I first told you I loved you and you said you already knew?' He pressed her to his chest so that she could feel his heart beating. 'It'll be the same. You'll know in your heart if I'm safe.'

And she thought their bodies might meld into one as they stood, rocking slightly, with Alfie's arms holding her ever more tightly. When he released her, he reached into the pocket of his trench coat.

'I wanted to get you something you can look at while I'm away and know I'm thinking of you.'

In his hand he held a gilded heart-shaped locket, the chain a fine golden thread draped over his strong, elegant fingers. He flicked open the heart to reveal a small photo of himself in one half and one of her in the other. She smiled, recognizing the photo of her, one of the few in existence, taken at the Labour Institute dance. Ida must have provided it.

He fastened it around her neck. 'Do you like it?'

'I love it, but Alfie you can't afford something like this. You'll need funds, out there.'

'Shh, it's what I wanted to do. Something to remember me by when I'm gone...'

And now the tears overflowed. 'Don't say that. You're coming back, Alfie, you promised!'

'I didn't mean it like *that*. I just meant – it's to help you remember what I look like while I'm away.'

'Sorry, sorry. I'm being silly.' She swallowed her tears and cupped his face in her hands. 'I'll remember you every minute you're away. And you'll remember that I love you, won't you, Alfie?'

There were no more seconds left; people were boarding, slamming doors along the carriages. Another urgent whistle, harsher this time, signalled he must let her go. He stepped up into the carriage, threw down the window and stuck his head out. He waved and she waved back, till the train turned a bend in the track and disappeared from her sight.

She turned and walked away, dashing tears from her eyes. She passed a newspaper stand by the platform. The vendor thrust a folded newspaper into her face and she brushed him away, but not before reading the headline displayed on the board.

Bloody battle for Teruel continues in Spanish conflict. British volunteers pledge to fight on against fascism.

She ran, blinded by tears. And when she stood at the tram stop she suddenly felt trapped, encircled by invisible walls made up only of absence. Alfie wasn't here and he wouldn't be back for a very long time, if ever. Grief at her mother's death had felt like this; a cell of loneliness that she couldn't escape.

During the first week without Alfie, Ruby saw Ida and Ocki every day. Being in his home, talking to people who missed him, somehow brought Alfie closer to her. It was on the Saturday after he'd left that Ida made her suggestion. They were in Ida's small kitchen making tea.

'Listen, you've got to keep yourself occupied, love,' her friend told her. 'This could go on for a long time and Alfie wouldn't want you to stop living. Besides, I need to get meself out of this house. Ocki's driving me mad. He's very down.'

Ruby knew what Ida meant. When Ruby had arrived, Ocki had looked up from his book and nodded a hello, but he hadn't spoken, or joined them as he normally would have.

'I'm plenty occupied!' Ruby said. 'I'm working all the shifts I can to keep Alice Nash off our backs and I'm run off me feet looking after my *two* kids!'

Ida's explosive laughter filled the kitchen. 'You're a saint the way you put up with Dodge,' she said.

'I can't help it. I love him, and it don't matter how many times I tell myself I'm finished with him—'

'You never are.'

Ruby shook her head. Once she might have put her loyalty down to being a good Christian, honouring her father no matter what his faults, but now she knew her feeling for what it was: a love borne out of shared grief. If her mother had been alive, perhaps she wouldn't have been so bound to Dodge, but since her death he was mother and father both. 'He's got a heart of gold, really,' she said.

'Hmm, pity you can't pay the rent with it,' Ida said, unimpressed. As they sat at the kitchen table, Ida returned to her suggestion. 'All right, you might be busy, but you need something that'll take you out of yourself, something that's about the future, not just struggling on day after day.'

'You've got a plan, haven't you, Ida Turpin?'

Ida leaned forward, grinning. 'I have, Ruby Scully! Remember how I taught you to read when you was twelve? Well, I think we should go to evening classes together. Get our matriculation! Alfie would be really proud of you when he comes back.'

'Has he been telling you about my silly dream of becoming a

teacher?' Ruby blushed; it was a secret she hadn't even shared with Ida, it was such a foolish idea.

'No! And why didn't you ever tell me about it?' Ida slapped her hand on the table in rebuke. 'But Alfie's always saying you're cleverer than you give yourself credit for. We'll go to the Bermondsey Settlement, they do evening classes. What about it?'

For the first time since Alfie's departure, the constant gnawing anxiety was replaced by the beginnings of hope.

'All right. I'll give it a go. But goodness knows how I'll find the money for books.'

'You can share mine, love.' Ida pulled out a matriculation text book from her bag and waved it at Ruby with a flourish.

'You got a book already!'

Ida looked pleased with herself. 'Bloody Girl Guide, me, always prepared! Besides, I knew you'd agree in the end.'

Ruby left feeling oddly cheered. The future no longer stretched itself out before her in a long line of fearful days until Alfie came home. And she wasn't doing it for him. She knew that he appreciated her for who she was, not who she could become. He'd made that clear in every conversation they'd had – long before he ever declared his love. She would be doing this just for herself and that would be enough.

Within days of Alfie's departure, she'd received news of his safe arrival at the International Brigade HQ in Spain. But it was only a pre-printed card, identical to the one every other worried woman would be receiving. Each day since then she'd hoped for a personal letter in his own handwriting and today, when she got home from Ida's, still with her spirits high, the letter was waiting for her on the mantelpiece. Dodge must have put it there. When she'd finished reading it she was almost sorry it had arrived.

It began and ended with loving words that warmed her heart, but in between she learned how the new recruits were lacking even the most basic military equipment, were without proper uniforms to protect them from the cold they'd be facing in the mountains and, crucially, there were not enough rifles or ammunition.

She tucked the letter behind the framed photo of Alfie she now kept on the mantelpiece, saying a heartfelt prayer for better news in the next letter which arrived a week later, hastily scrawled in pencil on a blank page torn from a printed book. '*Sweetheart, I am leaving today for Teruel,*' she read, remembering the newspaper headline at Waterloo that had declared Teruel the site of a bloody battle. He was heading for that. Gripped by a wave of nausea, she lowered herself into the armchair and felt a hand on her shoulder. Looking up, she saw her little brother standing beside her. Softly, he asked. 'Is it about Alfie? Is he dead?'

She saw his lower lip tremble and she grew strong. 'No! Don't be a silly 'apporth. He's just telling me where he's going. Sit here, I'll read it to you. And she patted the arm of the chair, so he could lean on her shoulder as she read.

'He says: *I am assigned to the Major Atlee Company, the finest bunch of men you could ever wish to meet. They are all in Spain because, just like me, they believe if we don't fight fascism now, we will only have to fight it later on. Don't worry for me, Ruby, my darling. They will have my back as I will have theirs. There's no conscription or coercion among us, we're all here because we want to be and morale is very high. The transport is waiting to take us now, so I must go. Give my love to Davey and tell him I'm relying on him to look after you!*'

She glanced at Davey, who was grinning and now put a protective arm around her shoulder. She read on to herself. *It's a just fight, Ruby. And, whatever happens to me, I want you to know I couldn't have done anything else. Always your loving Alfie.*

He finished with many kisses, which Davey made a mischievous point of counting. She was glad the little boy was with her, a reminder that she must be strong, if only for him. But as she rose and leaned over to tuck the letter behind Alfie's photo, she caught the frame which toppled to the floor, the glass cracking on the iron fender.

In an instant she was enveloped by that same feeling of dread she'd had on the day Alfie had left for Spain. It was a certain knowledge that the man she loved would not be coming home – a sign. Charles would have scolded her, saying she should have no truck with prophecies or omens, that the last prophets had died thousands of years before. But still...

'Don't cry, Ruby.' Davey reached up to wipe a tear from her cheek. 'He'll be all right. God won't let him die,' he said, with an innocent faith she'd once shared.

'No. You're right, Davey, love. God wouldn't do that.'

There were no more letters from Alfie. The only news she could glean were from newspaper and radio reports. One Saturday evening in February she was listening to a news bulletin about Spain and Dodge was talking over the announcer.

'Shh, Dad, I'm trying to listen, this is about where Alfie is!' Ruby said, turning up the volume.

'*The battle for Teruel is over!*' the reporter declared in a rousing voice. '*Franco's forces have inflicted a crushing defeat on the Republican army, including the British Battalion of the XVth International Brigade. With thousands dead and hundreds cut off, besieged by encircling Nationalists, it seems the Republican army may never recover. The retreat from the mountains has proved a tragic race against freezing conditions, lack of food, supplies and ammunition. Many who survived the Nationalist onslaught have succumbed to the harsh conditions...*'

'Turn it off, Ruby!' Dodge said, reaching for the knob. 'Don't listen to that, gel. It'll only upset you.'

'No, I want to!' she said, switching the wireless back on. But the report was over and the broadcast had switched to a musical interlude with Ken 'Snakehips' Johnson and his Rhythm Swingers orchestra.

'You're looking a bit queasy, love. Stay there a minute.'

Dodge felt about in a corner cupboard and pulled out a bottle of brandy. He poured a fingerful into a cup and made her drink it. She gagged as the fiery liquid burned her throat and only then realized that he had given her strong drink and she'd broken the pledge. It didn't seem important.

She lay awake for most of the night, till she ran out of tears and prayers and succumbed to a fitful sleep. In the early morning, St James's bells woke her with their pealing and she remembered how hard Alfie had worked to repair the frame, so that the bells could carry on ringing. She closed her eyes and, in spite of their clamour, felt a blanket of peace settle around her. Today the bells were ringing and she had to live as if he was still safe.

At night school, Ruby discovered that she was surprisingly good at arithmetic. Ida told her it was all those years of counting pennies and checking her pawn tickets. Dodge told her it was in the blood. She came from a long line of gamblers and anyone who liked a bet, he said, was good at arithmetic. But her great delight was the English section of the matriculation paper.

She was grateful when Ida got them a new job on salad cream. The bottling line was slow and she and Ida could work as a team, with Ruby wrapping the bottles in paper before Ida stacked them into corrugated boxes. The easier daytime job meant she was at least able to stay awake during her evenings of study, and her teachers had told her she would certainly matriculate if she kept up with the assignments.

It was on one Saturday evening, when she'd fallen asleep over her essay on *The Pilgrim's Progress,* that she was awoken with a start by a loud banging on the front door. Her mind still groggy from sleep, she stumbled along the passage. Dodge was at the pub, Davey fast asleep. She hadn't lit the gas lamps in the passage, but as she approached the front door, the feeble hope grew like a glimmer of light – what if it was Alfie? Perhaps he'd been invalided out? She opened the front door an inch and in that instant it was shoved violently, smashing into her face, knocking her off her feet. She was flung back and lay sprawled on the linoleum floor as a dark figure blocked the doorway. He slipped inside, clicking the door shut behind him. Even in the gloom she knew the shadowy outline. Solid, unmoving, unspeaking, he stood there while she scrabbled to get up.

'Charles! Why did you do that? I would have let you in!' she said.

He didn't answer, but took a step forward, placing his foot on the hem of her dress, pinning her like a butterfly to a mount.

'Let me get up, then,' she said, feeling a surge of panic.

With a sudden swoop he dropped to his knees beside her, as if he were praying. He leaned forward to trace a finger down her cheek, stopping at the corner of her mouth. Now he was closer, she could see that he was smirking. He let his hand fall to her breast.

'I could've had you, any time,' he breathed into her ear, 'but I had *respect*!' He spat out the word as if it was dirt in his mouth. 'And where did that get me? You ruined my life, you know that, Ruby?'

Pushing away his pawing hand, she scrambled to her feet and ran along the dark passage but he lunged after her, catching her by her hair.

'Oh, no. You're coming with me.' He frog-marched her into the kitchen and forced her onto a chair, shoving his face so close that his lips were almost on hers as he spoke. 'You ruined my life. Now, you're going to sit there and listen while I ruin yours.'

'What are you talking about, Charles? I didn't ruin your life! You left me, remember?'

'You keep your mouth shut! Or I'll drag your grubby tyke of a brother out of bed and make him listen while I ruin his life too. Understand?'

She nodded, cringing as he gave her hair a vicious twist.

'You! You!' he hissed, his rage so intense he could find no other words.

'What have I done, Charles? I told you there was nothing between Alfie and me! Not when you accused me,' she added.

'But there is now!' He clutched at her admission, seeming triumphant.

'But not what you think. I'm not a whore, I'm not!' Her voice rose and she tried to calm herself; the last thing she wanted was Davey walking in on this. Charles was looking and acting like a madman and she had to treat him like one.

'Why don't you sit down, you look worn out, Charles.' He was pacing up and down in front of her now, propelled by fury. At each turn he pounded a balled fist against the mantelpiece. 'Have you travelled from Derbyshire today? I'll make us some tea,' she said in a sing-song tone she hoped would soothe him.

'I am a bit tired,' he said, stopping, suddenly meek. He wiped sweat from his forehead, took off his hat and scarf and collapsed into Dodge's armchair.

She rose and walked slowly, carefully, to the scullery. With shaking hands she made him tea, cut a slice of bread and found a square of cheese. When she came back in, he was still seated, his red-rimmed eyes staring into the last embers of the fire.

She placed the tea and food by the hearth. He was like a slumbering dragon she didn't want to wake, so she sat opposite him and waited while he gulped the tea and wolfed down the bread. When he'd finished, he began to mutter something in a low voice, so low she had to lean forward to catch it.

'*Do I not hate them, O Lord, that hate thee*? Psalm 139:21.' His voice grew louder as he went on, '*And am not I grieved with those that rise up against thee?*' He stared at her as his voice turned into a deep, almost animal growl, '*I hate them with perfect hatred: I count them mine enemies!'* His eyes were hard, pale stones, lit by pure loathing.

'Me? You hate me? But I've not turned against God. If anyone's life was ruined it was mine! You lied about me at the Mission and they believed you. I had to leave!' She waited for a response, but he stared, almost unseeing, with the same pale abhorrence. '*You* can still come and go there as you please, you're still at Bible college, still going to the mission field. What's ruined?'

He leapt like a big-boned cat, grasped her throat. 'A woman is not permitted to speak! You want to know what's ruined? I can't go to the mission field now! You and your deaconess friend saw to that.' With his other hand he pulled a letter from his coat pocket and read in a hoarse voice. '*Charles Best is no longer deemed suitable for the mission field; his minister has withdrawn his recommendation. Accusations of dishonesty and spreading malicious gossip cast doubt on his character.*' He slapped her face with the letter. '*You're* the liar, *you're* the whore of Babylon posing as an angel of light! *You* perverted God's will and now my ministry is finished. So yes, Ruby Scully, yes!' He slumped to the floor and through lips taut with venom, he finished, 'I do hate you with a perfect hatred.'

Ruby daren't speak a word or make a move. The clock ticked and the embers sighed to ashes in the grate, the gas mantle hissed and Charles stared into nothing. When he came to himself, he looked around, as if he'd forgotten where he was, then rose, straightened his jacket and pulled another document from his pocket.

'Now for you.' He went back to sit in the armchair and angled the paper, so that light from the gas mantle fell across it. 'Your mother, Rachel Scully, you told me she died in childbirth?'

'Yes, she did,' she answered in a rasping whisper, not understanding this interest in her mother.

He flicked the paper with his index finger. 'This is your mother's medical record from the Mission's Mother and Baby

Clinic. And it proves that either you're a wicked liar or your precious father is!'

She rose out of her chair, but he pushed her down, so that she tumbled to her knees. Putting a wide hand on the back of her head, he forced it forward, so that she could see what he read. '*Rachel Scully, safely delivered of a baby boy* – see the date?' It was indeed the date of Davey's birth. 'Does it say she died in childbirth?'

She shook her head, straining against his hand. 'No. But she didn't die on the same day Davey was born. I found that out from her Bible – she'd written his birth date in the front. She died afterwards.'

'Let's see what else it says, then. See this date, one month later? You read it. No! Out loud.'

It was painful to speak, but Ruby read in a rasping whisper. '*Rachel Scully diagnosed with milk fever.*' Her eye moved to the next entry, about a week after that. '*David Scully, five weeks old, brought into the clinic with head injuries by his father, who informed us the child's mother, Rachel Scully, had stamped on her baby's head in an attempt to kill him. In her ravings she said she'd mistaken the child for a rat.*'

Ruby looked up into Charles blank eyes. 'No! This ain't right, this is about another woman, not my mum. Dad never said nothing about her hurting Davey. She loved him!'

'Read,' he said, and she found herself wishing with every fibre of her being that Ida had never taught her to read, wished that the words could have stayed a jumble of impenetrable symbols.

'*Rachel Scully, diagnosed with insanity due to childbirth and declared a danger to her children, was admitted to Cane Hill Mental Hospital for an indefinite period.*'

He let her go and Ruby had hold of the record now. She stared at the document, searching for understanding. 'But – but how did you know to look for this?'

He looked pleased with himself. 'Something my drunkard father said once, years ago, when he was beating my mother.

He told her if she didn't do as she was told, he'd stick her in the looney bin, like his mate had done to his wife. I'm not sure when I first put two and two together, perhaps when you first introduced me to your father.'

'So, you sneaked in to the clinic and stole this? For what? Revenge? Just so you could hurt me?'

She looked at him for some sign of pity but saw only exultation. The pale light sparked in his eyes. *'I hate them with a perfect hatred!'* He paused, studying her. 'So, Ruby, how do you feel about your dear old dad now? The man you put before me, the man you wouldn't give up when I told you he'd drag you down? He's been lying to you all these years!'

Her whole body began to tremble and through chattering teeth she managed to say, 'He didn't lie. He just didn't want to tell us she'd died in a mental hospital. He wanted to protect us.'

Charles laughed. 'He didn't want to protect you! He just couldn't be bothered with her. She's not dead, she's still there!'

The words seeped into her understanding like a slow bitter poison. 'Still there?'

He nodded slowly, his eyes fixed on hers, their expression almost hungry. 'Alive. All these years, alive. And he told you she was dead.'

The fire had died and he knelt beside her. He scooped up a handful of ashes and smeared her forehead with them. 'This is what it feels like to have your life ruined, Ruby Scully.' He smeared her lips with the ashes. 'And this is what it tastes like.'

And then he rose up and walked out, leaving her rocking herself slowly beside the dead fire.

22

The World Turned Upside Down

February 1938

Alive! Her mother was alive. All those years without her, all those grief-stricken nights when she'd cried herself to sleep. 'Mum, oh, Mum,' she keened, over and over. What did she care if Rachel Scully had been declared insane? Her mother was in the world. She lived, she walked, she breathed the air, she was near! Ruby could have seen her face at any time, could have touched her hand, been held in her arms. And Dodge had robbed her of that, knowingly, year after year. She didn't care what his reasons were for lying to them, and he would have reasons, so many reasons. One after the other he would trot them out, she knew him, until she was forced to agree that it was a reasonable thing to have done. *But it wasn't!* He'd cheated Ruby of her mother all these years. In this thing Charles had been right – Dodge had never been worthy of Ruby's love. She would have done anything for him, and all the time he'd told his stories of the war and his hard childhood and sat in his armchair and cried over his dead wife, and it had all been lies.

Ruby got up. She went to Dodge's bedroom, opened his wardrobe and pulled out his clothes, slinging them in a pile onto the bed. One by one she grabbed the shirts and, with great rending rips, tore them to shreds. The suits were harder. She got a knife from the kitchen, stabbed and tore at the trousers, hacked at the jackets, sliced the ties. She pulled out his good shoes and slashed at the leather till they were gouged with holes. Then she stood on his bed and reached up to his hiding place on top of the wardrobe. She tore up every banknote he had stashed there. She worked methodically and in complete silence so as not to wake Davey.

After there was nothing of his left to destroy, she put everything into a laundry bag and walked downstairs to Aunt Nancy and asked her to listen out for Davey.

'Are you all right love? You had a visitor?'

'Charles.'

'That bastard! Did he hurt you?'

Ruby shook her head. 'No. He's not going to the mission field now.'

'Well, the poor black babies have been spared, that's all I can say.'

Out in the street she forgot, for a moment, why she was there. And then she remembered. As she walked through the darkening streets she was aware only of the bag slung over her shoulder, banging rhythmically against her back. She kept her eyes fixed on the pavement, sometimes looking up and wondering for an instant where she was going, and why, and then the bag strings would dig into her shoulder and she'd hurry her steps.

Eventually she came to the World Turned Upside Down. She passed the children waiting outside for their parents, and pushed through the young men standing in the street, blocking the doorway. One of them spoke to her, but she didn't understand him and he turned to his mates, putting a finger to his head, murmuring, 'Nutter.' Inside, she scanned the room. At the tables sat toothless old women in black hats with pints of Guinness and the bar was blocked by tightly packed men's bodies. She was used to worming her way through a crowded pub with a collecting tin, but the bulky bag hampered her, so that she drew stares and complaints.

'Ain't you in the wrong place, love?' An old man with leathery skin peered at her. 'You should be down the bagwash with that!' Others around him laughed, but she stuck out her elbows and pushed through, feeling beer bellies and muscled backs alike giving way to her.

He sat at the bar, with a gramophone on his lap. His blond hair fell forward over his forehead as he demonstrated to a potential buyer that the machine was in working order. The record playing was 'It's Only a Paper Moon' and the voice singing '*but it wouldn't be make-believe if you believed in me*' had slowed to a low, distorted wail. Dodge wound up the machine while the record still played, and the crooner's voice speeded up to a ridiculous high pitch. A silly grin crossed Dodge's face. At that moment he looked up and saw her.

'Hello, gel, what's the matter?' He handed the gramophone to the punter, with an invitation to try it out, slipped off the bar stool and tried to steer her towards one of the tables. But she couldn't move. 'Ruby, love. You ill? What you got there?'

She pulled the laundry bag off her shoulder, opened it and tipped out the contents onto the dirty pub floor. It was a moment before Dodge recognized the scraps of material.

'What you done to me fuckin' suits?' He gathered them up, his face white with shock. 'And me shirts! Ruby! You gone mad?'

By now a ring of silence had formed around them.

'No, Dad.' Ruby found her voice, though it didn't sound like hers. It was harsh and hoarse, her vocal chords damaged from Charles's throttling. 'It's not me that's mad. It's me mother that's in Cane Hill, ain't it?'

His face went rigid with shock and his eyes widened with fear.

'No! Hang on, gel, who's been telling you lies?'

'You!' she roared, ignoring what felt like ground glass in her throat. 'Me mum's *alive*! And you let us believe she was dead, you lying, useless, miserable coward. You're not my father. You're *nothing*. Here's your clothes and here's your filthy money. I don't want you coming home to me. I don't want you anywhere near my brother. Give me your key.'

Dodge put his hand into his trouser pocket, almost as if someone else were controlling him, and put the front door key into Ruby's outstretched palm.

'You told me my mum was dead. Well, now my dad's dead too.'

As she turned and walked away from Dodge, someone began clapping. A few cheers echoed around the bar and the door slammed behind her. No doubt it had been the best entertainment the World Turned Upside Down had seen in many years.

When she got home, she went to Dodge's bedroom and put all the cufflinks and tiepins, his best watch, everything that hadn't been pawned, into an old box. She could have pawned them, but she felt nauseous even touching them; she wanted nothing of his in her life. She found his shaving gear and Brylcreem and put those into the box as well. Then she went down to put them into the dustbin. Aunt Nancy came out into the yard, ostensibly to throw cold cinders into her own dustbin, but Ruby knew she was curious.

'Aunt Nancy, Dodge ain't coming back here again. I'm not letting him in and I've taken his key. If he comes knocking at your door asking you to let him go upstairs to our flat, don't.'

'What's he done? Has he gone too far?' Aunt Nancy asked.

'He's done the worst thing in the world. I've found out my mum's not dead. She's been in Cane Hill all these years!'

'In Cane Hill? The nuthouse? What are you talking about? Rachel's dead. Your dad told me the doctor was sending her to Fairby Grange to convalesce because she was so worn out having your Davey. Dodge took her down to Kent himself and

I'll never forget his face when he come back here to me, sobbing his heart out. She'd died and they'd buried her down there. He was in a terrible state.'

'Crying for himself, Aunt Nancy. That's why Charles come to see me. He showed me the medical record. They said Mum went mad because of childbirth and tried to kill Davey, so they locked her away. But she's alive!'

'Oh, that wicked, lying bastard, how could he do that to his kids? You poor darlin,' come here.'

Aunt Nancy hugged her. But Ruby felt no impulse to cry or seek comfort. A numbness had stolen over her heart that froze any pain threatening to surface. Under the ice it was fixed and manageable. She seemed to be looking down on herself, encased, like a picture of Sleeping Beauty she'd once seen during one of Ida's reading lessons. She didn't want to wake up; she hoped to stay there, embalmed forever.

'I won't let him set foot in my place, Ruby. He won't get in this house if it's got anything to do with me.' Aunt Nancy shook her head. 'I can hardly believe it, the wickedness. Poor Rachel, she was a lovely woman, your mum.'

'Is. She *is* a lovely woman, Aunt Nancy.'

'Ruby, you don't know what state she might be in. Cane Hill...' Aunt Nancy gave a shudder. 'If you wasn't mad to start with, that place would make you. They've kept her in for a reason, darlin'. Just don't expect too much when you see her. Do you want to see her?'

And it was only then that Ruby understood she had a choice. 'Of course I want to see her!'

The following morning Ruby went upstairs to see Mrs Nash. The upper floor of the house was like a foreign country. The lino of Ruby's passage gave way to an old burgundy patterned stair carpet, the walls were painted in the dark greens and browns of an earlier age, even the smells were different - a combination of dust and lavender. She knocked at Mrs Nash's sitting-room door and waited. There was a sound of someone shuffling about inside, but eventually the door opened and old Mrs Nash's black wig emerged. It had been put on hurriedly, showing wisps of what remained of her own white hair poking out from under it.

'Oh, is that little Ruby? Come in! My Alice is out.'

Ruby hadn't seen much of Mrs Nash since her daughter had come and she was surprised at how frail she looked. The old lady had a shawl wrapped around her bony shoulders and was already tottering towards a couch that had been made up as a bed.

'I'm sorry, Mrs Nash, I didn't mean to get you out of bed.'

The old lady lowered herself with a groan onto the couch. 'Have you come about the rent? Alice told me your father wasn't happy about the rise, but she says it's fair.' The old lady took a few deep breaths and exhaled through pursed lips. She was in pain.

'Can I get you something, Mrs Nash, a drink?'

'I'm all right, dear. Come closer.'

Ruby took a step forward.

'You've grown up into a lovely young woman, Ruby. You've got your father's colouring, but you're the face cut off your mother. How is she? I haven't seen her for a long time. Is she keeping well?'

Ruby paused. 'Yes, Mrs Nash. She's fine.'

Just then the sitting room door opened and Alice Nash walked in.

'What's all this?' she asked suspiciously.

'I just wanted to ask a favour.'

'I've told you, you either pay the rent or I'll find someone else—'

'I *will* pay the rent! I just want you to take Dad off the rent book and put me on it and I'd rather you didn't let him in if he knocks. I don't want him in the house.'

'You had a falling out?'

'I'm just fed up with him not paying you,' Ruby said, hoping to convince Alice she was on her side. Instead the woman curled her lip.

'So, how will you manage on Crosse's wages?'

'I'm doing extra shifts...'

Alice looked doubtful.

'Alice,' her mother said, in the strong voice that Ruby remembered, 'she's a good girl.'

'All right, then,' Alice relented. 'I'll give you a month. I can't say I'm sorry Dodge's gone. I've got enough to do with looking after Mother, never mind chasing him every week.'

'Dodge and Rachel, that's it,' Mrs Nash said with a vague smile, remembering. 'They're a lovely young couple. Got a sweet little girl. I said to my Albert, when they asked for the rooms, they won't be no trouble...'

Alice Nash shook her head and lost her habitual look of guarded suspicion. 'Her mind's going,' she mouthed. And Ruby felt sorry for Alice Nash, realizing she was, after all, a daughter too.

But Dodge wouldn't have been Dodge if he couldn't talk his way round a woman. She didn't think Aunt Nancy would have crumbled so it must have been Alice Nash, obviously not as immune to his charms as she liked to pretend. He'd left it a few days. Perhaps he'd thought Ruby would have calmed down, regretted her decision, so when she came home from work she was immediately alerted by the smell of cigarette smoke. He was sitting at the kitchen table, a Woodbine burning down between his fingers.

'Get out,' she said in as even a voice as she could manage; it made her feel sick just to look at him.

'Where's me little boy?' he asked. 'Have you told him about his mother?' He looked scared.

Davey was out playing football and she hadn't told him about Rachel, but she wouldn't give Dodge the satisfaction of an answer.

'Get out!' she said, in a louder voice.

'I ain't going nowhere till I explain.' His strained face, uncombed hair and crumpled suit suggested he'd been sleeping under the bar of the Upside Down or on Uncle Jim's floor. She looked at him with loathing.

'I don't want to hear what you've got to say. It'll all be lies.'

'I know I've hurt you, Ruby, but you don't understand, gel. Your mum wasn't your mum any more. Might as well have been dead, after what she done. It was kinder on you kids, kinder. I didn't want you hoping you'd get your mum back. She'd gone!' He began to sob. 'I missed her too.'

Ruby put her hands over her ears. 'Don't start snivelling, it don't mean nothing to me no more.'

But his weeping continued, deep and long, like some great sobbing violin, with every indrawn breath another deep moan came up from the depths of his chest. She walked over to him and slapped him hard across the face.

'You're only feeling sorry for yourself.'

She could see him clearly for the first time. There was not an ounce of love in him. He was selfish to the core.

The slap shocked him into silence. He put a hand to his reddened cheek. 'No. I loved your mum, really, I did. But I couldn't help her. I had to think of me kids.'

'You? Think of us? *I've* brought up your kids! You've done nothing but been a drain on us ever since Mum die—' She stopped short. 'See, Dodge, what you did was, you killed my mother.'

His wretched eyes pleaded with her. 'I never wanted to speak ill of my Rachel. I never wanted you to know what she did. But she tried to kill our baby boy…' He lowered his head, wiping away fresh tears with his knuckle. 'She was a danger to all me kids – the doctor said!'

It was strange to feel nothing; he'd always been able to touch her heart. 'Really? Well, I've seen it with new mums in the child welfare clinic, and they're not mad, they're ill! They can get *better*. But you never give her a chance. I'll never forgive you. Now, get out, and I mean it, don't come back.'

He stood up and tried to put his arms around her, but she punched him away. He turned to avoid her blows and she battered his back all the way to the door, yelling, 'Get out, get out, get out!' until he was gone.

Afterwards, in the quiet, she went to the fireplace and leaned her head on the mantelpiece and wept for everything that had been taken from her: Alfie, her brother Eric, the Mission, her childhood – and most of all, the lost years she might have had with her mother.

When she finally raised her head and wiped away the tears, she saw in the mirror a ghost: a ghastly ashen face; a halo of whitish hair; eyes red-rimmed but lit by a pale fire that reminded her of Charles's eyes.

'The ghost of Ruby Scully,' she said to her reflection, in a voice thick with tears. But when her gaze fell upon the photograph of Alfie, she felt ashamed, for although she'd wept for all the things taken from her, she feared that there was one thing she'd lost all by herself, and that was Ruby Scully.

Ruby was seated in front of Dr Scott, the young woman doctor who'd once prescribed her with a nerve tonic.

'Ruby, I am so sorry. I can't think how Charles Best got hold of that record. It's highly confidential.'

'He's trusted here. He must have got in through the church's connecting door, probably on a Sunday.'

'I'll certainly be speaking to the minister about this,' she said, frowning. 'But what about you, Ruby? It must have been a terrible shock for you.'

Ruby didn't want to talk about how she felt. 'Did you know

my mother was alive?' she asked, feeling that everyone must have known except her.

'I didn't, Ruby. I came to the Mission after your mother was admitted to the mental hospital.'

Ruby nodded slowly. 'I want to visit her. Can you help me?'

Dr Scott took off her spectacles and tapped them on her desk. 'I would advise waiting – just until I've spoken to the superintendent of Cane Hill and have a clearer idea of your mother's current mental state. It could be very upsetting for you, Ruby.' She paused. 'Perhaps I should have that back.'

Ruby looked down at the screwed-up medical record. To Ruby it felt like the only proof she had that this wasn't all a dream. 'Couldn't I keep it?'

A flicker of pity crossed the doctor's face. 'I daresay you could. I'll telephone today and let you know what he says. And Ruby, you might want to think about who you could take with you. I wouldn't advise going alone.'

Ruby got up. 'I know what sort of place it is, doctor.' Cane Hill was always spoken of with a sensational horror. Those admitted were often given a life sentence without a trial and the place had the reputation of being darker and more forbidding than any Victorian prison building.

'You've heard, but you can't know. Believe me. I spent a year working in a similar place. Take someone.'

There was only one person she'd feel comfortable taking with her, but she hadn't told Ida about her mother's resurrection. She wasn't sure why. Perhaps because her friend would have forced the real Ruby Scully out of hiding and she wanted to remain encased in ice. Besides, Ocki's depression had continued to deepen and Ida was at her wit's end. No. Ruby would go alone.

It didn't take long for Dr Scott to find out about her mother's condition. She was, the doctor explained to Ruby, in a ward of quiet patients, not disruptive or violent at the moment, being kept calm and comfortable with the help of various therapies. *Calm and comfortable* sounded beautiful to Ruby. It was a balm to her tortured imagination to know that her mother wasn't being chained to her bed as she raved in a straitjacket. Cane Hill, she knew, was somewhere in Surrey, but when Dr Scott gave her the exact address, it brought back a memory. Coulsdon. She'd once caught Dodge out in a lie when she'd found a train ticket to Coulsdon in his pocket. He'd told her he was on a driving job up north at the time. What if he'd been visiting her mother? If he had, it made his deception even harder to bear. He could have taken Ruby with him.

She didn't put any money in the gas meter for a week. Davey enjoyed it, thought it was an adventure to go to bed with a candle. But the saving was enough for a return ticket to Coulsdon and on the day she walked to London Bridge, glad that she wasn't catching a train from Waterloo, where she'd said goodbye to Alfie. She didn't want to face the memory of him today. She wore her best dress and coat and had washed her hair, rinsing it in vinegar so that it shone. Her nails were clean and trimmed nicely and she'd polished her shoes, grateful that no one could see the cardboard stuffed inside the soles. Her mother had always said they might not have much money but soap and water didn't cost much. Ruby thought she would pass muster.

On the train journey she stared intently out of the window, ticking off all the stations as the train steamed out into the Surrey countryside. Rows of new semi-detached houses began to appear between the fields as they approached Coulsdon and her palms began to sweat. Many passengers got off at the little station which looked innocuously pretty with its scalloped-edge wooden canopies over the platforms. A handful of people headed for a covered walkway and Ruby followed. The sign read *To Cane Hill Mental Hospital*. For those who were ashamed of having relatives there it must have been torture, but to Ruby it felt like a secret passage to happiness. She noticed she was the only one smiling and, as the little band trudged up an incline, she felt her heart beating so fiercely she thought it would thump through her chest.

A number of shallow steps curved up to the arched entrance of the main hospital building. Patterned brickwork and tall chimney stacks gave it the look of a country manor house. There was a central two-storey block, topped by an octagonal white clock tower. The windows were tall and ornamented with elaborate stone pediments and two wings protruded on each side of the central block. This was not the forbidding place she had been expecting.

As a man in front of her held open the door for her, she took a deep breath. Dr Scott and Aunt Nancy had both warned her not to get her hopes up, but she felt her heart soar. Who ever got such a second chance? She remembered the Bible verse about Jairus's daughter: *She is not dead but sleepeth*. Ruby knew how he must have felt. It was a miracle. In a matter of minutes, she would see her mum again – alive.

At the reception desk she was told Matron wanted to see her and a young nurse showed her to the office. Matron, a middle-aged woman with a kind, round face sat behind a large desk. She wore the usual dark blue uniform, with a tall, white pleated hat. She reached over to shake Ruby's hand.

'I understand this is the first time you will have seen your mother in...' She looked down at a file.

'Ten years,' Ruby offered.

'And how old were you when you're mother was admitted?'

'Ten.'

'And you were told that she had died?' She tilted her round head and gave a small, understanding smile. 'It's often the case that families wish to forget—'

'I didn't want to forget!' Ruby said, fiercely.

'Of course not. But it's my job to prepare you. Your mother has been able to improve due to certain therapies our doctors have recommended, but she will not be the mother you remember.

Today, for example, she will not be able to hold a conversation with you.'

'Has she lost her voice?'

The matron shifted in her seat uncomfortably. 'Perhaps it's best if I take you to her.'

'Yes, please.' Ruby jumped to her feet.

It was only as she followed the matron out of her office that she got an idea of the vastness of the hospital. They walked for at least five minutes, following a single horseshoe shaped corridor with dozens of two and three storey ward blocks radiating out. Eventually matron stopped and pulled out a key from a bunch hanging on her belt. She unlocked the door and led Ruby past a day room, where she glimpsed patients sitting in armchairs or at tables; there was a huge bay in the room, but only a dim light filtered in through the tall windows. The radiating blocks were so close together they shaded each other and it felt as if she was walking through a perpetual twilight. They arrived at a long, dark ward containing at least sixty iron-framed beds, many of them curtained off. There was an unnerving silence hanging over the room and Ruby kept her eyes firmly on Matron's back as she led her to a screened-off bed halfway along the ward. She swished aside the curtain and beckoned to Ruby.

Stepping forward, Ruby looked down at a grey-haired woman, whose thin face was ashen, but her fine features were undeniably beautiful. She was asleep.

Ruby took in a sharp breath. 'That's my mum!' Ruby went closer and leaned over the bed. 'That's my mum,' she repeated softly and reached out tentatively to touch her mother's hand which was warm and a little clammy. Tears pricked Ruby's eyes.

'Can we wake her up?'

'It would interfere with her therapy, I'm afraid. But as you can see, she's quite calm.'

Ruby felt an instant deflation and then a quick infusion of fire. 'I can't see no therapy.'

Ruby had had some idea that a calming therapy would involve crafts, basket-making perhaps, and warm baths. Some doctors at the clinic recommended their frazzled mothers to take warm baths – something Ruby had always questioned silently, for most of the mothers attending the Welfare Clinic had no bathrooms in their homes.

'This *is* the therapy.' Matron indicated the sleeping Rachel. 'It's called prolonged narcosis. It helps to keep patients comfortable and calm and restores them to a peaceful state.'

'What's narcosis?' Ruby asked.

'Sleep,' Matron replied.

Ruby's gaze returned to her mother. 'How long's she been having this therapy?'

Matron looked puzzled. 'You said she was admitted ten years ago.'

Ruby nodded.

'Then, ten years. She would have been started on prolonged narcosis immediately. You see, your mother was suffering delusions and she was very violent towards others and to herself. But look at her now. So peaceful.'

'She's been asleep for *ten years*?' Ruby's anger, hitherto reserved for Dodge, now exploded into the kindly face of the matron. 'So how do you know she's not got better in all that time?'

'Shh, you'll disturb her; there's a certain amount she will be aware of, especially emotional upset and raised voices. Really, my dear, you haven't any idea what these patients are like when not sedated.'

Ruby would once have felt rebuked and stupidly in the wrong, would have followed whatever rules Matron issued. Not now.

'How do you know she's not better?' she repeated.

'Because periodically we do bring the patients into a lighter state of sleep, and on those occasions she has been very agitated.'

Ruby felt like screaming. Instead, she stroked her mother's hand and said, 'I'd be agitated if someone had kept me drugged in a bed for ten years.'

She ignored Matron's impatient, 'Tsk' and, leaning over the bed, whispered in her mother's ear. 'It's Ruby, Mum.'

Matron started to speak, but Ruby cut her off. 'Can I have a minute on me own with her?'

Matron nodded. 'I do have other duties.' She turned to go and then paused. 'I'm sorry, my dear, it's possible your father was right to keep you ignorant.'

After she'd left, Ruby stroked her mother's hand and let the tears fall freely. 'I'm sorry I never come before. They told me you was dead. If I'd known I would have come, I wouldn't have just left you.' A tear fell onto her mother's hand and Ruby wiped it away. 'I'm here, Mum. You can wake up now.'

23

Not Dead But Sleepeth

February–March 1938

Ida was understandably hurt. 'Why didn't you tell me? I'm your best mate.'

'You're more than that, Ida. You're like a sister to me. You know me better than anyone and maybe that's why I didn't want to tell you. I've chucked Dodge out – for good. I thought you'd say I was wrong.'

'Chucked him out? I never thought you'd harden yourself up.' Ida looked shocked, then added, 'You'll regret it.'

'See! That's what I meant. No. I won't.'

'Oh, Ruby, you've had a shock. You don't know what you're doing. To think you went to Cane Hill all on your own, you poor thing.' Ida gave her the hug she'd been dreading and like a burst dam Ruby's sobs broke.

'Shh, darlin'. It'll take time. You don't know what to feel, do you?'

And Ruby shook her head, wetting Ida's blouse front with her tears. 'I only know I'll spend the rest of my life making her happy.'

Ida let her go. 'That's what I mean about the shock. You can't make a promise like that now – you can't just give up your future. Besides, you've got Alfie to think of. He wants a life with you when he comes back.'

Ruby saw the wisdom of Ida's words. 'I know. And we will have a life.'

But a storm of conflicting desires spun her in every direction. In any minute of the day she could find herself veering from elation to despair and she didn't know why. Part of her unease was because of her brothers. She would have to tell them.

It had been five months since she'd seen Eric; she assumed he was still at Black House in Kensington. She decided she would have to go there, but whether she'd be allowed to see him was another matter. This time she went straight to the stone-arched front entrance. She was stopped by two young Blackshirts guards, but when she mentioned Eric's name and that it was an emergency, they let her in. Ruby was surprised to be greeted by a polite young woman in a grey skirt and black beret who told her to wait while she found him. The uniform ban must only apply in public. Eric would be happy. At least he could dress up in his beloved uniform here. And at that moment he came walking down the wooden staircase, black-shirted and booted, followed by the young woman. He didn't look pleased.

'What's the emergency?' he asked.

Ruby glanced at the receptionist, now back behind her desk, pretending not to be listening. A group of young Blackshirts barrelled through the entrance hall.

'Can we go somewhere quieter?'

'All right. Follow me,' Eric ordered and she felt like a subordinate.

He led her up the stairs and along a polished wooden corridor to a large room with high, mullioned windows that overlooked the parade yard. The room was comfortably furnished with a collection of easy chairs and tables, a bookcase and a wireless on a sideboard.

'Elite Squad mess room,' he explained, and she hated his

clipped tone, with its fraudulent, recently acquired posh vowels. 'Sit.' 'So, why've you come? Has something happened to Dodge?'

'I've chucked him out.'

Eric gave a bitter laugh. 'Not before time. What did he do, steal the rent money? If you've come for a handout, the answer's no, you had your chance.'

She shook her head. 'I don't want your money – and he's done something much worse than steal the rent. Eric, sit down, you're not on parade.'

'I haven't got much time,' he said, but sat down opposite her. They were seated beside one of the windows and she could see a group of Blackshirts being drilled by an instructor. She turned her gaze back to Eric.

'I found Dad out in a lie.'

'Well, that's nothing new, it's Dad, what d'you expect?'

'Eric, you need to prepare yourself for a shock.' She took a deep breath. 'He's been lying – the biggest, most wicked lie you could ever imagine about our mum. She's alive.'

He froze. For what seemed like minutes nothing about him moved. She even thought he had stopped breathing. And then he blinked. 'Are you sure?'

She nodded. 'I've seen her.'

'Where?'

She reached over for his hand. 'Eric, she's been in Cane Hill all these years.'

He groaned. 'Oh, Ruby, no, no. Not our mum.' He gripped her hand so tightly she felt the blood pumping back to her heart.

'Do you want to see her?'

Eric looked at her, pale-blue eyes pooling with tears. He nodded and in his old voice he asked, 'Will you come with me?'

'Of course I will. But there's something I need to explain about Mum.'

*

Eric had taken the news of their mother's being alive better than she'd hoped. She'd expected him to be angry, wanting to hurt Dodge, but instead she'd seen a softness in his face she hadn't seen for years. Even when she'd told him about the sleep therapy, his reaction was muted. It was as if hearing their mother was alive had forced a crack in the hard BUF shell Ruby hated so much.

Telling Davey was another matter and, as she faced this, she began to understand why Dodge had decided to lie. For Davey, their mum was a comforting dream that Ruby had conjured for him. But the reality was a sleeping woman he didn't know and who, if she stayed in that state, he would never know. Ruby asked herself which was kinder, the dream or the reality. Just as, she supposed, Dodge had asked himself. She decided to tell Davey the truth.

In the following days she tried several times to broach the subject to him, but at ten, he had a life of continual urgent appointments. He was either out in the backyard with Aunt Nancy's boys, where they spent hours teasing her chickens, or building camps, or playing football up in the cage atop the Time and Talents building, or venturing down to the Thames foreshore searching for treasure. He hadn't ever been the strongest of boys but he did have a great spirit. And it gave her hope he would cope with the news.

Still, she put off telling him till the last minute, the day before she was due to visit Cane Hill again – this time with Eric. It was a Saturday evening. She'd given up her half day to do an extra shift in the butchery at Crosse's, her least favourite job in the whole of the factory. She'd spent the afternoon stripping chicken carcasses into breasts and legs for the chicken soup and cleaning off any other flesh for the chicken pastes and potted meats. The only way she got through it was the thought of Alice Nash's surprise when she handed over the rent money on time.

She hurried home and found Davey putting the finishing touches to a model bi-plane. Alfie had donated his balsa wood and modelling tools and given Davey a few lessons before he'd left. It was a hobby Davey loved so much that his half of the ceiling in their bedroom looked like a huge mobile, with model planes suspended over his bed.

She opened a tin of Crosse's sausages and put on a potato to boil. Sausage and mash was a favourite of Davey's. After he'd polished off his dinner, she stopped him from dashing back to his model.

'Wait a minute, Davey. I've got something to tell you. Davey, you know Dad hasn't been here lately?'

He shrugged.

'Well, he ain't coming home again.'

The boy's eyes widened. 'Is he in nick?'

She wished he was. 'No. I asked him to leave and not come back, because he's done something really bad to us.'

Davey sat down and rested his elbows on the table, looking serious now. 'What?'

'You know how Dad said Mum died when she gave birth to you?'

He nodded silently.

'Well, that was a lie. Our mum's not dead, Davey. She's in hospital; she's been there ever since you were a little baby.'

His eyes fixed on hers, held her with the intensity of concentration he reserved for his wooden models, and then he sprang, launched himself around the table and in to her arms. He squeezed her hard, his round head, with its soft brown hair nestling into her throat. 'I've got a mum!' he whispered, his voice tight with happiness. 'I've got a mum!'

She felt some invisible, long-carried burden lifting from her. Yes, Davey had a mum and it wasn't Ruby, and she no longer had to live as if she was.

Eric came to the house the following day and looked as if he was going to a wedding, with his best suit on and a hanky sticking out of the top pocket, highly polished shoes and freshly cut hair. She was pleased he wanted to dress up for Rachel. She'd made Davey wear his best grey shorts and the scratchy V-neck jumper he hated, the only one without darns.

As Ruby and her brothers made the trip to Cane Hill, it was oddly comforting to have them with her. She'd tried to explain to Davey that their mother would be asleep and that it might be better to wait until she woke up before he visited. But it had been like trying to put the genie back in the bottle. He was irrepressibly happy and excited. The one thing she hadn't had the courage to tell him was how Rachel had come to be in the mental hospital. She'd said only that it was soon after his birth and had explained that Dodge thought it would be painful for them all to see her in such a place. Davey was well aware of what sort of hospital she was in. It was a common method of teasing among Bermondsey kids to suggest that someone belonged in Cane Hill.

She led them along the covered walkway from the station, along with the other visitors, and she could see that Davey was overawed by the massive place. He moved in a little closer and grabbed her hand as they presented themselves at the reception. They were allowed to go to the ward, where they waited to be shown in by a nurse. The long row of beds seemed to stretch away into infinity and she felt Davey's hand tighten as she stopped halfway along the ward. She glanced at Eric as the nurse pulled aside the screens. Eric took a step forward and bowed his head. He went to hold their mother's hand, but glanced hesitantly at Ruby.

'Go on, it's OK,' she said.

He lifted the limp hand and then bent down to kiss Rachel's pallid cheek. He was eight when he'd last seen her. 'Mum,' he said, 'it's me, Ricky.'

Ruby stared intently at her mother, looking for any sign that she'd heard. But she slept on peacefully, seemingly unaware of Eric's presence, just as she had been of Ruby's. Now Ruby led

Davey to the other side of the bed. She put an arm around him and leaned in close to Rachel.

'Mum, this is Davey. Your little boy.'

Instantly Ruby saw what looked like a ripple of anxiety cross her mother's impassive face and Rachel's inert body jerked. Davey jumped back into Ruby's arms.

'It's all right, Davey. Sometimes she wakes up a bit; it's like when you have a dream and then you wake up with a start.'

He peered at his mother and then, bolder, went to her side, putting a hand to her cheek.

'Hello, Mum, I love you,' he said, simply.

Ruby saw the anxiety fade from Rachel's face. But where there had been blankness, the calm of her features was now infused with something indefinable. Ruby could only think of it as a knowing. She was sure her mother had heard Davey – and she hoped with all her heart that Rachel Scully had felt forgiven.

Before they left, Ruby asked the receptionist if she could speak with the matron. She would need an appointment, she was told, and realized that what was new and wonderful to her, the rediscovery of her mother, was just another case in the matron's workload. She made the appointment and returned to her brothers.

They had to run for the train. The dark green doors were being banged shut one by one as the guard went along the carriages, blowing his whistle. Davey spent the train journey happily identifying the different engines and rolling stock used by the South Eastern Railway as they steamed through the countryside. Ruby was astonished at how easily he'd accepted their mother's return. Eric, on the other hand, was unusually quiet. She decided it was best to leave him to his own thoughts but as they neared London Bridge, he asked her why she'd spoken to the receptionist.

'Oh, I made an appointment to see the matron. I'm going to ask her if Mum really needs to be asleep for the rest of her life.'

Eric looked sadly at her. 'I wish she could be awake, Ruby. I wanted to tell her I'm sorry I didn't go to see her and that we're all right. I was expecting her to hear our voices and wake up...'

'So was I.'

'Life ain't like that, is it?'

'Sometimes it is,' she said, wondering if what she'd seen crossing her mother's face had been a figment of her imagination.

'Still believe in miracles, then?' Eric asked, but his voice held no hint of mockery.

One evening during the following week, Sister Evelyn came to visit.

'I don't want to intrude,' Sister Evelyn said, 'but Dr Scott has told me about your mother.'

Ruby instantly felt guilty that she hadn't told Sister Evelyn herself, but it had been the same feeling as with Ida. It was an event too momentous to fit easily into Ruby's everyday, normal life. It seemed to make her a different person.

'Come in, Sister Evelyn.' She ushered the woman along the passage, dark because she wanted to save money on gas, to the kitchen where she had been darning Davey's socks by candlelight. 'I'll make us tea,' she said.

The deaconess glanced at the candle. 'No, my dear, I've just come from a family who plied me with a whole pot! I came to say that it's wonderful news about your mother, but the circumstances! You must have been in turmoil since. You could have come to me.' There was a gentle rebuke in Sister Evelyn's tone.

'I know. I should have.'

Sister Evelyn nodded. 'But the way you heard! Dr Scott has made a formal complaint against Charles Best. The minister made some inquiries and it seems Charles was seen going into the clinic through the connecting door after service one Sunday evening. The minister's reported the matter to the college and Charles has been asked to leave.'

'So, he's got something else to blame me for,' Ruby said. 'Poor Charles, he can't be a missionary or a minister now – he'll be lost.'

Sister Evelyn gave a low hrrmph. 'Some of us think he was already lost,' she said, and it was the closest Ruby had ever seen her come to openly judging another human being.

'Perhaps, but he wanted to be good so much.'

'Mark 10:18. *Why callest thou me good?* Jesus asked the rich young ruler. None of us are good, Ruby, dear, but we can all try to be kind. Now, I must be off, but I want you to promise to let me know if you need anything.' As she said this, the woman took Ruby's hand in her own.

'I will. And I wanted to say I'm sorry I can't come with you to home visits any more, I'm having to do Saturday afternoon shifts.'

'I'm sorry too – and I'll send you some coal out of the emergency fund.'

Before Ruby could protest, Sister Evelyn kissed her and, giving her hand a parting squeeze, said, 'You're a good girl,' contradicting both herself and Mark 10:18 in one breath.

It had been almost a month since she'd heard of the Battle of Teruel's bloody end. Finding out about her mother had forced her to push her fears for Alfie to the margins of her life, allowing them out like fierce dogs only for those moments of the day when it was darkest – as she fell asleep or in the hours before dawn. Then she would imagine him mangled and bloody, abandoned on a Spanish mountainside, and the pain would be as bad as if a mad dog really had gnawed at her from the inside. The rest of the time she worked and struggled to make sense of the mixture of happiness and grief that seemed to have taken over her life since her mother had been returned to her.

Then came the letter bearing exotic Spanish stamps, looking as if it had been soaked in brine and wrung through a mangle. She could barely read the address and wondered how it had ever found its way to her. She tore it open, almost fearing to read the words, and then she felt her whole body trembling with relief. It was from him. Alfie had been one of the lucky ones; he'd come down from the freezing mountains of Teruel, not unscathed, but at least alive. A sniper's bullet had grazed his temple and he'd sprained his wrist falling down a rocky slope. Hence his appalling handwriting, he explained, apologizing. He seemed more worried about his penmanship than his head wound. He might make light of it, but all she could think of was the scant inches between the bullet and his brain.

She knew there was so much he wasn't telling her, but at least he promised to send her as many letters as he could write while he was recovering at the Brigade HQ in Albacete. But they would only be there for a brief time, while the company regrouped. They had lost many fine men, he said, men that had become his good friends, who had all gladly given their lives for the cause. And she whispered to the letter: *don't give your life, Alfie, don't give yours.*

Her next visit to Cane Hill wasn't on a regular visiting day, so she'd thought it best to go alone. She wondered at herself; who was she, Ruby Scully, to be questioning the doctors? But her work in the Mission's Welfare Clinic had given her an insight into the way medical decisions were made, and if Cane Hill was anything like the clinic, then much came down to time. How little there was of it, how many people to see, or how long the doctor had been a doctor or the nurse a nurse. Time and luck. And she felt her mother had been at the losing end of both so far.

'Yes, I remember your mother's case – Rachel Scully, prolonged narcosis therapy,' Matron said, as if it had been years since the name last came up. She waited for Ruby to speak.

'That's what I wanted to talk to you about. I want her to come off that therapy.'

'Well, my dear, I'm afraid that is not your decision to make. The doctors believe this is the best treatment for her.'

'But I don't agree. When I brought my little brother last time, he spoke to her and she definitely heard him. I saw it in her face. She was *pleased* he was here. If you could just bring her out of it for a few weeks? What if she just didn't get better because we never came to see her? My father abandoned her! What if she just had nothing to get better for?'

She wanted to cry at the thought of it, because she believed it was true. Ruby hadn't meant to get emotional, she didn't want to be seen as the hysterical daughter of the would-be child killer in Ward C. But something in what she'd said must have struck a chord, for the matron said, 'Don't upset yourself my dear. You were a little child, you had no say in the matter, and as soon as you found out you came to see your mother. There's no blame on your part. I understand what you're saying and I will certainly raise your concern with the superintendent. He would want to get your father's approval, though, before changing Mrs Scully's treatment.'

'But Dad's got no interest.'

'I think you're wrong about that.' She took a leather-bound book from a shelf behind her and flicked through. 'Here it is. Rachel Scully, visitor record. It appears Mr Scully has visited once a year, always on her birthday.'

The train ticket to Coulsdon! She'd found it in his pocket around the time of her mum's birthday. She was shocked and oddly disappointed. She wanted more reasons to hate him, not less. And acknowledging that his meagre yearly visit meant he loved Rachel was something she wouldn't do.

'Once a year? That's just so he wouldn't feel guilty,' she said.

Matron, who Ruby was beginning to feel had a soft spot for her, allowed her ten minutes with her mother. Unlike visiting day, the ward had a much more frenetic air. Nurses rushed up and down the long narrow ward with bedpans and rubber sheets and the smells made Ruby's stomach heave. She could see some white-coated doctors moving down the length of the ward, spending just seconds at each bed.

The curtains around her mother's bed had already been pulled aside, obviously ready for the doctors' visit.

A nurse with a trolley full of medicines stopped and spoke to Ruby. 'I don't know what Matron was thinking, letting you in during rounds. We'll have to rush you, I'm afraid.' She glanced at the approaching doctors and dumped a bottle and a syringe on her mother's bedside table.

Ruby went quickly to her mother's side. 'They're rushing around today. I ain't got long, Mum. I just wanted to tell you that I've asked them to let you wake up.'

She studied her mother's face, but there was no flicker of understanding. 'I think you'd prefer it, being awake, so you can see our Davey. He's such a lovely little boy. I looked after him for you.' And there, taking her by surprise, though she'd been hoping for it, came a spasm of what looked like discomfort on Rachel's face.

'Mum, I don't blame you. I know why it happened. You was ill...'

And her mother let out a long breath. *Dear God, she can hear me. She understands!* Ruby felt a rising panic that she could not free her mother, here, now. She looked anxiously towards the doctors as they approached the bed. They were talking amongst themselves. Ignoring her.

'This is my mum!' she burst out, 'And she can understand everything I say to her. She don't want to stay asleep any more. Can you stop that?' And she pointed a shaking finger at the doctor who'd picked up the bottle and syringe.

But the nurse came towards her at a half run and hustled her out, saying she was disturbing the patients. But Ruby suspected the only ones she'd disturbed were the doctors.

And a week after her visit, she received a letter from Cane Hill, saying that Rachel Scully's case had been reviewed and it had been decided that prolonged narcosis was by far the best therapy available. There would be no change in the treatment plan. She held the flimsy letter in her hand and seemed to hear the clanging of the prison door shutting on her poor mother. But then, not for the first time in her life, the story of Jairus and his dead daughter came to her, sparking hope in her heart, and she whispered to herself, *Weep not; she is not dead, but sleepeth.*

24

When Your Lover Has Gone

March–September 1938

Through the spring and into early summer, Ruby watched her mother's inert form beginning to change. Tasks that had once belonged to the nurses, Ruby now gladly made her own. She cut her mother's hair, trimmed and filed her nails, saved for a pot of Atkinsons' moisturizer and smoothed the cream over her mother's pale papery face and hands. She spoke to her mother as if she were awake, sometimes telling her about the previous week, sometimes about the past decade, fleshing out for Rachel the lives of her children through all the lost years. She watched and rejoiced at each sign that her mother knew she was there. But the moments of joy were mixed with torment too, for Rachel Scully remained locked in a prison within a prison, one which Ruby believed her mother desperately wanted to escape and she vowed never to give up pestering the doctors, not until she could look once more into the long-remembered, loving eyes of her mother.

No one was more surprised than Ruby to find an ally in her brother, Eric, and he had an undeniable advantage over her when speaking to the doctors: he was a man. And although still only eighteen, he was used to giving orders and making speeches. It was what the BUF was training him to do – their blue-eyed, working-class boy. Ruby wondered at the ways of God, that Eric was now using his fascist-groomed skills in service of his mother.

But, just as they seemed to be making progress, Eric's attention was diverted. After one particularly hopeful visit when the nurse had informed them Rachel's therapy was coming up again for review, Eric explained, during the journey home, that he couldn't visit again for a while.

'I know you won't like the reason, but we've got another mass rally planned and the top brass want me up the front,' he said.

'Oh, Eric. Don't take a gun this time!'

He tutted impatiently. 'Don't start. If you must know, I won't be the one providing protection for the speakers – I'll be one myself!' he said with undisguised pride.

Ruby would have been proud too, if the subject of his speech hadn't involved persecuting the man she loved. She bit her tongue, valuing the change she'd seen in Eric and not wanting to diminish it.

'Where is this rally?' she asked.

'Bermondsey.'

Ruby groaned. 'Not again!'

It had been almost seven months since the Battle of Bermondsey, and now Eric said their leader had decided the time was ripe to pass through the borough again. Mosley had told them that it was a humiliating failure that they'd never managed to set up a BUF branch in Bermondsey and now, Eric, as a Bermondsey boy himself, had been charged with rallying all the others to join the cause.

As soon as they were home, she left Davey with Aunt Nancy and hurried to see Ida and Ocki.

'We've heard the rumours,' Ocki said when she explained about the BUF's plan to march through Bermondsey again, 'but up till now we haven't known the date, Ruby.'

'Will the League of Youth block it again?' she asked.

'They're thinking of following Dr Salter's advice this time,' Ida said, 'asking everyone to stay home, boycott the rally. The idea is the fascists will just end up in a cordon talking to themselves.'

'Bloody appeasement!' said Ocki in disgust. 'It's everywhere. We've given Ethiopa to Mussolini and next we'll be giving half of Europe to Hitler. I know Dr Salter's a true pacifist, but what's my brother risking his life for if we can't even be bothered to stop a piddling few thousand Blackshirt thugs on our doorstep?'

'Ocki! Don't shoot the messenger, it's not Ruby's fault!'

It was a shock to see Ocki reacting so bitterly. Ruby had never witnessed him so agitated; his manner had always been so gentle and amused. 'Don't worry, Ida. I'm not offended. I'm frustrated, to be honest. Eric's been so different since Mum came back to us, I thought he might give up the bloody BUF for good.'

Ocki came and put a conciliatory hand on her shoulder. 'Sorry, Ruby. You're the last person I should be angry with; you gave up a lot to stand with us. Truth is, I'm angry at everyone – with the fascists, with Alfie for going to Spain, most of all with myself for not going.'

But although Eric was taken up with planning this new rally, she saw more of him around Bermondsey. She'd often spot him while she was shopping in the Blue Market, his familiar blond head standing out in a group of Blackshirts. They were leafleting Bermondsey relentlessly. Every passer-by, all the shops along The Blue, all the pubs – they seemed to be everywhere she looked. If he saw her, he would nod, nothing more.

One Saturday afternoon she was looking for end-of-day bargains at the fruit and veg stall. She had Davey with her, so that he could carry a bag, heavy with potatoes and greens. She was distracted by the sales patter of the fish man, offering her skate she could ill afford, when she became aware of raised voices. Looking around, she saw a group of Blackshirts haranguing a Jewish shopkeeper who was telling them to clear off. Davey dumped the bag at her feet and was now running toward the Blackshirts – he had seen Eric was at their centre. She refused the skate, picked up the bag and ran after Davey.

Eric spotted her and continued with what he'd been saying to the shopkeeper. 'We've got every right to our free speech and if I want to give these leaflets out I will.' His face was close to Mr Marks, the shopkeeper. As children Ruby and Eric would run in and out of the shop just to look at the assortment of oddities on display, everything from zinc buckets to glass goblets. They obviously never bought anything, but Mr Marks had never chased them off.

'Come on, Davey. Eric's too busy to talk to us today,' she said, giving Eric a disdainful look. 'And *you* ought to have a better memory, Eric. Mr Marks never turned you away on a cold day when you'd got nothing better to do than hang around his shop!' She was surprised to see a sudden look of shame cross her brother's face. And then he took charge of his little troop.

'Come on, we're wasting time here. We've got all of Tower Bridge Road still to do,' he said, and the group walked away.

'And they won't want you there, neither!' Mr Marks shouted after him, then looked at Ruby, shaking his head. 'It's all right, love, we can't choose our families, can we?'

Which only made her feel even more ashamed of Eric and the new blackshirted 'family' he had chosen for himself.

That night, when a knock came at the front door, she feared it was her father. Uncle Jim had told her he'd given Dodge a place to stay and had brought her a message from him, begging Ruby to give him a chance. She'd sent Uncle Jim away with her answer and since then Dodge hadn't tried to get in touch again. But it wasn't like him to give up and she'd been half expecting him. She pushed aside her night school science homework and went to answer the door. It was Eric.

'Can I come in? I let the van go back to Black House without me.'

Ruby hesitated with the door only half open.

'Can't I just stop for a cuppa?'

She let him in and when she'd set his cup of tea on the table, she waited for him to speak.

'What's all this?' he said, pulling her homework towards him. 'Since when are you interested in chemical bonds?'

'It's part of the science paper for my matriculation.'

'Matriculation! You? Why?'

She gave him a sour look. 'Because I want to get a better job one day and I can't do it without a Certificate of Education.'

'I didn't think you even liked *reading*,' he said.

'I was too busy wiping your snotty nose to find out if I did or not!'

'Hmm.' He flicked through her text book. 'I came to say – about earlier – I don't want to fall out with you. Not now we've got Mum back. But, Ruby, you've got to let me believe what I believe. Same as I do you.'

She looked at him as he ate one of the jam tarts she'd made for Davey. 'But I don't think they *are* your beliefs. Not really. I think there are people high up feeding you, using you. You're a Bermondsey boy, you've got Dad's looks and you've got the gift of the gab, same as him. You're just useful, Eric.'

He looked offended. 'Well, what if I am! I *want* to be useful.'

'But not for this – this hatred. You do know that my Alfie is Jewish? And what about your own grandfather?'

'It's not all about race. Fascism's a fairer system, with strong leadership and power for the people instead of the bankers and the rich.'

She waved an impatient hand at him. 'So, when your strong leader comes along and says he's decided all people with Jewish grandads are banned from the BUF, what then?

'That won't happen; look at me!' He pointed to his sky-blue eyes and pulled at a strand of his blond hair.

'All right, then, what if it's all mad people that are the next ones on the list to be got rid of. Are you going to march up to Cane Hill and turf out your own mother?'

He opened his mouth and closed it again. 'Don't say that.'

'Why not? Ocki told me they're already doing it in Germany.'

'Mosley's different, he wouldn't.'

'No?'

He licked his lips. 'No system's perfect. But I'm not arguing with you. I just wanted to tell you to stay away from the rally. It'll get nasty, really nasty. We'll be better prepared this time.'

'Oh, don't worry. I'm staying away.'

She didn't add that the whole of Bermondsey would be staying away too. That would have spoiled the surprise.

And in May, when the day of the mass rally came, the boycott had its effect, just as Dr Salter had predicted. The change in the anti-fascists' tactics had been kept quiet and when the Blackshirts marched into Bermondsey this time, they were immediately corralled by the police without any opposition from stone throwers or barricades. Curtains were tweaked along the route and front doors opened a crack to give the curious a view of the Blackshirt ranks marching past, escorted by their own armoured vehicles. But there were no crowds of jeering protestors on every street corner to greet them. Mosley – and Eric too – were left speaking only to their own followers, as all of Bermondsey stayed away – all, that is, except Ocki Diamond. He'd told Ida that he owed it to his brother to turn up and make a stand and he had come home with a bloody nose, but in a better frame of mind, Ida said cheerfully.

In the following days, Ruby looked out for newspaper articles about the rally, but there were only a few small columns and she was glad that Eric's speech had gone unreported. It might discourage him from making another. When she next saw him, he didn't mention the march and neither did she, but he did promise he'd start visiting Rachel again.

It wasn't until July that Rachel's doctors finally agreed that her children's visits had had a calming effect and promised they would reduce the drugs which kept her asleep. Ruby's elation was short-lived, however, for July was also the month when Alfie's battalion marched off to join what was being called the Battle of Ebro. She'd heard news broadcasts that the International Brigades, along with the bulk of the Republican forces, were mounting a last-ditch attempt to push back Franco's Nationalist army. Alfie had managed to write one letter while on the march to the battleground on the banks of the sprawling river Ebro. Ruby sensed a new, worrying note of resignation in the letter. Alfie told her, in all but words, that the war was already lost.

Ocki followed the Battle of the Ebro obsessively, which was difficult as reports were sporadic and conflicting. The only consistent story coming out was that the Republicans were being slaughtered in their thousands by Franco's men, who, with help from Hitler's air and artillery forces, seemed to be blasting them into oblivion.

There was nothing Ocki could do to help his brother, so as the summer wore on, he made it his mission to thwart Eric's attempts to set up a Bermondsey BUF branch. If Eric was giving out leaflets in the streets, Ocki would be close behind, tearing them up; if Eric was on a soapbox in Bermondsey Square drumming up followers, then Ocki would be standing close by, heckling or making a speech of his own.

Ruby understood why he was harrying Eric – better to do something than nothing. The feeling of powerlessness was the worst. She spent days and nights in a state of rigid fear, so that by morning her muscles ached and her teeth hurt from clenching her jaw tight. Her thoughts had turned into one unceasing prayer for Alfie. The only relief she felt was in visiting Rachel and, oddly, in the difficult process of trying to matriculate.

On night school evenings, Ida usually came to St James's Road and the two friends walked to Bermondsey Settlement together. But this evening, Ida had told her she would meet Ruby there because she needed to make sure Ocki went out to the Labour Institute and didn't spend all night glued to the wireless, waiting for reports from Spain.

The class had already begun by the time Ida arrived and the teacher gave her a reproving look. 'If you can't be bothered to be on time for my classes, Miss Turpin, I'd rather you didn't come at all.' Miss Sloane was the strictest of all their teachers, most of whom had been patient with them, knowing that to carve out a few hours for study took a monumental effort after a day in the factory. Ida apologized – quite meekly for her – and sat in the seat Ruby had saved.

Ruby pointed to the place they'd reached in the maths text book.

'Old cow,' Ida muttered.

'What happened to you?' Ruby whispered.

'Ocki. We had a row. I told him he's got to sort himself out or I'm off.'

'No!'

Miss Sloane turned around sharply and, catching Ruby's guilty look, said, 'As Miss Scully has been paying such close attention, perhaps she would like to come to the front and complete the equation.'

With a burning face, Ruby did as she was told. Her hand shook as she picked up the chalk, but looking at the board she realized she'd worked out this very problem in her home work the night before. She finished the equation with ease and put the chalk down, looking to Miss Sloane.

'Yes, very good,' the teacher said, ruffled. 'Well, quickly, Miss Scully, back to your seat!'

'Shot her right up the arse,' Ida said under her breath as Ruby sat down. And Ruby put a hand over her face, masking a grin.

After class, as they walked home, Ida explained what had happened with Ocki.

'He comes home from work every night, on goes the radio and he's got a bloody map out at the tea table, marking off this battalion and that, and he's jotting it all down in a little notebook. Sometimes I want to say to him, just go yourself! Go and fall arse over tit in a Spanish river for the cause!'

'You don't mean that.'

'Course I don't mean it. I love him like crazy, but I don't know how to bring him out of it.'

'What did he do, when you said you'd leave?'

'First laugh I've got out of him all week. Says I'd miss him before I was out the door, starts singing that sad song you and me used to like when we started getting interested in *romance*, you know – 'When Your Lover Has Gone'?'

'Oh, I remember how it goes,' Ruby said, and began to sing the plaintive song about lost love.

When you're alone, who cares for starlit skies?
When you're alone, the magic moonlight dies
At break of dawn, there is no sunrise
When your lover has gone...'

'Except he's tone deaf, and he sounded like this,' Ida began singing off key and Ruby joined in.

What lonely hours the evening shadows bring,
What lonely hours – with memories lingering
Like faded flowers; life can't mean anything
When your lover has gone.

By the end of the song they were both laughing at their joint disharmony. 'Only that was better than his version!' Ida said, slipping her arm through Ruby's. 'He was right, though. Even if he is a misery these days, I couldn't do without him now. Same as you couldn't do without Alfie.'

'No,' Ruby said, feeling a tightness creep across her chest. 'I can't even bear to think of it...'

Ida looked stricken. 'Oh, Ruby. I didn't mean that; me and my big foot.'

'It's all right, Ida. I'd rather we talk about him as if he's just going to be sitting in your kitchen when you get home. It's better than all the other pictures I've got in my head. I just wish I knew exactly where he was...'

It wasn't long after their conversation that Ruby found out exactly where Alfie was, and then she wished she hadn't. The news came with one of Alfie's comrades, who'd been invalided home. He was a Suffolk boy, but instead of going straight home, he made a special trip to see her when he got back to England. He stood at the door, introducing himself as Johnny Bray. He seemed a nice boy, round-faced and stocky, with a thick Suffolk accent that made her think of farms and fens. As he sat at her kitchen table, drinking tea, she couldn't picture him in Spain, nor fighting with anything other than a pitchfork and spade. He didn't look capable of killing anyone. He must be a farmer's son, she thought, but was surprised when he said no, he'd been on the fishing boats out of Lowestoft, before volunteering.

'I've got news of Alfie,' he said, and she wanted to put her finger to his full, rosy lips, wanted to send him back to Suffolk without ever hearing another word from him.

But she sat down opposite and said, 'Go on.'

The hill had no name except 481, he said. They'd got there by crossing the river Ebro in boats and pontoons. Full of hope they thought they'd smash Franco's men.

'But it were us ended up smashed to pieces.' His accent had such a cosy warmth about it. And then he told her about the constant bombardment during the unbearable heat of the Spanish summer.

'I han't never heered nothin' like it. Went on day an' night. And the heat! T'were hotter an' hell.'

With their water supplies running out, they'd been pushed back to the river, bombed by German planes and Spanish artillery all the way, till they'd lost every bit of ground they'd gained.

'No retreat, that were the order they give. No retreat.'

'And Alfie, what happened to him? Did you leave him there, on the hill?' she asked. Her teeth were chattering and she knew she could not stop the trembling in her limbs, so she gripped the kitchen table in an attempt to steady herself.

'Leave him? No fear! He couldn't walk, so we dragged him back to the river on a stretcher. Waited till it was dark and we put him on one of our boats that was evacuating wounded back across the Ebro.'

'So, he went to a hospital?'

The young boy twisted his International Brigade beret around and around. 'Honestly? I couldn't say for sure. He warn't at the hospital they sent me to later on, when I got this,' he patted his own wounded leg, 'but that don't mean nothing, though. Last time I seen him was on the river bank and he warn't dead. He give me this – for you.'

The boy handed her a piece of grubby paper, folded tightly.

'I han't looked at it,' Johnny said and she believed him.

She folded it in her palm, which was clammy and cold. She couldn't read it in front of the boy, so she tucked it into her apron pocket.

'But no one's heard anything since?'

He shook his head. 'It was chaos. I got shipped back to England with a couple of hundred others invalided home. Alfie could still be in one of the other hospitals, waiting till he's fit enough to travel. T'won't be long before all the boys come home, though. The war's lost.'

Before he left, she gave him sandwiches to keep him going on his journey and her hand shook so much that half the cup of tea spilled into the saucer, but he didn't seem to mind and drank what was in the saucer first. He wolfed down the sandwiches.

After he'd gone, she took out the folded note. She sat for a while, gripping it in her hand, frightened to read it. Eventually she unclenched her fist. It ached. She let her fingers open gradually till her palm was flat and the small piece of folded brownish paper lay there like a crumpled dead flower. She teased it open. The pencil Alfie had used had been blunt and the writing was faded in places. The long journey in the boy's pocket had etched the creased folds with dirt. She spread the paper onto the white deal table and bent to read.

My Darling Ruby,
I wish I had more time and words, but must hurry. I have been wounded in the battle, taken a bullet in the back, but I wanted you to know that I'm alive and I will come home to you when this is all done. They are evacuating me tonight. I know you will be happy to see me safely out of the battle. You are the strongest, bravest girl I know. Keep the faith, Ruby, my love, keep the faith.
Always yours, Alfie.

Faith? Which faith did he mean? Faith in the cause, faith in him, faith in God? There were too many faiths and all who held them believed them to be the one true faith. Eric kept the faith, Charles kept the faith, but that hadn't stopped either of them from being cruel. Perhaps she could have faith in love? Ruby got up, tucked the letter, with the others, behind Alfie's photograph, then went to her bedroom. She lay down on the bed and, curled into a small ball, cried till she had no more tears to shed. She wasn't strong, she wasn't brave, and Love had made her weaker and more defenceless than a newborn baby.

*

She hardly knew Alfie's parents. But now she had to go to them. She could have passed on the news through Ocki, but she felt it would strain him to breaking. Besides, she thought it might be some comfort for them to see his letter. It was a love letter, of sorts, but she didn't mind them seeing it. There was nothing she was ashamed of in hers and Alfie's love.

Ruby went straight from work. She walked past the Central Hall and felt the pull of all the comforting certainty it held, but that had belonged to a different Ruby Scully. All her certainties had been shattered. She hurried on up Bermondsey Street and cut under the thundering, soot-filled railway arch into Barnham Street.

It was strange going back there. Her last visit had been for Charles's father's funeral. Ruby had got the Diamonds' door number from Ida, who'd agreed it was best not to send Ocki. The courtyard of Barnham Street buildings stank. The large rubbish bins were overflowing with rotting food and waste and there was a puddle of something slimy in her path. She skirted the smelly pool and dodged the vocal group of kids who asked her where she was going and offered to show her the way if she gave them a penny.

She told them she didn't have a penny but was looking for the Diamonds' flat and after some good-natured teasing, they pointed it out without payment. She hadn't rehearsed what she would say, but when the door was opened by an older, greyer version of Alfie, she lost all her nervousness. The tiny flat was very different to Charles's mother's. There were two well-worn armchairs and a table with a threadbare velveteen cloth on it, and the sideboard was crammed with photographs of Ocki and Alfie growing up. She could immediately see where the brothers had got their love of books, for there was the unusual luxury of bookcases lining the walls. The place was crowded enough without the little library and she could imagine how hard it must have been for them all when Alfie and Ocki lived there, sleeping in this kitchen, while their parents had the only bedroom.

Alfie's mother's face crumpled when she introduced herself.

'Is it my Alfie you've come about?' she asked. And the fear in her eyes broke Ruby's heart. She wished she didn't have to confirm it. But she nodded and the woman put a hand over her mouth. 'Is it bad?'

Mr Diamond made his wife sit down and offered Ruby the other seat, pulling up a kitchen chair for himself.

'One of his comrades came to see me,' she said, getting the note out of her bag. 'He give me this.' She handed it to Mr Diamond who read it aloud. Mrs Diamond wept quietly while he read. He folded it and handed it back to Ruby.

'Thank you for letting us read it. I'm glad he had you to think about – while he was out there.'

'Oh, I begged him not to go. What am I going to do if my boy don't come home?' Mrs Diamond asked, rocking herself slightly back and forth.

And Ruby, understanding now what Alfie had meant in his letter, said, 'He wants us to keep the faith.'

As the summer wore on, Ida decided to join Ruby on her extra Saturday shifts in butchery. She needed to start earning a bit of extra money and besides, Ocki was spending most of his Saturday afternoons with anti-fascist work and today was no exception.

'He's seemed a lot better lately, though,' Ida said as she plucked the wings from a chicken and twisted off the legs.

'That's good, Ida. His mum and dad told me they were worried about him when I was there. They don't need to be worrying about both their sons.' Ruby scooped a carcass she'd picked clean into a bin, ready for making into stock. She began chopping up the meat for chicken soup.

'Where's Ocki going today?'

Ida chuckled. 'He's going to make sure your Eric has a bloody bad day!' And she explained how he planned to stalk

Eric and his group of Blackshirts along Tower Bridge Road as they leafleted shops and stalls. He'd already alerted many of the Jewish shopowners and they'd promised to be outside their shops, seeing off the Blackshirts and generally making it difficult for them to linger and talk to people.

'Well, I'd be happy if Ocki does chase Eric off. The thing is, Ida, I don't think he's a bad boy, he's just—'

'Stupid?'

Ruby laughed. 'That too, but more like gullible. He trusts these people and they're good at twisting the truth.'

Ida sighed. 'Sometimes I think it's the same on our side too.'

'Really?' Ruby had never heard a disloyal word from Ida about the socialist cause.

'They're all at each other's throats.'

'But not Dr Salter?'

Ida smiled indulgently. 'Even he got in trouble for losing his rag and had to put an apology in the paper for saying some party members were as bad as fascists!'

'Eric says I have to let him believe what he believes.'

'Not when people start dying because of it.'

Ruby stared down at the bloody board and paused in her chopping. 'They're dying in Spain...'

They worked steadily through the piles of dead birds until Ruby was nauseous with the smell of offal and flesh and longed for a lungful of fresh air.

'You've gone green, love, not long to go now.'

Ruby looked up at the clock. It was ten past four. She could survive another twenty minutes.

'My Ocki's coming to meet me after work – we're going to see his mum and dad.'

'That's nice, they need a bit of company.'

Ida gave a small smile. 'Ain't just that – we've got a bit of news to tell them.' Ida paused, and began clearing up her bench. Their shift was at an end, so Ruby had to wait until they'd been to the cloakroom before asking Ida about her news.

'There's another reason Ocki's been happier, Ruby. We're getting married!' Ida grabbed her around the waist and tossed her up in the air, a habit that always caused Ruby to giggle, though it did attract a few stares from the other women in the cloakroom.

'Oh, Ida, I'm so happy for you! You kept that quiet. But I thought you didn't care about marriage?'

Ida put her down. 'Not for myself,' her friend said, putting a hand to her stomach. 'For the baby.'

Now it was Ruby's turn to hug her friend. She couldn't lift her off the ground but she jumped up and down with joy. It was the sort of news they all needed at the moment.

As they emerged from the 1924 building they were met by the shouts of men running across the barrel yard. They were going in that direction anyway, so Ruby and Ida followed quickly to see what the commotion was about. It was as they rounded the corner and the 1927 building came into view that they saw a ring of men had formed around something on the floor.

'What's going on, Tom?' Ruby asked a young cooper she recognized as Alfie's workmate.

'Oh, Ruby, no! Don't go over there, love.' Tom barred their way, arms outstretched.

'Why not?' she asked as the young man looked around for help.

'There's been an accident. Looks like someone's fallen off the roof.'

Ruby automatically glanced up to the flat roof of the seven-storey building. When she looked back, Ida, never one to follow an order, had slipped past Tom. 'She can't see that,' he said, dashing after her. But Ida was already elbowing her way to the front of the group.

Tom lunged forward, caught her arm, trying to drag her back, but he was too late. Ida's scream split the air. Ruby's blood froze. She charged through the crowd to find Ida on her knees, with her arms wrapped around the broken body of Ocki Diamond.

25

Like Faded Flowers

September–October 1938

Ida would not be parted from Ocki, so the men had to pick him up with Ida's arms still around him and carry him to the nearby Medical Mission. They laid him on a treatment bed and, for the first time, Ruby dared to look at him. Although the men carrying him had put him down so carefully, his arms were now as twisted as his withered leg. His misshapen body had been smashed in the fall and the dark hair on the crown of his head was plastered and sticky with blood. Yet his pale, youthful face was untroubled by the turmoil that had plagued him over the past months and was without blemish.

'I'm sorry, my dear, but there's nothing we can do for him. I'm afraid it looks like a suicide,' the doctor said gently to Ida. 'Some of the men who brought the young man here said he'd been depressed lately.'

Ida looked up fiercely. 'No! My Ocki wouldn't do this, not now. We was getting married. I'm having his baby. He wouldn't! Would he, Ruby?' Ida looked wildly round and held out a bloodied hand for Ruby, who went to her friend and held her tightly. She wished that the strength of her embrace could be enough to staunch Ida's pain, like pressing a finger on a bleeding wound. But Ida's heaving sobs could not be contained and she laid her head against Ruby's shoulder. 'Oh, Ruby, Ruby, I can't bear it. He's gone.'

Ruby looked up into the doctor's eyes and with a trembling voice declared, 'Ocki wouldn't do this to Ida. He *loved* her.' And at those words, Ida's cry of agony seemed to rend the small room apart so that all the light around them was sucked out into the blackness of empty space.

Ruby looked up to heaven, wishing the rippling waves of light and love that she'd felt on the day of her conversion would come now and enfold Ida. But if Ruby saw anything at all through the rip in the room, it was only darkness. There was no light that she could make out at all, not for herself, nor for her friend.

'I'm sure he loved her,' the doctor said, laying a hand over Ruby's. 'I'll leave you two here and let you know when the police arrive.'

Ida brushed Ocki's forehead with one hand and gripped Ruby's hand with the other.

'He didn't do it, Ruby. He didn't kill himself,' Ida said, choking on her tears. 'He was so happy about the baby and—' Suddenly Ida went very still and she fixed wide eyes on Ruby. 'Someone else done this to him! And when I find out who it was I'll kill them with my bare hands.'

It seemed to take an eternity for the police to arrive, but it was probably no more than twenty minutes. Ruby sat with her arm around Ida, who held and kissed Ocki's hand. Sometimes Ida would let out the deepest, heart-wrenching groan and then Ruby would hold her close, but in the face of this death, Ruby had no words of faith or comfort to offer; she simply felt as if she were being frozen from the inside out.

Eventually the doctor returned with a policeman, who asked them questions about their relationship to Ocki and what they thought of his state of mind. The constable said he had already spoken to the men who found Ocki and was now going on to the factory to question more witnesses.

'So, there is nothing that might have caused him to take his own life, in your opinion, Miss Turpin,' he asked.

Ida shook her head violently. 'No! Nothing. He was happy,' she managed to say.

'And you, Miss Scully, you were a friend of Mr Diamond; is there anything you can think of?'

Ruby had to believe he wouldn't do this to Ida. 'No, nothing,' she replied.

He made some notes and told them that Ocki's body would be taken to the police morgue. There would have to be a coroner's investigation and it would be better, he said, addressing Ruby, if she took Ida home.

When the policeman had gone, Ida looked at her imploringly. She seemed smaller somehow, shrunken and frail. Her strong, bold friend was broken. 'It's all right, Ida. We don't have to go home. We'll stay here till they come to take Ocki away.'

They sat vigil for another hour. A nurse from the clinic brought them hot, sweet tea and, as the minutes passed, Ida's trembling grew less. They sat while Ocki's body grew cold; their own breathing, hers and Ida's, seemed to synchronize, and then the peace that Ruby had prayed for descended like an invisible mist into the room. Ida looked into Ruby's eyes and nodded. Ida had felt the peace too and now she spoke, not to her lover's dead body, but to the space around him.

'It's all right, Ocki, I know you love me. And I'll look after our baby. You can go now, darlin'. You can go.'

It was dusk before Ocki's body could be taken away and, as they stepped out of the Medical Mission's side door into Crimscott Street, Ruby took hold of her friend's arm. She felt Ida lean heavily on her for support.

'It's me legs,' Ida said, 'they've gone to water.'

'Take deep breaths. There's no hurry,' Ruby said, and while Ida recovered her balance, Ruby looked towards Grange Road and the early evening traffic swishing past. People rushing about their business, eager to be home for teatime and the pools results on the wireless, while tragedy played out just yards away in this little side street.

As she turned her attention back to Ida, her eye was caught by a movement in the gathering dusk. Ruby felt a cold chill in the pit of her stomach, for she recognized the familiar figure standing on the corner, looking on, white-faced and lost, his pale hair falling across a bloodied forehead. As soon as he realized he'd been seen he darted back into Grange Road and disappeared. At first, she couldn't work out what he could have been doing there, but as she and Ida began walking to the bus stop, she could only conclude that if anyone knew what had happened to Ocki that day, it would be Eric.

Ruby searched Ida's face for any indication that she'd seen him, but she had an almost blank, trusting expression. Her brave friend had gone somewhere else and was reliant upon Ruby now. 'You're coming home with me tonight,' Ruby said.

Ida nodded. 'But what about Ocki's mum and dad?'

'I'll go round later; let's just get you home first.

Back at St James's Road, she was relieved that Davey wasn't there. He'd left a note saying he was downstairs at Aunt Nancy's. At least she wouldn't have to explain to him what had happened in front of Ida. Now, she helped Ida off with her coat and made her tea and while she drank it Ruby made up a fire. It was midsummer, but Ida felt cold to the touch and shivered continuously. The doctor had given Ruby a sleeping draught for her friend, which she made her drink down. When she'd warmed up her own bed with a hot water bottle, Ida got in fully clothed and Ruby lay on top of the covers, stroking her friend's hair till she fell asleep. She waited until Ida's breathing was deep and steady and then she eased herself off the bed.

Downstairs she explained to Aunt Nancy and Davey what had happened. Her little brother's face was solemn as he assured her he would be all right staying with Aunt Nancy. 'You go and look after Ida. She needs you,' he said, in a grown-up way that made her proud of him.

'I will, but first I've got to see Ocki's mum and dad,' she told him.

All the way to Barnham Street she was trying out ways of telling Ocki's poor parents that he was dead. She wished it hadn't fallen to her, but she told herself she was doing it for Ida – and for Alfie. Alfie! She hadn't even had time to think what this would do to him when he found out. But how would he find out? 'Oh, Alfie, where are you? We need you here,' she whispered to him as she walked.

Ruby's face, when she arrived at the Diamond's flat, proved more eloquent than any of the words she had rehearsed. Both parents knew instantly that their son Alfie had died. There was a look of almost resignation at the inevitability of it. They had prepared themselves. But then Ruby was forced to lacerate their preparedness with an unforeseen pain, the bewildering news that it wasn't Alfie who had died, but their younger son Ocki.

Their grief was quiet, shocked and unbearably dignified. They were sparing her, she knew it. She told them all that she knew, which was little enough, and left them to grieve in private.

Her whole body felt numb as she left the flat and her legs wouldn't carry her any further. She sat on one of the damp, clammy steps, letting herself weep for Ocki and for Alfie and Ida. Her bones felt as if they had melted within her and only willpower enabled her to get up and walk down the stairs. It wasn't only grief she felt. She was terrified. If Eric had anything to do with Ocki's death, then either Ida or Alfie would kill him, and if they didn't, she feared she might do it herself.

The following day Ruby went with Ida to Arnold's Place to tell her parents what had happened and left Ida in her mother's care while she went to fetch some of her things from Fort Road. When Ruby had suggested it wasn't wise for Ida to be alone in the home she'd shared with Ocki, her friend had given in without much of a fight. As there was certainly no room for her in Arnold's Place, it was agreed she would stay with Ruby.

Ruby went to Ida's bedroom and the poignancy of Ocki's death hit her as she opened the wardrobe. Ida's clothes were mixed up with his in a comfortable jumble so that Ruby felt guilty just to be disentangling the frocks from the shirts. The chest of drawers told the same story. There wasn't a part of their lives that hadn't intertwined. Ruby was reminded of the gnarled old cherry tree she'd once seen in Southwark Park; a rambling rose had grown up through its branches, but the tree had died and as the branches had given way, the vibrant, living rose had collapsed too, breaking and dying itself. And now Ruby wondered if Ida, like the rose, would simply collapse and die without her lover.

As she passed Alfie's bedroom, she put a hand on the door knob. She hesitated, knowing that whatever she saw would be a painful reminder of him. She turned the handle and walked in. It smelt of him. Looking round at the neat room she went to his wardrobe and opened it. Alfie had left his good clothes behind. She unwound the scarf she was wearing, kissed it and then carefully draped it over his best jacket.

On Monday, Ruby stayed home from work to look after Ida. Her friend could eat nothing for breakfast, but Ruby had just made her some tea when the constable who'd questioned them at the Medical Mission arrived.

'I spoke to a number of witnesses of the accident,' he said. 'Some people actually witnessed the fall – it's possible he deliberately threw himself from the roof.' Ida blinked and looked at Ruby, who took her hand.

Ida spoke slowly, as if she were dredging up words from a deep well. 'I told you before, he wouldn't; he had no reason to kill himself.'

'I believe his brother is fighting in Spain. Some of his colleagues said Mr Diamond had been worried about him.'

'Yes, he was worried about Alfie, but we all were!' Ruby interrupted.

'I see. I should also tell you we're investigating another theory. A few witnesses came forward saying they'd seen a group of men running from the 1927 building minutes after Mr Diamond fell.'

'Did they recognize any of them?' Ruby asked quickly.

'Not individually. But the men were wearing black shirts beneath their jackets.' He paused, letting the information sink in. 'They said Mr Diamond was a staunch anti-fascist; was that the case?' he asked Ida.

'Blackshirts?' Ida's dull eyes sparked a sudden fire and she shot a look at Ruby. 'Eric?'

All the occasions when she'd tried to pull Eric back from the path he'd chosen flashed before Ruby in an accusing stream of images. If she'd been stronger, more persuasive, would Ocki still be alive? Her feelings of guilt must have shown on her face, for the policeman leaned forward, alert.

'Is there something you know, Miss Scully, about these Blackshirts and what they might have been doing at the factory?'

She looked at Ida and nodded slowly. 'I saw Eric outside the factory, as we carried Ocki to the Medical Mission. He run away.'

Ida groaned. 'Oh, Ruby. If it's him…'

'We can't be sure he's involved,' Ruby said, while realizing that things looked very bad for him.

'Who's Eric?' the policeman asked.

'My brother. He's a member of the BUF and he was in Tower Bridge Road leafleting that day. Ocki was there too – trying to stop them.'

The constable sat back in his chair. 'Ahh, I see. Do you think it's possible your brother and his fellow Blackshirts could have harmed Mr Diamond?'

'I can't speak for anyone else, but my brother? No, I don't think he would have.'

'Well, I'll need to interview him; does he live here with you?'

'No. He lives at Black House – in Kensington,' Ruby replied.

'If you see him, I'd urge him to come to the police station Miss Scully. It'll be better for him if he comes in voluntarily...'

When the policeman had gone, silence hung between them. Ruby broke it. 'Ida, I was going to tell you I'd seen Eric, but I wanted to talk to him first, get his story. I know what he is, but I don't think he's capable of doing this to Ocki, to you.'

Ida was staring into the tea that had now gone cold. 'You said yourself he had a gun at the march last year. You don't know what sort of bloody monster they've turned him into, Ruby. He's not your little brother any more.'

'No, he's not. And if he really did have something to do with this, then he'll never be my brother again, Ida.'

She wouldn't have been surprised if Ida had wanted nothing more to do with her now Eric was implicated in Ocki's death, but her friend's sense of justice hadn't been skewed by her grief. When Ruby asked if she'd prefer not to stay with her, Ida looked puzzled.

'If I find out Eric killed my Ocki, I won't rest till he swings for it. But you're not your brother's keeper, Ruby, even though you always tried to be. He's made his own choices. I'm not holding it against you.

Ida put out one of her large hands and Ruby took hold of it. It felt tremulous and feeble, not like Ida's hand at all.

Ruby resolved to seek out Eric and make him go to the police. But when or how she didn't know, for Ida needed her constantly by her side. It seemed another lifetime ago when Eric had agreed to go with her when she next visited their mother and when Sunday came round and he didn't turn up, she was hardly surprised. Ida's younger sister came to sit with her and promised not to leave until Ruby returned.

Ruby took the train to Cane Hill alone. The possibility of perhaps seeing her mother more conscious and aware this time had been a secret joy she'd been holding for a while. Even Ocki's death couldn't completely dim her anticipation.

The nurse showed her in as usual. Rachel was still in her screened-off bed and Ruby was disappointed.

'I thought she'd be sitting up by now,' she whispered to the nurse.

'Oh, no. It would be too traumatic for her to bring her to full consciousness all in one go! Small steps, my dear. You should notice some tiny differences. Try to be patient.' And the nurse was gone, leaving her alone with Rachel.

Ruby found herself longing to pour out her worries about Eric. But the doctors had stipulated there must be no shocks or emotional stresses placed on her mother. Instead she sat and spoke about Davey; how grown up he was, how clever, how kind. She told her about Alfie and how happy he made her and she mentioned nothing of Spain. But sitting there, holding her mother's hand, searching for all the good things in her life to tell her, made her feel calm in a way she hadn't since Ocki's death. It was as if her mother's silent voice was assuring her that, somehow, all would be well; there was nothing they couldn't get through together. Perhaps it was an illusion, but Ruby felt a small pressure from her mother's hand as it rested in hers and she let an unseen tear of gratitude trickle down her cheek.

It was as she walked away from the hospital, in the semi-darkness beneath the covered walkway leading to the station, that someone came up behind her and spun her around. His face wore a shocked, spectral pallor, there was a golden stubble on his chin and his hair looked greasy. He had the crumpled look of someone sleeping rough.

'Eric!' She gripped him by the arms, shaking him. 'What have you done? Did you hurt Ocki?'

He opened his mouth, but no sound came out. She shook him again. 'You'd better tell me. You and your bully boys have gone too far! Ocki's dead and it's destroyed Ida. My Ida! Do you understand?'

He looked blankly at her and then said in a flat voice, 'Ida? Oh, Ruby.' He dropped his head, covering his eyes to hide his tears. 'I deserve what you think of me. But I wouldn't do that to Ida. I tried to stop them!'

It was hard to believe he wasn't involved in this, but she needed to find out exactly what he'd done. She pushed him forward. 'Come with me. You need to tell me everything, Eric.'

She hurried him on, taking him to a pub opposite the station. They slipped into the saloon bar and Ruby sat him down. The barman gave her and Eric a curious stare and, when she went to buy a brandy and a bitter lemon, he made it plain he didn't like serving a woman. The prices in the saloon bar were steep, but she didn't care if it left her with only sixpence in her purse; she needed to revive Eric to get some sense out of him.

He took a gulp and coughed, avoiding looking at her. She grabbed his arm. 'Eric, look at me. They're trying to say that Ocki killed himself. It's not true, is it?'

He shook his head miserably. 'Oh, Ruby, I've been going mad all week. I couldn't go back to Black House. I don't know what to do!'

'Do you know how it happened?'

'I think so.'

'Then tell me.'

'Ocki was making a nuisance of himself all that afternoon, stirring up people against us, like he always did. I wasn't bothered, just told my lot to ignore him and carry on with the leafleting. But there's this new bloke, Digger. He's a nutter, Ruby. There's plenty of hard men in the BUF, but he's one vicious bastard. So, by the time Ocki's followed us all the way up and down Tower Bridge Road, Digger's had enough of him, starts shoving him around. Well, I was fed up with Ocki too, but he's a cripple!' Eric's hand shook as he lifted the brandy to his lips. 'I told Digger to lay off him, but he ignores me and starts geeing up the others. They start chucking old bits of veg from the market at Ocki, then it was broken crates, anything they could find. In the end, Ocki's surrounded and they're poking at him and so he runs for it.' Eric dropped his head and rubbed at his eyes.

'What happened next?'

'He might have been a cripple, but he must have been terrified, because he pelted down Grange Road and they all went after him. I tried to stop them, but they was like a pack of dogs. It was my fault, Ruby. I was in command. I should've stopped them!'

'You tried?' Ruby said hopefully.

He nodded. 'Yes, but I wasn't quick enough! By the time I got to Crimscott Street I'd lost them. I thought Ocki must have run into Crosse's.'

'He thought he'd be safe there.'

'Well I looked around a bit, but there was no sign of them in the yard, so I was walking away and all of a sudden my troop come shooting out of Crosse's gates. I grabbed Digger, but he give me this.' Eric pointed to a scabby bruise on his forehead. 'He knocked me out cold, and when I come to I was in the airey of a house in Grange Road. They must have chucked me down there. I was just going back to the yard, when I saw you all carrying Ocki out. I panicked! I know running away makes me look guilty, but I swear I had nothing to do with what happened to him.'

Ida had said he wasn't her little brother any more, but looking at him now he seemed pathetically young. Others had used his youth and gullibility for their own purposes, had pushed him to a place beyond his years or understanding; and now he'd bear the guilt for the rest of his life.

'Ruby, tell me what to do!'

Go to the police. The copper said it'd be better if you came in before they found you.'

'Digger'll kill me.'

'Would you rather it be Jack Ketch?'

He shuddered at the mention of the legendary hangman. 'No.'

Back in Bermondsey they went straight to Tower Bridge Road police station, where Eric made his statement. Afterwards, he told Ruby the detective had asked for his address. When he'd said no fixed abode, he was told he might have to stay in the cells overnight.

'So, I gave them your address. Can I come home with you, Ruby?'

'Ida's staying with me. Can you face her?'

He bit his lip and nodded. 'I've got to.'

Once home, she left him in the passage, and went to tell her friend she had Eric in tow.

'He's here?' Ida stood up, swaying slightly. Her little sister put out a steadying hand.

'He knows what happened to Ocki and we've been to the police already. Do you want to see him?'

'I'll hear what he's got to say for himself,' Ida said. 'The worst thing's been not knowing how it happened.'

Ruby beckoned Eric in and again was struck by how young he looked. His eyes brimmed when he saw Ida, but Ruby was glad he didn't cry. The only one in the room who deserved to spill tears was Ida.

'I'm so sorry, Ida. It wasn't me killed Ocki. I tried to stop it, but I couldn't…'

Ida listened with rapt attention, stopping Eric every now and then to ask for a detail. Did he know why Ocki had come to the factory? Had he heard Ocki cry out? What had he said, what were his last words? Had he looked scared? Had he fought back? Most of the questions Eric didn't know how to answer. But one thing he said, which seemed to give Ida peace, was that it was only a matter of minutes between the time Eric lost sight of the pack of Blackshirts and when they'd come rushing out of the factory gates. Whatever had happened on that rooftop had happened quickly.

When he'd finished telling her all he could, she gave a satisfied nod and dropped her head. 'Thanks, Eric. It's better to know.'

It seemed extraordinary that Eric should be sleeping under the same roof as Ida. But the effort of hearing about Ocki's last minutes had depleted all Ida's reserves and when Ruby asked if she minded Eric staying she barely had strength to answer.

'Whatever he's done, he tried to save my Ocki. Of course I don't mind.'

And Ruby felt that in all her years of church going she'd never seen a truer or more simple example of forgiveness.

Not long after Ocki's funeral, Ruby received a letter from the International Brigade's British Battalion welfare committee. After investigating her request for news of Alfred Diamond they were able to confirm that the hospital train in which he had been travelling had been destroyed by shelling. The survivors had been transported to various military hospitals and clinics in the region. They noted, with a hint of compassion, that during the withdrawal from the Ebro, record-keeping had been patchy. All searches of the likely locations had uncovered no trace of Alfred Diamond and they therefore had to regretfully list him as missing in action.

So that Ida wouldn't be alarmed, she'd gone to the scullery and descended the rickety wooden steps to the small backyard. The silver birch tree her mother had planted was outgrowing its mean space, and its graceful, swaying filigree of fine branches had begun to shed its leaves early, so that a few fell like bronze pennies around her feet. She leaned her face against its bright trunk and squeezed her eyes tight shut. When she'd first known Alfie he'd been as slender and fresh as this tree was in spring. She'd loved the way he walked with such easy grace and, once he'd acknowledged his love for her, she'd loved to be held by those long, strong arms, or to intertwine her legs with his as they sat together talking of all they would do in the future. Peeling slivers of silver bark scratched her cheek and she pressed her flesh into the sharp edges. Better to feel this physical pain than the amorphous mist of grief that descended around her along with the bronze, dead leaves.

She couldn't go inside and mourn in front of her friend. She remembered the song they had sung together, so flippantly, so insouciantly, never fearing it would one day be their story.

What lonely hours, the evening shadows bring
What lonely hours with, memories lingering
Like faded flowers, life can't mean anything
When your lover has gone

With a balled fist, Ruby stifled the groan that came up from the pit of her stomach and clutched at the tree for fear that she would fall to the ground and never get up. She never heard the footsteps behind her, but when she felt Ida's hand on her shoulder, her resolve to keep her own sorrow to herself vanished. 'We've lost them both,' she sobbed, crumpling the letter, and letting her head fall on Ida's shoulder. The two friends clasped one another tightly, drawing strength from each other, as they always had done.

26

Resurrection

Winter 1938

Ida had confessed to Ruby that, but for her unborn baby, she would gladly have followed Ocki to the grave. Eventually she knew she would have to begin picking up the unravelled threads of her life and the only way to do that, she said, was to return to work and home to Fort Road, and Ruby found it hard to let her go. Looking after her had helped ward off her own grief. She had no dead body as evidence and told herself she should be able to keep hope alive, yet most days Alfie felt as lost to her as if he'd been buried with Ocki.

Her mother became the single point of hope in her life. The process of reducing Rachel's medication had taken so long it had felt like weaning a child, but the doctors had now completely stopped the prolonged narcosis and the day was approaching when she and Eric would be able to hear their mother's voice and see expression on her beautiful, wasted face.

'Are you nervous?' Eric asked Ruby as they got off at Coulsdon station and approached the hospital.

Ruby nodded, dry-mouthed. 'She might not even recognize us. We're not ten and eight-year-old kids any more.'

'I think she'll know us, but Ruby, I'm worried about something else. What if she's still – still mad?'

Ruby hadn't let herself think about that possibility. She'd concentrated all her efforts on making sure her mother simply had the chance to wake up.

'I don't think it was ever a permanent thing. If she hadn't been chucked in here... Anyway, even if she is still mad, at least she'll have us to fight for her now.'

They were led to a different ward block from their last visits and, as they hurried to keep up with the orderly, Eric asked her, 'Do you think we should tell Dad that she's awake?'

'No!' Ruby snapped. 'He left her to moulder in this place for years – he doesn't deserve to know.'

'What if Mum asks for him?'

'She won't.'

She hadn't told Eric about her father's yearly birthday visits to Rachel and she couldn't allow herself to soften towards Dodge. He'd given Rachel so little, it seemed worse than if he'd given her nothing at all. And she was sure that her mother would agree with her.

The orderly handed them over to the nurse in charge of a smaller, lighter ward than Rachel's previous one. It was more like a day room, with some patients sitting around tables, others sitting up in day beds. They followed the nurse to a bed drawn up into a large bay window. Rachel was propped up on pillows, her face turned towards the window. She hadn't seemed to hear their approach. They stopped at the bed and still Rachel didn't look round. The anticipation was almost unbearable, yet Ruby felt almost too shy to speak.

The nurse put a hand under Rachel's chin and tilted her face towards her children. Her eyes were still closed. Ruby looked at the nurse in confusion.

'Is she still asleep?'

'I thought the doctor had explained.'

'No! Why's she not woken up?'

'Oh, my dear, I know it's disappointing for you, but sometimes this happens with patients who've been under narcosis therapy for a very long time. She's been taken off all medication and there's absolutely no reason for her not to have woken up. She's simply forgotten how to. The best thing you can do is sit and speak to her gently. She'll wake up when she's ready.'

Eric looked as disappointed as Ruby, who felt a sharp pang of envy for all those visitors now chatting to their relatives. Even the occasional hoots and uncontrollable high-pitched laughter coming from one corner seemed better than this silence.

She leaned forward. 'Hello, Mum. It's me and Eric. Don't you want to open your eyes and see us? Eric's a handsome feller. He's grown up now and so am I...' Ruby had felt less inhibited talking to her when she was deep in her induced coma. Now it felt she was talking to someone who didn't want to respond, not to someone who couldn't. Eric was even more tongue-tied than she was. He looked helplessly at Ruby.

He could hardly tell Rachel that he was due in court to testify against a psychopath who'd killed Ruby's friend, so she suggested, 'Tell Mum about your new job.'

He leaned forward and awkwardly addressed his sleeping mother. 'I learned how to drive, Mum, and I've got a job at Peeks, driving a delivery van.'

The BUF had at least given him a useful skill so that now he could survive without them, but Ruby wished it hadn't come as a package with firearms training.

'And I'm still at Crosse's,' Ruby added, 'but I've been going to night school. It'll take me another year but if I matriculate I might...' She glanced at Eric, hoping he wouldn't mock her, and continued in a rush, 'I might even go to Goldsmiths and become a teacher.' She hoped that by sharing her most precious, secret dream she might nudge her mum into a response. But her steady, deep breathing continued, and not a flicker of recognition crossed Rachel's face.

'Davey's looking forward to seeing you,' Ruby played her trump card, 'but we've said it's better if he waits till you're properly awake...'

The hoots and laughter from the other side of the room punctuated their silences as Rachel slept on, unmoving and seemingly unmoved.

'You couldn't have done any more, Ruby,' Eric said as they followed the orderly back around the labyrinthine web of corridors linking the ward blocks. There was a sticky, dull, grey light filtering through the windows and she felt as if she had left her mother caught like a fly in gossamer, wrapped and cocooned by sleep and unable to break free. She didn't like Eric's resigned tone.

'I ain't giving up yet!'

Eric shook his head. 'You heard what the nurse said. She don't *want* to wake up. And she was always stubborn – like you.'

'I'll come back every week if I have to, till she opens her eyes again.'

She was grateful when they left the fusty building and walked back to the station. In an unusual display of brotherly affection Eric took her arm and slipped it through his own. 'You ain't got to fight all the battles on your own no more, Ruby. We can take it in turns coming to visit Mum. I've had enough of trying to put the world to rights. I'm concentrating on me own family now.'

She believed his change of heart was real. A combination of finding their mother was still alive and guilt over Ocki's death had freed him from the fascist nightmare he'd been sleepwalking in for so long. Rachel might still be asleep, but at least Eric had woken up.

Ruby was glad of the small patch of peace to be found in her backyard today. The slender birch branches were bare now and the gold and copper coins of its leaves carpeted the scrubby square of grass.

Ruby and Ida had gone together to the Old Bailey that morning for the last day of the Blackshirts trial. They sat anonymously in the gallery, listening to the summing up, and when the verdict finally came, Ruby clasped her friend's hand and Ida let out a cry of triumph. Digger and the other Blackshirts in Eric's troop were found guilty of Ocki's murder. And Eric, in spite of being head of the troop, was cleared of any involvement. Though nothing could bring Ocki back, Ida seemed to take palpable strength from the verdict. Ruby could almost feel the power rising like sap into her friend's hand which gripped Ruby's as they walked towards St Paul's. She and Ruby might have been certain that Ocki wouldn't voluntarily leave her and their baby, but now the rest of the world would know it too.

Ruby leaned against the birch tree. Her mother had told her when she was a child that if you listened very carefully you could hear the sap of a birch tree rising. She pressed her ear to the trunk, hearing the thump of her own blood pumping through her veins and perhaps a faint whooshing sound. She looked up through the branches. The late afternoon had a mildness that made her want to linger, as a low white sun glanced into the yard, outlining the birch branches with a silver thread, glinting off the scattered leaves at her feet. The air felt muffled – perhaps rain was coming. And then into the quiet came the sound of a bell, tolling. The St James's ringers must be practicing, but it was odd to hear just the one bell. The birch and the bell both made her think of Alfie. The trial, her mother, her studies – all could block out his memory, for an hour, sometimes two. But when she was alone, it lit her thoughts, like this sun on the birch.

She began walking to Aunt Nancy's back door, needing to collect Davey, who'd gone there after school. She was swishing her feet through the pile of leaves, not hurrying, when Aunt Nancy poked her head out of her scullery window.

'Someone's knocking on your door upstairs, gel,' she called. 'I've got me dinner on. Davey can stay – it's his favourite – meat puddin'!' She pulled her head back into the steamy scullery as Ruby thanked her and hurried up the outside wooden steps. She ran along the passage to the front door. Eric had gone for a drink with Malchy Mongey after the trial, so she wasn't expecting him home. She threw open the door, breathless.

The weather-bronzed face had a dark stubble on it and, as he squinted against the low sun, the creases at the corner of his dark eyes looked dusty. Black strands of hair curled from beneath a battered beret and a dirty cravat was tied loosely around his throat. A shapeless blue jacket hung on his broad shoulders and every inch of him looked lean and hard. It was seconds, or perhaps centuries, or perhaps no time at all before she recognized him.

She moved towards him and stepped out of one world and into another, the world of loss and grief gone in an instant as she melted into his arms and found herself in the new world where Alfie was alive again.

'Alfie? Oh, Alfie! But how?' She let her head fall onto his chest and felt his heart beating against her cheek. 'You're alive!' she sobbed as he curled her into his arms.

'Yes, I'm alive, darling Ruby. I'm alive. Didn't I tell you to keep the faith?'

'I'm sorry I – I couldn't. It's just...'

'Oh, Ruby, you're forgiven a hundred times over.' He kissed the top of her head and she heard him gasp, as if he was a dying man and she his last breath. 'I kept the faith for both of us because I knew this day would come.' They stood on the doorstep, Ruby fearing that if she moved he would disappear and she would be forced to wake up from her dream.

'Can we go in?' he asked, eventually.

She nodded, but wouldn't let go of him. She kept his arm around her and in the kitchen she touched his face, familiarizing herself with its changed contours, chiselled by war. She put his slender, broken-nailed hands to her own cheek and then felt how the calloused fingers brushed through her silver blonde hair, catching on the fine strands. She kissed his dry, cracked lips, asking questions all the while. 'Where have you been all this time? How did you get here? Why didn't you let me know?' And not waiting for answers, she wept tears of happiness and relief till he lifted her up into his arms and carried her to the armchair by the hearth, where she sat intertwined with him, in a silence more eloquent than any words of love.

When they finally moved, she made him tea and scolded him for not warning her he was coming so that she could have made something decent and he smiled at her, seeming to enjoy the scolding.

'I didn't stop to telegram because I wanted to keep on the move! Every minute I was standing still – it was agony, Ruby. I just wanted to get here – to you!'

She forgave him instantly and then, often stumbling over the painful memories, he told her how, in the confusion after the hospital train was shelled, he'd been transported to a rural clinic miles from anywhere. He owed his life to the skill of a humble Spanish doctor who immediately recognized that his back wound meant he must be kept immobile, or risk paralysis. At this she gasped, thinking how close she'd come to losing him, and he quickly took her hand.

'They looked after me for months, Ruby, hid me, when the Nationalists were overrunning the place,' he explained, in a voice full of admiration. 'They tried to get word out to the battalion, but to be honest, by that time there wasn't much left of it.' Shaking his head, his eyes brimmed with tears. He brushed them away. 'I promised myself I wouldn't do this. But so many brave men – we lost so many.' Anguish dimmed his joy at being home and seeing her once more.

'You told me in a letter once that they were all in Spain because they *wanted* to be, the same as you.'

'Yes, like me. But, Ruby, I didn't know a thing when I volunteered. And now I wonder what it was all for. Do you know our side even ended up fighting each other? The anarchists attacked the communists and the Irish volunteers wouldn't serve with the British. That was while me and all those smashing blokes I joined up with got sent out to be slaughtered. We didn't mind dying if it'd stop fascism overrunning Europe, but what happened? Chamberlain went and signed a deal with Hitler! We knew we'd lost, that day he came back with his bit of paper. We should have all packed up and come home then. We'd lost the war and they told us, no retreat!'

She'd never heard such bitterness in his voice. She knew what it was to feel betrayed by the cause you'd given your heart and soul to.

'In the end, Alfie, it don't matter what anyone else did – the politicians and the generals – it matters what you did and why you did it. That's all you can rely on in the end.'

He smiled, his dark eyes bright with adoration. 'I love you Ruby Scully.'

He pulled her to him and they kissed again and she felt hungrier than she ever had for his kisses, knowing that, in spite of all her Christian principles, if Davey hadn't been downstairs and likely to barge in on them, she would have given herself to Alfie in a heartbeat. But there would be time for them later. For now, she had to face shattering his world as soon as he'd regained it.

He hadn't immediately been struck down by grief as she'd feared. It was more like bewilderment. She'd had to repeat the details of Ocki's last day twice over, but each time she reached the most painful part of Eric's involvement it was as if he couldn't comprehend.

'So, Eric did it? Your *brother*, Eric?'

Like a stuck record she repeated, 'No! It was his troop – but not Eric, he tried to help...'

There was a noise of scuffling in the passage. Alfie was in no state to greet Eric, so she turned to intercept him. She was too late and the door was flung open.

'Thank Christ that's over and done with!' Eric strode into the room and, registering the bronzed stranger, threw a questioning glance in Ruby's direction.

Alfie leaped out of his chair and, with an almost animal power, launched his combat-muscled body straight at Eric, knocking him to the floor.

'I'll kill you, fascist bastard!' Alfie screamed in rage and grief, pummelling him. Ruby stood by horrified, watching what war had done to the sensitive man she loved. She had no doubt Alfie would kill Eric if she didn't stop him right now.

She put her arms around Alfie and pulled him away, but his fist smashed into Eric's face again. She clung onto his neck, but he shook her off, like a dog savaging a rat. He didn't know who she was. His only feeling seemed to be hatred for his enemy. Not only Eric, but all the enemies he blamed for the death of his comrades.

While Ruby tussled with Alfie, Eric rolled over and sprang to his feet, pounding along the passage and out into the street. Alfie followed hard on his heels and Ruby ran too, calling after him, 'Listen to me, Alfie, listen. It wasn't Eric!'

Her brother hurtled across the road and disappeared into St James's churchyard. She ran after them, rasping breaths scraping her lungs until she skidded to a halt in front of the church. Alfie sat slumped on the pink granite edge of the portico steps. The polished stone, used as a slide by generations of Bermondsey children, was spattered with fat drops of ruby blood. It dripped from Alfie's knuckles onto the rosy granite surface. His chest was heaving and a hoarse groaning came from his throat.

'What have you done to Eric?'

He covered his face with his hands, the slender fingers wet with blood. She lowered herself to the step, not touching him. 'Alfie, where's my brother?'

He lifted a hand, pointing towards the Gregorian Arms pub on the corner. His reply was barely audible. 'He ran in there.'

'Alfie, listen to me. My brother didn't kill Ocki. Eric tried to save him! He went to the police, told them who did it, and he's been in court today – as a witness. He got the guilty ones convicted and they'll pay now. But you can't punish Eric any more than he's already punished himself.'

'Oh, no,' he groaned. 'I'm sorry I hit him. It's me to blame...' He tilted his head back and looked up at the old dragon atop the tower, twisting slowly in the wind. Tears streamed down his face and he bit his lip till it too was dripping blood. 'So it was fascists killed Ocki.' Alfie spoke almost to himself. 'I'm out there saving Spaniards from fascists and all the time I should have been here, protecting him!' Suddenly he grabbed her hand.

'I can't breathe down here, Ruby. Come with me.' He led her to the side door and with a practiced shoulder-barge against the door he opened it and they climbed up the dusty stairs to the bell tower.

Up in the ringing room it was cool and calm. The wind sang through the louvres in the tower above them and set the bells humming. Ruby's heartbeat slowed and Alfie's breathing calmed.

'I'm sorry you saw me like that, Ruby. Fighting, killing – it makes you find a switch inside. You switch off all your compassion and you switch on something else – you have to, and now it'll always be there, that switch. It frightens me.' He drew up his knees and folded his arms around them.

'You'll be yourself again, Alfie, don't worry. I remember something you said to me once; you was telling me Charles was a dictator and you said – *they're all the same, Hitler, Mussolini, whatever their names are*. You told me, *They'll rob you of your people, rob you of your power and if you're not careful they'll rob you of yourself*. You said that one day I'd turn around and there'd be nothing left of me – and you were right. So Franco won and the Blackshirts killed Ocki. But don't lose yourself, Alfie. Ocki wouldn't want it and I couldn't bear it.'

He gave a shuddering sigh. 'You're right, Ruby.' He stood up and helped her to her feet and they peered out of the high circular window, looking across Bermondsey to Tower Bridge, which stood like a castle drawbridge across the Thames as it wound its way eastwards to the docks and the sea. 'We're going to need to remember who we are when the war comes and all this goes up in smoke.'

'And if it comes, we'll remind each other who we are then,' she said, taking his hand.

Alfie hadn't waited until war broke out before reminding Ruby who she was. A few weeks after his return he made it plain he was disappointed in her.

He'd been astonished and delighted when she'd told him about her mother, but his immediate reaction was that she should have told Dodge that Rachel now had the chance of waking up.

'I'm not saying it wasn't wicked of him to keep you all believing she was dead. But Ruby, do you really want your mum to wake up and find out you've sent Dodge packing? It's not like you to be so unforgiving, and you only get one family. Go and make it up with your dad.'

If it had been anyone else asking her, she would have ignored them. But Alfie's plea was powered by his own regret at leaving his brother. He'd put his principles before those he loved and he didn't want her to make the same mistake. She promised to think about it, but she wasn't even sure where Dodge was living and besides, she'd told herself so often that what he'd done was unforgiveable that the thought of seeking out her dad made her feel physically sick.

In the end she didn't have to seek him out. One evening, just before Christmas, he came to the door holding out an unplucked turkey.

'Here y'are, gel. I been over Leadenhall market, bought this for your Christmas dinner,' he said, with wide-eyed innocence.

She knew he hadn't bought it. 'How many more of 'em fell off the back of the lorry?' she asked, before remembering she'd vowed never to speak to him again.

The turkey swung between them. 'It's a decent size.' He peered at it. 'Enough there for you to invite your new chap round and his family – and me.'

She stared at him, ready to slam the door, but then remembered Alfie's plea. She took the turkey. 'You'd better come in.'

He told her he was still living at Uncle Jimmy's, but it had become a bit cramped since Uncle Jimmy moved in a young woman he'd met in the Upside Down.

'Lovely girl, don't get me wrong, but she's made it plain she don't want me there.' He looked around the kitchen hopefully.

'Eric's back. He's sleeping in your room with Davey,' she said. Even if she could forgive him, she doubted it would be wise to let him back in the house.

'Oh, is he? He's packed in that BUF shit?'

She nodded.

'Thank Christ for that. What changed his mind? Get fed up when they took his uniform away?' he said, grinning.

She found herself telling him about Ocki and Ida and how Alfie had come back from Spain so angry he'd nearly killed Eric with his bare hands.

'You been through the mill, gel, ain't you?'

'I've coped.'

'Yeah. You always cope. You ain't had much choice with me as a dad.' He looked down and tapped an unlit Woodbine on the kitchen table. 'I'm sorry, Ruby. Truly sorry. I just want the chance to make it up to you.'

'And Mum, what about her? How can you make it up to her?'

He shook his head sadly. 'What can I do? If you've been to see her, you know what she's like. It's what I was trying to tell you: I lost my wife, Ruby, and if I could do anything to get her back I would. But them doctors in Cane Hill told me she ain't never coming back.'

There was no sound in the room but the continued tattoo of Dodge's cigarette on the table and the clock's faint tick. Perhaps it was time.

'And what if the doctors told me different?'

He paused with his cigarette in mid-air and he spoke in a voice devoid of his usual flippant tone. 'If I ever got her back, I'd be a better man, a better husband, I can promise you that, Ruby.'

She nodded. 'They've taken her off the sleeping medication. They said she can wake up now, but she hasn't – so far. We don't know why. They tell us to talk to her. Will you come with me tomorrow when I visit her?'

'Yes, love,' he replied, eagerly, 'I will.'

So, Ruby, Eric and Dodge made the journey to Cane Hill. Eric had been surprised by Ruby's forgiveness of Dodge, but he'd agreed to bury the hatchet for the sake of their mother. The journey had been awkward and chilly, not made any easier by Dodge's vociferous admiration of Alfie.

'I hear your lot are calling themselves the Peace Party these days,' he said to Eric, who ignored him. Undeterred, Dodge went on, 'I met Ruby's chap. He's a brave feller, going out to Spain, getting stuck in. Sounded worse than the trenches. I said to Ruby, it's not all words with him.'

Eric didn't rise to the bait, for which she was grateful. He still bore the marks of Alfie's attack and, though they'd shaken hands after it, she didn't think they'd ever be best friends. She just wanted to get this first visit with Dodge over with. She prayed it wasn't a suggestion she'd regret. If it upset her mother, it could undo all the progress they'd made.

Rachel was in the same smaller ward, propped up in the same bed by the bay window. Ruby's heart sank. She'd hoped to see some small improvement. They drew up chairs and Ruby tilted her mother's head to face them. She turned to Dodge, who looked like a rabbit caught in headlights.

'We've brought someone to see you, Mum,' Ruby said, nudging Dodge.

He coughed and shifted in his seat. 'Hello, darlin'. It's me. You ain't got to stay asleep no more, Rachel. Do you think you could open your eyes, talk to me and the kids?'

Rachel's pale face remained impassive and she could have been taken for dead if it hadn't been for the rhythmic rising and falling of her chest. Dodge coughed and spoke again, louder this time.

'I done a bad thing by our kids, Rachel. But our Ruby and Eric, they've forgiven me...' He paused and Ruby saw a teardrop spill onto his cheek and drop onto Rachel's hand. 'I've come to ask if you can forgive me too.' His voice broke into a sob and he dropped his head.

Ruby had been staring at him; this was a father she had never seen. She'd seen him sentimental, she'd seen him mock-penitent, but she'd never seen him full of such painful remorse. She turned back to Rachel. Her mother's hand, wet with Dodge's tears, moved. Ruby gasped. 'See that?' she asked Eric, who shook his head. 'Wait.' The movement came again, the merest flutter as if her mother's fingers were butterfly wings.

'I saw that!' Eric said, and Dodge's head shot up.

Ruby saw her mother's eyelashes tremble and then she opened her eyes.

Warm brown eyes, so like Davey's, sleepy at first, blinking at the sunlight filtering in through the bay. She looked from Ruby to Eric, wonderment in her face, and then her eyes rested on her husband.

'Is that my Dodge?' She moved her hand on the cover, not strong enough to lift it. Dodge took it and put it to his lips and kissed it and then he leaned over the bed and kissed Rachel on the lips.

'Welcome back, darlin'. I never thought I'd see the day.'

Rachel smiled. 'Have you come to take me home, my love?'

It was a short visit. The ward sister insisted that Rachel must be brought gently back into the world of the living. Anything too taxing could send her retreating back into her somnolent state. And Ruby, more than anything, wanted to keep her mother awake. She gave only the briefest accounts of her life, nothing about Alfie or his painful return, nothing about her rift with Dodge, nothing about Eric's Blackshirt activities. She held Rachel's hand and shared her with Eric and Dodge and listened to her mother's weak voice, remembering with a shock how sweet and musical was its tone. Mostly she enjoyed her mother's smile as she looked at Ruby. It lit Rachel's pale face with a glow, warmer than the sun and full of love.

The bell was rung for the end of visiting and they stood up to go. Rachel lifted a weak hand and beckoned Ruby closer. 'Did I dream it, or did you tell me my Davey's all right?'

'Yes, Mum, I did tell you. He's well and he can't wait to see you.'

'I had a nightmare when I was asleep, darlin'. Terrible nightmare. That I killed him.'

'You never killed him.' Ruby stroked her hand. 'He's ten years old.'

Rachel gave a small, disbelieving smile. 'My baby's ten? I've been here ten years?'

Ruby nodded, expecting her mother to be anguished, distraught at her loss. But instead she nodded and a serenity shone from her eyes. 'I'm so grateful. So grateful my baby's all right. Bring him with you next time – and Ruby, I don't know how to thank you, sweetheart.'

'What for, Mum?'

'For looking after them all while – while I was gone.'

'I just did what I thought you'd do. I felt you helping me...'

Her mother nodded and fixed her with those gentle brown eyes she'd so often described for Davey. 'But now I'm back, Ruby, I want you to do something else for me.'

'Of course!'

'I want you to go and live your own life, not mine. Promise me you will?'

'I will.' And she bent to receive her mother's kiss, her heart bursting with love and gratitude.

The bells of St James's were ringing for Christmas morning. A full peal, bursting from the bell tower, reverberated along St James's Road and filled the little room where Rachel Scully sat in Dodge's armchair, still weak in body after her long sleep, but undoubtedly strong in mind. She'd been declared sane and released from Cane Hill Mental Hospital just in time for Christmas Day. From her seat, she gave Ruby detailed instructions for cooking Dodge's turkey and reminded her when to put the Christmas pudding on to boil and how to roast the best potatoes. Ruby happily pretended she didn't know how to cook a roast turkey dinner and paused in her preparations to listen to the bells. She smiled to herself, remembering all the mornings when she'd woken to feel she was just like a resting bell, waiting for something or someone to set her into motion. She caught Alfie's eye and he put a hand to his ear.

'Don't they sound beautiful?'

She nodded, thinking of the hours he'd spent working in the tower. 'They wouldn't be ringing if it wasn't for you!'

He smiled at her. 'They're ringing the changes, Ruby Scully!' And Ruby smiled back, knowing, as she looked round the room, that it wasn't only the bells of St James's that had been brought to life.

It was Christmas and Hanukkah rolled into one. Ruby had invited Alfie's parents as well and, although they weren't particularly strict, he explained that as it was the last day of Hannukah, the Festival of Lights, he would bring the many branched candelestick, so they could light the eighth candle. Mrs Diamond had brought with her the traditional doughnuts and chocolate pennies for Davey, who sat contentedly by his mum's side reading a Christmas annual Dodge had bought him. Ida was there as well. She said her mum would be only too happy to have one less Turpin mouth to feed in Arnold's Place that Christmas.

It was a Christmas of sorrows and a Christmas of blessings. Ocki was not there in body, but he was remembered in everything they did. He was there in Ida's visible pregnancy. He was there in Eric's changed heart. He was there in Mrs Diamond's fond reminiscences of her clever son and in her delight at soon being a grandmother. He was there in Alfie's determination not to let bitterness sour his life.

And although Rachel's mother had lost years of her life, she too was untainted by bitterness. Dodge's tears of regret had woken only forgiveness in his wife's heart and now Ruby allowed herself the joy of glancing up from her tasks to see Dodge fussing around Rachel, making sure she was warm enough, that she wasn't getting too tired. Davey seemed the least touched by all their past tragedies, remembering nothing of his part in them, only grateful now that he had a mum to call his own.

Once everyone was seated, Ruby looked around the table and reflected that this was indeed a Christmas of sorrows and a Christmas of blessings. One of dark and light intertwined, inextricable, the one unable to exist without the other. Much like life.

Acknowledgements

I would like thank my agent, Anne Williams and my editor, Rosie de Courcy, for their continued invaluable support and advice. Also, my copy editor Kati Nicholl, whose keen eye and skill have helped make this a much better book. Thanks also to the talented team at Head of Zeus for their enthusiasm and professionalism in bringing the book to publication.

Thanks to Violet Henderson, Lillian Piddington and Jennifer Stroud for generously sharing their family stories and Bermondsey memories; to P.J. Mawson for his detailed help with the history of Methodism, and to the librarians at Southwark Local Studies Library for their patience and help with my research.

Many thanks for all their support to my writing pals at Bexley Scribblers and to my wonderful family. And finally, to Josie Bartholomew, who, as ever, deserves special thanks for making it all possible.

Author's Note

You can find out more about the little-known Battle of Bermondsey in *Rebel Footprints* by David Rosenberg. Published by Pluto Press, 2015.

The history of Bermondsey Central Hall is very well documented in *The Bitter Cry Heard and Heeded* by John D. Beasley. Published by South London Mission, 1990.

Crimscott Street, Colin Metcalfe's memoir of his years working at the Crosse & Blackwell factory in Bermondsey has been particularly useful and can be found at Southwark Local Studies Library.